INTO THE RIVER DEAD

DETECTIVE INSPECTOR SIMON WISE CRIME THRILLER
BOOK 4

MICHAEL DYLAN

Sunday 1st January

1

Happy bloody new year, the man thought, as he lay awake listening to his girlfriend snore. A glance at his phone told him it was 4 a.m. and that just irritated him even more. He should've been asleep long ago, but the racket Justine was making was off the charts. In fact, it was so bad, he was surprised the neighbours hadn't been around to complain.

They'd gone to bed at just past 1, and she'd fallen asleep straight away, helped no doubt by the bottle of Prosecco she'd drunk nearly all by herself. He'd known earlier that the alcohol was going to cause problems, but he'd kept quiet, conscious that it was New Year's Eve, after all. Especially since he'd refused to go with her to any of the parties she'd been invited to. 'It's our first New Year's Eve together,' he'd said. 'I just want to be with you. Not fighting a crowd trying to kiss you at midnight.'

That wasn't really why he'd not wanted to go out, but it was a far more acceptable reason than the truth. And, in the end, they'd had a lovely evening. He'd cooked Justine a delightful dinner of filet mignon with a red wine sauce, seasoned with garlic and shallots, and finished the meal off with individual portions of crème brûlée. She'd oohed and aahed, of course, and told him he should've been a professional chef, but he'd heard it all before. Personally, he didn't think he had any great talent as a chef but if he was going to do something, he was going to do it well.

There was no hiding the fact that he was a perfectionist. He paid attention to the details other people don't notice. He cared about things being exactly as they should be, and he never ever accepted second best.

Like a girlfriend who snored loud enough to wake the dead.

In fact, Justine's snoring was so bad, she'd warned him about it when they first met over drinks at a pretentious tiki bar. She'd laughed and giggled and just dropped it into the conversation like it wasn't the deal breaker that it was. A perfect woman admitting to one tiny, inconsequential flaw. 'Are you a sound sleeper?' she'd asked. 'Because a few people say I snore.'

And he'd laughed it off like it wasn't going to be an issue. After all, she was a stunner. An eleven if ever there was one. Tall, athletic, blonde, with big bright blue eyes — what was there not to like?

He'd been so happy after they'd first met and got chatting. Enjoying the playful banter that followed and getting excited by the flirty text messages. They'd got on so well, in fact, that he'd thought he'd found his soulmate at long last. The one that would make him behave and forget all his bad, old ways. Justine seemed like someone he could settle down with and they could grow old together.

He'd even told his mum about her.

Then they'd met again in that stupid tiki bar for drinks. It was her choice of venue, not his, of course, and he should have spotted that red flag straight away. But she was more than good-looking and that overruled any worries that the venue created in his mind.

And, in her defence, she'd warned him about the snoring again before the first time they spent the night together. No joking this time. She was dead serious about it. Offering him an out, a chance to escape. But what did she really expect him to say? As if any man would turn down the opportunity to sleep with someone who looked like her over something as trivial as snoring?

So, he'd said it wasn't a problem. They'd had amazing sex and then they'd both fallen asleep, wrapped up in each other's arms. It was lovely. Perfect.

For about five minutes.

Until she started snoring. Just like she said she would. But no words could ever describe how truly bad it was.

It had taken all his self-control not to end it there and then. But he was a gentleman, and it would've been wrong to walk away after their first night together, especially after everything he'd said. He didn't want anyone to think he was just after a one-night stand.

The next morning Justine had look so worried when she asked if he'd slept alright. Of course, he'd laughed and said he had. He claimed he'd not heard a thing, and she'd smiled like she'd won the lottery. She looked so happy, in fact, that he reckoned that if he'd proposed there and then, she'd have accepted. Maybe in her mind she was already picking wedding dresses and venues because she thought she'd finally found someone who wouldn't go insane sleeping next to her.

But it really did bother him. It'd bother anyone with ears who wasn't dead.

He knew then it wouldn't last. How could it? A man had to sleep.

It was a shame though. She could've been the one. But that was life. You had to kiss a lot of frogs until you found your princess and all that. Of course, his mother was going to be so disappointed when he told her yet another relationship was over. She claimed he was too fussy about everything. His mum always got so fed up that he found something wrong with whoever he was seeing. In fact, he could hear her moaning now. 'No one's good enough for you. You'll end up alone if you're not careful.'

Well, he'd rather be on his own than put up with that foghorn for the rest of his life. If he was going to marry someone, he couldn't compromise on anything. He had standards. Needs. And sleep was pretty high up on that list.

Even so, he'd suffered for six weeks so no one could say he didn't try. But each night, it got worse and worse and now, he was at his wit's end.

It was over.

He'd didn't care that it was New Year's Day.

Anyway, now he was awake and had made up his mind, he might as well get on with things.

First of all, though, there was her flat to clean. He hated mess almost as much as he hated her snoring.

He slipped out of bed and headed into the kitchen. Delving into the bag he'd brought his cooking kit in, he produced a brand new pair of bright yellow Marigolds and put them on. After flexing the fingers, he started in the kitchen section of the open plan living/dining space of her apartment. He'd already cleaned up after dinner, but there was a big difference between what most people considered clean and what was actually required in this particular situation. He sprayed every surface and wiped them all down, removing every mark, every stain, until everything gleamed. Bending down so he was eye level with the marble countertop, he examined it carefully, looking for any spot he might've missed and found none.

'Good enough to eat off,' he whispered.

He moved to the dining table next with the polish, really bringing out the wood, humming to himself as he worked. Loud enough to almost forget about the racket coming from the bedroom. Almost but not quite. He ran the cloth over the chairs and even wiped the underside of the table and the legs. 'Leave no spot unpolished,' as his dear old mother would say.

Enjoying himself, he worked on the living area next, cleaning the coffee table and the sofa and chairs, checking under the cushions in case anything had found its way down between the cracks. Even the remote controls got plenty of love and attention. He hated seeing dust and fluff caught in the buttons. Bits of who knows who and God knows what.

He paused to check on her, before he started on the bathroom. Just in case. Even though he could still hear that wall-shaking foghorn coming out of her mouth from the other side of the flat. Watching her from the doorway, he couldn't help but think what a shame it all was because she really was quite extraordinarily beautiful. Really up amongst the best of his girlfriends or, rather, ex-girlfriends.

Oh well, time to get back to work.

The bathroom always took longer, after all. He had to get into the plug holes with the bleach, making sure there were no stray hairs left, no bits of skin or other nasty things like that. He wiped the taps and faucet until they shone so bright, he could see himself reflected in them.

The toilet was the worst to do. The job he hated most. But if you were going to do something, you had to do it properly. Thank God he had the gloves on. On his knees, he scrubbed away, trying not to breathe in that faint, sickly odour from the bowl. Still, when he was done, the stink was gone, and the thing was bloody spotless. Even his mum wouldn't find fault with what he'd done, and she was a fussy one. No wonder he'd ended up the way he was.

'As good as new.' He smiled, feeling proud.

But he knew he couldn't procrastinate anymore. It was time to let Justine know the bad news and say goodbye.

He headed back into the bedroom and climbed into bed, naked except for the gloves. There was no point taking them off now.

He watched Justine for a few minutes, as she lay there oblivious to him, her blonde hair splayed out across the white pillow, one arm out of the duvet, half-reaching for his side of the bed. He could imagine a painter capturing the moment on canvas, recording her beauty. A goddess for the ages. Aphrodite herself.

If it wasn't for that fucking awful noise coming out of her throat, he'd almost be sad to say goodbye. As it was though ...

He sat up, rolled his neck and loosened his shoulders. Breathing deeply, he could feel a tingle of excitement in his gut. A stirring of lust in his groin.

Most people hated breaking up with their partners, with all that heartbreak and shattered dreams. But not him. If he was really being honest with himself, and he knew it was wrong to say this, it was his favourite part of every relationship he'd ever had. In fact, he'd got really good at finishing things. He knew how to make it fun. After all, he'd had enough practice.

He picked up his pillow. It was nice and firm, made with goose down. Just the way he liked it. He had no idea how anyone could sleep with one of those synthetic numbers or, heaven forbid, something from IKEA. You could scrimp and save on most things but not when it came to having a good night's sleep.

He placed it beside her head, close to hand and then straddled her, but keeping his weight off her for the moment. 'Justine,' he said gently. 'Time to wake up.'

She stirred but her eyes remained close.

'Justine,' he repeated, firmer this time. 'Wake up.'

'Wha ... hmm,' she mumbled but the bitch wouldn't open her eyes.

He slapped her. 'Wake up.'

That did the trick. That got her eyes open. She struggled to focus on him, her face no doubt stinging if the red handprint on her cheek was anything to go by. 'What ... what are you doing?'

He smiled. 'I'm sorry but this isn't working out. We have to break up.'

'What?' She looked confused. Maybe even a little scared. Actually, she was petrified. She'd seen the gloves, after all.

'I know I'm supposed to say it's not you, it's me, but I can't. It *is* you. *Your* snoring, in fact. It's a deal breaker.'

'I don't ... I don't understand.' Her lip quivered. A tear popped up in the corner of her eye. God, it made him hard. Why do beautiful women look so damn attractive when they're terrified?

Still, there was no going back now. The decision was made.

He picked up the pillow.

Holding it tightly in both hands, he shoved it hard over her face. She clawed at it, at him, desperate to get it off her, but he pressed down harder, grateful for the bed's firm mattress pressing back.

She bucked, trying to throw him off but she had no hope. What followed was inevitable. It was just a matter of being patient now and maintaining the pressure.

And, just like that, he could feel her slowing down, her legs twitching more than kicking, her hands flailing more than clawing.

Still, she wasn't dead yet and, as much as he wanted to, he knew he shouldn't prolong things. To do that was cruel and he never wanted to be one of *those* men. He shifted his weight so most of it was in his upper body and pushed down even harder.

And, just like that, her hands twitched only once more before falling to her side. Her left foot shifted an inch, then nothing.

Still, he didn't stop. He had to be sure. If a job's worth doing, it's worth doing well. He hummed *Happy Birthday* to himself. Not that it was his birthday but, just like singing it twice while washing your hands killed all germs during Covid, he found a couple of renditions were more than enough to guarantee someone was really dead once they stopped moving.

With that done, he slowly lifted the pillow off her face. Bloodshot eyes stared back at him. Her mouth open but silent at last.

Thank God.

Tossing the pillow aside, he climbed off her corpse and wandered through to the bathroom. Turning on the light, he checked himself for any cuts or scratches. There were a couple of marks but nothing too bad. Still, he'd have to give her fingernails a good scrub later. Make sure she didn't have any of his DNA on her.

He went back into the bedroom, singing that Elton John and Dua Lipa song, *Cold Heart,* as he did so. He wasn't normally a fan, but it was a catchy tune and, somehow, it seemed apt. And he could really go for it now that he didn't have to worry about waking anyone up and there was no snoring to put him off.

He dressed then walked over to her make-up table and picked up the pair of silver earrings that Justine always wore. Yes. They would do. He always liked to keep something to remember his girlfriends by and it wasn't as if Justine would miss them now. He slipped them into his pocket as there was still plenty to do and no time to dally.

First of all, he dragged Justine off the bed, letting her drop to the floor with a thud. Now she was out of the way, he had the bed to strip, the sheets to wash and dry, and the floors to do before he took the garbage out.

Tuesday 3rd January

2

For most people, it was the first day back to the drudgery of working a nine to five after the Christmas break, of getting up in the dark and coming home in the dark, and, somehow, trying to survive the weeks ahead with a bank account that was already empty if not overdrawn. Back to a reality determined to crush whatever hope people had that this year was going to be better than the one gone by. After all, the trains were still on strike, the NHS was on the verge of collapse, the war in Ukraine was still rattling on and the cost-of-living crisis wasn't showing any signs of calming down. Not when the average heating bill was now the price of a small car not so long ago.

Of course, Detective Inspector Simon Wise wasn't back at work just yet. That was tomorrow's fun thing to look forward to.

Today, he had a funeral to get through.

A funeral of a fellow police officer killed in the line of duty. A funeral of a colleague, a friend.

While the vicar said nice things about a man he didn't know, Wise glanced around at the other mourners. A good crowd had turned up to say goodbye to a good man. Wise knew a lot of them from his many years in the Metropolitan Police. He'd spoken to a few earlier and nodded at others.

Naturally, his whole team were there. Or what was left of them, anyway. It was their friend in the box, after all.

Detective Sergeant Hannah Markham, hair tied back as ever, stood to his right. She had a long black overcoat on over a black dress, instead of her usual combo of jeans, motorbike jacket and what Wise's dad would've called Bovver Boots. Then there was Trainee Detective Constable Callum Chabolah next to her, wearing what looked like someone else's suit because it didn't quite fit. The lad looked like he'd aged five years since Wise had last seen him two weeks ago. Then again, death had that effect on everyone.

Case in point, Detective Sergeant Roy 'Hicksy' Hicks was on the other side of the grave, his arm around the dead police officer's widow, his scowl deeper than ever above that crooked nose of his, what was left of his hair more white than grey now. If ever there was a man who looked ready to retire, it was him.

DC Alan 'Brains' Park was next to him, head down and eyes hidden behind those big glasses of his. Finally, there was DC Ian 'Donut' Vollers, who actually looked like he'd made an effort for once and showered to go along with a nice new suit.

The top brass was in attendance too. DCI Anne Roberts stood in the second row, despite being suspended pending an investigation into the Ollie Konza murders just before Christmas. She'd run over two gunmen in her Audi to stop an armed ambush from killing two police officers and, apparently, the higher-ups weren't as impressed by her quick thinking as Wise had been at the time. They thought she should've stopped, then identified herself as a police officer, before taking any other action. Of course, she would've been killed if she'd done that. Wise too. But that didn't seem to matter to the pencil pushers at New Scotland Yard. Heaven forbid some common sense got in the way of a time consuming and costly enquiry that kept good coppers off the street.

Detective Chief Superintendent Walling was by her side, though neither was talking to the other. Walling oversaw everyone at

Kennington Police Station, where Wise was based. He'd never been the most popular of people, but Wise was starting to see him in a new light.

Finally, Wise looked down at the last member of his team. The one in the coffin. The one they'd come to say goodbye to.

DS Jonathan 'Jono' Gray.

He'd been murdered just before Christmas by someone in Konza's gang. Maybe by Konza himself. The killer wouldn't be identified now, of course, because they were all propping up daisies themselves. Roberts had killed two of the gang when she'd run them over. The other three were shot by Armed Response Officers in a short, but very brutal, gun fight.

Jono had only returned to duty a few days before, after undergoing treatment for lung cancer. He was supposed to be on desk duty, but Jono had done everything he could to get back into the action, even turning up to the arrest of a murder suspect. Because Wise was short of manpower, he'd sent Jono to watch a suspect's house instead of sending him home, under strict orders not to leave his car, thinking it would be an easy, safe job for a man in Jono's condition.

It was a decision that cost Jono his life, and, needless to say, his death would haunt Wise for the rest of his days.

Like so many others.

Wise sighed. He was going to miss Jono so damn much.

When he looked up, he realised that the vicar, a small man with a pinched face and round glasses, was bringing the service to a close. 'We have entrusted our brother, Jonathan Grey, to God's mercy, and we now commit his body to the ground.'

Jono's widow, Pat, let out a sob and Hicksy squeezed her shoulder. Wise could imagine only too well the pain she was going through. The grief — such a simple word to describe a sensation so overwhelming that it could make breathing feel like an impossible task.

'Earth to earth, ashes to ashes, dust to dust,' the vicar went on. 'In sure and certain hope of the resurrection to eternal life through our

Lord Jesus Christ, who will transform our frail bodies that they may be conformed to his glorious body, who died, was buried, and rose again for us. To him be glory for ever. Amen.'

'Amen,' everyone else chorused, playing their part. Even Wise, who wasn't a believer. There was comfort in the theatre of it all, of course, but he'd seen too much evil in the world for him to even consider the possibility of a higher power looking out for everyone.

With the final words said, there was an awkward pause as everyone looked from one to the other, wondering if the funeral was indeed over. This was only broken when the vicar walked over to Pat and said some last words of comfort, before heading back to wherever vicars go when their jobs were done.

Hicksy then led the crying widow over to the first of the hired cars and helped her into the back seat.

'Are you going for a drink with everyone?' Hannah asked as everyone else started to drift off to their own cars.

Wise nodded. 'I'll pop in for a quick one. It's at the Spirit of Hackney, right?'

'Yeah. On Mare Street.' Hannah watched him for a moment, in that way of hers that made Wise think she could see past the mask of normality that he always wore now. 'How are you holding up?'

Wise raised an eyebrow. 'Peachy.'

'That good, eh?'

'Yeah. That good. What about you?' Wise hadn't seen Hannah since the ambush three weeks before. Konza's gang had driven a van into the side of the car Hannah was in and she'd been badly bashed about. The doctors had told her to take the rest of the month off while she recovered from the concussion.

'I still have my moments,' Hannah said, 'but I've been given the all-clear to come back to work. I'll be in tomorrow.'

'It'll be good to have you back.' Wise noticed that Roberts was still by the graveside. When he caught her eye, she motioned with her head that she wanted a word with him. 'I'm just going to have a quick word with the boss,' he said to Hannah. 'I'll see you at the pub.'

'Okay. I'll catch up with you there.' Hannah followed the others to the cars, leaving Wise alone.

'You're looking well,' Roberts said, coming to join him. Her tightly cropped silver hair looked even more severe than normal when contrasted with her black dress uniform.

'Looks can be deceiving,' Wise replied. 'How are you?'

Roberts rolled her eyes. 'Oh, I'm just a bundle of fun to have around. The holidays are bad enough without everything else that's gone on.'

'Any updates on the enquiry?'

'It's starting this week.'

'I'm sure it'll be over soon,' Wise said. 'You saved everyone's lives by doing what you did.'

'Perhaps. But I'm also the DCI who had two bent coppers on her team that she didn't know about, one of whom got Jono killed.' Roberts sighed. 'No one likes that. Not even me.'

Wise said nothing. One of those bent coppers was his best friend and partner, DS Andy Davidson, and the other was his right hand, DC Sarah Choi, a fact that reflected even worse on Wise than it did his boss. The only thing that had saved his career was the fact that the top brass in the Met knew the problem went far beyond his team. Apparently, there was a whole squad within the Met made up of dodgy coppers working for the very people they were supposed to be putting away. And, according to Specialist Crime and Operations Ten, or SCO10 as it was known, the secret unit investigating the problem were all working for Wise's twin brother, Tom.

'Anyway, I heard who they are bringing in to cover for me while I'm stuck at home,' Roberts said. 'And I thought I'd better give you a head's up.'

'Who is it?' Wise asked, a sinking feeling in his gut.

'DCI Douglas Riddleton.'

'Shit. Seriously?' The man was a grade one arsehole, and the last person Wise needed to be dealing with right then.

Roberts nodded. 'I'm afraid so. As you know, he and Walling are good friends.'

Riddleton had joined the force around the same time as Wise, but he'd progressed further and faster due his ambition and deft political manoeuvrings. Walling had brought him in to take over the investigation into the Motorbike Killer back in the autumn of the previous year, but Riddleton had cocked up everything, sending the whole team on a wild goose chase, while Wise and Hannah went after the real killer against his orders.

'The man's a dick,' Wise said in the understatement of the year so far.

'As if that's ever stopped someone's career from being fast-tracked,' Roberts replied. 'In fact, I'd say that's a prerequisite for doing well these days. Anyway, keep your head down and, hopefully, I'll be back before dear old Doug can wreck too much havoc.'

Wise gave her a look that told her what he thought about that. It had taken Riddleton all of twenty-four hours last time to get Wise taken off his own case and for things to go horribly wrong. 'Are you coming to the wake?' he asked instead.

'No. I'm going to head home,' Roberts said. 'Say hello to everyone for me, though.'

'I will.'

'Any news when Sarah's body will be released for burial?'

'Not yet. No one's agreed a cause of death yet.'

Roberts eyebrow shot up. 'I thought it was suicide.'

'I think there's going to be another autopsy this week,' Wise said. 'Hopefully, we'll know more then.' There was more Wise could tell her, not least the theory that Tom was behind Sarah's death as well as so many others but, at his meeting before Christmas with SCO10, the need for secrecy had been stressed on everyone. The fact that no one knew exactly who could be trusted made everything so much more difficult. After all, before he knew of Andy and Sarah's betrayals, Wise would've trusted both of those police officers with his life.

'Well, keep me updated,' Roberts said, 'and I'll see you when I see you.'

'Look after yourself, boss,' Wise said.

Wise watched Roberts walk away and then he was alone by Jono's graveside. He bent down and picked up a handful of dirt. It was hard to imagine his friend inside the coffin. Jono had always been such a character to be around. Larger than life in every way. And now?

He was just another body in a box. Another friend gone too soon.

'I'm sorry, mate. I really am. I'm going to miss you,' Wise said, letting the dirt fall from his fingers onto the coffin. He could almost hear Jono telling him not to be such a soft git, that it was all going to be okay.

Wise only wished that was true. The way things had been going, though …

Straightening up, Wise tilted his face to the winter sun and closed his eyes, enjoying the feel of it on his skin as he took long, deep breaths of cold air. There were going to be long, hard days ahead and he needed to be strong.

Because, no matter what, he didn't want to stand over any more graves, staring at coffins with his friends inside or, heaven forbid, his family.

It wasn't going to be easy though. Not in the slightest.

He had a war to fight, after all. Against his own brother.

3

It was gone 6 by the time Wise made it home. He pulled up outside his house, with its red door, feeling exhausted after Jono's funeral and wake. Turning off the car engine, he sat still for a moment, watching his home, taking in the dark windows and the lack of life within.

It was stupid but he didn't want to go inside. He didn't want to face what he'd find on the other side of the door — or rather not find there. In fact, if he could think of somewhere else to go right then, Wise would've quite happily turned the engine back on and driven off.

But there was nowhere to go. Nowhere to hide.

He couldn't even go to his dad's because his father wasn't talking to him at the moment. They'd not spoken since his wife, Jean, had told his dad that Tom had threatened the lives of Wise's children and was now under investigation by the police for even more serious crimes.

The silence between them wasn't for want of trying on Wise's part, though. He'd called his dad every day since, only for his father to either decline the call or let it go to voice mail. Wise had left messages when that happened but, again, his father had just ignored them. Even his text messages went unheeded.

Rain started to fall, pitter-pattering against his windshield as Wise watched a food delivery person whizz by on an electric scooter. Across the road, a neighbour manoeuvred his car into a parking spot outside a house that was all brightly lit and welcoming.

Wise shifted in his seat as the cold from outside wormed its way into the car now the engine was off. He really should go inside. It was stupid sitting where he was. Really bloody stupid.

His phone beeped. It was a WhatsApp message from Jean. *The kids want to FaceTime you.* Wise stared at the message, reading so much into those six words, especially the way Jean had said *the kids* and not *we*.

Just parking the car. I'll call in 5, he typed back and hit send. The whoosh of the message filled the car for a heartbeat, then Wise unbuckled his seat belt, grabbed his jacket and coat off the passenger seat, and got out of the car. He walked quickly to the front door as if needing the momentum to keep going, to hold his nerve. He had his keys ready, so he almost didn't need to break his stride to get inside the house.

But he still wasn't quick enough. Memories came back of Jean greeting him at the door, full of smiles, asking him how his day was, cooking smells wafting out of the kitchen, Ed and Claire playing somewhere, laughing and causing chaos. Now though?

The house was empty and painfully silent. Wise switched on the hallway light the moment he was through the door, eager to banish the darkness lurking in every corner. Dropping his coat on the end of the banister, he moved over to the thermostat and cranked up the heating to get some warmth back in the place, so he could at least pretend things were normal.

His MacBook Air was already set up on the coffee table in the lounge, left there after his chat with the kids the day before, so Wise sat down on the sofa and typed in his password. A picture of the whole family filled the screen, everyone all happy and grinning away, showing off their tanned skins with blue sea and sky behind them.

Taken on a family holiday in Lanzarote a year or two ago, Wise had been using it as his laptop wallpaper ever since. Looking at those faces now, he wasn't sure if he recognised any of them. They all looked so happy, for one thing. Not a care in the world between them. Full of love for each other.

And now? They were in separate homes in different parts of the country with no idea when or if they would ever be reunited.

It was all such a mess.

He opened up FaceTime and called Jean's number. It was answered almost immediately by Ed and Claire, their faces jostling to fit into the picture frame.

'Daddy!' they both cried in unison, big grins springing up on their faces.

'Hey!' Wise called back, doing his best to be as carefree as he once was. 'How are you both?'

'Good,' Ed replied. 'We miss you.'

'And I miss you, too,' Wise replied. 'Are you behaving yourselves for Mummy, Nanna and Grandad?'

'I am,' Ed said, 'but Claire's not.'

'I am,' his sister shot back, giving her brother a good elbow at the same time. 'Ed just keeps picking on me.'

'I don't,' Ed said, elbowing her back. 'You're naughty.'

'Hey, you two,' Wise said. 'Be nice to each other.' He couldn't help smiling though. Just seeing the kids made him feel better, like there was a point to life after all. 'What did you do today?'

'Mummy took us shopping for school clothes,' Claire replied. 'It was boring.'

'Why do we have to go to school here anyway?' Ed asked. 'I liked my old school.'

'We've talked about this,' Wise said, trying to keep his voice jovial. 'Mummy wants to spend some time with Nanna and Grandad in Leeds for a while, but you still need to go to school while you stay there.' It wasn't quite the truth, but it was the best alternative he and Jean could come up with to explain his family's move north. Obviously, they couldn't tell the kids that Jean was worried about

Tom hurting the kids and they'd gone to her mother's to be out of harm's way. Originally it had only been for the Christmas holidays but, when Wise had gone up to spend Christmas itself with them, Jean had announced she wasn't going back to London until everything was sorted out with Tom.

If ever.

The kids exchanged looks. Neither looked happy with his answer. 'We don't like it here. It smells funny,' Ed said in a whisper. 'We want to come home.'

'We miss you,' Claire added. 'And I miss my room and my toys. I have to share a room with Ed here.'

And, just like that, the burst of happiness Wise had felt evaporated, leaving only the heartache that seemed his constant companion these days. 'It won't be forever, honey. Be patient. You'll be home before you know it.'

'Tea's ready,' Jean called out from somewhere in the background. 'Say goodbye to Daddy.'

Both kids glanced over the top of the phone to wherever Jean was, then looked back at Wise. 'Bye, Daddy,' Ed said.

'Bye, son. Talk to you soon,' Wise replied.

Tears sprung up in Claire's eyes and her chin began to wobble. 'Bye, Daddy.'

'I love you, honey.'

The screen went blank, and Wise was alone once more, the silence heavy around him.

He turned on the TV, needing the noise to keep him company and drown out his maudlin thoughts. There were some Premier League games starting in just over an hour, so he flicked over to Sky Sports to watch the pre-match discussions. Arsenal were playing Newcastle, hoping to extend their lead at the top of the table. As a die-hard Chelsea fan, it was the last thing Wise wanted to happen. Especially since the Blues were having a season to forget under Graham Potter and the new owners.

But it wasn't enough. He stared at the TV, trying to listen to the pundits talking nonsense, but the ghosts were lurking around in the shadows of the room. His best friend, DS Andy Davidson, was there as he always was, half his head missing thanks to a police sniper's bullet. DC Sarah Choi was with him too, bloody streaks running down her arms and legs from her slashed arteries, a suicide no one believed. The pair of them had been bent, working for his brother, selling secrets for cash and much worse besides. Some said they'd got what they deserved, but both Andy and Sarah had been Wise's friends as well as being a part of his team, and he couldn't help but think Tom had targeted them because of that fact.

And there was Jono, of course, with a hole in his forehead. A good man in the wrong place. He'd died alone and so utterly needlessly. Murdered by Konza and his gang. Killed by one of Tom's crews.

Wise could feel the anger building in him. The hate. His hands curled up into fists without thinking, growing tighter and tighter until his knuckles turned white against his skin. The TV became a blur as the ghosts moved closer, whispering in his ear.

'You don't know what I am,' Andy says.

'You can count on us,' Sarah adds. 'We won't let you down.'

'What do you need me to do?' Hicksy asks.

Wise jumped up from the sofa and marched through the house and out of the back door and into the garage. He had a small work out area set up there. A bench, some free weights, a mat for sit-ups and press-ups, and most importantly, his old punch bag dangling from a chain fixed to the roof.

He didn't bother turning the light on. He just headed straight to the bag, ripping his shirt off on the way, not caring as buttons pinged left, right and centre.

The bag was twenty years old and looked as ugly as a thing could get. The leather was worn and cracked where it wasn't patched up, and its sides were just a series of lumps and bumps from the punishment Wise had inflicted on it over the years. Jean had always hated it and had wanted it gone from their home from the moment he'd hung it up.

But now she was gone? It was all he had.

Wise didn't bother putting on gloves. He didn't bother warming up. He was too furious for any of that. He put all his weight, all his strength, into the first punch. His fist sank into the leather and the shock of the impact rattled up his arm. But Wise was already swinging his left in, driving it into the bag.

There was no discipline in what he was doing. No real technique. Just the crack of his skin against the leather, the chain rattling with each punch. Right. Left. Right. Left. Right. Left. Right. Left. On and on and on he went. Punching, punching, punching.

Wise screamed as he beat the crap out of the bag, his rage out of control, the beast within set free. A storm of fury lashing out, wanting to hurt the world, smothering his pain with more pain.

Wednesday 4th January

4

A noise woke Wise up. He didn't know where he was for a moment, as his brain tried to kick into gear. He was on the sofa in the living room, the TV still on but muted, his phone buzzing away on the coffee table. He didn't remember falling asleep there and a part of him was glad about that. He was cold though, still bare-chested from his workout in the garage, still in his suit trousers from the day before. His hands ached from battering his punchbag, his knuckles red and raw.

He reached over and picked the phone up, ignoring the pain. It was Kennington Police Station.

If they were calling him at 6:45 a.m, there was only one reason.

Someone was dead.

'Detective Inspector Wise,' he said on answering. God, his mouth was dry.

'Oh, hi. I'm Katherine — Kat — Galley,' a woman said, a hint of Yorkshire in her voice and far too bright and breezy for Wise to cope with right then. 'I'm your new Ops Manager.'

Wise vaguely remembered being told there was a civilian joining his team. 'What can I do for you, Kat?' He got to his feet and padded through to the kitchen. He needed water. He needed coffee.

'I've been asked to contact you and your team, sir. There's a body we need you to look at. An IC1 female.'

'A body? Where abouts?' He grabbed a glass from a cupboard and filled it up at the sink.

'She's caught up on an old jetty off Cousin Lane, sir,' Kat said. 'Some treasure hunter was waiting for low tide so he could go looking for Roman coins or something. As the water dropped, he spotted her.'

'And we think it's suspicious?' Wise downed the water in two gulps, then refilled the glass.

'Apparently, she's naked and wrapped up in a net, sir.'

Wise sighed. 'Alright. I'll head over. You called anyone else yet?'

'Not yet. I thought it best to call you first, sir,' Kat said.

'I'm flattered,' Wise said. 'Tell the others to meet me there as soon as they can. And Kat?'

'Yes, sir?'

'Please don't call me "sir". Save that for the Chief Super. You can call me "Simon" or "Guv".'

'Yes, sir — I mean, Guv,' Kat replied.

'Thank you, Kat. I'll see you in Kennington later and we can say hello properly then.'

'I'll see you then.'

Wise ended the call. It certainly was all change for the new year. Wonderful.

Wise drank the second glass of water, then popped a capsule into the coffee machine. He tried to roll the kinks out of his neck while it gurgled away, filling up a cup. The machine cost a fortune but, as far as Wise was concerned, it was worth every penny. His daughter Claire might not be impressed by how environmentally unfriendly it was, but for Wise, its fast delivery of quality coffee was worth the damage to the planet. Once he was armed with caffeine, he then headed upstairs to make himself look, if not feel, vaguely human.

Ten minutes later, showered, shaved, suited and booted, he stepped out of his front door into a cold, dark, damp world, shrouded with fog. As he climbed into his battered Mondeo, he realised that he'd not eaten since lunch time the previous day. God only knew when he'd get a chance to grab something, though.

At least the coffee was doing its job, and his brain was starting to clear up. He couldn't say the same for the weather, though. The fog clung stubbornly to the roads, reducing visibility to little over five or six metres in front of his car in some places. There was no way he could put his foot down in such conditions. He might be feeling down about life, but he didn't have a death wish anymore.

To take his mind off the conditions, Wise turned on the radio as he drove. The local news was on. There'd been a robbery at the London International Diamond Exchange in Hatton Cross over the New Year's Eve weekend and the thieves had taken three million pounds worth of rare and uncut diamonds. For some reason, the radio show hosts were talking about the robbers as if they were people to be admired. They raved about their audacity in carrying out the crime, like they were some sort of modern-day Robin Hoods out stealing from the rich.

Wise wondered which team from the Flying Squad was investigating the robbery. He didn't envy them handling such a high-profile case with the media watching their every move. In fact, Wise couldn't think of a single time in his whole career where the press' involvement had helped an investigation. In a case like this robbery, every step the detectives took would be dogged by reporters. Every move they made would be observed and criticised. And, if they didn't get a result, the media would go to town, tearing the Met apart, looking for someone to blame, acting as if it was the police's incompetence that was to blame for any failures. No one ever mentioned that the rising crime rate in the capital was in direct proportion to the cuts in manpower and resources made by the government. After fifteen years of the Tories, the sad truth was that only six percent of crimes were solved with charges brought against the perpetrator.

The fog made the traffic worse than ever as Wise fought his way up the A3 along with all the weekday commuters. In the end, he had to put his blues and twos on, hoping to speed things up. Slowly, cars edged themselves out of his way and he began to make better progress. But it was only when Wise looped round Elephant Square that the fog and the road opened up enough for him to make decent progress. He shot past the world's worst Weatherspoon's, and then headed straight up Tower Bridge Road and over the river. After that it was left by the Tower of London and he drove down Lower Thames Street.

On the surface, London was as modern as any other world capital, with its tall, glass-fronted office buildings slowly taking over the skyline and replacing history with modernity. But there were still plenty of monuments from the past lurking here and there, and with the fog swirling around, it almost felt like he was traveling back in time to days long gone by.

He passed Sugar Quay, where the trading ships used to dock, full of sugar cane from the West Indies. That was right next door to the Old Billingsgate Fish Market, built back in 1850 to get the fish sellers and their stink off the streets and into one place. Both buildings now had expensive apartments hidden within them but, once, they'd been vital cogs in the city's economy, hustling along all day and night.

He drove past more and more iconic venues; the monument to the Fire of London, the Church of Saint Magnus the Martyr, the Fishmongers' Hall and, of course, London Bridge. It was a journey Londoners had been making for centuries, whether by foot, horse, carriage or car. He couldn't help but wonder what life would've been like back then, then realised that things hadn't changed that much. London had been and always would be a city of two halves. Full of glamour for the wealthy and privileged and bloody hard going and unforgiving for the rest. He'd read somewhere that over twenty-five percent of Londoners were living in poverty, with that number rising to nearly fifty percent in single-parent households. And, with costs spiralling out of control, Wise knew things were only going to get worse for most of the people who called London home. He could already feel the rising tension in the city as every service struggled to cope with the increased demands placed on them, all while being stripped of staff and investment. It didn't matter if it was housing services, the NHS, the police, the fire service or social services, they were all overworked and underfunded while the government blamed anyone other than themselves for the mess they'd created.

Still, he pushed those thoughts from his mind. As Wise approached Cannon Street Station, the police cars and forensics vans parked up along the side of the road told him that he'd arrived at Cousin Lane. It was time to go to work. He had a job to do and a possible murder to investigate.

5

Wise managed to squeeze his Mondeo into an available spot between two marked cars. After turning off the engine, he sat for a moment, gathering himself, making sure none of his team could see the cracks running through him. His team needed him to be strong. The dead needed his full attention. Everything else was a distraction, noise to be ignored, problems to be buried.

Of course, that was easier said than done. Sometimes, he felt so fragile, a huff and a puff could blow him down.

God, he wished he had another coffee.

With a deep breath, Wise grabbed his phone and coat from the passenger seat and got out, immediately feeling the cold. He welcomed it now, though, needing its sharp touch to wake him up and keep him alert.

Putting on his overcoat, he headed down the lane towards the water. The buildings on either side of the lane trapped the fog, creating a good old-fashioned peasouper for Wise to wade through. He couldn't help but think how many times over the centuries a police officer had wandered down this particular alleyway on their way to see a dead body. It had, after all, been one of the main crossing points for people to get from one side of the Thames to the other.

The real world returned quickly enough, though, as blue and white police tape closed off the lane halfway down. A crime scene manager stood with a clipboard taking down everyone's details before they were allowed access to the actual crime scene further on. As Wise produced his warrant card, he heard someone approaching from behind. He turned to find Hannah jogging towards him, motorbike helmet in one hand.

'Morning, Guv,' she said, coming to a halt.

'Morning, Hannah,' Wise replied. He nodded towards the helmet. 'I'm surprised you rode your bike here in the fog.'

She smiled but, somehow, it didn't seem to reach her eyes. 'It keeps things exciting.'

'Better you than me. It was hairy enough getting here in my car.' Wise and Hannah handed over their warrant cards to the officer at the tape and waited while their details were taken down.

'Do you know what we've got?' Hannah asked as they walked on, past a set of ornamental cannons outside a gym, to the end of the lane where a small army of police officers waited by the entrance to the Thames.

'Probably as much as you — that there's the body of an IC1 female caught up on an old jetty. No doubt this lot can tell us more.' Wise nodded towards the gaggle of uniformed officers and Scene Of Crime Officers already dressed up in their white forensic suits. They were waiting at the end of the lane, next to a pub called The Trader.

Wise spotted Hicksy with his shoulders all hunched up and his chin buried in the folds of his coat. An elderly man sat at a table nearby with a cup of something hot clutched in his hands and a silver thermal blanket wrapped around his shoulders.

'Guv!' Hicksy walked over to meet them. The man looked even more tired than Wise felt. Even the bags under his eyes had bags. He nodded at Hannah. 'Diversity.'

'Diversity' was Hicksy's nickname for Hannah, a bad joke of his that she was only on the team to make up some sort of representation quota. Normally, Wise would've pulled him up about it, but he was too tired to say anything. Besides, Hannah could more than take care of herself.

'Morning, Hicksy,' Wise said instead. 'What have we got here?'

'Naked blonde wrapped up in a net and snagged on a post,' Hicksy said. He nodded back towards the man with the cup. 'Dermot there spotted her while he was waiting for the tide to go out. Apparently, this bit of the river is a good site for treasure hunting.'

'Treasure hunting?'

'According to him, you can find anything from clay pipes to Roman coins down in the mud if you look hard enough.' Hicksy sniffed. 'It's called "Mudlarking", apparently, but it's a weird bloody hobby if you ask me. It obviously floats Dermot's boat, though. Anyway, there he is, watching the water go out and up pops our mysterious lady. Tits up and arse down.'

Wise glanced over at the officers all standing about. 'What's everyone waiting for up here? Why haven't we gone down for a look yet?'

'We're waiting for the okay from the Port Authority. Apparently, it's not safe to go wandering about until the tide's completely out.' Hicksy pointed to a woman standing on the top of the sea wall. Tall, thin and with a pair of glasses perched on the end of her nose, she wore a bright red jacket with the Port Authority logo on the front of it. Her eyes were fixed on the water, ignoring the comings and goings on the dry side of the wall. 'Her name's Vivian. She says that people like dear old Dermot go down on to the foreshore, dig big holes looking for treasure and then don't bother filling them in. Then the tide covers the holes with silt, hiding them but not filling them up, and then the next unsuspecting sod comes along, steps in the hole and ends up breaking a leg. So, we gotta wait for the tide to go out so we can see where we're stepping.'

'Great. How long before we get the okay?'

'Apparently, low tide is 8:29 a.m.' Hicksy glanced at his watch. 'Five minutes.'

'Who's in charge of the SOCOs?' Wise asked.

'Do you know Helen Kelly?'

'Yeah. She was working on the Konza murders last month.'

Hicksy flinched at the reminder. 'Of course. I should've remembered.'

'We've all had other things to think about,' Wise said.

'Ain't that the fucking truth. Anyway, she's with the pathologist,' Hicksy said. 'I'll walk you over.'

'The pathologist is here already?'

'Yeah, time and tide wait for no man — or woman.' Hicksy winked at Hannah as he said it. 'We've got less than an hour to get everything we need before the river starts coming back in.'

'Who's the pathologist?' Wise asked.

'You'll be happy.' Hicksy led them into the midst of the other officers, who all straightened up and moved out of the way when they saw Wise and Hannah approaching. As they did so, they revealed a diminutive figure in a white forensic suit standing in the middle of them all, deep in conversation with Helen Kelly. Neither had pulled up their hoods or put on a mask, but Wise would've recognised Doctor Harmet Singh even if she was dressed up in a clown's outfit. And Hicksy was right. He was glad to see Singh. She was smart and damn good at her job.

'Inspector!' the Home Office pathologist said with a smile. 'We meet in all the best places.'

'Doctor,' Wise said, with a nod of greeting to the two women. 'Helen. How are you both this fine morning?'

'All good,' Singh replied. Then her face became serious. 'I was sorry to hear about your colleagues.'

Helen nodded. 'Me too.'

Wise had to look away for a moment. He never knew what to say when people offered their condolences. 'Have you had a look at the body yet?' he asked instead.

'Not up close yet. We're just waiting for the tide to go all the way out.' Singh pointed to the stone steps at the end of the lane. 'Come. Let me show you.'

Leaving Hicksy behind, Wise and Hannah followed Singh and

Helen up the five steps to the top of the tidal wall where the woman from the Port Authority waited.

'Vivian,' Singh said. 'Can I introduce you to Detective inspector Wise?'

The woman gave a start as if surprised at being spoken to, then turned to face the small group. 'Hello.'

'Hello,' Wise said. 'And this is Detective Sergeant Markham.'

'Hiya,' Hannah said.

Vivian gave a small wave back.

Climbing onto the top of the sea wall, Wise looked down over the Thames. Southwark Bridge was off to the right, just visible in the fog, and London Bridge was to the left, with the Shard looming high above it, almost lost against the grey sky. Wise couldn't remember ever seeing the Thames at low tide like this before. The water level had dropped about seven metres from where it normally was at high tide, judging by the water marks and green slime that marked the river walls. Steep steps descended to a pebbly foreshore, swapping from stone to metal about halfway down, still glistening from the water that had washed over them mere hours before.

The foreshore itself was made up of pebbles, rocks and shingle of various colours. Lumps of stone and concrete jutted up through the mist, alongside the occasional wooden or metal pole. They were all that was left over from the various piers and jetties that had once lined up along the shore, allowing wherries to dock as they took passengers from one side of the Thames to the other.

However, Wise's eyes were drawn to the naked, bloated body of a blonde, Caucasian woman trapped against one of the wooden poles. She was caught up in netting that left her dangling like some obscene catch of the day. The woman's skin was purple and black and half-covered in mud, suggesting she'd been in the water for a while at the very least.

No wonder the man who'd found her looked so shocked.

'Well, she's definitely dead,' Wise said. 'The question is whether she ended up like that by accident, suicide or murder.'

'I'd infer that she didn't fall into the Thames by accident from the fact that she's naked,' Helen said. 'She wouldn't have gone for a walk naked and just fallen in and this isn't the weather to go swimming. The removing of her clothes is a deliberate action — so she either meant to kill herself or someone else stripped her and threw her into the water.'

'What a way to go,' Hannah said.

The woman from the Port Authority shivered. 'It would've been quick at least. Water that's between ten to fifteen degrees centigrade in temperature can kill you in less than a minute, if not quicker — and the Thames is about three or four degrees at the moment. She would've been dead in seconds.'

'Hypothermia can set in that quickly?' Hannah asked.

Vivian shook her head. 'Hypothermia is the least of your worries at that temperature. Basically, sudden immersion sends your body into cold shock. It's like being hit by lightning. Most people's immediate and uncontrollable reaction is to gasp for air — a huge gasp as you try to fill your lungs with air. If you're already underwater at this point, obviously your lungs fill up with water instead and you sink instantly. If your head is above the surface, then panics sets in and you lose the ability and strength to swim and down you go.'

'Shit,' Hannah said.

'Shit indeed,' Vivian agreed.

'So, we can rule out a pleasure swim gone wrong then,' Wise said. 'That just leaves us with suicide or murder.'

Singh nodded. 'And that's why we're here, all dressed up.'

'We're going to give everything a good sweep when we go down,' Helen said, 'but anything we do find, we'll have to treat as circumspect as it could've washed up from anywhere and not actually be associated with the body. The foreshore was under water an hour ago and the body's been submerged for God knows how long, so it's highly unlikely there'll be any random DNA to be found near the body or fingerprints to lift.'

'Great,' Wise said. 'It gets better and better.' He stared at the poor dead woman, wondering how she'd ended up in the river. Helen's description of death by water shock playing over in his mind. Death might well have happened in seconds, but they would be long, terrifying seconds and a truly awful way to die.

'I think it's safe enough for you to go down there now,' Vivian said. 'But please be careful where you step. The ground can be quite treacherous.'

'We will,' Helen said.

'Are you going to come down and have a look, Inspector?' Singh asked after Vivian had left them.

'Of course.' Wise held up his boots. 'I've come prepared.'

'Well, get suited up quickly,' Singh said. 'We've an hour before the tide's back so the clock's ticking.'

Wise glanced over at Hannah. 'You heard the lady.'

'I certainly did,' Hannah replied.

Vivian gave Wise a tight smile. 'If it's okay with you, I'd rather not go down myself.' Her eyes flicked over to the body. 'I think I'll be having nightmares about this for a long time as it is.'

'Certainly, but would you mind waiting here, though?' Wise asked. 'I'll probably want to talk to you after I've had a look myself.'

Vivian shuddered. 'I'll go and wait at one of the tables.'

'Thank you,' Wise said.

'Right. I'd better rally the troops,' Helen said. 'The clock's ticking.'

They all followed Vivian back down the steps to the lane.

'Can I have your attention please,' Helen called out to the greater group as they did so, making every head turn her way. 'We've been given the go-ahead to go down to the foreshore. We only have an hour, so move quickly, act smartly and go over everything thoroughly. And watch where you put your feet. I don't want to fill out any accident reports because someone put their big foot where they shouldn't. Any questions?'

No one spoke.

'Good! Now haul your arses and let's get this done,' Helen said, clapping her hands. Her team sprang into action, moving quickly up the stairs and over the top of the tidal wall.

Wise glanced over at Hannah. 'Let's get our party outfits on so we can join them. We've got a dead body waiting for us.'

6

Hannah took a deep breath as she followed Wise back over to where Hicksy waited with the others. The doctors might have signed her off as fit for work but she certainly didn't feel ready.

There was the permanent headache she'd had since she'd been hurt in Konza's ambush, for one thing. Right now, it was just a dull ache at the back of her skull but, sometimes, it got so bad that all she could do was curl up in a ball and cry.

Then there was her concentration. Everything just seemed ... off. Sometimes, she'd just miss snatches of conversation, a TV show would jump forward to a new scene without her noticing, or it'd be a completely different show altogether. It wasn't ideal, obviously, and more than a little frustrating when she was sitting on the sofa at home. However, this morning she'd been riding her Ducati Monster to Cousin Lane when everything skipped forward in a blink of an eye. She'd run a red light and nearly got taken out by a black cab. Now, the thought of getting on her bike — her love and joy — petrified her.

Finally, there was the paranoia. She didn't know if that was another side effect of the concussion or just the result of being ambushed by armed men with the intent of killing her. However, it made her see danger everywhere. A man who just happened to glance at her walking down the street was obviously a hitman out to get her. The woman reaching into her bag was going to produce a gun. The people who got into the lift with her intended to kidnap her. On and on it went. From morning to night.

It was stupid, of course. Her mind playing tricks on her. She knew that but it didn't make her feel any better. And she couldn't ignore it either. Because the moment she let her guard down, someone would get her.

Her hand drifted to her back and felt the bulge of the knife she had tucked away under her leather jacket. The next time someone tried to kill her, she'd not need to rely on a collapsable baton to defend herself. No way.

Even now, surrounded by police officers at a crime scene, she didn't like the fact she could get to the knife if she had to, trapped as it was under her SOCO protective over-suit, but there was no way she could walk around with it in her hand. That would get her busted off the job straight away.

Of course, Hannah was also aware that a knife wouldn't be much good if someone came after her again with a gun.

Shit.

'What do you think?'

The voice startled Hannah, snapping her back to the present. It was Hicksy but he was talking to Wise, not to her, thank God.

'It's not pretty down there,' Wise replied.

'Someone should've told her that skinny-dipping in January was a bad idea.'

'Alright,' Wise said with a wince. 'Have some sensitivity.'

'I'm not sure I've done that course yet,' Hicksy replied.

'Maybe you should get it booked in.'

'You know what they say about old dogs, Guv,' Hicksy replied with no hint of a smile. Normally, what Hicksy considered banter would've driven Hannah up the wall, but Jono had been his partner and best friend, so she made a mental note to cut him some slack.

Donut and Callum had turned up as well, standing just behind Hicksy, clutching coffees in their hands.

Of the two, Hannah liked Callum a lot. He was smart, ambitious, and a damn hard worker.

Donut, on the other hand, she wasn't so sure about. The man never actually seemed to contribute much. Tall and painfully thin, Donut seemed happy being told what to do and often found himself doing a lot of the grunt work that modern policing depended on.

However, even as she thought that, she noticed there was something different about the man. His hair, normally a bird nest on a bad day, was cut short and styled, and he was clean-shaven for a change. And, if she didn't know any better, Hannah could've sworn the man had a new shirt on. The collar certainly looked white instead of frayed and yellow like it normally was.

Brains wasn't with them, of course. He'd be back at the incident room in Kennington Police Station, doing what he did best — digging through the digital world.

Normally, Sarah Choi would be with him, getting everything set up for the start of a new investigation, keeping everyone organised and the balls rolling. But Sarah was dead, just like Jono.

A wave of sadness washed over Hannah. Sarah had been one of the first people she'd worked with at Kennington, and Hannah had liked her no bullshit attitude to life. It was hard to believe she'd killed herself in hospital. There'd been plenty of gossip in the pub about why she'd done it, but no one really had a clue — or, if they did, they weren't the ones doing the talking.

'Well, for now, I want the three of you to check out any cameras near here,' Wise said to Hicksy and the others. He pointed to one above the door of the pub. 'Start with that one. It looks like it covers all of the tabled area up to the stairs. I doubt our body was dumped here but you never know. Maybe we'll get lucky and see someone leading the victim down the lane, killing her and then throwing her over the side.'

'Fucking hell,' Hicksy said. 'If they did that, they might as well have left a note with their name and address on it.'

That got a chuckle from the others, but Wise ignored it. 'I also want full statements from the chap who found the body and any other witnesses.'

Hicksy nodded. 'We'll get on it now.'

'Good man,' Wise said.

'Come on,' Hicksy said to the others. 'You heard the governor.'

As they headed off towards the pub, Wise and Hannah walked over to the table where a SOCO was handing out forensic over-suits.

'It doesn't feel right seeing Hicksy without Jono by his side,' Hannah said as she climbed into her suit.

'I know,' Wise said as he struggled with the one-size-fits-all forensic suit. He was a big man and the suits always looked tight and uncomfortable on him. 'He was a good man.'

Hannah noted the sadness in Wise's voice and cursed herself for bringing Jono up. Yet again, she'd put her big boot right in it. 'Sorry, Guv.'

'It's alright,' Wise replied, but he didn't say any more than that and Hannah was smart enough to keep her mouth shut this time.

Once they were all suited up, they walked back up the stairs. The foreshore was already a hive of activity as the SOCOS combed the scene despite the fact that, as Helen Kelly said, there was little chance of finding anything that would help them.

The truth was that all their hopes rested with the body and what it could tell them.

Following Wise, Hannah concentrated as she climbed down the steep steps to the foreshore. There was no handrail to hold onto and it was easy to imagine falling off the stairs to the riverbed below. It wouldn't be a soft landing, either. Not with all the rocks and stones jutting out. She'd be lucky to only break a limb or two but, knowing her luck, it'd be her neck that went.

Again, Hannah felt the world shift around her and her sense of balance disappeared with the wind. She stopped to catch her breath, concentrating as hard as she could on moving down to the next step. Thank God, Wise was in front of her and couldn't see her struggling.

Halfway down, the steps turned from worn stone to modern steel just to make things worse. Mud and silt covered each step to keep everything treacherous. She could feel sweat pop out across her back despite the cold as she gingerly went from step to step, cursing all the way. A five-year-old could've done a better job of going down those stairs right then.

She glanced down as Wise moved confidently on the wet steps, graceful despite his big bulk, his forensic suit straining with every step. Enough people had told her that joining his team would be career suicide after what had happened to his last DS, but she was glad she'd ignored them all, despite what had happened to Jono and Sarah.

Whatever doubts she had about her own abilities, she had none when it came to working with Wise. Being on a Murder Investigation Team might be a thousand times harder than anything else she'd done since she'd joined the Met but, at long last, she had a governor who treated her with respect and wanted her opinion. In fact, the cold ambitious part of her was well aware that with Jono and Sarah gone, he'd need her more than ever.

She just needed her brain to start doing its own job properly so she could do better at hers.

When she reached the bottom of the stairs, she nearly gave a cry of joy, but she quickly realised the going was just as tough on the foreshore. The SOCOs had already set up a clear path to the body, marking the approach with cones, but every time she put her foot down on the silt, it sank in, and she had to tug it free. The process quickly became exhausting. She could imagine how dangerous it would be if she stepped into one of the holes they'd been warned about. Cursing herself for not thinking of it straight away, Hannah used rocks and half-buried bricks as stepping stones as she made her way over to the dead woman. But her balance was still off, so she had to hold her arms out wide to try and compensate. God only knew what the others must've thought of her stumbling along like that, though.

Singh was already at work with her examination of the body, while one of her assistants took pictures and video of the scene.

Stopping near Wise, Hannah watched as Singh lifted the head up, moving the hair away from the victim's face.

A shiver ran through Hannah when she saw the woman's bloated facial features for the first time. It was hard to imagine what she must've looked like when she was alive because immersion in the water had not been kind to her. Her skin had taken on a purple-ish marble colour and decomposition had been cruel to her features.

There was a stink in the air as well that only came from something dead and rotting but, thankfully, the breeze off the Thames stopped it from becoming too overwhelming. Throwing up in front of everyone because she couldn't handle the smell of a corpse was the last thing Hannah wanted to do, on top of everything else.

'Can you take pictures of this?' Singh said to the photographer, holding the head up and pointing to the neck. As her assistant snapped away, the doctor looked over at Wise. 'You might want to have a look.'

Wise gingerly made his way over and Hannah followed. She wasn't going to wait for an invite from Singh. Of course, when she got up close, a big part of Hannah wished she hadn't. She'd never seen a body in such a state and her stomach churned in protest. Hannah closed her eyes for a moment, gathering herself, angry that the sight of a dead body could upset her so much. What sort of murder detective was she going to be if she got upset every time she saw a corpse? Still, it didn't make it any easier when she opened her eyes again.

'It looks like the victim was dead before she went into the water.' Singh carefully lowered the woman's head and moved around the body. Singh pointed to the black stains on the victim's skin that ran along her spine. 'The marks on her back would indicate she was left somewhere, lying on her back, after she was killed and before she went into the Thames. Long enough for all the blood in her body to congregate here, causing the skin to discolour. I'll know more when I open her up. If there's water in the lungs, we'll know if she was still breathing when she went in. But on my first impressions here, I'd say not.'

'Any idea how long she was in the water?' Wise asked.

'Not that long. Two or three days perhaps. Long enough for her skin to start to slip but not long enough for anything too serious to start nibbling on her.' Singh held up one of the victim's hands. It looked like she had the remains of a white latex glove on, with the woman's fingernails, painted a deep purple, poking through it.

'What do you mean by "long enough for her skin to slip"?' Hannah asked, even though she wasn't sure she wanted to know the answer.

'Skin slippage is a part of the decomposition process. The top layers of skin become disconnected from the layers below and "slip" off the body. On land, this process can take weeks,' Singh said. 'In this case, water's soaked through the top layers of skin, making the cells holding the layers together separate far faster. It normally occurs after twenty-four hours of being submerged.' Singh pointed at the remains of what Hannah had thought was a glove. 'As you see here, the epidermis has begun to shed and the skin has literally slipped forward until it's broken away in chunks. Once we remove this, the layer of skin beneath it won't be as developed, making our chances of finding a fingerprint very difficult indeed.'

Hannah's jaw nearly dropped. 'That's her skin?'

'What's left of it,' Singh said. 'It's lucky we found her when we have, though. Another day or two and we could probably pull her whole birthday suit completely off.'

'Christ,' Hannah said. 'What a way to end up.' She stared at the woman, her skin hanging off her hands like a snake's. Whoever this woman was, she'd had a life, with friends, family, maybe a loved one, a job perhaps doing who knew what. Only for some bastard to come along and put an end to it all. Then he threw her into the river like she was trash. Leaving her with no dignity. Leaving her to rot.

Once more, Hannah felt the weight of responsibility fall on her shoulders. Whoever this woman was, she deserved justice for what happened to her. She just hoped she could deliver it. One thing was for certain, though, she'd not forget how this poor woman ended up. It was what nightmares were made of.

'Let's get this poor woman moved,' Singh said to one of her assistants. 'We can have a proper look at her back at the morgue.'

'Where are you going to take her?' Wise asked.

'King's College,' Singh replied. 'I try not to go too far north of the river unless someone gets my colleague suspended.'

Hannah looked up, only too aware of whom Singh was referring to.

'Technically, I didn't get him suspended,' Wise said, his voice just a little bit colder than normal. 'How is dear old Dodson anyway?'

Doctor Harold Dodson was another Home Office pathologist. He'd been sent to a murder of a homeless lad back in November that Wise and his team were investigating, but he'd turned up to the crime scene drunk — and it wasn't the first time that had happened. Wise ordered two uniformed officers to breathalyse him if he tried driving home afterwards but Dodson had refused the test, resulting in his arrest. Afterwards, he'd taken stress leave, probably to avoid a suspension.

'Still on leave,' Singh said. 'I don't think he'll be back for a while.' She stepped away from the corpse as her team began the grizzly task of unhooking the body from the wooden pole. They had to take their time to ensure they didn't damage the body further. 'There's talk he may take early retirement.'

'Might be a good thing,' Wise said. 'The Job can take its toll on people.'

The governor had a point. It was hard enough being a detective but, watching Singh and her team at work, Hannah had no idea how they did their job. Singh and her team spent every day, all day prodding and examining bodies in all sorts of desperate states, looking for clues hidden within them. Hannah wasn't sure she'd be able to get out of bed if she knew that was what she'd be doing all day.

'Hannah,' Wise said, breaking her from her thoughts. 'Let's go find the person from the Port Authority and ask her a few questions. I want to know where the currents come from around here. If we can work out a direction our victim could've drifted in from, we can narrow down where to do a CCTV search.'

'Sure, Guv,' Hannah replied, happy to get off the foreshore and away from the body.

Wise turned back to Singh. 'Any idea when you'll do the postmortem?'

'Sometime this afternoon. I'll have someone call you to confirm the time,' Singh said.

'Thanks, Doctor,' Wise said.

'Anything for you, Inspector. You know that.'

'It's appreciated,' Wise said.

Hannah followed Wise back towards the stairs, happy to be heading back to solid ground, even if it meant climbing those stairs again. Traipsing about on the foreshore had knackered her out and she could feel the headache building behind her eyes.

'Everything okay?' Wise asked as they reached the stairs.

Hannah nodded. 'Yeah.'

'You sure?'

'Sorry. I'm just a bit tired. I've not been sleeping well since the attack.'

'I know that feeling,' Wise said, indicating with his hand that Hannah should go up the stairs to Cousin Lane first. 'Why do you think I drink so much coffee?'

'I had wondered,' Hannah replied, not taking the invitation. 'I've never known anyone to drink as much as you do.'

'As bad habits go, it's not the worst,' Wise said. He must have realised she wasn't going to go first, because he started climbing up the stairs. 'Anyway, if you're not feeling up to being back at work just yet, tell me. We can always sort something out.'

'I will,' Hannah replied, knowing she wouldn't. In fact, she was annoyed he'd noticed she was struggling. Thankfully, it was easier going up than it had been going down. She had to use her hands a few times like a mountain climber, but she managed to keep pace with Wise.

Even her headache seemed to ease off once they reached street level and she had some good old-fashioned concrete beneath her feet and the stink of the corpse wasn't in her nose. She and Wise removed their forensic suits and handed them back to the SOCO responsible for them. They would be bagged and tagged along with anything that might be found at the scene, before they were eventually disposed of.

They found Vivian sitting on a bench, her eyes focused on a cup of tea in her hands.

'Do you mind if we join you?' Wise asked.

Vivian looked up, startled, then relaxed a fraction when she saw it was Wise and Hannah standing in front of her. 'Please,' she replied, waving at the bench on the other side of the table.

'Thank you,' Wise said, sitting down. Hannah took a place next to him. 'It must be very traumatic when you get called out to things like this.'

'It doesn't happen that often, thankfully,' Vivian replied. She swirled the tea around and around in its paper cup. 'And my team and I take it in turns to come out when it does. This is my first time in about three years. I still wish, though, that it wasn't me here.' She looked up, her eyes wide with shock despite her best efforts to be brave.

'I can imagine,' Wise said. He was using that soft tone of voice of his that made people almost forget he was six foot something tall and built like a brick shithouse. 'How long have you worked at the Port Authority?'

'I joined straight out of school, so it's been about thirty years now,' Vivian replied. 'A long time.'

'And what made you decide on it as a career back then?'

Vivian gave a little snort of laughter. 'I'm not sure we thought too much about careers in those days. The moment I'd done my exams, I went down to the job centre to see what sort of job I could get. There was no big thinking behind it. The port had a vacancy, the money was half-decent and the work itself seemed easy enough, so I applied and that was that.'

'You enjoy it, though?'

'Yeah. Apart from days like today.'

'Well, we won't keep you much longer,' Wise said. 'What we're really curious about is where do the currents come from around here? Where should we start looking for possible places the body could've gone into the water?'

'It's really hard to say,' Vivian replied. 'The Thames is a tidal river because we have water coming from the North Sea, which causes the high and low tides that you've witnessed today. They happen twice a day. Then there's the fresh water coming in from over fifty tributaries with currents of their own. And, of course, there's the boats going up and down and all the general traffic. So, basically, it's one big continuous swirl twenty-four hours a day. That's why the water always looks so dirty. It's just the silt being stirred up non-stop. The Thames actually has relatively clean water these days.'

'You're saying the body could've gone in anywhere?' Wise asked.

'Well, not anywhere. The Thames is two hundred and fifteen miles long and there are locks and weirs and things like that, which would stop a … a body from floating down river.' Vivian looked from Wise to Hannah and back again as if seeking reassurance in what she was saying. 'But I think the area you should look at is what we call the Tideway. That covers the river from Teddington Lock down to the Pool of London, which is this area here, and ends about five miles past London Bridge.'

'Just in case the killer used a boat to dump the body, is there CCTV covering the river we could look at?' Hannah asked.

Vivian flinched at Hannah's choice of words. 'Er … yes, there is. I'd need to know the time period you'd be interested in, but I can get that for you.'

Wise smiled. 'Thank you, Vivian. We'll call you later today with some dates.'

'Right. Okay.' Vivian rustled about in one of the pockets of her big red jacket and produced a card. 'Here's my number.'

Hannah took the card and glanced at it, noting the woman's full name was Vivian Carr. She resisted commenting that Vivian was working in the wrong transport industry with a name like that. 'Thank you.'

'We'll let you go now,' Wise said. 'Try not to dwell too much on what you've seen today. I can promise you this sort of thing doesn't happen that often.'

Wise and Hannah both stood up and, a few heartbeats later, Vivian did too. 'Right. Well. I'll speak to you later,' she said.

'Take care,' Hannah said. Once Vivian had scurried off, Hannah turned to Wise. 'What do we do next?'

'We need to put a name to our unfortunate lady in the river. Once we know that, we can work out who wanted to kill her,' Wise said. 'Let's get back to Kennington.'

Hannah nodded, already thinking about getting on her Ducati. She just hoped she'd not kill herself on the way to the station.

7

Wise was glad to have another case to focus on. It gave him another person to think about other than himself and his own problems. It was a chance to forget about the mess his own life was in.

Wise drove over Southwark Bridge and headed towards Borough, taking his time as he made his way through the various road works along the route. Like everywhere in London, Southwark was going through the gentrification process at a rapid rate. Modern buildings mingled with Georgian terraces, an old fire station had been converted into apartment blocks with a cafe taking up the ground floor, and the old building next door was now a posh school for rich kids.

Just after Wise passed an old pub that had been brightly painted to advertise the fact it was now an art school, he turned right onto Great Suffolk Street and then left into Webber Street. There were more glass-fronted buildings on one side and a wall of portacabins encircled a construction site on the other. After the tunnel, it was just a mishmash of housing lining both sides of the route, from new deluxe accommodation on one side to council houses in desperate need of repair on the other and everything else in between. It was modern London in a nutshell.

Wise took another left, this by The Stage Door pub, and drove down Gray Street and Morley Street, grateful that the back roads were relatively free of traffic. He had to slow as he passed the London Ambulance Station as yellow and green vehicles of every description were parked along the side of the road. Then it was along Baylis Road to Kennington Road and finally to the nick. Thankfully, the whole journey had taken him all of ten minutes for once.

After parking his car, he wandered over to Luigi's to pick up a coffee before going to the station. It was quiet inside and there was only Luigi's wife, Maria, and one of her daughters, Sofia, working behind the counter. Maria wasn't one for customer interaction and she didn't offer even the merest suggestion of a smile when Wise walked up to the counter.

'Yes?' she asked.

For some reason, Wise felt compelled to over-compensate for her brusqueness. He grinned like a five-year-old on Christmas day. 'Hi, happy new year. All good?'

Maria grunted. 'You want coffee?'

'A double espresso and a large Americano, please,' Wise replied, then remembered his empty stomach. 'And a bacon sandwich as well.'

Maria looked over her shoulder. 'Sofia! Double espresso, a large Americano and bacon sandwich.' She then turned back to Wise. 'Nine pounds, ninety.'

He held up his debit card and got another glare as Maria slapped down the payment machine and inputted the price. When Wise looked down, he saw the option for a tip displayed. They started at twenty percent. It was a bit much, considering the service had been all but hostile. However, Luigi's served the best coffee, and Wise was willing to forgive a lot for his caffeine fix. So, he added the tip to his total and tapped the card to authorise the payment. 'Luigi not here today?'

Maria gave him a look that seemed to doubt both his sanity and his ability as a detective for even asking such an obvious question. 'Get your drinks there,' she said, indicating to her right with a nod of her head.

Wise smiled again. 'Great chatting with you, as ever.' He moved to the other end of the counter before Maria tried murdering him with her death stare.

At least Sofia gave him a smile as she handed over his drinks and the sandwich, wrapped up in grease-proof paper. 'Dad's in bed with a cold,' she whispered. 'Mum thinks he's being a wimp for not coming into work.'

'Well, give him my best and I hope he gets better soon,' Wise replied, picking up his order.

'I will.'

Balancing the sandwich and the double espresso in one hand and holding the Americano in the other, Wise left the warmth of the cafe and immediately felt the bite of the cruel wind that whipped its way up Kennington Road. Grey clouds grumbled overhead, threatening more rain to add to the overall misery of the day. He just hoped it held off until he got inside the station. A soaking was the last thing he needed.

Not that things were much better once he was inside the nick. After all, the building's glory days were long gone by. No longer open to the public, it was home to pencil pushers and paper chasers for the most part, as well as housing five Murder Investigation Teams, one of which Wise ran. Normally, each team would consist of ten detectives and some civilian admin support, but it had been a long time since Wise had that number working with him. In fact, there was a part of him that wondered if he'd have a team at all for much longer. Yesterday's news about Riddleton returning hadn't exactly filled him with confidence about the future.

Wise's team operated out of Major Incident Room One, or MIR-One as it was known, located on the third floor of the station. Always one to avoid using a lift if he could, Wise trudged up the concrete steps, nodding at a few familiar faces as he passed.

Wise felt a sense of trepidation growing as he approached the incident room, only too aware of who wasn't going to be waiting for him inside. He'd lost over half his team in the last six months. Three were dead, one had transferred out and the other had quit the Met for good.

Of course, he knew there was fat chance of getting any extras in. He doubted there was a single part of the Met that was fully staffed these days, apart from the accountants and data boffins. Somehow, in today's police service, crunching numbers had become more important than solving crimes. It didn't help that the Home Secretary was only worried about TV opportunities where she could go on about how she was going to 'Stop The Boats', in an effort to appeal to the far right that made up her voting base. Wise sincerely hoped she and the rest of the useless government got voted into oblivion at the next election. With any luck, they'd get someone in charge who would want to build up the police again instead of stripping it to its bare bones.

At least, when he walked into MIR-One, he immediately spotted Brains at his desk, his face illuminated by his monitor's warm glow. The bespectacled officer looked up as Wise entered and gave him a nod in greeting before going back to tapping away on his keyboard.

Normally by now, Sarah would've started putting information up on the three whiteboards that covered the far wall. One said, *What do we know?* The second said, *What do we think?* and the third, *What can we prove?* Now, though, they were blank, ignored by the three newcomers huddled by one of the desks on the right-hand side of the room.

One of them was a middle-aged man, with strands of hair poking up in every direction in what looked like an attempt to hide the fact that he was losing more on top than he was growing. He was big too. Not like Wise was big, though. Maybe once he'd played rugby or something similar but now Wise wouldn't be surprised if most of his exercise was done down the pub, sinking pints while playing snooker or darts.

The two women were younger than the man. One looked like she was in her early thirties, with fire-engine red hair tied into a ponytail, revealing that the left-side of her head was shaved down to the scalp and a tattoo of a dragon crawling up her neck from beneath the collar of her denim shirt. Wise presumed she was Kat Galley, the civilian co-ordinator, who'd called him that morning, because no serving police officer would be allowed to look like that. The other woman, on the other hand, definitely looked like a police officer. Her blonde hair touched her shoulders in a neat bob and she wore a white shirt under a black jumper, matched with black trousers. Wise put her age around her mid-twenties.

He walked over. 'Hi. I'm DI Simon Wise.'

The redhead stepped forward. 'Hiya. I'm Kat. We spoke this morning.'

'That's right,' Wise replied. 'Thanks for getting everyone up and out.'

'That's what I'm here for. Did you want a cup of tea or anything?' she asked.

Wise held up his purchases from Luigi's so she could see them. 'I'm okay, thanks.'

Despite that, the other woman held out her hand to shake. 'I'm DC Millie Buchanan. I was transferred over from Hammersmith with DS Palmer.'

'Right,' Wise said. He put down his Americano and shook her hand. 'Great to meet you, Millie.'

'And I'm DS Palmer,' the man said, making a show of sticking his own hands in his pockets.

'No first name?' Wise said, doing his best to ignore the man's gruffness.

'I do, but everyone calls me Palmer.'

Wise nodded. 'Palmer it is then. Who were you working with in Hammersmith?'

'Doug Riddleton,' Palmer said. 'He asked us to come over with him.'

'Ah. That's good to know,' Wise said.

'Actually ...' Kat held up a finger as if asking permission to speak.

Wise smiled. 'Yes, Kat?'

Her cheeks coloured. 'DCI Riddleton asked if you could see him the moment you got in.'

'Of course,' Wise said, keeping his face impassive. 'Have they given him an office yet?'

'He's on the second floor. In the old DCI's office,' Kat replied.

'Okay. Can you let him know I'm on my way? I'll just drop my things in my office.' Wise indicated the door in the corner of MIR-One.

Kat nodded. 'Righto.'

'Thank you. And good meeting you all,' Wise said. 'I'll get you all briefed on the new case when I get back from seeing the DCI.'

Millie smiled and Palmer grunted in reply. Leaving them, Wise headed into his office. To call it small was probably being generous. There was barely enough space for his desk and the two chairs on either side of it, both of which had their backs against their respective walls.

And, right then, Wise felt the same.

He was under no illusion that Millie and 'everyone calls me Palmer' were there to help him. They were Riddleton's people, and they'd be reporting everything he did back to dear old Doug. Hopefully though, he wouldn't have to put up with them for long. The enquiry into Roberts had to exonerate her for what she did. Her actions had saved lives, after all.

After putting his coffees down on his desk, he took off his overcoat and hung it over the hook on the back of his door. He then prised the lid off the espresso and downed it in one gulp. Luckily, the walk from Luigi's had allowed it to cool down just enough, so it was comfortably hot rather than scalding. Immediately, he felt better as the caffeine worked its magic.

He then ripped open the wrapping to his sandwich and demolished it quickly with big, hungry bites. Like everything Luigi's made, it tasted divine. The bread was just the right thickness, soaking up some of the bacon fat and melted butter, and the bacon was crispy without being burnt.

Once that was gone, Wise felt just about human again. Maybe, he felt strong enough to face Riddleton.

He picked up his Americano just in case he needed an extra boost and left his office.

'Doctor Singh has called,' Kat said when she saw him reappear. 'She's doing the PM this afternoon. She asked if you could come down around two to go over whatever she's found.'

'She's not wasting any time,' Wise said. 'That's good.'

'Anything you want me to be getting on with until then?' Kat asked.

Wise glanced over at Brains. 'Have you met Alan yet?'

Kat followed his gaze. 'We said hello.'

'Well, we call him Brains. It's not very original but very apt. He's your man when it comes to HOLMES and anything technical. Let's get him started on trawling through Missing Persons for IC1 females. Concentrate on any reported missing in the last week or so. You never know, we might get lucky and find who our lady in the river is.'

'What about CCTV?'

'Wait until we get a better idea of the victim's time of death. I don't want you drowning in footage unnecessarily.' Wise winced. 'Sorry. Not the best choice of words.'

'I'll forgive you,' Kat said.

'Can you chase Hicksy and the boys up as well? Tell them to be back here for five for a debrief. Hopefully, we'll have some information from the PM to share as well.'

'Will do, Guv.'

Wise nodded. He pointed to the blank whiteboards. 'I like having everything recorded on those boards. Put Jane Doe down for our vic's name until we get a real one for her, plus where she was found and anything else we know now. And make sure they stay updated as the investigation progresses.'

'No problem.' Kat smiled like she'd just been given the best job in the world to do. Wise had to admit it was a welcome change to his own dour mood. He had a feeling he was going to like having Kat around.

'Thank you,' Wise replied. 'Now, I'd better go and see my new boss.'

8

Wise didn't hurry as he made his way down to the second floor to Roberts' old office. He knew he was being childish, but he'd never liked Riddleton from the very first moment they'd met on a course at Hendon. The man was a political animal and Wise's complete opposite in nearly every way. What was worse, the man had a smugness to him that irritated Wise on a primal level. Every time the men had met, it had taken a miracle to stop Wise from plunging his fist into Riddleton's face. It didn't take a genius to work out that the more time that he and Riddleton spent together, the harder it would be to stop himself from acting on that impulse.

He only hoped that it wasn't going to be today that he lost that battle.

Roberts' office door was closed, so Wise knocked.

'Enter,' Riddleton's voice boomed out, sounding like some lord of the manor.

'Don't hit him,' Wise whispered to himself, then opened the door.

Even though he knew Roberts wasn't going to be there, it still felt strange walking into his old boss' office and not seeing her behind her desk, glasses perched on her nose, battling with a mountain of paperwork.

Instead, there was dear old Doug Riddleton behind her desk. He didn't look up as Wise entered, keeping his attention focused on whatever was on his monitor. He might've been reading something important, but it could just have as easily been a weather report or a game of solitaire on his screen. Either way, the effect was the same. It was the DCI's way of letting Wise know that Riddleton was an important man with important things to do and Wise, being less important, could wait for a moment of his attention.

Sitting down, Wise kept his face impassive, determined not to let the man wind him up. He had enough to deal with without making matters worse for himself. Grateful he'd brought his coffee with him, he took a sip while he waited, noting that Riddleton hadn't changed much in the months since they'd last seen each other. He'd grown a goatee, perhaps to compensate for the ever-increasing bald patch on the top of his head. He was tanned, though, and Wise had to hide a smile as he pictured Riddleton spraying on his bronzed skin.

Still not looking at him, Riddleton tapped away at his keyboard for a moment, then made a dramatic act of pressing the return key. 'And done.' He leaned back in his chair, making eye contact with Wise for the first time. His beard twitched as he smiled. 'Simon. Happy new year.'

'Doug. You're looking well,' Wise replied, doing his best to sound like he meant it. Wise had no doubt that whatever feelings he had towards Riddleton, those feelings were mutual on his new boss' part as well.

'I managed to escape with the family to the Caribbean over the break,' Riddleton said. 'Did us the world of good.'

'I imagine it would.' Wise thought of his own Christmas, of the coldness growing between himself and Jean, the tears shed by his children when they realised they weren't all going home together.

'I hear your team had an early call out this morning.' It was a statement, not a question. Riddleton's way of letting Wise know he was keeping tabs on him, perhaps?

'A woman's body washed up on the side of the Thames as the tide went out,' Wise said.

Riddleton nodded. 'And it's one for us?'

'She either killed herself or someone killed her. PM's this afternoon. We'll know more then.'

'Right. Right. Who's the pathologist?'

'Doctor Harmet Singh.'

'Any good?'

'The best,' Wise replied.

Riddleton nodded. 'Are you going?'

'To the PM?'

'Yes.'

'Yes.'

Silence fell between them. It was uncomfortable in every way as each man watched the other. It was an old interrogator's trick to get someone to talk. When the pressure of no one speaking got too much, the idea was that the suspect would start blabbing away. But Wise knew that game only too well. He simply sipped his coffee and waited.

In the end, it was Riddleton who spoke. 'What time's she cutting?'

'Doctor Singh asked me to be there just after two.'

Riddleton opened up a leather diary on his desk and made a show of reading his appointments for the day. When he looked up, he was smiling, and Wise didn't like that. 'Excellent. I'll come with you. We can take my car.'

Wise raised an eyebrow. 'It'll be a pleasure to have you but are you sure you don't have too much to oversee here? DCI Roberts always found it difficult to get away.'

White teeth flashed behind Riddleton's thick beard. 'I'm not like DCI Roberts. I run a tight ship, and I like to know everything that's going on with my teams.'

Wise smiled. 'Wonderful.'

'Have you met Palmer and Buchanan yet?'

'A couple of minutes ago,' Wise replied.

'They're good coppers,' Riddleton said. 'They'll be assets to your team.'

'I'm sure they are.'

'And I know they're not bent,' Riddleton said. 'Which will make a change for here.'

Wise ignored the barb, his mind going back to the meeting at Hendon with SCO10. He'd been given some idea then about how widespread corruption really was within the Met. He'd found out then that there were hundreds of police officers taking backhanders, doing dodgy deals and providing protection for the very worst criminals in London.

Like his brother, Tom.

If Riddleton thought keeping his eagle eyes on the problem was going to make a difference, he was going to be very sadly mistaken.

'Playtime is over, Simon. We're going to run things differently here from now on. No more cowboys going off doing their own thing. No more corrupt cops selling us out.' Riddleton lowered his head so he was looking at Wise from under his eyebrows. 'Do I make myself clear?'

'Like crystal ... sir,' Wise replied.

'Good. Now, I expect updates every day on your cases. When do you do your Daily Management Meetings?'

'Normally, first thing in the morning,' Wise said. 'However, we're having one this afternoon once everyone's back, so we can make a good start tomorrow.'

Riddleton nodded. 'I'll attend the ones I can. If I can't make it, you're to find me immediately afterwards and brief me.'

'Got it.'

'You'd best get back to it,' Riddleton said, waving him away. 'I'll meet you downstairs at 1:30.'

'Can't wait.' Wise stood up, imagining the satisfaction of driving his fist into the man's face. He'd break Riddleton's nose, maybe take some teeth out as well. It would be quite satisfying but not worthwhile enough to lose his job over.

He left the DCI's office and headed back towards the stairs. With any luck, Riddleton's plan to be all over Wise like a nasty rash wouldn't last long. The man had four other teams to oversee after all, each as busy as Wise's.

He was halfway up the stairs when his phone rang. Fishing his mobile out of his pocket, he saw the caller ID said, *DCI Heer*. It gave him a rush of excitement to lift his mood. Heer was the senior officer at SCO10, the team investigating Tom.

He answered the call. 'Morning.'

'Simon,' Heer replied. 'Happy new year.'

'Is it?' Wise replied. He stopped on the half-landing between the second and third floors and gazed out of the window. Dark clouds lay across the top of the buildings, smothering any hope of seeing the sky.

'Probably not,' Heer replied. 'But we can live in hope.'

'So, you don't have good news?'

'No but what are you doing tomorrow at 7 a.m.?'

'Well, normally I'd be getting ready for work at that time. Why?' Wise could feel his heart beat faster.

'Fancy meeting me at the Travelodge in Finsbury Park?' Heer said. 'There's someone I want you to meet. Can't say any more than that right now.'

'I'll be there.'

'Okay. Speak then.' Heer ended the call.

Wise stood staring at the phone in his hand for a moment, his mouth dry, wondering just who Heer wanted to introduce him to.

And Heer had rung at the right time. A reminder of what was important. Let Riddleton play his games, his politics. Wise had a dead woman who needed his help and, more importantly, he had a brother who needed to be stopped.

Everything else was noise.

9

Wise was lost in thought when Hannah knocked and stuck her head around his door. 'You ready to head down to the morgue?'

Glancing at his phone, Wise saw it was 1:25 p.m. He looked up and smiled. 'I am indeed.' He stood up, put on his suit jacket and walked around his desk before unhooking his coat from the back of the door. 'Oh, just so you know — Doug Riddleton is joining us.'

'Fantastic,' Hannah said, looking as enthusiastic about the prospect of spending the afternoon with the new DCI as Wise felt. That wasn't surprising. The last time Riddleton had been running things during the Motorbike Killer investigation, Hannah had gone rogue with Wise. They may have found the real culprit, but they'd also made Riddleton look like a fool in the process.

Wise just raised an eyebrow. 'Maybe keep how you feel to yourself, eh?'

'I'll do my best, Guv,' Hannah replied.

'You feeling better after this morning?' he asked as they walked through MIR-One. 'You looked a little peaky down at the crime scene.'

'I'm fine,' Hannah replied, looking away. 'The sight of the body just turned my stomach a bit.'

'I'm not surprised. It was pretty bad.' Wise glanced around the incident room. Most of the team were still down at Cousin Lane but Brains was beavering away at his desk and Kat was on the phone to someone. There was no sign of Palmer or Millie, though. Maybe they'd gone out for lunch or something.

They took the stairs down to the ground floor. 'Apparently, Doug's driving,' Wise said.

'I'm not surprised,' Hannah replied. 'Your car's seen better days.'

'It's knackered but it does its job,' Wise said. 'A bit like its owner.'

Hannah laughed. 'I think you're holding up a bit better. At least you haven't got any dents in your face.'

'My wounds are all hidden,' Wise said, hiding the truth in the joke.

'I wonder what the DCI drives.'

'Something flashy, no doubt.'

'Mercedes E-Class,' Hannah said as they reached the reception area.

'You sound quite sure about that,' Wise said with a chuckle.

Hannah pointed through the window into the car park. Riddleton was standing next to a black Mercedes E-Class, talking to Palmer and Millie. 'They look the best of friends.'

'Yeah,' Wise replied. 'They are. Watch what you say around them. I've got a feeling that they haven't got our best interests at heart.'

'Wonderful.'

Riddleton looked over as Wise and Hannah stepped out into the car park. 'Ah, Simon. Good to see you here early.' He then fixed his gaze on Hannah. 'DS Markham.'

'Hello, sir,' Hannah replied. 'It's good to see you again.'

'Is it?' Riddleton replied coldly. 'Where are you off to?'

'Hannah always comes with me to the PMs,' Wise said.

'Well, there's no need to today,' Riddleton said. 'Between myself, you and DS Palmer, I think we'll have more than enough people in attendance. I'm sure there's something else more useful that DS Markham could be getting on with.'

Hannah stopped walking. 'Oh, right.' She looked to Wise, unsure of what to do.

'With all due respect,' Wise said, doing his best to control his temper, 'I'd rather Hannah was with us. I value her opinion and she's been invaluable in solving our more recent cases.'

Riddleton scoffed at that. '*I* think you'll find DS Palmer will be more ... invaluable.'

Wise glanced at Palmer, who wasn't embarrassed in the slightest at what was going on. In fact, he looked like he was enjoying himself. 'Sir, I'd really ...'

Hannah put her hand on his arm. 'It's alright, Guv. I'll catch up with you later.'

'It's not alright,' Wise said.

'Don't play his game,' she whispered.

Wise took a breath, knowing she was right. He nodded. 'Alright. I'll catch up with you later.'

'I'll come up with you,' Millie said to Hannah. She turned to Riddleton. 'Good catching up with you, boss.'

'And you.' Riddleton flashed his teeth at Wise. 'Shall we be off? Palmer's driving.'

'Sure,' Wise said.

He walked over to the Mercedes and went to open a rear door, but Riddleton pointed to the front passenger seat. 'You can go up front with Palmer. I've got some work to do while we drive.'

Wise smiled, while once again imagining what it'd be like to punch Riddleton in his smug face. But Hannah was right. It was best not to react. The man obviously wanted to wind Wise up. However, it was up for debate whether he wanted to put Wise in his place or provoke him, instead, into doing something stupid that would get him kicked off the force.

So, Wise climbed into the front passenger seat like a good little boy and buckled up. Palmer got into the driver's seat without saying a word and Riddleton sat in the back, immediately getting his phone out 'to work'.

No one spoke as they made their way down to the morgue at King's College Hospital in Camberwell. The traffic was its normal mess, but Wise had to admit the Mercedes was a comfortable car to while away the time in as they inched their way forward. Certainly a damn site better than his own car. Somehow, he doubted it was issued by the Met — not unless Riddleton had some really serious friends looking after him. Then again, Wise knew how much a DCI earned. It wasn't enough to be able to afford a car like that.

Then again, maybe Riddleton was independently wealthy. Or had another revenue stream to bolster his pay. Of course, in light of how both Andy and Sarah were 'earning' extra income, that also raised some questions, but Wise doubted that Riddleton was dodgy. If he was, he'd have to be an idiot to display so publicly any ill-gotten gains.

After signing in at the morgue, one of Singh's lab assistants came to meet them and took them to get dressed in protective clothing before leading them over to where Singh was carrying out the postmortem.

Singh and her team were hard at work in Examination Room Two. They all wore green smocks, hats, masks and gloves. One assistant helped Singh while another videoed the procedure.

The victim lay on a metal table with her organs already removed and weighed. The woman's face was now visible, but it was bloated from its time in the water and her skin was a mottled mess of purple and blue. The thought of asking her parents or loved one to identify her flashed through Wise's mind and he hoped that was a task that science could spare them all from going through. No one should have their last memory of whoever this woman was to be the sight of her like this.

'Inspector,' Singh said without looking up. 'You're on time for once.' She was checking the fingernails of the victim's left hand. 'That makes a pleasant change.'

Wise winced. He hated being late for anything, but London's

traffic made that that an inevitability more often than not. 'Good to see you too, Doctor.'

'You've not got DS Markham with you,' Singh said.

'No,' Wise replied, still annoyed that she wasn't there. 'This is DCI Riddleton and DS Palmer.'

'I'm honoured,' Singh replied. She glanced up then, running her eye over both men.

'I'm pleased to meet you, Doctor Singh,' Riddleton said, stepping forward. For a moment, Wise thought he was going to try to shake Singh's hand. 'I've heard good things about you.'

'And so you should,' Singh said, dropping her head back down to concentrate on what she was doing. 'Our victim is Caucasian, mid to late twenties in age, one hundred and seventy-three centimetres tall —that's five feet seven inches in old money. Weight's fifty-eight kilos. If she wasn't dead, she be very healthy. No diseases or signs of any substance abuse that I can see. Lungs are pretty clean so she wasn't a smoker, just someone who's lived in a city all her life. No old injuries to note. No operation scars. Even her teeth are pretty damn near perfect, with just the one filling on a bottom left molar.'

'Do you know how she died?' Riddleton asked.

'Of course,' Singh said, raising an eyebrow. 'We haven't just been standing around gossiping over this poor girl's corpse.'

'And?'

'She died of asphyxia,' Singh said.

'She drowned,' Riddleton replied.

'I said she died of asphyxia,' Singh repeated. 'I didn't say she drowned. They are very different ways of dying.'

Wise had to force himself not to grin as Riddleton made a humph noise behind his mask. Wise could've sworn the man's cheeks coloured as well and his fondness for Singh only grew.

'More specifically, her killer smothered this poor woman to death, probably with a pillow or something similar,' Singh continued. 'Now before you ask, I'm not making a lucky guess at this but going by the evidence in front of me. First of all, there was no water in the woman's lungs. So, that rules out drowning.

'Next, there are subconjunctival haemorrhages in her eyes. This is caused by suffocation or, to use its technical term, asphyxia. Plus, we've also found high levels of carbon dioxide in the blood that's caused as the body uses up what little oxygen there is, and the victim can't exhale. There's also bruising on her torso that indicates the killer straddled her as they did it. However, there's no bruising around her neck, so she wasn't strangled. Therefore, my most humble suggestion that someone, most probably a man, used a pillow, or something similar, to kill her. And there are no defensive wounds either.' Singh rattled off the information like a boxer delivering a flurry of blows to an out-matched opponent and Wise loved every moment of it.

'No defensive wounds?' Wise repeated. 'So, she felt safe with the killer. She let him climb on top of her.'

Singh nodded. 'Either that or she wasn't aware that they were doing it. Perhaps she was unconscious or asleep.'

'Or drugged,' Riddleton added.

'Perhaps. We'll know more when we get her blood work back,' Singh said.

'But this definitely wasn't a fight or argument that got out of control?' Wise asked.

'No. Not at all.' Singh's tone changed now she was replying to Wise. 'Whoever did this was quite precise in what they did. Even their actions afterwards suggest very calm, calculated behaviour. For instance, the victim's fingernails have been cut far too short to have been done by the victim. I would imagine this was done by the killer to ensure there was no DNA trapped beneath them. They then left the poor girl lying somewhere on her back for anything from twelve to twenty-four hour hours — going by the postmortem lividity of the skin.'

'Waiting until it was safe to move the body,' Wise said.

'I would imagine so.'

Wise stared at the corpse on that cold, metal table, imagining her last moments, the terror she must've felt as someone sat on her and pressed a pillow against her face, fighting for her life, feeling the air run out. It was no way to die.

Then he thought of a person who could do that. The coldness in them — no, in him. It had to be a man. Bigger and stronger, the woman trapped beneath him, unable to escape no matter what she did. He took care in the way he killed her and then in the way he dealt with the body. Not hurried. Not scared. Taking his time. Making no mistakes. 'Why dump her in the water, though? Why not bury her? Or burn her?'

'I can't tell you that,' Singh said. 'Maybe it was just easier? But, by throwing her in the river, they ensured the body was cleaned of any stray forensic evidence that might have been left on the body, as well as making it impossible to fingerprint the victim. I've taken x-rays of her teeth and extracted a DNA sample, so we have something to identify her with but that's it.'

'Only if her DNA is in our database,' Riddleton said.

'Quite.' Singh sighed. 'Thank you for telling me that.'

'I don't like this,' Wise said. 'I don't like this at all. Most murders are messy affairs, acts of spontaneity carried out in the heat of the moment. But not here. The killer's done a great job of covering up for themselves.'

'You're not making excuses already, are you?' Riddleton said.

'No, not excuses,' Wise replied. 'Just trying to get an idea of who we're looking for.'

'The only other thing that might help identify our victim is that she has a tattoo on her right ankle,' Singh said.

'What of?' Wise asked.

'No idea,' Singh said. She walked to the bottom of the body and Wise followed, aware of Riddleton and Palmer on his heels. 'If you look here, you can see ink marks on what's left of the skin but, again, the slippage has made it difficult to tell what the actual design was.'

Wise peered at the ankle. Amongst the ripples of skin, he could make out blue blurred lines, leading into a larger area filled in with more ink. 'Is there any way to smooth out the skin so we can get a clearer image?'

'That sort of thing only really works on TV, Inspector.'

Wise sighed. 'Should we give Nikki Alexander a call then?'

'This isn't the time for flippant remarks, Simon,' Riddleton said.

'I wish I had better news for you,' Singh said, ignoring the DCI.

'Any idea when she was killed?' Palmer asked.

Singh glanced over at him. 'Even that's hard to narrow down. The water's not our friend when it comes to the usual guides we use to judge these things. The best I can say is three or four days ago.'

'You said earlier that you thought the victim had been in the water for two or three days,' Wise said.

'And I still think that,' Singh replied. 'The skin slippage and general state of decomposition backs that up.'

Wise nodded. 'So, she was murdered either Saturday or Sunday, left somewhere for up to a day, then moved and dumped in the Thames.'

'That's right,' Singh said.

'Okay. That's something at least,' Wise replied. 'What about the net she was in?'

'Actually, I'm not sure if she was wrapped up in the net by the killer or if it was something she just got caught up in after she'd been dumped in the water,' Singh said. 'We've sent it off to the lab anyway. Maybe they can work some magic and tell us something useful.'

'Thanks,' Wise said, feeling disappointed. He knew it wasn't Singh's fault, but he'd really hoped she'd have something more that he could work with.

'Contents of her stomach are interesting, though,' Singh said. 'It looks like she had a nice meal before she died.'

'How nice?'

'We found traces of beef, a bit of potato, some other vegetables.'

'As last meals go, it's not the worst,' Wise said.

'And that's all I have for now,' the pathologist said. 'I'll be in touch with you, Inspector, if we come across anything else that might help you.'

'I hope that'll be soon, then,' Wise said.

Wise, Riddleton and Palmer left the examination suite and

headed back to the changing room to dispose of their forensic suits and retrieve their coats.

'I'm not sure I liked that woman's attitude,' Riddleton said. 'I'll be having words with her bosses.'

'She is very good at what she does, Doug,' Wise replied.

Riddleton fixed him a look. 'I think we should keep things more formal now you're officially working for me. You can call me 'Boss' or 'Sir', if you must.'

Wise nodded, screwing up the suit and shoving it into the waste bin. 'As you wish, *sir*.'

As they headed back to Riddleton's Mercedes, Wise let the other two walk in front of him. It been good to see that Riddleton was the one who'd got riled. He really did owe Singh a drink for that.

Still, he had more important things to think about other than petty point scoring with his new boss. Whoever had killed that poor girl back in the morgue was a cold and calculating killer who knew exactly what they were doing. They had to kill that woman for some reason, so they did exactly that. No more, no less.

He had a feeling this was going to be another nasty one to solve.

10

Thankfully, Riddleton didn't want to join Wise for the catch up in MIR-One and left them on the second floor as Wise and Palmer headed up to the incident room on the third floor.

'How long have the pair of you been working together?' Wise asked once they were alone.

Palmer looked at Wise briefly as they climbed the stairs. 'About six years now. We've been based out of Hammersmith mainly but the Brass move him about a bit, so we've worked at most stations at one point or another.'

'You been working mainly on murders?'

'Nah,' Palmer replied. 'We done all sorts — fraud, robberies, blackmail, the odd drug bust — but they've all been high profile, if you know what I mean.'

That bit of news didn't surprise Wise. Riddleton had always been a headline chaser. 'How come you didn't join Doug when he took over the Motorbike Killer investigation?'

'I was on holiday with the missus in Tenerife.'

'That's as good a reason to miss out on the fun as any,' Wise said with a smile as they reached the third floor.

Palmer looked at Wise again, his eyes twisted in a scowl. 'Yeah? Well, maybe if he'd had someone helping him who was a team player, things might've turned out different in that case. Instead, it sounds like he was sabotaged at every turn by a right bunch of cunts.'

Palmer walked off before Wise could reply. Wise watched him go into MIR-One, both flabbergasted and outraged at the man's bluntness. Wise and the others had hardly sabotaged Riddleton's handling of the Motorbike Killer investigation. Wise himself had been taken off the case and sent home, while Riddleton had Hannah answering phones. The DCI had then set a course of action that went against everything Wise had uncovered at that point. He then made massive assumptions based on hare-brained psychology that had eventually been proved to be about as wrong as a theory could get. Granted, Riddleton had come out of things looking a right arse, but he'd achieved that all by himself.

Still, like all of Riddleton's games, Palmer's attitude and opinions were a distraction he had to ignore. He wouldn't let anyone think they could rattle him. Taking a deep breath, Wise fixed his face into a mask and followed Palmer into the incident room.

Everyone was there, waiting for him. He walked straight over to Kat. 'Can you write up on the boards all the key points that come up, please?'

'Of course,' she replied, grabbing a marker.

Wise turned to face his team. 'Evening, everyone. I won't keep you long tonight as we all had an early start this morning. First of all, I'm sure you've already met each other but we have some new faces on the team. Kat is our new Ops Manager. She's a civilian so make sure you're all nice to her — especially you, Hicksy.'

Hicksy held up both hands. 'You know me, I'm always as good as gold.'

That got a laugh from the old hands.

'We also have DC Millie Buchanan and DS Palmer — who doesn't have a first name. They've come from Hammersmith nick, where they worked with our temporary DCI, Doug Riddleton.' Wise looked over at the two detectives, who were standing side-by-side against a wall. 'I'm really grateful you're here and I know you'll be invaluable to us in our investigations.'

'It's good to be here, Guv,' Millie said. Palmer just deepened his scowl.

'Right, now the introductions are done, let's get down to business,' Wise said. 'As you know, we were called out this morning because the body of an unidentified IC1 female was discovered on the foreshore off Cousin Lane. As of this moment, we still don't have a name for her, but Doctor Singh has confirmed her height as one metre and seventy-three centimetres, her weight as fifty-eight kilos and her age as somewhere in her mid-to-late twenties.' As he spoke, Kat started writing down the information on the board under the heading of *What do we know?*

'What about cause of death?' Hicksy asked. 'It's definitely suspicious?'

'Doctor Singh believes our victim was smothered by a pillow apparently sometime on either Saturday or Sunday night, left somewhere for up to a day and then dumped into the Thames,' Wise replied. 'So, yeah — it's definitely murder.

'Obviously, identifying her has to be our number one priority. Unfortunately, her submergence in the water means we won't have any fingerprints to help us. We'll have her DNA data back tomorrow but that won't do us much good unless she was arrested at some point. The only other identifiable mark we know is that our victim has a tattoo on her right ankle but, again, water damage to the skin means we don't know what the design was.

'Once we know that, we can start building up a picture of her life and work out why she ended up in the Thames and who did it. Brains — have you found any possible MisPers for us to look at?'

'A few,' Brains said, standing up from behind his monitor. 'But it's not that straight-forward.'

Of course it wasn't. 'What do you mean?' Wise asked.

'Well, one hundred and eighty thousand people are reported as missing in the UK every year. That means a new case gets logged every ninety seconds.' Brains paused for a moment to let those figures sink in. 'And this being London, we get the biggest chunk of those calls — a staggering one hundred a day. Luckily, most of those are cleared up within a few hours. Normally, the supposed MisPer has just gone down to the shops without telling anyone or stayed late at the pub or snuck off to spend the night with their boyfriend or whatever, without telling their parents. That's why we don't respond to a lot of the initial calls straight away. There's just no point. Then, out of the remaining cases, nearly all get cleared up within two or three days. Only three percent of cases are still ongoing for a week or more. And, of course, there's plenty of people who just disappear, and no one even notices they've gone, let alone reports them missing.'

'Right, but what does that mean for us?' Wise said.

'Well, if we assume that our victim wasn't a long-term MisPer and only concentrate on people who have been reported missing this week, we've had two hundred and twelve cases. Out of those, a good number are already no longer missing while more new cases are being reported every minute,' Brains said. He bent down, tapped at his keyboard, then checked his screen, before standing up once. 'But, working within those moving figures and using the data Doctor Singh has given us as per their age and ethnicity, well, at this moment, we have seven possibles.'

'Bloody hell,' Hicksy muttered. 'You could've just said that.'

'That's good. Seven's a manageable number with our resources,' Wise said. 'You got pictures?'

Brains tapped away at his keyboard and seven headshots appeared on the big screen by the whiteboards. Seven women with blonde hair in their twenties. Wise stared at them, trying to recognise the person he'd seen in the morgue. It was hard, though, as the images of the women were so full of life, taken at various social occasions or just reacting to whoever was taking the picture. He could see a part of the victim in each of them but there wasn't one that jumped out as if to say: 'It's me'.

'Let's start checking them out,' Wise said. 'Hopefully, we can narrow the possibles down even more.'

'There is the one proviso though,' Brains said. 'There's a chance our victim's not been reported missing yet. Depending on what type of life she led, she might not have friends or family to notice she's gone. If she had a job, her employers might think she's just got a cold or something and they're not too worried she's not turned up for work. Maybe she doesn't even have a job or she's a contract worker. Maybe she was homeless.'

'Well, let's work with what we've got so far,' Wise said. 'Hicksy?'

Hicksy slid his foot off his knee and leaned forward. He didn't stand. 'I'm not saying we wasted the day but, except for sore feet, we've got fuck all to show for it. No witnesses to anything. No CCTV footage of anything. The pub had a camera overlooking the lane and their tables that also had a good view of where the body turned up. But, when we went over the week's footage, the first time we see the body is this morning when the tide goes down. There's no one carrying a body and chucking it in the drink.'

'Alright. Thanks for doing that,' Wise said. 'Can you help Brains go through the MisPers? Callum and Donut can crack on with gathering CCTV footage. We're looking at Sunday or Monday night as possible drop times. Start with the nearby bridges and riverbanks on the north side of the Thames, heading east, and go from there.'

'Absolutely,' Callum said, eager as a puppy.

'Millie?' Wise said. 'Can you give the boys a hand with that?'

'Sure,' Millie replied. 'That sounds like fun.'

'Hannah, keep an eye out for the DNA results,' Wise continued. 'Doctor Singh said we should have them by tomorrow afternoon.'

Hannah nodded. 'Will do, Guv.'

'Alright, everybody. It's a slow start but necessary,' Wise said to the team. 'Once we know who the victim is, things will pick up. Let's call it a night now and go hard again in the morning.'

No one needed telling twice. Even Hicksy was up on his feet quicker than normal, shoving his pack of cigarettes in his suit pocket, eager to be off. Before Wise could head back to his office, though, Hannah came over. 'Did everything go okay at the PM?'

Wise knew she wasn't talking about Doctor Singh's work. 'Just the usual nonsense. Sorry you got caught up in that. You know I'd have preferred for you to be there.'

'It is what it is,' Hannah said. 'I'll see you in the morning.' Her voice was quiet. Subdued.

'Are you sure you're okay?' Wise asked.

'I'm fine,' she replied.

Wise knew she wasn't being honest, but he let it go for now. He had enough worries of his own. 'See you tomorrow.'

Alone in his office again, with the door shut, Wise once more gazed out over Kennington Road. The pub opposite was busier now, its windows casting a flickering orange glow out over the concrete world outside as more people bustled through its doors. He could almost hear the laughter inside, the raised voices fighting to be heard over the chink of drinks. He remembered days gone by when he'd be in somewhere similar, enjoying the good times, when his only concern was who was buying the next round.

Now, though? He had enough worries to last him a lifetime.

Hopefully, his meeting in Heer in the morning would be a step towards solving some of them.

Thursday 5th January

11

Wise arrived in Finsbury Park fifteen minutes early for his meeting with DCI Heer. The Travelodge had its own carpark, but he ignored it, driving on until he found a spot around five minutes' walk away in in Coleridge Road. He walked back towards the Travelodge on Isledon Road, pulling his overcoat tight around him.

It was still dark and bitterly cold, but there were a few people out, hustling along to wherever they had to go. Most had their heads down and were avoiding eye contact with anyone who might be passing, in the way that all true Londoners did. Even so, Wise checked out everyone as subtly as he could, feeling more than a healthy dose of paranoia as he headed to his clandestine meeting with DCI Heer. He didn't need to be told that there was a good reason why they were meeting at an anonymous hotel instead of anywhere more official. Everything Wise had learned of his brother's business dealings so far had reinforced the fact that Tom took his own security very seriously and would act ruthlessly to protect it.

Wise was on the opposite side of the street to the hotel when his phone beeped. It was a message from Heer. *Room key waiting for you at reception. In the name of Andrew Simon.*

Putting his phone back in his pocket, Wise jogged across the road to the brown-brick Travelodge. It was sandwiched between a set of rundown Georgian terrace houses on one side and a modern curved building offering student accommodation on the other, but the moment Wise walked through its doors, he could've been in any Travelodge in the country with its very corporate and anonymous interior design.

A tired-looking woman stood behind the brightly lit, blue reception desk, with the word *Welcome* running along its front. She looked up as Wise approached, the harsh lighting doing her no favours.

Wise smiled. 'You should have a key for me? The name's Andrew Simon.'

The woman looked down at her desk behind the counter and produced a key card. She placed it into a little card wallet, wrote a room number on it and passed it to Wise.

He looked down, saw that he had to go to 717. He was about to ask where the lifts were but the woman simply pointed to her right.

'Thank you,' Wise said but the woman was already looking at whatever was on her desk. He wasn't going to complain. The receptionist's lack of interest was a good thing. She'd probably already forgotten what he looked like.

Wise entered the lift and only hesitated for a second before pressing the button for the seventh floor. It wasn't that he was claustrophobic, he just hated being in confined spaces. As the lift made its juddering way up, he found himself holding his breath and staring at the floor numbers above the door, willing each one to illuminate faster than the one before it. It was either that or scream.

Even so, each second took an hour, each floor an age. Sweat broke out on his forehead as the walls moved ever closer and the space got ever tighter.

Damn, he should've taken the stairs.

Thankfully, the number seven finally lit up above the door. The lift announced its arrival with a ping and the doors opened. Wise moved quickly, stepping out into the corridor, very happy to have space around himself once more. He set off, following the signs towards his room. The carpet looked like a million people had walked up and down it in its time, leaving a worn and faded path down its centre.

When he reached 717, he knocked rather than use the room key, not wanting to surprise anyone inside. He heard someone get up and walk to the door. A shadow fell over the spyhole momentarily, then bolts shifted and the door opened.

'Come in,' Heer said, stepping aside. The previous times Wise had met the DCI from SCO10, she'd been wearing suits, looking very much like the stereotypical police officer. Today, though, she was dressed in jeans, with a black hoodie and a watch cap pulled down over her ears.

'Shouldn't I have worn the suit?' Wise said as he walked past her. There was a small corridor from the door to the bedroom, with a space to hang clothes and store a small case on the left and the bathroom on the right.

'The suit's okay,' Heer replied. 'That's how I know it's you.'

The bedroom itself had grey walls and a large window that overlooked Finsbury Park tube station. Two beds, separated by a small table with lamps, took up most of the available space, but there was another table by the window, with two chairs arranged around it.

A man was sitting on one of them. Caucasian, in his mid-to-late thirties, his scalp was shaved down to the bone. He gave a start when he saw Wise and his hand went to the small of his back as he jumped to his feet.

'It's okay, Jamie. He's the one on our side,' Heer said, moving quickly to stand between Wise and the man.

The man — Jamie — stared at Wise. 'Are you fucking sure?' There was a glint of a silver tooth as he spoke. The man wasn't tall but he was bulky and appeared more than capable of looking after himself. Like a bulldog with a bad temper.

Wise held out his hand. 'I'm Detective Inspector Simon Wise. I take it you know my brother?'

'You really are fucking identical,' Jamie said, his eyes wide. He reluctantly brought his hand back out from under his bomber jacket and shook Wise's.

'So I've heard,' Wise said, trying not to think what the man had behind his back. A gun, maybe, or a knife?

'Simon, meet Sergeant James Aspinal,' Heer said. 'He's from National Intelligence, specialising in Organised Crime Gangs.'

'Only my mother calls me James,' the man said, sitting back down. 'It's Jamie to everyone else.'

'Good to meet you, Jamie,' Wise said.

The man pointed at the other chair. 'Take a pew.'

Wise pulled the chair out and sat down while Heer perched herself on the corner of the nearest bed. 'I told you we had a UCO in your brother's organisation,' she said. A UCO was the abbreviation for an undercover officer.

'The one who took the picture of Tom,' Wise said. 'The one who was killed.'

'Well, he wasn't the only one,' Heer said. 'Jamie has been working with Tom's crew for nearly a year now. He's got in deep with them.'

Wise was impressed. 'That can't be easy for you.'

'It certainly stops life getting boring,' Jamie replied, still unable to take his eyes off Wise.

'The only people who know about Jamie are me, DS Murray and Deputy Assistant Commissioner Steel,' Heer continued. 'And now you.'

Wise smiled. 'I'm honoured.'

'Don't be. I wasn't too happy about it,' Jamie grunted. 'That bastard of a brother of yours has too many cops on his payroll and, I can tell you, if he gets word that I'm a plod, he'll have my balls in my mouth quicker than Bernard Matthews can carve up a turkey.'

An image flashed through Wise's mind, of a young drug dealer murdered in his home. 'I thought that was Ollie Konza's party trick.'

'Ollie was a mad motherfucker, but he picked up a whole new bag of tools once he started working for your brother.' Jamie sniffed. 'Tom's in a different class altogether.'

Wise sat back. The information wasn't anything new, but it still stung to hear it.

'If we're going to start using you, Simon,' Heer said, 'then you need to become an expert on everything we know about Tom's operations and the people he works with. We can't have you walking into a place and not knowing who's who.'

'I've worked some bad OCGs before,' Jamie said, 'but no one has the security measures Tom has. He suspects everyone all the time. You slip up and he'll spot it. If you're not killed on the spot, you'll wish you had been. His crew won't give you any preferential treatment just because you're their boss's brother.'

'How did you get in with them?' Wise asked.

'I was working another gang when Tom's crew came along and took them over. And when I say "took them over", I mean they came along and whacked the blokes running my gang, then offered the rest of us a very simple choice — to work for Tom or to get whacked ourselves.'

'Not much of a choice.'

'It's worked out well for us,' Heer said. 'It's allowed Jamie access we couldn't have hoped for at this stage of our investigation. Your brother has an eye for talent.'

Wise didn't ask what Jamie had done to get talent spotted by Tom. It certainly wouldn't have been anything good.

But every officer knew UCOs walked a very thin, dangerous line, often breaking laws themselves to protect their cover and their lives. The trouble was that more than a few UCOs over the years went so deep undercover that they became criminals themselves or behaved in ways that were totally inexcusable both morally and in the eyes of the law.

When some of those actions came to light, Theresa May bowed to public pressure and launched the Undercover Policing Inquiry in 2015 to look into the deployment of police officers as covert human intelligence sources in England and Wales, and to review undercover policing practices, identify lessons learned and make recommendations about the way it was conducted for the future.

However, eight years later, that inquiry was still ongoing. An interim report was promised by the summer but, it was fair to say, no one was in a rush to see it completed.

On top of that, some thirty million pounds had been spent by the Met in its dealings with the inquiry. For a lot of officers, seeing that kind of expenditure, when the rest of the service was so cash-strapped, really hurt.

Jamie reached down and picked an envelope up off the floor. He opened it up and took out a series of photographs. Each one was of a different man or woman. 'So, Detective Inspector, are you ready to start learning?'

Wise took a deep breath. 'Yeah. Let's do it.'

12

The man sat at his kitchen island, eating avocado on toast and scrolling through his phone. It'd been nearly a week since he'd broken up with Justine and it was about time he saw what else was out there. And who knew? Maybe the next one would be The One.

He certainly hoped so.

As much as he enjoyed playing the happy bachelor, even he knew it was time to settle down. God, it would make his mum so happy if he got married and had some rug rats of his own for her to spoil.

He took a sip of tea and opened the Sparks app. He liked that one the best. He found it had better quality women to choose from. His latest profile on the site was proving to be as popular as his last one had been. Of course, after his breakup with Justine, he'd thought about adding 'no snoring' to his turn offs but had resisted the urge. No one could be as bad as Justine in that regard.

Anyway, if he were to list all the things he considered dealbreakers in a relationship, then he'd never meet anyone.

Looking back now, it might even be fair to say that, maybe, he'd been a bit hard on some of his ex-girlfriends. After all, he'd finished with Rachel because she ate with her mouth open. Then there was

Emma who'd worn crocs all year round. Yukari had spoken English with a terrible accent. Sarah had never seen a Bond film and had no intention of ever seeing one. And Anna had been a Spurs fan. At the time each of those traits had seemed a big enough issue to end things but none of those were anywhere near as bad as Justine's snoring.

His mother claimed he went into relationships already looking for reasons to end things, but he didn't believe that. He was just a man with standards, who wouldn't compromise on anything. That's what had made him successful at work, after all, so why shouldn't he apply it to his love life?

He took a bite of his avocado on toast. He had it most mornings when he was at home, savouring the tang that a squeeze of half a lime gave it, but it needed something more this morning. He jumped off his stool and wandered over to his spice cupboard. Opening it up, he quickly spotted the jar of red chilli flakes and picked it up. Returning to his seat, he carefully sprinkled some over the rest of his toast. Just enough to give it a kick but not too much of one. He didn't want to go to work sweating.

He took another bite and sighed. Perfect.

The man knew he was fussy. He always had been. When he was younger, his mother said he used to fly into terrible rages if everything wasn't exactly how he liked it, whether that was how his food had been put on his plate, or if the outfit he'd wanted to wear was in the wash instead of ironed and hanging up in his wardrobe. Looking back now, he knew he had put his mum through so much. But, no matter what he'd done, she still loved and cared for him. The woman truly was an angel.

It was no wonder he was looking for someone as perfect as she was.

Picking up his phone, he began to look for Miss Right.

She was out there somewhere and he'd find her, no matter what it took.

13

Looking back now, Hicksy might've made a mistake finishing off the bottle of Johnnie Walker the night before. It wasn't as if he'd been out having a good time. No, he'd been on his Jack Jones at home indulging in his new favourite pastime of misery drinking. Something he did oh so well. Drinking until there wasn't another drop to drink in his flat. Drinking until he couldn't think anymore, until he passed out in his chair like the sad, old sod he was.

Still, getting drunk and crying in the dark on his own was better than letting anyone else see that he was falling apart. Of course, he had an excuse for his rapid descent into alcoholism. His partner, his best friend, Jono, had been murdered, after all, and it was fair to say Hicksy missed him something bad.

They'd been joined at the hip for as long as Hicksy could remember, busting heads in the Flying Squad together before moving over to Major Investigations and a murder team. When they weren't working, they'd be out drinking or Hicksy would be round Jono's gaff having a lovely meal, curtesy of Jono's missus, Pat. Christ, he'd even spent the last ten Christmas Days there, never once feeling like a third wheel — just part of the family.

He'd hoped the funeral would've somehow lessened the pain but seeing Jono lowered into that hole, then spending the afternoon at the wake with Pat, feeling like two strangers suddenly thrown together with nothing in common, had only made everything feel a thousand times worse.

It was no wonder he needed the booze to numb the world.

But that blessed relief came at a price.

Now, Hicksy's mouth tasted like someone had taken a big, fat dump in it and his head felt like that same evil someone had hammered a spike through his brain. Even the bloody fluorescent lights in MIR-One were making his eyes hurt.

He opened his desk drawer and fished around the mess of papers inside until he found a small packet of Neurofen. There were only three tablets left in the blister pack, so he popped them all out and shoved them in his mouth, then washed them down with the last of his tea. It'd gone cold at some point just to make matters worse, and he grimaced as he swallowed. He felt his empty stomach clench and, for a horrible moment, he thought he might puke the lot back up. That would just be his bloody luck.

To top it all, Hicksy really hated the job the governor had given him. Even on a good day, when he was feeling super-dooper, calling the families of MisPers to find out if it was their loved one's body in the morgue was not his idea of fun. He'd made two calls already that morning and the only result he'd got was to reduce some old girl to tears.

The fact of the matter was that it needed a delicate touch to do those sorts of calls and Hicksy's style was much more of 'a bull in a China shop' approach to everything. Why Wise hadn't asked anyone better suited to the job to do it was beyond him.

The governor had turned up half an hour earlier. Hicksy was about to go ask him to find someone else to do the calls but one look at the Guv's face told him not to. It had been the right call too. Wise had gone straight to his office without speaking to anyone.

Still, that meant he was stuck making misery calls on top of his hangover. With a sigh, Hicksy looked at the next name on the list.

Jill O'Brian. Age twenty-two from Sydenham. Mrs Carol O'Brian, her mother, reported her missing on Saturday.

Hicksy picked up his desk phone and punched in the number. The line rang and rang to the point that Hicksy was about to hang up, when someone answered.

'Yeah?' A woman answered, her voice barely audible over the background noise of a fruit machine rattling away.

'Is that Mrs O'Brian?' Hicksy asked, incredulous that she was on the one-armed bandits at 10 in the morning.

'Who wants to know?' The woman's voice was confrontational, rather than inquisitive. There was the sound of more coins being dropped into slots. She was a woman on a mission and not even a phone call was going to stop her playing the machines, apparently.

'This is Detective Sergeant Hicks from Kennington Police Station,' Hicksy said, mustering all the patience he could.

'Whatever it is, I didn't do it, and I didn't see nobody who did do it.' Now she sounded bored.

'I'm ringing about your daughter, Mrs O'Brian.' Hicksy had to all but shout as the sound of a fruit machine whirred into life with a multitude of pings and beeps.

'I know nothing about whatever she's done neither,' Carol O'Brian replied. 'Now, I'm bus—'

'You reported her missing, Mrs O'Brian.'

'Missing? Oh yeah. Well, don't you worry. The slag's turned up again, more's the pity. And she's still not got the money she owes me. Must think I'm NatWest or somethin'.' More coins went into the slots, then the line went dead.

'Nice speaking to you too,' Hicksy said, then slammed the phone back in the cradle. He glanced over at Brains. 'Mrs O'Brian was a right charmer. Apparently, her daughter — *the slag* — isn't missing anymore.'

'I'll make a note on her file,' Brains said without looking up from his monitor.

Hicksy picked up the list again. Next up was a Jennifer Wilkins.

Reported missing by her husband on Monday. Hicksy dialled the contact number.

This time, the phone was answered in a nanosecond. 'Jennifer?' a man said, sounding as desperate as could be.

'Er, hello. Is that Mr Wilkins? Raymond Wilkins?' Hicksy asked.

'Yes. Yes. I am,' the man said.

'Detective Sergeant Hicks from Kennington Police Station ...'

'Oh my God, have you found her? Please tell me you've found her. That she's alright. She is alright, isn't she?'

'Mr Wilkins,' Hicksy said. 'I just need to ask a follow up question. That's all. About distinguishing marks.'

'What about them?' Wilkins said with a barely concealed sob.

'Does your wife have any distinguishing marks?'

'What? Like a birth mark or something?'

'Yeah, or a scar or a tattoo or something like that.'

'Er ... er ...er. I don't ... I ...' Wilkins was openly crying now. 'I can't remember.'

'Take your time, Mr Wilkins,' Hicksy said. 'There's no right or wrong answer. We just need to know for the forms.'

Wilkins just cried some more.

As he listened, Hicksy rubbed his temple. The blasted Neurofens hadn't kicked in yet or, if they had, they weren't making a blind bit of difference. He really needed to pack the drinking in.

'Mr Wilkins?' Hicksy tried again, keeping his voice as soft as possible.

'Y ... yes,' the poor man managed.

'Did your wife have any distinguishing marks?'

'She has a scar from when she ... she had her appendix out.'

'And that's it? Nothing else. No tattoos?'

'No. Nothing.'

'Okay. Thank you very much,' Hicksy said. 'I'm sorry to have disturbed you. We'll be in touch if we have any news for you.'

'You haven't found her?' Wilkins said.

'I'm afraid not, sir.'

'Then why did you ring me? Why all these questions? Do you know how upsetting it is?'

'We just needed some more information, sir. To help us find your wife.'

When Wilkins started wailing, Hicksy hung up the phone. How many more calls did he have to make? He looked at the list. Four down, three to go.

'Brains,' Hicksy called out. 'Scrub Wilkins off your list. Or delete it. Or whatever you techno boffins do.'

Brains looked over the top of his monitor. 'Sometimes you act like you've never seen a computer, let alone used one. I bet you've got one of those old flip phones instead of a smartphone.'

Hicksy leaned back in his chair and held up his iPhone. 'So much for that theory, Brains. But listen, I'm old enough to remember what it was like without one of these things controlling our every move and, I've got to tell you, life was better for it.'

'Yeah, yeah. Was that back when life was in black and white, and you had to trudge ten miles uphill in the snow just to get a pint of milk?'

'Aw fuck off,' Hicksy chortled. He stood up, then instantly regretted it, as his head swirled with the sudden motion. 'I'm going to get another cup of tea. Want one?'

'Yeah, that'll be good,' Brains said. 'Oh, and Hicksy?'

'Yeah?'

'You might want to pick up some mints or something,' Brains said, his cheeks colouring at the same time.

'Mints?' Hicksy was confused for a moment, then his whisky-addled brain cells kicked in and he got the message. 'Right. Yeah. I will do. Thanks.'

'It's alright, mate.' Brains gave him a look that was all sympathy and Hicksy hated it.

'I'll be back in a minute with the tea.'

But Brains wasn't paying any attention. His eyes were fixed on his screen. He'd probably used up his whole quota of human interaction in that conversation.

Hicksy went to leave but Brains held up a finger, stopping him. 'Hicksy, have a look at this. I think this is our Jane Doe.'

14

Someone opened Wise's door without knocking. 'Guv,' Brains said, his face flushed with excitement. 'We've just had an interesting MisPer report come in. I think you should take a look at it.'

Wise stood up. 'Show me.'

'I put a flag in the system,' Brains said as they headed back to his desk. Hicksy was waiting by it, looking as pleased as punch for the first time in an age. 'For any new MisPers came in that match our Jane Doe and I think we've got a good possibility.' He slipped behind his desk and tapped away, then nodded towards the big monitor.

Wise turned to face the screen. The others in the room did too, sensing something important was up.

A picture of another smiling blonde haired woman appeared on the screen. Unlike the other possibilities, where Wise thought that there was the odd similarity with the body they'd found, the moment he saw this woman's face, he knew in his gut it was her. No wonder Brains and Hicksy were excited.

'Battersea nick had a call from the parents of Justine Mayweather, age twenty-seven,' Brains said. 'She's an account manager at Green, an ad agency in Soho. The parents are on holiday in Tenerife at the moment, but they've been trying to get hold of Justine since the weekend. They thought it was unusual that she didn't call or text to wish them a happy new year and she's been unreachable since. They got worried as she's due to pick them up tomorrow from the airport and they couldn't confirm pick up times with her. Her phone goes straight to voicemail and, when they rang her work, they said they'd not seen her all week.'

'The timing fits,' Wise said.

'She's five feet six as well,' Brains added. 'Same as our girl. And she has a tattoo on her ankle that she got in Thailand when she was nineteen. Her parents described it as "some tribal thing".'

'She's ticking a lot of boxes,' Wise said. 'We got an address for her?'

'Yeah — a flat in Warriner Gardens,' Brains said. 'Battersea sent a couple of uniforms around but there was no answer.'

'It's her, isn't it?' Hicksy said.

'I think it is,' Wise agreed. 'Justine.' Just saying her name felt right. The corpse had now become a person.

He turned to face the room. 'Right, everyone. We've got a good possible here but that doesn't mean we skip what we were doing. Let's eliminate the other MisPers like we planned. Donut, you and your team keep on the CCTV. Brains, look into Justine. Let's find out who she was and what she did. Let's get her phone details and track where it was last. Maybe she's just ignoring her parents and she's off at her boyfriend's or something. Check her bank account too. See if she's been spending any money.'

'Will do,' Brains said.

'I'll go with Hannah to check out Justine's apartment,' Wise added. 'Is there someone with a key that can let us in?'

'I'll check with the parents,' Brains said.

'Good — and find out what time they're back tomorrow. We'll send someone to meet them off the plane. Oh, and be sensitive when you speak to them. It might not be their daughter in the morgue.'

'I'm not Hicksy,' Brains said.

'Mate, I don't think a blind man would get us confused,' Hicksy said.

Palmer walked over. 'I'll come with you to check out the MisPer's home.'

'It's alright,' Wise said. 'I'd rather you help out here until we know for sure it's her. Once we get that confirmed, you can help with the door-to-doors.'

Palmer gave Wise a look that told him exactly what he thought of that, but the man had the common sense not to say anything out loud.

'I'll call you the moment I need you,' Wise said with a wink, just to rub it in. After all, he'd not forgotten the man's comment the day before.

With a shake of his head, Palmer stropped off back to his desk.

At least Wise could see an immediate buzz of excitement spread around the incident room as everyone set to work. If the victim was Justine, then it would give their whole investigation focus and more clues would surface.

Wise caught Hannah's attention. 'I'm going to see the boss. After that, we'll head out to Justine's flat.'

'I'll be ready,' Hannah said.

Wise headed straight out of MIR-One and took the stairs down to the second floor and headed straight to Riddleton's office. Updating the man was the last thing he wanted to do, but orders were orders. It was one thing to wind Palmer up, but Wise wasn't going to give Riddleton a chance to go after him if he could help it.

Still, Wise hesitated before knocking on Riddleton's office door. He needed to put his mask on and ready himself for whatever provocation came his way.

'Come in,' Riddleton called out.

Wise entered. 'Morning, sir,' he said, doing his best to sound bright and breezy.

'Simon,' Riddleton replied with all the warmth of a dead fish.

'Do you have five minutes? I just wanted to fill you in on the body we pulled out of the water yesterday.'

Riddleton looked at his watch. 'Sure. I can give you exactly five minutes and no more.' He pointed at a chair opposite.

Wise sat down. 'It looks like we might have got lucky. A MisPer turned up that looks like our victim. Same height, weight, tattoo on her ankle as well.'

'That sounds promising.'

'Her name's Justine Mayweather. She's not been heard from since the weekend so the timing fits.'

'It was New Year's Eve at the weekend. She could just be hungover somewhere.'

'We're going to check out where she lives. Maybe she'll be sitting at home, watching TV but, if it looks like she's in the morgue instead, I'll call in the SOCOs to give it the place a thorough going-over.'

'Who are you taking with you?'

'Just Hannah for now. I'm short of experienced people to chase other leads so I'd rather the others stay here for now and keep everything on track.'

'Hmph, I would've thought you had better people than that to help you,' Riddleton replied, his eyebrows knotting. 'I went to a lot of trouble to get you more resources, Simon. I hope you're using them ... wisely.'

'Of course — and I appreciate all that you've done.' Wise smiled like he meant it.

Riddleton stared at him for a moment, his moustache now twitching to go with the furrowed brow, no doubt thinking, quite rightly, that Wise was taking the Michael out of him.

Seconds passed.

'You best be getting on,' he said in the end. 'Don't fuck it up.'

'I'll do my best,' Wise replied, standing up. 'I'll leave you to it.' Wise gave Riddleton another smile and did as he was told, happy to leave the man and to get on with his job.

15

Justine's flat was in an old, converted warehouse building halfway down Warriner Gardens in Battersea. Justine's parents had given Brains the number of the management company that looked after the property and he'd arranged for someone to meet Wise and Hannah and let them into the apartment.

As they entered the lobby area, Wise spotted a very anxious young lady waiting by the mailboxes that ran along one wall. She was in her early twenties by the look of things, wearing a suit that was far too old for her. The moment she spotted the police officers, she darted forward. 'Are you ...'

'The police,' Wise said, finishing her sentence. 'Yes. I'm Detective Inspector Wise and this is DS Markham.'

'I'm Simone Sakal, the property manager for the building,' the woman said, her cheeks reddening. She held out a hand to shake, thought better of it and withdrew it, then offered it again after a second thought.

Wise shook hands. 'Thanks for coming to help us. I take it my colleague informed you of where we need to see?'

Simone looked away again. 'Er. Yes. Um. Miss Mayweather's apartment. He said she's gone missing?'

'Her parents can't get hold of her,' Hannah said. 'We just want to put their minds at rest.'

'Right. Okay. Well.' Simone looked lost for a moment, then pointed to the lifts. 'Her flat's on the sixth floor.'

'Shall we?' Wise said, gesturing to the metal doors, as if to say, 'After you'.

'Of course, of course,' Simone replied. 'This way.'

As they followed Simone, Wise glanced around at his surroundings. The ground floor was kitted out in a type of industrial chic, with wooden floors and exposed iron beams that might have once been a part of the original warehouse, offset by a purple velvet sofa placed against an exposed brick wall, while a chandelier dangled above it from a ceiling covered with more exposed pipework. It was quite the difference compared to the Travelodge that he'd been in earlier.

Wise was glad to note that there was a security camera overlooking the whole of the ground floor area. Hopefully, that could provide some useful footage if it came to it.

'I've not met Miss Mayweather myself,' Simone said, more to herself than to Wise or Hannah. 'I mainly deal with emails about faulty plumbing or rubbish pickups. Not that we really have any problems here. I mean it's so new, nothing should go wrong. My biggest headache is chasing people to pay their maintenance fees.' She glanced at Wise. 'I've never had to deal with the police before.'

'We're not as bad as people think,' Hannah said. 'Unless you've done something wrong.' She said it with a smile and a jiggle of her eyebrows, but Simone looked petrified.

'When you say new, how long has the building been open?' Wise asked, trying to keep her focused.

'Oooh. Er. About six months, I think,' Simone said. 'Give or take a week or two. We've done very well, though. We're already at ninety percent occupancy and should be completely sold out by the spring. It's not surprising though. A building of this quality, this location … I mean, it sells itself, doesn't it?'

'I wouldn't know. I'm not much of an expert on London property.'

All Wise knew was the capital was becoming more and more of an outrageously expensive place to live. He and Jean had bought their house in Clapham fifteen years ago when it only cost them an arm and a leg. Now though? There was no way he'd be able to afford something similar. Not on his salary. If they ever sold the place, it would be to move far out of London and that wouldn't work with his job.

Of course, if he couldn't fix things between the pair of them, he'd have to sell it anyway. Then, he'd probably have to move back to his dad's — if his dad was speaking to him by then.

The building had flats on eight floors, but Wise noticed there was a floor marked P below the ground floor on the control panel. He pointed at it. 'Is that the parking level?'

Simone looked over, startled. 'Yes. Yes, it is. All the residents have one dedicated parking spot. Of course, some of the residents don't think that's enough. They want two or three or even four car park places and they can be quite demanding about it. They don't seem to understand that there's limited space. The floor wasn't designed for car collectors, but they think it's my fault. That "I'm being difficult".' Simone did the air quote bunny ears thing as she said it. 'They think I'm saying no to their requests just to annoy them or something like that. It's so frustrating.'

'How do they access the car park?' Wise asked.

'Residents have a door pass that gives them access to everywhere in the building, from the front door to the car park,' Simone replied. 'All they have to do is wave it in front of the scanner at each entrance.'

'Is there a record of who uses the cards when?'

'Er ... perhaps. I think so. I'll have to check. The building's still very new and I'm still trying to get to grips with everything. A lot of things we have planned aren't quite ready yet but, you know, it's a work in progress. Rome wasn't built in a day as they say. In fact ...'

Simone went on but Wise wasn't listening too closely. The doors to the lift had opened and the three stepped inside. Simone pressed the button for the sixth floor as Wise squidged to one side. The sign said eight people could fit in the tight space, but he couldn't see how that would be possible. Not unless they were all midgets. There was certainly no way eight people his size could squeeze inside the glorified coffin.

He took deep breaths as he waited, maintaining his composure. There was another camera above the control buttons, and he wasn't going to make a fool of himself for whoever was watching.

Thankfully, the lift moved quickly and there was the welcome ding as it reached the sixth floor. Wise let out a sigh of relief as the doors opened. He still let Simone lead the way out, though, into a corridor with very white walls that contrasted with the worn and scuffed wooden flooring. He could almost hear his father wondering 'why they couldn't afford a carpet' but this was obviously a look that people who lived in converted warehouses liked.

Wise couldn't see any security cameras though. That was a shame.

'Each floor has three units. A three-bedroom, a two-bedroom and a single bedroom apartment.' Simone stopped by a door on the right-hand side. 'This is Miss Mayweather's. A single.'

The door was made of ash wood, like the others on the floor, with a spy hole in the centre at head height. There were no marks or scuffs that Wise could see that would indicate forced entry of any kind.

He rang the doorbell, despite Simone having her keys already in hand. As she looked quizzically at him, Wise smiled. 'Just in case she's come home from wherever she was,' he explained. 'It's best if we're polite.'

'Right. Right. Of course,' Simone replied.

They waited but no one answered. Wise rang the bell one more time but, this time, he was already putting on blue latex gloves, the sight of which made Simone's eyes bulge. 'If you could let us in,' he said once he had them on.

Simone dutifully unlocked the door's two sets of locks with shaking hands.

Hannah, gloved up as well, turned the door handle and pushed the door open. 'Miss Mayweather?'

No one answered. Not that they expected her to. Not if she was the body in the morgue.

'If you could wait here, please,' Wise said to Simone. 'We won't be long.'

Looking relieved at being asked to wait outside, Simone nodded and stepped out of the way.

Wise and Hannah entered the flat. The door opened onto a hallway that appeared to run the length of the apartment, with more white walls setting off nicely against the wooden floorboards. Pictures from holidays abroad were hung at even intervals along one side. In the first of which, Justine grinned away in skiwear while holding up a glass of champagne against some epic, snow-covered mountain scenery.

Wise stood for a moment in the threshold, getting a feel for the place. It was cold, as if the heating hadn't been on for a long time, and quiet too. There were none of the noises that normally ticked away in the background of a home. In fact, the only sound was of muted traffic from outside. And there was a smell in the air, a sort of chemical flowery scent that Wise couldn't quite place. At least there wasn't the stink of a rotting body waiting for them. Wise had walked into plenty of homes to be greeted by that.

The first doorway to the right led into the living area. It was the sort of space that developers liked to call 'open plan,' but really it was just a kitchen, living room and dining room crammed into a single room that always felt cramped with more than two people in it. It was the sort of room Wise would go mad in.

A large white sofa, with perfectly plumped cushions, faced a large flat-screen TV mounted on the wall. There was a wooden cabinet underneath it, with more framed photographs of Justine in various exotic places, either alone or with other women, posing and pouting. Two remote controls were neatly lined up on the glass coffee table.

'This is the tidiest home I've ever stepped foot in,' Hannah said.

Wise looked down the length of the room to the kitchen area. There was nothing out of place. Nothing that gave away the fact that someone actually lived there. 'It looks like a show flat. How long has Justine lived here?'

'Four months.'

'That's not that long but still. It shouldn't be like this.' Wise opened the fridge but there wasn't even a wilting lettuce or a half-drunk bottle of milk. In fact, it was as clean as the rest of the flat. Holding the door open, he stepped aside so Hannah could see.

'That's not normal,' Hannah said. 'Even if she didn't cook, there should be some half-forgotten condiments in there or a bottle of wine or something.'

Wise checked the kitchen worktops, noting how much they gleamed. Even the sink had been scrubbed so it shone. 'Nothing feels right.'

Leaving the kitchen, they crossed the hallway and entered the main bedroom. If this was where Justine had been murdered in her bed, no one would know. The sheets looked box fresh on a perfectly made bed, with pillows plumped so well that they would've looked good in a photoshoot. Even the corners of the bed were perfectly folded. Wise's father was a stickler for things being just so, but even he'd be impressed by what had been done there.

The ensuite bathroom was as spotless as the rest of the apartment. Even Justine's toothpaste and make up were positioned in a straight line so labels faced outwards, and all the bottles lined up exactly.

No one in their twenties lived like this.

'Either Justine's got terrible OCD or this place has been thoroughly cleaned from top to bottom,' Wise said.

'Maybe she has a service come in during the week,' Hannah suggested. 'To keep things tidy.'

'I've never come across a cleaner this good,' Wise said. 'Most of the time, you're lucky if they empty the bin, let alone plump up your pillows. You could eat your dinner off these floors.'

'You reckon the killer did it?'

'I think we definitely need to get the SOCOs in — I just don't think they'll find anything.'

'I'll go make the call.' Hannah headed out into the hallway while Wise wandered back into the bedroom. He looked around the room once more, convinced now that it was a crime scene, despite how innocuous it all appeared.

There was a picture next to the bed. Justine with an elderly man and woman, her parents no doubt, all laughing together in a restaurant. Happy times gone for good now. He felt that familiar pain as he looked at Justine captured so full of life and remembering how he last saw her lying on a steel table, all bloated from the water. Her whole future stolen away.

He looked at the bed, so impeccably made and imagined her lying there, while some bastard held a pillow over her face, wondering why he'd done it. What could Justine have possibly done to deserve such a fate?

But Wise knew killers didn't need a reason. The fact Justine was young and beautiful was enough of a thrill to make it worthwhile.

With a shake of his head, he left the bedroom and headed for the front door.

Hannah was at the far end of the hallway on her phone while Simone waited by the door, looking more worried than ever.

'Is everything okay?' Simone asked.

'I'm afraid we'll need to do some more work here,' Wise said. 'We'll let you know once we're done and return the keys to you.'

'Oh, right,' Simone said. She didn't move though until Wise held out his hand for the keys. Only then and very reluctantly, she dropped them in his palm.

'Thank you,' Wise said. 'I'm also going to have to bring more officers down here to interview the other residents.'

'You will?' Simone looked utterly petrified at that prospect and Wise had to wonder how difficult some of the people living in the building actually were.

'I'm afraid so,' he replied. 'And we'll need access to all your CCTV footage.'

'Ah,' Simone said. 'That might be a problem.'

'Why's that?'

'Our cameras don't work at the moment.'

Wise stared at her as if she'd just spoken in Urdu rather than English. 'What do you mean?'

'As I said earlier, we're a new building and we're still getting all the systems set up. We have cameras but they're not actually connected to anything. Yet.'

'Do your residents know this?'

'Some do.'

'Some?'

'It's not as if we're keeping it a secret, but we've not exactly gone out of our way to let everyone know, either.' Simone looked awkwardly around as if worried who might overhear in the empty corridor. 'But if anyone's asked, we've been very honest about where we are in the development process.'

Wise shook his head. It was unbelievable. 'Right,' he said, barely able to control his frustration. 'I want a list of every resident who lives here — and add a note if they knew about the cameras. I also want a list of every person in your company that has anything to do with this building and who might've come into contact with Miss Mayweather, plus the names of any contractors who have been working here as well.'

'Right. Okay,' Simone said, looking up wide-eyed at the tall detective. 'That's quite a list.'

'By the end of the day, please,' Wise added. 'And, if you are keeping a record of who uses their access card, I'd like a list of everyone who came and left the building from Friday to Monday.'

'Er. Yes. Of course. I'll get onto it straight away,' Simone said.

'Thank you.'

Simone scuttled off to the lift and pressed the call button a dozen times quickly as if that would magically make it appear.

Hannah rejoined Wise. 'SOCOS are on their way. I also called the incident room to help with door-to-door interviews. Hicksy said he'll come down too, with Palmer.'

'Let's get some uniforms here as well. I've got a feeling we'll need all the help we can get.'

'I'll get on that now.'

'Good. Because we've got a killer to catch.'

16

Wise and Hannah didn't have to wait too long before Helen Kelly arrived with her team of SOCOs, all dressed up, ready to play, in their blue jumpsuits. Wise filled her in on what they'd seen so far and what he feared.

'If there's something to be found, we'll find it,' Helen said. 'No one's that good at cleaning up after themselves.'

'I hope you're right,' Wise said.

'Well, you know what they say,' Helen said. 'Absence of evidence is evidence in itself. If they have left the place spotless, that tells you that you're dealing with someone who's very forensically aware.'

'These days that's anyone who watches TV.'

Helen winked at him. 'Just because they watch *CSI*, it doesn't mean they know all my tricks.'

'I hope you're right about that.'

'I'll come grab you once we have anything to share.'

As Helen's team got set up, Wise turned to Hannah. 'Do you want to have a look at the car park with me?'

'Sure,' she said. They walked over to the lift and Wise pressed the call button. It stirred into life and the floor numbers lit up above the lift doors as it shot up towards them.

A minute later, they stepped out into the building's car park. It already had that aroma of petrol, oil and rubber that all car parks had but it still felt new. The walls were clean, half painted a shiny grey until a hard line of black and yellow separated it from the raw concrete ceiling above.

The car park was about a quarter full, with the usual mix of vehicles that people in London drive, when they could afford flats in the half million to a million-pound range.

'No Ducatis,' Wise said.

'It's not really the vehicle of choice for banker wankers,' Hannah said.

'It's not what you expect a detective to drive either,' Wise said.

'Says the man with a car that looks like it belongs on the scrap heap.'

'Hey! I love that car. It's just showing its milage.'

Hannah arched an eyebrow. 'For someone who's always so smartly dressed, I would've thought you'd have had it fixed up by now.'

'I know, but it's become this superstitious thing. You know, "it takes a licking and keeps on ticking" sort of thing. In fact, maybe I relate to that a bit too much,' Wise said. He looked around the car park. 'Not even the pretence of cameras down here.'

'No doubt that's something else on Simone's list of things to do later,' Hannah said.

'The killer could've brought her body straight down in the lift and put it into the back of a car without being seen.' He walked along, looking at the parking spaces. Each one was marked with an appropriate apartment number. 'What was Justine's flat number?'

'6C.'

Wise followed the numbers until he found the space marked with her flat number. It was towards the far side of the car park. There was a black BMW Three series parked in her spot. 'Nice car.'

Hannah took a picture of the number plate with her phone. 'I'll run an ANPC check.'

'What did Brains say Justine did for a living?'

'She was an account manager at an ad agency, apparently.'

'How much do you think that pays? Seventy or eighty grand?' Wise said.

'If that.'

'The apartment must be about eight or nine hundred k minimum, plus all the exotic holidays, and a Beamer to potter around in? Where does that cash come from?'

'Rich parents? Rich boyfriend?' Hannah suggested.

'Maybe — or she's got a side gig that pays better than her full-time gig.'

'She's a good-looking girl.'

'You reckon she could've been on the game?'

'If she was, she wouldn't be the first bright young thing to do it. But maybe she just had a sugar daddy looking after her? There are plenty of websites offering to hook up young women with rich old men.'

Wise went over to the BMW and peered through the dark windows. There was a Starbucks coffee cup in the drink holder and some receipts and unopened letters on the passenger seat. 'If it is her car, it's not as tidy as her flat.'

'I'll go upstairs and do the DVLA check,' Hannah said. 'I haven't got a signal down here.'

'If it's hers, I want the SOCOS to go over it as well,' Wise said.

Hannah nodded. 'I'll let Helen know.'

'Great. I'll meet you upstairs in a minute.'

As Hannah headed back in the lift, Wise stood in the car park, letting his imagination run over what might have happened. If Justine had been killed upstairs, the killer had to get her out of the apartment somehow. The body had been left lying somewhere for nearly a day. Waiting for night again. Waiting for some peace and quiet to move the body. Did they know the cameras didn't work in the building? Maybe the killer wrapped up Justine in something, carried her to the lift and brought her down here to the car park unseen and into the back of a car?

Justine's car?

The Beamer was big enough to fit Justine in the boot.

Wise headed back upstairs, the lift mercifully less claustrophobic now he was on his own.

Hannah was waiting for him when he reached the sixth floor. She was dressed in a white forensic suit. 'That Beamer belongs to Justine. I've got Callum doing a check on it now so we can see where and she was last out in it.'

'Well done,' Wise said. He nodded towards her change of outfit. 'You going somewhere nice?'

'Helen said get dressed up. She wants to show us something.'

Wise was halfway in his forensic suit when Helen herself came out to see them. She pulled down her hood and took off her face mask, revealing a red and sweaty face. 'You were right about the clean-up job in there.'

Wise winced. 'I was hoping to be wrong.'

'Yeah, well, I shouldn't have been so cocky. Whoever did it left the place bloody spotless,' Helen said.

'Can we come in and have a look?' Wise asked, zipping up his suit.

'Of course you can.' Helen chuckled. 'I didn't ask you to get all dressed up for nothing, did I? You know the rules, though. No touching.'

'I promise to be good,' Wise replied.

'In that case, come with me to the bedroom.' Helen headed back into the flat.

'That's quite the offer,' Hannah said as they followed the SOCO, both pulling up their hoods.

The SOCOs had set up ultraviolet lights in the bedroom and angled them onto the bed.

'I like what you've done with the place,' Wise said. 'Very Berlin chic.'

'You know me, I'm just a slave to fashion,' Helen said. 'Now, normally, these lights will pick up every sort of human-made stain that exists in the world. But ...' Helen pointed to the bed, awash in purple light. The bedding shone back blemish-free There wasn't a mark on them.

'Are they new?' Wise asked.

'No. Even new sheets will have some marks, even if it's where they were folded,' Helen replied. 'These have been washed, bleached and God knows what else and then ironed before they were put on the bed.'

'Who irons bed sheets?' Hannah said.

'Only a psycho,' Wise muttered, only half-joking. 'You have any luck with fingerprints?'

'No.' Helen walked over to the vanity table in the corner. 'This is obviously where Justine did her make-up. You'd expect to find at least hers here, whether on the tabletop, the mirror, her brush or on her actual make-up — but look.'

The table was coated in aluminium powder but, as Helen shone a light over the surface, Wise could see the powder hadn't picked up a single print. 'Shit.'

'I've had a chat with the others. No one's found so much as a hint of DNA or trace elements anywhere. It's as if we're the first human beings to walk in here.'

'I'm not surprised,' Wise said. 'Any sign of a mobile phone or a computer or anything like that?'

Helen shook her head. 'Not that I've seen so far.'

'Maybe they went in the Thames with her,' Hannah suggested.

'Yeah. Maybe.' Wise turned around looking at the room, still unable to shake the feeling he'd had earlier. 'This is the crime scene, isn't it?'

'Yeah. I'd say so,' Helen said. 'We'll keep looking, obviously. And, as I said earlier, the lack of evidence is evidence in itself.'

Wise let out a big sigh. 'Please tell me you've found something to match Justine's DNA with the victim at least?'

'We've already sent her toothbrush and hairbrush off to the lab for DNA sampling, so we'll be able to confirm if your body is Justine or not,' Helen said.

That was something at least. 'Alright, we'll leave you to it. Let me know if you do find anything.'

'Sorry, Simon.'

'It is what it is.' Wise gave the SOCO a smile of appreciation, then he and Hannah left the flat for the second time.

'What do you think?' Hannah asked as they removed their forensics suits.

'What do I think?' Wise rubbed his face. 'I think this is another nasty one. Do you remember what Doctor Singh said about George Bartholomew?' He'd been killing homeless people until Wise and his team caught him a few months back. He'd been getting them to play a sick game of hide and seek before cutting their throats with a Kukri knife.

'Yeah — that no one got that good at killing without plenty of practice.'

'I think it's the same here,' Wise said. 'The way he killed her, then the way he cleaned up the flat, taking his time, doing such a good job of it. So perfectly thorough. This wasn't the actions of someone who has just killed for the first time. There's no panic. No mess. No mistakes.'

'You think it's a man then?' Hannah asked.

'Definitely.' Wise looked back at Justine's flat. 'There are no signs of forced entry either, so Justine invited the killer into her home and, considering how she died, maybe she invited them into her bed too. So, at the very least, it says the killer was someone she knew and trusted.

'Now, that in itself doesn't necessarily mean it's a man we're looking for, but to smother someone like Justine, who appears to have been a fit and active woman, also takes strength and probably a greater body weight. Finally, if we assume her murder was the actions of one person, then it takes strength again to carry someone from her apartment down to wherever they had a vehicle, whether that was out in the street or in the car park.'

'That all makes sense,' Hannah said.

Wise nodded. 'Yeah — but maybe there's something else. We need to know where her money came from. She's living beyond her means. As you said, it could be she was on the game or doing something else dodgy to bring in cash.'

'Christ, if she was working then anyone could've killed her,' Hannah said.

'Let's hope that's not the case,' Wise said. 'Let's hope.'

17

The only good thing about the day so far was that Hicksy's hangover had faded to the point he could just about think without too much trouble. However, he'd been saddled doing door-to-doors with the new bloke, who could only be described as a right pain in the arse.

Every attempt Hicksy had made at small talk had earned a grunt back and a look that suggested Hicksy was something unpleasant to be avoided. Not that Hicksy was taking it personally. Palmer obviously had no interest in making friends with anyone on the team. And, to top it all, the man was marching around like he had a rocket shoved up his jacksie, as if he was out to break the world record for doing the most door-to-doors in the shortest amount of time. It was taking all of Hicksy's self-control not to trip Palmer up as he sped off towards the next flat.

To add to the misery, most of the people who lived in the dead girl's building appeared to be out, either at work or just off being rich. So far, they'd knocked on eight doors and only spoken to three residents. If it carried on like that, he'd have to suggest calling it a day and coming back after six. To which Dickhead Palmer would no doubt say no and insist on knocking on all the doors just in case.

What a twat.

As he followed Palmer to the next flat, Hicksy could almost hear Jono laughing at his suffering. 'Serves you right, you moaning old git,' he'd probably say. 'You should've been more grateful to have me as a partner.'

Yeah. And he'd be right about that. Jono was one of a kind. The best.

Shit. He couldn't go thinking that. He'd end up crying. And, not for the first time that day, Hicksy wished he had something on him to wash away the thoughts and memories. Just a nip of something strong.

Hicksy was still thinking about whiskey when Palmer pressed the doorbell to 5C.

They both waited, staring at the ash wood door, not talking. The last time Hicksy had felt this uncomfortable was when he'd taken a would-be girlfriend out for a steak dinner only to discover she was a militant vegan. There hadn't been a second date.

Anyway, 5C seemed to be another bust. 'Looks like another empty —' Hicksy said just as Palmer pressed the door buzzer again.

This time, the door opened. A man peered out. Tall, he had tussled, artfully grey hair, with one of those beards that needs professional grooming every other day. Dressed in black trousers and a black t-shirt, he'd sprayed himself with something citrusy that made Hicksy's nose twitch. 'Hello. Can I help you?'

Both Hicksy and Palmer held up their warrant cards. 'Police. Can we ask you a few questions, sir?' Hicksy said.

'If this is about that parking ticket, I thought I had until next week to pay it,' the man said. Hicksy placed him in his mid-forties perhaps, but it was hard to tell. The man obviously took care of himself with a physique that came from the gym and not long hours in the pub. His skin had the gleam of moisturisers and probably a bit of Botox.

It was no wonder Hicksy took an instant dislike to the man. 'It's not about your parking ticket, sir,' he said. 'We'd just like to talk to you about one of your neighbours. Can we come in?'

'And I'm not in trouble?' the man asked, with a jokey smile.

'No, sir. We just need you to help us with our enquiries, as they say.'

'Right. Come in. The living room is just on your right.' The man stepped aside to let the two detectives enter.

Considering all the flats in the building followed the same floor plans, Hicksy was amazed at how each owner had personalised their particular home. Out of the apartments they'd been into so far, decor ranged from Swedish minimalism to gaudy vulgarism. It would appear the owner of 5C was going for a kind of gentleman's club look and feel.

The hallway had been painted a sort of blueish-grey. A pop art painting in a gold antique frame dominated one wall. The living room was also painted in the same grey, with brown leather sofas and armchairs to sit on and cowhide rugs on the floor. Hicksy noted two photographs in frames on top of a drinks cabinet were of the man and another man, both with arms around each other, beaming brightly for the camera.

'Please, have a seat,' the man said, sitting down in one of the armchairs. He crossed his legs, showing off a bare foot that wasn't a mess of cracked dry skin like Hicksy's own slabs of meat. No doubt he moisturised his feet too.

'I'm DS Hicks and this is DS Palmer,' Hicksy said, getting out his notepad. 'And you are?'

The man smiled, showing off perfect white teeth. 'Marcus Short.'

'Have you lived here long?' Hicksy asked.

'We were one of the first to move in,' Short said. 'It was finished on the tenth of July and we moved in on the fourteenth.'

'"We"?'

Short smiled again. 'My partner and I. George. George Meadows.' He glanced over at the photos on the drinks cabinet with eyes full of love.

Of course. That explained all the grooming and moisturising. The man was a poofter. Hicksy should've twigged it straight away. There was no way a straight man could care so much about his appearance. He glanced over at Palmer but the dickhead ignored him.

'Do you see much of any of the other residents?' Palmer said instead.

'There are a few I know well enough to say hello to — normally when we're sharing a lift together. That sort of thing,' Short said. 'Otherwise, everyone keeps to themselves. Thank God. I can't be doing with all that "let's be friends" nonsense just because we live in the same building.'

'Did you ever meet Justine Mayweather?' Jono asked.

Short cocked his head to one side. 'Justine Mayweather?'

Hicksy pointed to the ceiling. 'She lives in the flat directly above yours.'

'Blonde girl?'

'That's the one.'

Short leaned back in his armchair and crossed his arms, chewing on his bottom lip as if he was thinking about how to defuse a nuclear bomb. 'Well, if it's who I think it is, then I know her well enough to say hello to but that's about it.'

'Do you remember the last time you saw her?' Palmer asked.

'Oh, I don't know. That's not the sort of thing I tend to keep track of. Maybe last week sometime. It would've only been in passing after all,' Short said. 'I'm sorry but it's not like I make notes about who I see.'

Hicksy tried giving Palmer a glance that said it was a waste of time, but the man ignored him and pressed on. 'Did you ever see her with anyone — friends, boyfriends ... girlfriends?'

'I'm sorry. George says I'm an introvert when he's being kind, and antisocial when he's not,' Short replied. 'I like my privacy and respect other people's.'

'What about your ... partner?' Hicksy said, doing his best to be PC about it. 'Is he more ... sociable?'

Short laughed. 'Of course. Everyone loves George. I think he's on first name terms with most of London.'

'Is he at work at the moment?' Palmer asked. 'Perhaps we could talk to him when he gets home?'

'He is at work, but he won't be home until early next week,'

Short said. 'He's on a shoot in Berlin. He's been there since Thursday last week and won't be wrapped until Tuesday, I think it is.'

'A shoot?'

'Yes. But he shoots fashion, not guns. He's a photographer. I don't know if you read Vogue or Elle much, but, if you do, you'd recognise his work.'

Hicksy wasn't sure if Short was taking the piss or just stuck so far up his own arse that he didn't realise that people like Hicksy didn't read women's fashion magazines. And, glancing at Palmer in his Mister Byrite suit, he reckoned that twat didn't either. Still, he'd had enough. Hicksy stood up. 'Well, we've taken up enough of your time, Mr Short. We'd best be off.' He produced a card with his name and number on it. 'If anything should occur to you or if George knows anything, please call. We'd appreciate it.'

Short took the card between finger and thumb and held it like it was covered in dog shit. 'Of course. Let me show you out.'

Hicksy held up a hand. 'It's okay, sir. We can find our own way out. You relax.'

The two detectives left Short in his armchair and headed for the front door. Neither spoke until they were out in the corridor again. With the front door shut behind them, Hicksy let out a bark of a laugh. 'What. A. Fucking. Poofter.'

'Oi,' Palmer said. 'Watch your manners.'

'Oh, come on,' Hicksy said. 'Did you smell him? I mean, did he bathe in that cologne or what?'

Palmer shook his head. 'Just be professional, alright? Or is that too hard for anyone to do in this Mickey Mouse outfit?'

Suddenly, all the humour went from Hicksy. 'I'd watch what you were saying if I were you. Now's not the time to go throwing insults around.'

Palmer cocked his head to one side. 'Oh yeah? Is that a threat? You some sort of tough guy?'

'Mate, you don't want to find out,' Hicksy replied, stepping closer.

'Oooh, I'm frightened.' Palmer waved his hands in surrender.

'Fucking grow up.' He didn't wait for Hicksy to reply, just spun on his heels, walked over to the next flat and rang its buzzer.

'I wonder if they're all light on their feet on this floor,' Hicksy muttered in his ear as they waited for someone to answer. 'Maybe you'd like that, eh?'

Palmer ignored him and buzzed the door again. No one answered, though.

They moved down to the last door on the floor. Flat 5A was on the left side of the corridor and was one of the building's three-bedroom apartments.

This time, Hicksy got to the door first. He ignored the buzzer and knocked on the door instead, giving it the full welly.

'What are you trying to do?' Palmer said. 'Wake the bloody dead?'

'Don't tell me I can't even bang on a door now?' Hicksy said. 'Did I miss that memo from your little woke mob?'

They heard footsteps approaching the door before Palmer could reply. Then the door opened a crack, a chain pulled taut. A sliver of a woman's face appeared. 'Yes?'

Even from the little Hicksy could see, he could tell that she was quite possibly one of the most beautiful women he'd ever encountered, all olive skin, full lips and startling bright eyes.

Hiding his shock, he held up his warrant card. 'Hello. We're from the police. My name's Detective Sergeant Hicks and this is DS Palmer. May we ask you a few questions?'

'I was just on my way out. I have a class starting in a few minutes,' the woman replied, with just a hint of the Mediterranean in her voice. Maybe she was Spanish or Italian. Wherever the accent came from, though, it only made her sound even more exotic.

'We won't take up much of your time,' Hicksy said.

The woman sighed like it was the greatest inconvenience in the world. 'One minute.' She closed the door, unchained it, then opened it again. 'Come in.'

If Hicksy had been a cartoon character, his eyes would've popped out of his skull and his jaw would've hit the floor when he saw the woman properly for the first time. And he'd been wrong in his initial assessment. She wasn't *possibly* one of the most beautiful women he'd ever encountered — she was *the* most beautiful woman he'd ever met. He had to force himself not to gawp as he stumbled into her apartment, feeling like a twelve-year old who'd discovered the beauty of women for the first time, barely aware of Palmer following on his heels.

Trying to compose himself, Hicksy forced himself to look around the woman's home, rather than look at her. Compared to Marcus Short's Gentlemen's Club look, this apartment was bright and white with dramatic lights dangling from the ceiling the length of the hallway. A mountain bike was parked to the left of the door next to two sets of skis leaning against the wall. They headed into the living area without being asked. It was twice the length of Short's with a long L-shaped white sofa set up against the main window. There were what appeared to be film lights set up in both the living area and in the kitchen, but there was no clue as to what the woman might be using them for. Immediately, his mind went to a certain type of home movie and Hicksy blushed at the thought. Thank God, Jono wasn't there. He'd be pissing himself at Hicksy's discomfort.

'So, what can I help you with?' the lady asked as she made a point of looking at the Apple Watch on her wrist. She remained standing and Hicksy didn't have to be much of a detective to work out he wasn't going to be offered a seat on her big comfy sofa.

'Can I ask what your name is?' Hicksy said, all but avoiding eye contact.

'Nicoletta Gallo.' Her accent turned her name into magical sounds that made Hicksy's heart go a flutter. He nearly asked her to repeat it just so he could enjoy hearing her say it once more.

'How long have you lived here?' Palmer asked, seemingly unfazed by Nicoletta's beauty.

'About a month.'

Hicksy looked around at the elegant furnishings. 'You look pretty settled already. I like what you've done with the place.'

The woman just stared at him as if he were an irritating madman.

She wasn't the first to do that, though, so Hicksy wasn't that bothered by her reaction.

'Have you met a Justine Mayweather since you moved here?' he asked instead.

'No.'

'She lives on the floor above.'

Nicoletta shook her head. 'No.'

Christ, the woman was hard work. She was just a step away from going 'no comment' on Hicksy. 'What about any suspicious comings and goings?'

'No.'

'Does anyone else live here? Perhaps we could talk to them?'

'I live here alone,' Nicoletta replied. 'Now, if that's all, I must be on my way.'

'Wow. It's a pretty big place for one person, isn't it?' Hicksy said. He pointed to the lights. 'What do you use those for?'

'I'm an influencer,' Nicoletta replied.

'An influencer? What's that?'

'I make videos for TikTok, Instagram, YouTube, talking about fashion, beauty and anything else that I'm interested in.'

'Right,' Hicksy said, still not sure what Nicoletta was on about. 'And that's a hobby or …'

'It's my job,' Nicoletta spat back, apparently utterly convinced now that Hicksy was a neanderthal and an idiot.

'Well, thank you for your time, Ms Gallo,' Palmer said. 'We'll let you get on with your day.'

Nicoletta simply pointed towards the front door.

Hicksy gave her one last smile just for the hell of it and then followed Palmer out of the apartment.

'If you can't speak without making a fool of yourself,' Palmer said once they were back in the corridor, 'I suggest you keep your mouth shut in future and let me do the talking.'

'Aw, fuck off,' Hicksy said. 'I haven't seen any pictures of you winning police officer of the year.'

Palmer glared at him. 'At least I'm a fucking professional that does his job.'

'And you're suggesting I'm not?' Hicksy stepped towards the other man, squaring his chest.

'Well, you tell me, Detective.' Palmer glared back, not backing down. 'Which one of us was homophobic towards one member of the public and then leering over another like a wannabe-rapist?'

'A wannabe-what?' Hicksy couldn't believe his ears. He jabbed a finger into Palmer's chest. 'You better adjust your attitude, son, or you'll have some serious problems to deal with.'

Palmer grinned like he'd won the lottery. 'Yeah? Go on, then. Hit me if you want. Then get ready to enjoy the rest of your life as a security guard or whatever washed up fools like you do …' he sniffed loudly, '… before you drink yourself to death.'

With an invitation like that, how could Hicksy say no?

Hicksy hit him straight in the nose.

18

Hannah closed her eyes for a minute, her head pounding. She and Wise were on their way to see Justine Mayweather's employers in Soho, but the journey had been a nightmare of stopping and starting, lurching forward then braking, then shooting forward for a few more yards before stopping again.

It wasn't quite 5 p.m. yet but the sky was pitch black and all the myriad of coloured London lights were on, making Hannah's eyes hurt on top of everything else. At one point, a white transit van had pulled up alongside them and she'd nearly screamed, thinking it was another ambush.

Thank God, she hadn't. Wise would've thought she was losing it. But maybe she was.

Wise's phone rang, making Hannah open her eyes. Hicksy's name was on the caller ID.

Wise answered. 'What's up?'

'Guv. You got a minute?' Hicksy sounded down, like the world was ending or something.

Wise glanced over at Hannah. 'Sure, but I've got you on speakerphone in the car and Hannah's with me.'

There was a pause before Hicksy spoke. 'Well, she'll hear about it soon enough, so she might as well hear about it now.'

Wise and Hannah exchanged looks. Whatever it was didn't sound good.

'What's happened?' Wise asked.

'I was doing door-to-doors with the new bloke, Palmer,' Hicksy said. 'And, well, words were said between us and I ... I hit him.'

'You did WHAT?'

'I punched him in the face, Guv. I didn't mean to, but he was being fucking rude and winding me up and ... and ... I think I broke his nose.'

'Christ. Why did you do that?'

'He called me homophobic and a wannabe-rapist and a few other things and I lost my temper.'

'Bloody hell,' Wise said. 'Where's Palmer now?'

'He's gone off to get his snout seen too,' Hicksy replied. 'Then he told me he was going to file an official complaint against me.'

'Shit. Alright. It's done now. We'll just have to deal with the fallout from it,' Wise said.

'He told me he was going to get me fired, Guv,' Hicksy said, his voice breaking.

'Look, you might get a slap on the wrist, but you won't get fired,' Wise replied. 'I won't let that happen. Everyone knows it's not been easy for you since Jono died.'

'Yeah, well, I'm sorry. I shouldn't have hit him, but he was being a right twat.'

'Go home now and write up exactly what happened and what was said before you lamped him. Hopefully that will show you were provoked, and we can make this all go away.'

'Sorry, Guv,' Hicksy said. 'I let you down.'

'Don't worry about it,' Wise said as he turned into Dean Street, where Justine's employers were located. 'Just get home and rest up.'

'Cheers, Guv.'

'And Hicksy,' Wise said before the other man hung up. 'Take it easy tonight. I need you to come in fresh and fit in the morning. Don't give anyone any more excuses, eh?'

'Understood,' Hicksy replied, then ended the call.

The Green advertising agency was on the corner of Dean Street, next to the NatWest Bank. It's 1950s red-brick exterior didn't look like much from the outside. There was no signage to say what went on inside, either. Only its bright green door suggested that Wise and Hannah were at the right location.

The parking gods were at least on their side as a black cab pulled away from outside the front of the building and Wise quickly zipped his Mondeo into the space.

'Shit, shit, shit,' Wise said as he turned off the engine. 'That's the last thing we bloody needed.'

'It sounds like Palmer was egging him on, though,' Hannah said.

Wise let out a cold laugh. 'Yeah, but if anyone hears that he called Hicksy homophobic, then they'd all agree with Palmer. It's hardly an excuse to hit someone.'

'Yeah, but he's not, though, is he? Not really,' Hannah replied. 'He's just a bit blunt and old-school in how he speaks to people. Half the time he's just winding people up.'

Wise glanced at her. 'I'm surprised you're defending him. He didn't exactly give you an easy time when you joined the team.'

'Yeah, but once you get past the whole Shrek persona he has going on, he's alright. And he's a good copper deep down.'

'You don't have to tell me that. Still, Riddleton will have a field day with this. I've got a horrible suspicion this is all part of his masterplan to get payback for what happened with the Motorbike Killer investigation.'

'What? When he made a complete tit of himself?'

'I think Riddleton is of the opinion that we made him look a tit, not him.' Wise shook his head and unclipped his seat belt. 'Anyway, that's tomorrow's problem. We've got other things to be concentrating on.' He glanced at the green door. 'Who are we seeing here?'

Hannah pulled out her notepad. 'The managing director. His name's Joshua McLean.'

'Sounds good.' They both got out of the Mondeo and Hannah shivered with the sudden change in temperature. Still, the cold felt good, and she could feel the pain in her head easing slightly.

They had to wait for a group of twenty-somethings to bustle out the door of the agency before they could enter the building. The reception area was a big, open space with a giant TV screen on one wall playing TV commercials while on the other, above the receptionist's head, was a quote from an Arthur Miller book. Something about 'the woods were burning'. It sounded like a load of pretentious nonsense to Hannah.

The receptionist herself was in the middle of packing up when Hannah and Wise approached her shiny black block of a desk. Nearly six feet tall, with long dark hair, she was wearing a pair of green dungarees with a black rollneck underneath. Despite the casualness of her attire, the woman still managed to look like a super model.

'Hi!' The receptionist said with all the enthusiasm of an eight-year-old kid high on sugar. 'Welcome to Green. How may I help you?'

They both held up their warrant cards. 'DI Wise and DS Markham,' Hannah said. 'We're here to see Joshua McLean.'

The woman stared wide-eyed at the warrant cards. 'You're the police?'

'That's right,' Hannah said.

'One minute,' the woman replied, her smile faltering only slightly. She picked up the phone, dialled a number. 'Mac? The police are here to see you,' she said when the person on the other end of the line picked up. She listened for a moment, then nodded. 'Okay. I'll bring them up now.'

When she looked up, her smile was back, as dazzling as ever. 'I'll take you up to Mr McLean now.' Coming out from behind her desk, she led the two detectives to the lifts. 'Can I get you anything to drink? Coffee? Beer? Wine? We have everything,' she said as they waited.

'I think we're fine,' Wise replied, doing that little two-step nervous dance that he did every time he had to get into an enclosed space. At least the lift, when it arrived, was large enough for them all to have plenty of room and the governor didn't look like he was about to jump out of his skin. He'd denied he was claustrophobic, but Hannah doubted that he even believed that himself.

Lonely by Joel Corry was playing over the speakers as they shot up to the fourth floor. It seemed more suited to a night club than an office, but what did Hannah know?

They walked out onto the fourth floor to find a set of glass-walled offices running around its sides with an open area in its centre, with various sofas and armchairs set up, all of which were filled with groups of artfully dressed people having what seemed like very serious conversations over God only knew what. More than a few had drinks in their hands and there were beer cans and bottles of wine on the tables. The music from the lift was playing even louder over speakers here too. Not what she needed with her headache thrumming away.

The receptionist saw Hannah looking. 'We have an office bar that opens at 5. There's often lots of us working late so Mac — I mean Mr McLean — likes us to enjoy ourselves while we're here.'

'That's nice of him,' Hannah replied. She wasn't sure that it was a policy that would help anyone's productivity but maybe it was what ad types needed to do their thing.

The receptionist led them to a corner office that was larger than the rest. Through the glass wall, Hannah could see a man with spiky, white hair sitting behind a steel-topped desk. Behind him, a bookcase dominated half the wall, full of what looked like awards in various colours and shapes. The rest of the wall was covered in framed pictures and photographs. Rather uncomfortable looking chairs and a velvet sofa were set up just to the right of the desk around a glass coffee table covered in giant hardback books.

The receptionist knocked, then opened the office door without waiting. 'Mr McLean — these are the police officers who want to see you.'

The man jumped up from his desk. 'Thanks, Naomi.' He rushed

over and stuck out a hand. 'I'm Joshua McLean — but call me Mac. Everyone does. And welcome to Green.'

Wise shook the offered hand. 'I'm Detective Inspector Wise and this is Detective Sergeant Markham. Thank you for seeing us at short notice.'

Despite his white hair, McLean looked to be in his early forties as far as Hannah could tell. He wore a pink shirt with the sleeves rolled up, and a pair of dark blue jeans with Chelsea boots.

'No problem. Anything to help,' McLean said. 'Please sit. Did Naomi ask you if you wanted anything to eat or drink? We have a full bar here.'

Wise perched himself on the edge of a black leather armchair. 'We're fine, thank you.'

McLean tapped a finger against his nose. 'Gotcha. You're on duty and all that. Right? Right?' He sat on the sofa, leaning back as if he didn't have a care in the world. That left a small, white leather bench for Hannah to sit on. She wasn't surprised to find it was as uncomfortable as it looked.

'Now, you said you wanted to speak about Justine? I hope she's not done anything wrong,' McLean said, the words rattling out of him so fast that Hannah wondered if he'd had a sniff of something illegal not long ago. 'She's a good girl. A right star. Bloody marvellous.'

'Don't worry. Justine's not done anything wrong,' Wise said. 'But her parents have reported her missing so we're just trying to track her movements.'

McLean's head pinged back from Wise to Hannah to Wise again. 'Missing? Oh my God. I can't believe it. Is she alright? I mean, you don't think ... oh my God.'

'When was the last time Justine came to work?' Wise asked.

'Right. Yes. When did I last see her? She was definitely here on Friday. I know it was the holidays and everything, but we've got a big pitch on. For a massive potential client, and when I say massive, I mean "let's go buy a yacht" massive if we win it. However, I know she's been AWOL this week and I thought that was very unlike her.'

'Were you worried when she didn't turn up?' Hannah asked.

'Well, if I'm being really honest, I was pissed off with her. I mean, it's an important pitch we're working on and to just not show up? Not even call? I thought it was out of order and I may have voiced my unhappiness about that to a few people. When I started working, that sort of thing would get you fired, and I can be a bit old-school about things sometimes — if you know what I mean.' McLean held up his hands. 'I feel terrible about that now. Obviously, I'm not going to win boss of the year with that sort of attitude.'

Hannah couldn't believe it. They'd just told him one of his employees was missing and the man was all *me, me, me*. 'I understand that Justine's an account manager here.'

'Yeah, that's right. She works on our big supermarket client.'

'What does that involve?'

'Everything, basically,' McLean said. 'Liaising with the client, getting their briefs, working out budgets, keeping them happy, organising meetings, getting the creatives to do some actual bloody work now and then. That sort of thing.'

'Sounds like a lot of responsibility.'

'Yeah, but Justine made ... makes it all look easy.'

'What sort of person is she?' Hannah asked.

'Hard-working. Loved a craic after work. I mean, everyone liked her, even the clients and they're difficult bastards.' Hannah didn't like McLean. He was far too in love with himself. And definitely a coke head.

Wise shifted on his seat, looking as uncomfortable as Hannah was on hers. 'And how long has she worked here?'

McLean chewed on his lips for a moment. 'Three or four years, I think. HR can give you the exact dates. We have three hundred and something employees working here so it's a bit hard keeping track.'

'What sort of salary does an account manager get?' Wise asked.

'They do alright,' McLean replied. 'They get something like eighty or ninety K but, again HR will be your best bet for exact details. I may sign the cheques, but I try not to look at the numbers. It gets too depressing.' He had a good chuckle at that joke, and it took everything Hannah had to not roll her eyes.

'Does Justine have any close friends here?' she asked. 'People who she might go out with or chat about things with?'

'Yeah, well, everyone gets on with everyone here,' McLean said. 'We're one big family. You know, looking out for each other, working hard and playing hard. I mean, the hours we work, we have to get on with each other. The job would be impossible otherwise.'

'It'd help us if we could speak to someone who works with Justine on a day-to-day level,' Hannah said.

'Of course. Of course.' McLean jumped up from the sofa and headed over to his desk. He picked up his desk phone, punched a few numbers and then winked at Hannah and Wise as he put his phone to his ear. 'Barry, mate. Yeah, yeah, all good. Just hoping you could help me with something. Justine's on your team, isn't she? Yeah? Cushty. Well, I've got two police officers here and they want to speak to anyone Justine might be friends with. Yep. Yep. I know her. She still here? In the pub next door? Well, can you give her a bell and ask her to pop back? Cool. Cool. Cheers, matey.'

McLean put the phone down. 'Apparently, she's good mates with Monique, one of our creative directors. She's gone to the pub but Barry's going to get her to come back.'

'We appreciate that,' Wise said.

'No problem,' McLean replied. 'You sure I can't get you a drink while we're waiting?'

'No, thank you.' Wise stood up. 'In fact, we can wait outside for Monique. I'm sure you've got plenty of things demanding your attention.'

'That's very kind of you,' McLean said. 'I'll let you know the moment Monique gets here.'

'Thank you again, for your time,' Wise said.

McLean's nose twitched. 'No problem. No problem. Anything to help. Just shout if you need anything else.'

Hannah got up too, grateful to be no longer perched on the leather bench, and followed Wise out into the common area. It wasn't as busy as it had been when they arrived, but the ones that remained were checking out Hannah and Wise, even if they were doing their best to pretend otherwise.

'We stick out like a pair of sore thumbs here,' Hannah muttered.

Wise nodded. 'They're probably worried we're about to carry out a drugs raid.'

'It's got that vibe, hasn't it?'

'What did you think of "call me Mac"?'

Hannah mouthed 'wanker' and Wise chuckled.

'I don't think you're wrong,' he said.

'I think he might have hoovered up half of Columbia before we got here.'

'What? You don't think he's normally that energetic?' Wise smiled.

'What about Justine? Eighty thousand's a good salary — but that's not enough to pay for that place in Warriner Gardens.'

'Yeah. I was thinking that too. Let's see what Brains can dig up for us later. We might need to have a proper nose about in her bank accounts. Maybe Justine was up to something dodgy to earn extra cash.'

19

As Wise and Hannah were about to sit down on a pair of sofas that looked a damn sight more comfortable than the ones in McLean's office, a woman came out of the lift all flustered and looking around. She was quite broad, with wild red hair erupting skyward out of a head scarf. She stopped in her tracks when she spotted the two detectives and then, after a quick pause, headed straight towards them.

'Are you the police officers?' she asked.

'That's right. I'm DI Wise and this is my colleague, DS Markham,' Wise said. 'Are you Monique?'

'I am.' Monique's eyes kept darting from Wise to Hannah and back again as if she couldn't believe she was actually talking to two real-life coppers.

'We're sorry to drag you out of the pub,' Hannah said.

'Barry said it was important,' Monique said. 'About Justine, yeah?'

Hannah pointed to a couple of now empty sofas away from everyone else. 'Shall we talk here?'

'Is it serious?' Monique said as she sat down.

'It might be,' Wise replied.

'Shit.' Monique's eyes went wide for a moment for a bit of added drama. Wise thought the woman was probably quite the actress.

'Do you know Justine well?' he asked.

'Yeah,' Monique replied. 'I think so. We're mates. We work a lot together and we like having a laugh together. You know what it's like when you're in the trenches and that. You form bonds.'

Wise knew exactly what she meant but, somehow, he thought 'being in the trenches' was a bit different in advertising compared to what the police were used to. 'What can you tell us about her?'

Monique blew out her cheeks. 'Well, what do you want to know? I mean, is she missing or something? She's not been at work all week.'

Hannah took a deep breath. 'No one's seen her since the weekend and her parents are worried.'

Monique covered her mouth with her hand. 'Oh my God. But she's okay? Right?'

'We hope so,' Wise said.

'We really need to know whatever you can tell us about Justine,' Hannah said. 'Anything that can help us build a picture of who Justine is and her life.'

Monica shook her head as if trying to kickstart her brain again. 'Right. Um. Justine. Shit. I can't believe this.'

'Mac said she was hard-working, and everyone liked her,' Wise said.

'Yeah, she was. This job can be a right pain in the what's-its, but Justine always helped keep it fun.'

'No arguments with anyone? No recent falling out with a colleague?'

'Not really. Tempers can get a bit frayed sometimes, but Justine tended to avoid that.' Monique shook her head. 'Advertising tends to attract narcissists and egomaniacs, but Justine was alright.'

'What about boyfriends or girlfriends or significant others?'

Monique looked up and Wise saw the hesitation before she answered. 'We need to know everything, Monique.'

The creative director winced. 'No judgement, alright? I mean, Justine's my friend.'

'Of course.'

'Justine was a serial dater, if you know what I mean. She was always looking for Mr Right — but she also wanted him to be Mr Rich as well. She liked the good life, you know? She'd grown up with money and was used to a very business class lifestyle. If she met someone and he wasn't earning over two hundred and fifty grand a year, she wasn't interested. There was no way she'd ever fly anywhere economy.'

'We've seen her apartment and car,' Wise said.

'Yeah. I think her dad helped her out with the deposit for the flat and, er, the car ... the car was a gift from some bloke she was seeing a while back,' Monique replied.

'Do you know his name?' Hannah asked.

'I think maybe his name was Danny or Derrick — something like that anyway.' Monique shrugged. 'It's been hard keeping track of Justine's fellas to be honest.'

Wise nodded. 'Was she seeing anyone at the moment?'

'She was, but ...'

'But what?'

'She was being quiet about this one,' Monique said.

'In what way?' Wise asked.

'Justine used to live her life on her socials. She used to post everything, everywhere and tell us all about it at the same time. You know? How she'd met this great guy, and he was the one this time and then, a few weeks later, it'd be all over.' Monique glanced out the window for a moment. 'But the latest one? She put nothing on Insta and kept dead quiet about him at work. When I asked her, she said she didn't want to jinx this one and her fella was really private about stuff. She wouldn't even tell me his name.'

'When was this?'

'Maybe six weeks ago.'

'Do you know where she met him?'

'Justine was on all the apps — Tinder, Bumble, Hinge, Sparks — you name it. But she'd only swipe right if they looked rich.'

'And did she meet this guy through an app?' Wise asked.

Monique shook her head. 'I really don't know. All Justine said was that he was a great guy, and she was happy. I thought she'd tell me more when she was ready.'

'Just one last question,' Wise said. 'Would Justine ever do anything else for money to support her business class lifestyle?'

Monique sat back, shocked. 'What do you mean by that?'

'I don't know really,' Wise said, making it all sound so innocent. 'As you say, she had expensive tastes, and her salary here could only pay for so much. I was just wondering if she had some side gigs to help with her lifestyle. Something like that.'

'She didn't have any other jobs as far as I know,' Monique said. 'Creatives can do freelance work on the side easily enough, but suits can't really.'

'Suits?' Hannah repeated.

'That's what we call account managers — in the old days they'd be the ones wearing suits and the creatives were in jeans and stuff.' Monique shrugged. 'Now everyone's pretty casual.'

'Would Justine do anything illegal for money?' Wise asked.

'Justine? No. Not at all,' Monique said. 'She was Miss Squeaky Clean. All prim and proper about everything. Not like a lot of people in this business.'

'By the way, what's Mac like to work with?' Hannah asked.

Monique glanced towards her boss's office. 'Mac?'

'Yeah, Mac.'

'Well, he's ... alright. Most of the time.'

'Most of the time?' Hannah repeated.

'Well, I'm not his type so it's not been a problem for me,' Monique replied. 'But some of the other girls ... well, let's say he often picks the good-looking ones for some personal mentoring, if you know what I mean. I'm not saying he abuses his position or anything like that but ... well ... you know?'

Wise did know. He knew the type very well indeed. 'Was Justine his type?'

Monique laughed. 'Mac? Let's just say she was good-looking,

blonde and had a heartbeat so yeah, she was his type. He tried it on a few times, I think, but Justine wasn't into married men.'

'That's good to know, Monique. Really good to know. You've been a massive help.'

'Yeah,' Monique said. 'Of course.'

'We'll let you get back to your friends for now,' Wise said. 'But we might need to have a follow up chat, if that's okay?'

'Sure. Anything to help.'

Wise stood up and the others followed suit.

Hannah handed Monique a business card. 'If you think of anything else, please call.'

'I will.'

As Monique headed back to the lift, something made Wise turn around.

Joshua 'Just call me Mac' McLean was watching them from his office. He didn't look happy at all.

20

Sam Wise had the news on the TV, but he wasn't paying attention. His half-eaten dinner lay on a tray by his feet, long gone cold. His Stella, now warm, stood forgotten on the side table by the sofa. He was dimly aware that he was cold, that he should get up and put the heating on or maybe get a thicker jumper or grab a blanket, but he couldn't summon up the energy to do anything.

Instead, he sat there, lost in his thoughts, drowning in sadness, wondering just how screwed up everything had got. He was just glad his wife wasn't around to see it all.

There was a picture of them all on the mantlepiece, from before she'd gotten sick, taken in the late eighties, when Sam still had his hair in that stupid mullet of his and the boys were nippers still. They were all smiling and laughing. Tom and Simon had their arms wrapped around each other and Jill, her hair all big and permed, was hugging the pair of them. A golden moment that Sam would give anything to revisit.

He knew he was looking back through rose-tinted glasses and all that but still. Times might've been tough but all he could remember now was the laughter and the love they shared. They used to call themselves the A Team after that TV show the boys loved. Tom had even wanted his dad to get a van like theirs, all black with a red stripe down the side.

They'd been a right, tight crew. A proper gang.

But now?

Jill was twenty-eight years dead, the boys were sworn enemies and Sam was alone, cut adrift amongst it all, feeling more lost than ever.

He'd not spoken to either Tom or Simon since the row back in December at Simon's house, when Jean had said all that stuff about Tom being a gangster.

About him being a murderer.

Shit no father should hear about their son.

Sam had spent Christmas alone in his house in Streatham, ignoring Tom and Simon's calls, and missing his grandkids so much it had felt like someone had cut out a piece of his heart. Even now, thinking of them in Leeds, so far away, broke his heart. There was no more popping by just to say hello or little trips out, just him and Ed and Claire enjoying a burger and a movie together. He'd FaceTimed them a few times, but it wasn't the same and the kids had questions that he certainly couldn't answer.

God, he didn't know if Jean would even let him visit. Not with everything else that was going on. Not with her accusations about Tom.

His eyes drifted to another picture. It was of his boys. Identical in every way except their personalities. Tom had always been a tearaway, excited by what trouble he could get into and happy to lead his brother astray. Left to his own devices, Simon was always the more serious of the two, the one who wanted to impress his mum and dad, happy to help when needed. Tom on the other hand would pinch money from both Jill's purse and Sam's wallet when their backs were turned. And how many times did Jill have to go down to school because Tom had been bullying some poor sod? She had to beg the school not to expel him the last time. They only relented because she was ill.

It was easy to say the lads went off the rails because their mum died but, if Sam was being honest with himself, Tom was always going to be a wrong 'un even if Jill had lived.

But, even knowing that, even knowing what he got put away for, he still couldn't wrap his mind around the thought of Tom being some sort of London Godfather.

Didn't want to get his head around it.

Christ, it couldn't be true.

Could it?

The thoughts rattled their way around Sam's head in the same way they'd rattled around his brain ever since that night at Simon's, when Jean had gone nuclear in that argument. God, he hated her for that. The way she just spouted out a load of nonsense, wanting to hurt Simon, not caring about the hurt she was dishing out to Sam in the process.

Sam felt like he was going mad, with no answers, no solutions.

The house phone rang, startling him back into the present. He stared at the thing, chirping away, wondering who it could be. No one ever rang the house phone anymore, apart from double glazing salespeople and con artists. Not like the old days when Jill could spend half the evening nattering away to her friends on the blower, while having a cheeky fag and a few glasses of wine.

He watched the phone ring and ring, not moving from the sofa, not going to answer it. Longing for it to stop.

Sam actually let out a sigh of relief when it went quiet and silence fell in the room once more. Grateful that whoever it was — the salesperson, the con artist — had given up.

Then it started again. Ring, ring, ring.

That surprised him. Salespeople and con artists didn't tend to call back. Not straight away, anyway. People only did that when it was important. An emergency.

The moment that thought entered his head, Sam shot up from the sofa, nearly stepping in his half-eaten dinner in the process, and snatched the phone up from its cradle. 'Hello. Sam Wise.' He didn't know why he'd answered it like that, like he was in an office job or something, but it seemed right, if it was an emergency.

'Bloody hell, Dad. Finally!' It was Tom. 'I've been trying to get hold of you for weeks.'

'Tom. How are you?' Sam's heart was still racing from the jump from the sofa and now he could feel the anxiety tickling his stomach, creating a sick feeling he didn't like.

'I'm a lot happier now I've got you to answer the phone,' Tom replied. 'I was starting to think you might've sold up and hot footed it to Thailand to find a girlfriend to love you long time.'

'I should be so lucky,' Sam said with a chortle and realised he'd missed speaking to his son.

'So, what's been going on then? Why the silence?'

Sam closed his eyes for a moment, taking a breath. 'No reason, son. I just had a cold and was feeling sorry for myself. You know how it is.'

'Not the old man flu?'

'Yeah. Terrible, it was. I was all snot and muck and a hacking cough. It wasn't pretty.'

'I can imagine. You feeling better now?'

Sam coughed to make it seem like he wasn't lying. 'It's not so bad. I should be match fit by the time the footie starts again.'

'You better be careful if you're planning on watching Chelsea. They're bad enough to send you straight back to your sick bed.' And, just like that, they were back in the old routine.

'The Yanks have really screwed the club up, haven't they?' Sam said.

'They've really Elon Musked it. Imagine spending all that money without a clue as to what you're buying. It's heartbreaking.'

'Did you have a good Christmas?'

'Yeah. It was good. Ate too much. Drank too much,' Tom said. 'The usual. You know how it is. What about you?'

Sam looked around his tiny living room where he'd spent most of December on his own. Thinking how sad it all was. 'It was alright. I was with a bunch of my mates. One of their wives cooked us all a nice bit of turkey.'

'That's good. I'd hate to think of you being on your Jack Jones.'

'There's no chance of that, son. My social calendar would put Kim Kardashian to shame.'

'Nice,' Tom said. 'Good to see my old man's still got it. Now, you around on Saturday? I've got some presents for you clogging up my house.'

'Saturday? Er …' Sam tried to think of an excuse, a good reason to say no, but his wits had deserted him. 'Saturday?'

'Yeah, Dad,' Tom said. 'It's the day after tomorrow. The start of the weekend. There's no football, thank God.'

'I do know what Saturday is,' Sam laughed. 'I'm not senile yet.'

'Good. Then how about a nice lunch somewhere? We can go for a steak and a Stella and you can tell me about all the old girls you're romancing at the moment. Sound good?'

'Yeah, it does actually,' Sam said, and he meant it.

'Lovely. I'll pick you up around twelve. Give you time to polish your shoes and press your trousers.'

'We going somewhere fancy, then?'

'Dad, you're the only man I know who wears a sports jacket to go to Aldi. But yeah, if you want. There's that new steak place in Peckham people are saying's worth a nosey. I'll book a table.'

'Sounds good,' Sam said. 'I'll see you Saturday.'

'Be good.' Tom ended the call.

Sam put the phone back in its cradle and realised he was smiling. It'd been good to talk to Tom, to have some banter about nothing. It was just like it always had been. The way it should be.

He had to forget all that other nonsense. Sam didn't know what was true and what wasn't, and it wasn't his business either. Jean was just being mean, most likely.

He bent down and picked up his dinner plate, then headed to the kitchen. Sam scraped the congealed leftovers into the bin, before washing the plate up in the sink and slotting it in the plate rack to dry. He gave the kitchen the once over, making sure everything was spick and span, then returned to the living room. It was still cold in there, so Sam put on the electric fire for a bit, aware that its little orange glow of warmth was probably going to cost him thousands the way energy prices were going.

Oh well, that was a problem for another day. He had enough to worry about for now.

Friday 6th January

21

It was 8 a.m. and Wise was in MIR-One, clutching a coffee, with Hicksy and Palmer. The latter had tape across his nose and heavy bruising around his eyes. Hicksy, on the other hand, didn't look hungover for once. Wise had asked them both to come in early for much needed peace talks in the hope that he could stop Palmer from lodging formal complaints against Hicksy. He'd already had words with Hicksy about what he had to say and do.

'I'd just like to say I'm sorry that I hit you yesterday,' Hicksy said to Palmer. 'It was wrong of me, and I regret my actions. All I can say in my defence is that I've been struggling since DS Jonathon Gray was murdered and a lack of sleep made me short-tempered. But I hope you can forgive me, and we can move past this.'

'You broke my nose,' Palmer replied.

For a moment, Wise thought Hicksy was going to start grinning, but the detective managed to keep his face straight and still appear contrite. 'I know and I'm sorry. I know it doesn't help but I didn't intend to hurt you.'

'This doesn't change anything,' Palmer said. 'By the time I'm finished, you'll be lucky to give out parking tickets.'

'Look,' Wise said. 'I don't think anyone here wants this to go further. Hicksy doesn't. I don't and, I would've thought you don't. From what I understand, the attack wasn't unprovoked.'

'I told your man here to be professional in dealing with the public,' Palmer spat back. 'Unless you condone homophobic and sexist behaviour.'

'So, you didn't actually ask Hicksy to hit you? You didn't call him a washed-up fool or tell him to go drink himself to death?'

Palmer sat back, crossed his arms and looked out the window.

Wise sighed. 'Alright. Do what you will. We'll see what the review board thinks about it. In the meantime, I expect both of you to behave professionally. Hicksy, keep your fists to yourself. Palmer, I suggest you think about your attitude. I know DCI Riddleton wanted you here, but I've seen nothing yet from you to suggest you actually want to be here. If that's the case, I suggest you ask to be transferred elsewhere.' He stood up. 'In the meantime, we've got a murder to solve. I suggest you both focus on that.'

Hicksy got to his feet as well. 'Understood, Guv. Sorry.'

Palmer said nothing. He just jumped up and stormed out of MIR-One.

'Dickhead,' Hicksy said after he was gone.

'Hey,' Wise said. 'I meant what I said. There are games being played here that could end all our careers if we let them and I don't want that. So rise above it. Be the bigger person.'

Hicksy nodded. 'I'll do my best.'

'You better.' Wise returned to his office, needing some privacy while he drank his coffee and got ready for the morning's DMM. He had no doubt that Palmer would be filling Riddleton in on the altercation at that very moment, and a summons would arrive sooner rather than later to explain what was going on. He was also one hundred percent sure that Palmer's attitude was part of Riddleton's plan to get his own back on Wise and his team after the Motorbike Killer debacle.

Twenty minutes later, caffeinated, Wise was back out front, facing a full house in MIR-One for the DMM. Hicksy on one side of the room and Palmer on the other, drawing more than a few crafty looks from the others, all keen to check out his battered nose.

Hannah was sitting on the edge of her desk, dressed as usual in jeans and her motorbike jacket, but Wise noticed her helmet wasn't in its usual spot on the floor by her feet. That was odd enough but then he spotted Donut sitting with Callum and Millie, looking like he had a new suit on and with freshly-shaved cheeks that practically glowed. That was four days in a row now that he looked clean and tidy. Was this some sort of new year's resolution on Donut's part?

Good for him if it was.

He took a gulp of the last of his coffee as he glanced at the information on the board so far. Under *What do we know?*, there was the picture of the victim, her physical statistics, plus Justine's name had been added with a question mark next to it. Kat had also stuck up some pictures of Justine from when she was alive as well. Comparing those pictures to the image of the victim, Wise had no doubts that it was the same person.

The other two boards, *What do we think?* and *What can we prove?*, were still blank, though. There was still so much to do.

Turning back to the troops, Wise clapped his hands together. 'Right. I know we all had a busy day yesterday —some more so than others — so let's quickly run through where we're at and then we can go hard at it again today.

'We're waiting for the DNA results to come in, but it is highly likely that Justine Mayweather is our body in the river. Brains — what can you tell us about her?'

Brains pressed a button on his keyboard, then stood up from behind his monitor. The widescreen TV to the side of the whiteboards flickered into life and a picture of Justine smiling appeared on the screen. 'Justine Mayweather. Born twenty-seventh of October, 1995 in Camberley. Father Lee is retired but was a money broker in the city back in the day and did well out of it. Mother Caroline was a stay-at-home mum. Justine went to an all-girls private school in Guildford, then went on to study Communications at

Warwick University. Came away with a Two Two in her degree — which normally means she was partying more than she was studying.

'She then did a year freelancing at various ad agencies before she got her job at Green's in 2019 and she's been there ever since. We've put in recs for her phone details and bank information,' Brains continued. 'We should have those back later today.'

'We've checked out her social media accounts as well,' Callum said, standing up. 'She's got accounts on nearly every site going. Her LinkedIn account is basically her resume. She often likes comments made by colleagues or her agency's clients and she reposts the work Green does but that's about it. No signs she's looking for a job or anything like that.

'She's on Facebook and Twitter but she's been pretty dormant on both of those for a while now. However, she was really active on Instagram until recently, posting video clips in her stories four or five times a day and sometimes even more than that. The reels are mainly of her out and about in town.' Callum turned to Brains. 'Can you play a couple of clips?'

'Here you go,' Brains replied, and a vertical video frame appeared on the incident room TV. It showed Justine in a club with three other girls, all posing and pouting for the camera as they danced. Another video came on next, of Justine in a restaurant, sitting at a long table with at least a half a dozen people on either side. Everyone toasted the camera. The third video was different. Just Justine and an older man on a hotel balcony overlooking Dubai. Justine was wearing a long see-through white shirt over a white bikini and the man wore white, loose-fitting trousers but was shirtless. Probably so he could show off his abs to the camera. Justine had added a glowing heart over the film.

'Who's the man?' Wise asked.

'His name's Stephan Askins. He works in the city, and it looks like they dated for a while at the end of 2022 to the middle of last year. This video was from one of many trips they took together,' Callum said. 'There are quite a few blokes she seems to be attached to if you go back far enough. Most of them are older than she is. Askins's got ten years on her.'

'Okay. Let's compile a list of possible boyfriends and start interviewing them, concentrating on the more recent ones first,' Wise said. 'Whoever killed Justine was known to her well enough that she let them into her flat and, maybe, into her bed. Maybe her killer is among them.'

Callum looked pleased with himself and held up a piece of paper. 'I've already got a list. I went back over the last two years and there's four blokes. I've been through their socials too. It looks like Justine has a type. They're all older than her, successful, go on plenty of trips and all of them are real players.'

'Players?' Wise asked.

'Yeah, you know. Players. They fancy themselves, and have a "new-woman-every-week" sort of thing.'

'Bit like you, eh, School Boy?' Hicksy cracked. 'A one-man love machine.'

Callum laughed. 'I wish.'

'Excellent work, Callum,' Wise said. 'Now, you said she was posting regularly until recently. When did she stop?'

'Six weeks ago, Guv,' Callum replied. 'She even stopped posting pictures of her meals.'

'Bloody hell,' Hicksy said. 'That should've been a red flag there and then.'

'When we spoke to a friend of hers yesterday, she said Justine had met a new man who was very private. That could explain the sudden silence on her socials,' Wise said. 'So, we need to find who's the new guy. Justine's friend said she was using all the dating apps. Maybe she met him on one of those. Have a look and see what you can find.'

'I'm on it.' Callum sat back down.

'The new boyfriend might be the killer, or it could be someone she met on New Year's Eve. We need to track down her movements in the time leading up to when she died. So, let's look at her phone use, messages, stuff like that,' Wise said. 'And Brains, let me know the moment you get the bank statements in. Justine had a very lavish lifestyle that she couldn't afford on her salary. Her friend said she only dated rich guys but see if there's anything dodgy going on. She was a good-looking woman. Maybe she wasn't averse to getting paid to date.'

'I'll have a look,' Brains said.

'Hicksy, Palmer — any luck with the door-to-doors yesterday?' Wise asked.

'It was a bit … hit and miss,' Hicksy said, drawing a few sniggers from the others. 'A lot of the residents were at work but the ones we did talk to were all relatively new to the building, and said they kept to themselves and so on. Only one bloke on the floor below her said he'd actually seen Justine or spoken to her, but he said it was only to say hello in the lift.'

'Right. Palmer, can you go back today and carry on? Millie, can you help him?'

Millie glanced over at Palmer. 'Sure.'

'And be careful. I don't want any more … incidents.' Wise turned to Donut. 'How are you getting on?'

Donut stood up and adjusted his jacket. 'I've just chased Simone Sakal for the full list of residents and the car park logs. She's promised to get them to me by lunch but, since she missed last night's deadline already, I'm not holding out much hope. I've got an ANPR request in for Justine's BMW so we can see where she went in that and when. The SOCOS said they'll start working on the car today, by the way. They said the car has an internal GPS tracker so, either way, we'll know where it went and when. Plus, I've just received the CCTV footage for Warriner Gardens. There's actually a camera overlooking the car park entrance that I'm hoping will show something interesting. Finally, I've got uniforms checking the area for any private CCTV — front door ring cameras, shop security. That sort of thing.'

Wise was impressed with the man's diligence. Maybe he was smartening up more than his appearance. 'Well done.'

'Thanks, Guv,' Donut said and returned to his seat.

'Hannah, do we have an ETA for Justine's parents' flight?' Wise asked.

'Yeah, Guv,' Hannah replied. 'It arrives at Heathrow at 2:45 this afternoon.'

'We'll go and meet them. Hopefully, we'll have the DNA results by then. If not, we can take them to the morgue to identify the body.'

'Sounds like a fun trip,' Hannah said. 'I spoke to Helen Kelly, by the way, for an update.'

'And?'

'It's as we discussed yesterday. The flat is spotless. She said that whoever killed Justine is incredibly forensically aware. Beyond anything she's come across before.'

'Does she think it could be someone on our side? Another SOCO perhaps?' Wise said.

'I asked her that. She said that everything anyone needed to know is on the internet. If the killer wanted to do the research, then they could teach themselves to become an expert — or as much of one as they needed to be.'

Wise took a deep breath, Singh's words echoing through his brain: *You don't become this good without practice*. The last thing he wanted, though, was another serial killer case. But ignoring the facts wasn't his style either.

He walked over to the boards. Under *What do we think?*, Wise wrote *Killer: Forensically aware. Male. Known to Justine. Lover? Mystery Boyfriend?* Then, in capitals, he wrote OTHER VICTIMS?

When Wise turned back to face the room again, all eyes were on him. 'I know none of us wanted another case with multiple victims, but let's think about this for a moment. This murder was premeditated — after all, no one learns how to remove evidence from a crime scene by accident and I can't believe someone just googled the information after killing Justine that night. So, it's information our killer has sought out ahead of time. People only do that when they know they are going to commit a crime and want to get away with it.

'But our killer hasn't just done a good job of removing all

evidence from the crime scene — they've done an excellent job of it. Taking their time. Not making mistakes. After killing Justine, he waits until he can move her safely. There's no rush. No panic.'

'He's not freaked out by what he's done,' Hannah said.

'Not in the slightest,' Wise agreed.

'And cleaning that flat that well would've taken hours.'

'I've not heard of any other bodies being dumped in the river recently,' Hicksy said. 'I think news of that sort of thing would get around.'

'The river could be a new thing,' Hannah said. 'Or he's just not done it in London before.'

'Brains, I know you have a lot on already, but can you have a dig around HOLMES and see if there's anything like our case tucked away in it?' Wise said.

HOLMES stood for Home Office Large Major Enquiry System. It was the database used by the various UK police services to help with the investigation of major incidents such as serial murders and high value frauds. It was initially launched in 1985 to carefully process the mass of information created during the course of a major investigation and ensure that no vital clues were overlooked. It was updated in 2004 to identify new lines of enquiry for detectives. However, it was still a beast to operate, especially with the antiquated computers that Wise's team had at their disposal. However, Brains was a magician when it came to digging out vital information from its database.

'I'll do my best, Guv,' Brains replied. 'But I could do with some help.'

'I know. And I'll do my best to get some,' Wise replied. 'I'll go and see the boss now.'

22

Riddleton didn't ask Wise to sit down. Instead, he left him standing while he looked up from his nice, comfy leather, ergonomic chair, with utter contempt on his face. 'You cannot be serious.'

'I'm afraid I am,' Wise replied.

'I only gave you two new officers on Wednesday — and one of them's already been beaten up by another officer on your team. I think that says a lot about your managerial style. Perhaps you're the problem, not the lack of resources.'

'I don't know what DS Palmer was like at his last posting, but he's gone out of his way to be antagonistic towards his colleagues since he joined us. Yesterday's incident was wrong and shouldn't have happened, but Palmer brought it on himself.'

'You're talking about one of the best officers I've ever worked with, Wise. I doubt the problem is with him.'

'If he wants to take things further, that'll be up to the review board to decide, sir. In the meantime, that doesn't change the fact that we need more help.'

'Because you've uncovered yet another serial killer?'

'I don't know for sure, but I suspect so.'

'Really? Because you seem to be making quite the habit of that little trick. From what I understand, you're in here every five minutes to announce you're on the trail of another mass murderer.' Riddleton shook his head. 'It would appear you can't even have a piss without uncovering another Jack the sodding Ripper.'

'Do you think I'm happy about this? I've got half a team run ragged as it is. This is the last thing any of us need right now.' Wise didn't tell Riddleton that was as true for him as much as anyone else. Maybe more so.

'Or is this just an excuse to get more officers? Is that what this is?' Riddleton snarled.

'Of course not,' Wise replied, trying not to get angry at his insinuation. 'Look, you're the DCI. Show me where I've misread the facts so far. I'm more than happy to be told I'm wrong. I really am.'

Riddleton just glared back at him. He might not like what Wise had said but Wise knew he couldn't argue with the logic of it all. 'Even if this is just a straightforward murder, you can't escape from the fact that I do need more people — even with the two extra officers you brought with you,' Wise continued. 'I'm supposed to have ten officers minimum on my team and I've got seven. And even if we were fully staffed, we'd still need more bodies on this. The CCTV and ANPR checks alone require at least two or three more people if we're going to get it done quickly enough. And Brains needs help with the victim's phone and bank details — not to mention looking for other possible cases.'

'Well, if you put it like that,' Riddleton said. 'Let me just pick up my phone and get more officers for you right away, Wise. Oh wait, I'll need my magic wand for that little miracle. Now where did I put it?' Riddleton made a show of opening his desk drawers. 'No. No. Not there. Is it in this one? No.' He looked up and gave Wise a real 'fuck you' smile. 'Sorry. It looks like I left it at home. No miracles for you today.'

Wise ground his teeth together, fuming. It was all a game, he had to remind himself. Riddleton wanted him to do something stupid like

Hicksy. 'Well, thank you for your time, *sir*. It's always a pleasure chatting with you, but I best be getting on'

Riddleton gave him a final glare. 'You do that.'

Wise stormed out of the DCI's office and headed back to MIR-One, absolutely furious. He wasn't sure how much longer he could go on working under Riddleton without killing the man.

What had he told Hicksy? Rise above it? Turned out that was a lot easier said than done. Still, he didn't have to see the man again that day. He could just get on with his job and forget he even existed until the next time.

'Guv,' Hannah called out as he entered the incident room.

'What is it?' Wise asked, walking over.

'We've got the DNA results back,' Hannah said.

'And?'

'Our victim is definitely Justine Mayweather.'

'Well, that's something at least.'

'There's more. Helen Kelly's been in touch again.'

'And?'

'They've found a lot of her DNA in the boot of her car. More than there would normally be,' Hannah said. 'She thinks the body was put in there before it was dumped.'

'Okay,' Wise said. 'Tell Donut to concentrate everything on where that car went the weekend Justine died. I want routes from ANPR, CCTV footage — everything. If she went out during the day, let's go to anywhere she stopped and see if anyone remembers her. Maybe she was with the killer during the day as well.'

'I'll tell him now.'

Wise looked at his watch. 'We better get a move on too. I want to get to Heathrow in plenty of time to meet Justine's parents and tell them the bad news.'

'At least we know now,' Hannah said. 'That'll spare them some pain.'

'Their daughter's been murdered,' Wise replied. 'Their pain is only beginning.'

23

Airport security was waiting for Justine's parents, Lee and Caroline Mayweather, when they disembarked from their BA flight from Tenerife. Security escorted the couple through passport control and took them to meet Wise and Hannah. Now, clutching cups of coffee in their hands, they sat shell-shocked opposite the two detectives in a small meeting room tucked away in the bowls of Terminal Five at Heathrow.

'I can't believe it,' Lee said, his voice still carrying a hint of his working-class roots. 'I just can't.' His bronzed skin set off his white hair, somehow making him look older than his sixty years of age. He was in good shape, though, and there was a hardness to the man that suggested he knew how to take care of himself.

Caroline, her hair a pale blonde, just cried into a tissue, her shoulders bobbing with each sob.

'I'm sorry, Mr Mayweather,' Wise said. 'Rest assured, we're doing everything we can to catch the person responsible.'

'My poor, beautiful girl. Who could do such a thing?' Lee said. 'She never hurt anyone.'

'When did you last speak to Justine?' Wise asked.

'A couple of days before we left for Tenerife. She was going to pick us up from the airport and give us a lift home.' Lee dabbed at the corner of an eye with the back of his hand. 'If I'd known that was going to be the last time that I spoke to her ...'

'A friend of Justine's said she had a new boyfriend. Did she mention anyone to you?'

'Only that she was well loved up. I think she'd been seeing him for about a month or so.'

'Did you she tell you his name?'

'No. She was being really secretive about this one. I said to Caroline that I thought there was something iffy about the bloke if he didn't want us to even know his name.' Lee put his arm around his wife and pulled her closer to him. 'I figured he was married or something.'

'Did Justine say where she met him?'

'No. It was probably on one of those dating apps, though. Sparks, I think she used.' Lee glanced at his wife for a moment. 'I never understood the point of those things. Once upon a time, you met people at work or in the pub but now? It's all strangers meeting strangers. No wonder this stuff happens.'

Caroline looked up then, eyes all puffy and red. 'I want to see her. I want to see my baby.'

Wise nodded. 'We can arrange that. On Monday, perhaps?'

Caroline fixed her eyes on Wise. 'Now. I want to see her now.'

'Wouldn't you rather go home first?' Wise said, keeping his voice soft. 'You've had a long flight and obviously this has been quite traumatic news for you to come back to. In the meantime, we'll assign a Family Liaison Officer to help you over the coming days and keep you up to date with the ongoing investigation.'

'I want to see her now,' Caroline repeated.

Lee squeezed her hand. 'Babe, maybe we should wait—'

'Now,' Caroline said again.

Wise turned to Hannah. 'Can you make a call? See if it's possible?' Hannah nodded, got up from her chair and left the room.

'Do you think you could answer a few other questions while we wait?' Wise asked.

Caroline had gone back to staring at her hands as she picked her tissue apart, but Lee nodded.

'Did Justine live alone in her flat in Warriner Gardens?'

'Yeah.'

'And she owned it?'

'As much as you do when you're mortgaged up to hilt.'

Wise nodded. 'I imagine it was expensive.'

'Nine hundred K for a one-bedroom flat,' Lee said. 'London prices are just stupid these days. Justine wouldn't have been able to afford it normally but her Grandad — my dad — had died and left her some money. I helped her out a bit too. Between us, she managed to scrape together the deposit.'

'Is that how she could afford the BMW too?' Wise asked.

Lee hesitated for a moment. 'That was a gift from a boyfriend.'

'That's some gift. It's a fifty grand car.'

'You've seen pictures of my daughter, Inspector. Men were always generous around Justine. Clothes, jewellery, holidays, cars. You name it, they gave it to her.' Lee gave Wise a hard look. 'There's nothing wrong with that.'

'I didn't say there was. Do you remember the name of the man who gave it to her?'

'Yeah. I met him a few times. Donny. Donny Reynolds. He was a nice bloke on the whole.'

Wise wrote the name down. 'Did she ever have any problems with any of her boyfriends asking for their gifts back after they broke up or from anyone she wasn't interested in?'

'Blokes would get upset when it was over, but everyone loved Justine. She stayed friends with all of them afterwards. Or so she told me.'

'That's very admirable.'

'Well, it's all different these days, isn't it? In my time, you didn't have friends of the opposite sex. You were either seeing someone or you weren't. You didn't hang out in big groups, swapping partners. You certainly didn't hang out with anyone after you broke up with them.'

Caroline looked up. 'You make it sound terrible. It wasn't like that. The world's moved on. People can be friends with who they want. Justine was a good girl.'

Hannah re-entered the room and gave Wise a nod. 'They're expecting us.'

Wise turned back to the Mayweathers. 'You can go and see Justine today, but I still recommend waiting.'

'I want to go now,' Caroline said without hesitation.

'Okay, if you're sure,' Wise said.

'I've arranged a car to take you both,' Hannah said. 'We'll follow behind you.'

As they left the meeting room, Wise whispered in Hannah's ear. 'Well done for sorting that out.'

'Somehow, I didn't think your knackered old car was suitable for grieving parents,' Hannah replied.

'You weren't wrong.'

An hour and a half later, they were all in the morgue's viewing room at the back of King's College Hospital in Camberwell. No matter how many times Wise had stood in that very spot with grieving family and friends, he'd never managed to become immune to the tsunami of pain that rushed out when they saw the deceased lying on the table on the other side of the glass.

Now, waiting there with the Mayweathers, the curtain still drawn across the window that separated the living from the dead, he could feel the pressure growing. Caroline Mayweather, despite her insistence on seeing her daughter, was being held upright by her husband, with tears flowing non-stop down her cheeks.

'We don't have to do this now,' Wise said again.

'Let's just get it over with,' Lee Mayweather said, his face set in a mask of his own, doing his best to hide his suffering.

Wise nodded and Hannah pressed the intercom switch. 'Can you open the curtain, please?'

An electric hum filled the room as the motorised curtain retracted, revealing a figure covered by a white sheet lying on a table on the other side of the glass. An orderly stood beside the deceased.

When the curtain was fully drawn back, he lifted the sheet and uncovered the victim's face.

Caroline let out a howl from the depths of her soul.

Lee held onto her as if his own life depended on it as he stared at his daughter's lifeless body. It was a sight no parent should ever have to see.

At least, Justine didn't look as bloated or disfigured as she had done when they'd pulled her from the water earlier in the week. In fact, she looked peaceful lying there, almost as if she were sleeping. Only the alabaster colour to her skin revealed the truth.

'Can I go ... can I go and give her a kiss?' Lee said, his voice cracking, his eyes watering.

'I'm sorry but it's not possible until we can release the ... until we can release Justine back into your care,' Wise said.

'When will that be?' Lee asked.

'Hopefully soon,' Wise replied. He nodded at Hannah, who pressed the intercom again.

'Thank you,' Hannah said. The electric hum returned as the curtain began to make its way across the glass again.

Lee helped his wife over to the chairs that lined one side of the viewing room and helped her sit down. 'Promise me you'll find the bastard who did this,' Lee whispered.

'I will,' Wise replied. 'I will.'

'I'll arrange a car to take you home,' Hannah said and slipped from the room.

Wise produced a business card and gave it to Lee Mayweather. 'You'll have a Family Liaison Officer to help you, but you can call me any time, day or night.'

'Thank you, Inspector.'

Wise's phone beeped. 'Excuse me.' Turning away from the Mayweathers, he pulled his phone out of his pocket and checked the screen. It was a message from Donut. *Got lucky with the CCTV. When U back?*

Heading back now, Wise typed and hit send.

Hannah returned. 'The car's ready.'

Caroline Mayweather needed all their help to get to the waiting police car. She appeared so utterly broken that Wise couldn't help but worry that the woman might never recover from her daughter's death. He knew only too well that the shockwaves of a sudden violent death could have that effect on people. He often thought that when the punishments were given out to perpetrators of these crimes, judges should take the suffering of others into consideration as well.

As he watched the Mayweathers disappear into the London traffic, Wise only hoped Donut had good news that would help bring this case to a swift conclusion.

24

Donut stared at his reflection in the gents' mirror and had to admit he barely recognised himself. The haircut, the new suit and shirts, the daily shave and daily shower had transformed him for the better.

He could already tell others were impressed with the new look and that made him feel good too. He'd had enough of being the butt of everyone's jokes, of having to smile at yet another cruel comment, of being given the shit jobs that no one else wanted.

And now he had some good news to tell the governor that would prove he wasn't an idiot, and that he was actually good at his job.

'Hello DC Vollers,' he said to himself, with just the hint of a smile, feeling proud. 'Well done.'

He left the toilets and headed back to MIR-One. Wise would be back soon, and he wanted everything ready for when he walked in.

As Donut entered the incident room, his eyes immediately went to Sarah's desk, half-expecting to see her there, and glad that she wasn't. The woman had been a bitch to him the whole time they'd worked together, bossing him about, and saying cruel things to him whenever she felt like it. He could still hear her now, spitting the words out, all that hate in her eyes, like he wasn't a human being with feelings. 'You stink, Donut, you dumb-arse. You stink so much I want to vomit.'

He couldn't admit this to anyone, but Donut had nearly danced a jig when he'd heard she'd killed herself. In his opinion, it couldn't have happened to a more deserving person. And, as far as he could tell, no one else seemed that bothered she was dead either. Not like they were with Jono.

There was the added bonus that the governor needed someone else to do what Sarah did, trawling through CCTV and stuff like that, finding the clues that caught the bad guys. And he was just the man for the job.

When Wise turned up twenty minutes later with Hannah in tow, they both came straight over to Donut's desk.

'What have you got?' Wise asked.

'We had a bit of luck with Justine's Beamer,' Donut replied, taking his time like he'd rehearsed. 'We're running ANPR checks like you said but her car had an internal GPS system and the SOCOs have extracted its data. It's got her last journeys on it — everywhere she went and when in minute detail.'

He could see Wise's eyes brighten. 'That sounds promising.'

'It's more than that, Guv,' Donut said, trying to control his excitement. This was his moment. His big reveal. 'When me and Callum had a look through the data, we saw that her car left her building at 4 a.m. on Monday morning after Justine was already dead. So, we got her route and started checking it.' He brought up a map on his screen, a red line travelling from Warriner Gardens through the city. 'As you can see here, her car travels along Battersea Park, crosses the river via Chelsea Bridge, heads east along Grosvenor Road and stops around here. A journey of seven minutes.'

Wise leaned in to get a better look. 'Pimlico.'

'St. George's Square, to be precise. So, we got hold of the CCTV footage and had a nose,' Donut said. He tapped away at his keyboard and a window with CCTV footage appeared over the map. 'Here's her car parking up.'

He hit play and they watched the BMW Three series reverse into a parking spot. A second later, its lights went out and someone got out of the driver's seat. Whoever it was wore a long black coat with a hood pulled up over their head. The driver went to the rear of the car, popped the boot open and reached in. The driver lifted a large sports equipment bag out of the boot and placed it on the ground.

'Is Justine in that bag?' Hannah asked.

No one answered as they watched the man, after closing the boot, heft the bag up and sling it over a shoulder, before walking out of shot. 'I don't know,' Donut said. 'But whatever's in the bag looks bloody heavy. The bloke's struggling with it. Now, we pick him up on another camera. This one's overlooking Grosvenor Road.'

The footage changed to another angle. The man waited for a car to pass, then crossed the road, disappearing through a gate on the other side. 'They've gone into Pimlico Gardens,' Donut said. 'There's only a small wall there separating you from the river.'

They continued watching the CCTV footage of Grosvenor Road for another three minutes before the driver returned into view of the camera. This time he held the bag by its handle in one hand. Whatever was in it before was now clearly gone.

'Is that how long it took to dump the body?' Wise said. 'Three minutes?'

Donut switched the camera angle back to St. George's Square. They watched the driver get back into Justine's car, turn on the engine and drive off. 'They drive back to Warriner Gardens and that's the last time the car moves.'

'So the killer goes back to her building, parks her car back in its spot and then does what? Carries on cleaning her flat? Walks out the front door?' Wise said.

'There's a street camera that has half of the front door but it doesn't cover all of it,' Donut said. Again, he tapped away, and another CCTV image appeared on his screen. Wise recognised Warriner Gardens. The entrance to Justine's building was to the right of the frame. 'I've not looked through it yet.'

'Shit. Is this the best we've got?' Wise asked.

Donut nodded. 'It is at the moment.'

'What about the camera overlooking the car park entrance you said you had?'

'I've got footage of the car leaving but that's it. Do you want to see it?'

'Go back to the driver getting out of the car, for now.'

Donut switched back to the St. George's Square clip. They all watched the driver climb out of the car, his head covered by the coat hood. The collar was turned up as well, revealing a white graphic of some sort.

'Freeze it,' Wise said. The image of the man was grainy, and he was more or less just a shadow under the streetlights. 'How tall do you think he is?'

'Hard to tell with that coat and the hood up,' Hannah said. 'Depends how padded it is.'

'Anyone recognise what type of coat that is?' Wise pointed at the man on the screen. 'What's that on the collar?'

'It looks like writing or some sort of pattern,' Donut said.

'It's pretty distinctive,' Hannah said. 'If we can find any images of people with Justine wearing that coat, we could have our killer.'

'I agree. Let's see if we can find out what type of coat it is,' Wise said. 'In the meantime, let's get this man's picture up on the board.'

'Leave it with me,' Donut said. He already had printouts ready.

'Have we got a list of residents yet for Warriner Gardens?' Wise asked.

'That came in this afternoon as well,' Donut said. 'There're forty flats in the building and thirty-six of them are occupied.'

'Let's put faces to the names — and I want everyone spoken to. Is Palmer still over there?'

'Yeah, he is'

'Ask Kat to pass him those names as soon as you can. He can handle all of that.'

Donut glanced around to make sure no one could overhear them. 'Did Hicksy really punch him?'

'Let's not gossip, eh?' Wise replied.

Donut immediately regretted asking, especially when he'd been doing so well. 'Sorry, Guv.'

'It's okay. This is good news about the car though. How far back does the data go?'

Again Donut winced, feeling stupid. 'I'm sorry. I didn't ask. They just gave me the car's last few trips.'

'Call them tomorrow. Let's get everything we can. Hopefully, we can track Justine's movements and then find CCTV to go with it. Who knows? Maybe you'll find a good image of her killer and we'll have him.'

Donut straightened up, buzzing off Wise's faith in him. The man had never taken the piss out of Donut like the others had but still, he knew the governor hadn't thought much of him. But now? He could feel his whole career changing, opportunities opening up. 'Yes, Guv. I'll get on it first thing.'

'Good lad.' Wise turned away, looking across MIR-One. 'Brains, have you got anywhere with Justine's bank and phone records?'

'No joy on the bank yet but her phone's come in,' Brains replied, taking off his glasses. He rubbed his eyes. 'I've just started going through it.'

'Good. I want to know where she went in the days prior to Saturday night and who she talked to,' Wise said.

'Okay, but is there any update on some help?' Brains asked.

'I put in a request with the boss,' Wise said.

'So, no chance then?'

Wise gave him a sad smile. 'I'm not hopeful. We're not exactly his favourite team at the moment.'

'Wonderful,' Brains replied. 'Oh well. Thanks for trying.'

'Sorry, mate.' Wise looked at his watch. 'Alright. Let's call it a night.' He put his hand on Donut's shoulder. 'Well done. I'm really impressed. You've come up with some good stuff here.'

Donut could feel himself swelling with pride at the governor's words. 'I just wanted to show you that I can do more than what I've been doing.'

'And it's appreciated,' Wise said. 'I know it can't be easy not having Sarah here.'

'I miss her a lot,' Donut lied. 'But the job still needs doing, right?'

'Yeah, it does. No matter what.'

'I'll see you tomorrow, Guv.'

Donut got his things together and headed out of MIR-One. As he walked down the stairs to the ground floor, he pulled out his mobile and rang his mum.

'Hello, darlin',' she said on answering.

'Alright, Mum,' Donut said, grinning from ear to ear. 'I'm on my way home now. Do you want me to pick up a curry on the way?'

'Yeah, that would be lovely,' his mum said. 'You have a good day?'

'Yeah, it's been brilliant.'

25

The restaurant was in what looked like a giant greenhouse in the grounds of a converted school. Round tables of various sizes, and covered in white tablecloths, were lined up along each side. Lights dangled from the glass ceiling, swaying ever so slightly to the rhythm of the rain drumming down.

Tall gas heaters fought the January cold trying to get in, aided by the mass of bodies squashed together, enjoying the privilege of eating in one of London's most sought-after restaurants. The place might be called The Canteen to go with the old school surroundings but there was nothing canteen-like on the menu.

Looking around, the man was glad he'd kept his reservation. He'd originally planned to eat there with Justine and had booked the table six weeks ago as the waitlist was so long. It seemed a shame to waste the booking just because he and Justine had broken up. Life had to go on, after all. The man could've eaten there on his own, of course, but again, he'd thought that it'd be nicer with company.

So, when Kelly had contacted him through Sparks and they'd chatted for a bit, he'd invited her along.

The table had been booked for 6:30. It was early, but the restaurant was one of those places that was designed for the convenience of its staff rather than its customers. The kitchen took last orders at 7:45 and kicked everyone out by 10. Still, he'd arrived at 6:20, just in case Kelly arrived early, as he hated the idea of her waiting on her own without him. But it turned out Kelly wasn't the sort of person who arrived anywhere early and now, he was the one sitting on his own, waiting for her to arrive.

He glanced at his phone. 6:48. She was eighteen minutes late and had sent no messages to explain why or to give him an ETA. Not the best start to the first date. He understood that it was easy to get delayed, especially in London, but he was never late for anything. All it took was a bit of planning. A bit of forethought. Maybe allowing an extra bit of time here and there just in case. That was all. He'd been taught that it was a sign that you cared about the other person, that you were considerate. Only selfish people were late when it came down to it. People who thought their time was more valuable than the people they were meeting.

He picked up the menu again and ran his eye down The Canteen's offerings. It certainly looked interesting — and pretentious; asparagus gribiche, confit garlic and goat's curd on toast, monkfish, chard and laverbread, lamb saddle, peas and green sauce. On and on it went, at prices that were beyond extortionate. A bowl of salted almonds was five pounds, for goodness' sake!

He sighed. Perhaps it had been a mistake to ask someone out so soon after Justine.

'Excuse me, sir,' a waiter said, breaking him from his thoughts. 'Your guest has arrived.'

The man looked up from the menu. Kelly was standing next to the waiter, an awkward smile on her face.

'Sorry I'm late,' she said and gestured outside. 'The traffic.'

He stood up as the waiter disappeared and kissed Kelly on both cheeks. 'It's always bad, isn't it?'

The man pulled back her chair and helped her sit like the gentleman he was, then returned to his own seat.

She looked around the restaurant as she unfolded her napkin and placed it on her lap. 'I've heard great things about this place.'

'I've been told the food is spectacular,' the man replied, happy that Kelly was even prettier in real life than she had been on her Sparks profile. Her dark skin set off her bright eyes and she had a smile to die for. It was just a shame that she obviously couldn't tell the time.

'Well, I feel very lucky to be here,' she said. 'It's not the sort of place most blokes take you on a first date.'

'You'll find I'm not like most ... blokes.' The man faked a smile, already knowing this relationship wasn't going to last.

Saturday 7th January

26

'Sorry to ruin yet another Saturday,' Wise said as he turned into Crayford Road, in Kentish Town. It was still dark, still cold, still miserable, but at least it wasn't raining. Yet.

'Don't worry about it,' Hannah replied, gazing out the window. 'I had nothing planned.'

'Sometimes, doing nothing is something special,' Wise said. 'It can be knackering being a police officer these days.' He hoped he sounded casual enough when he spoke but, the truth was, he was worried about Hannah. She looked like she'd lost weight and there was a nervousness about her that hadn't been there before. He of all people knew the toll that The Job demanded of officers at the best of times, and everything his team had been through in the last six months could hardly be called that.

'Yeah, well, when your partner's idea of heaven is not moving from the sofa all weekend while stuffing her face with takeaways, doing nothing can get pretty irritating,' Hannah replied. 'I'm happy to be out and about. What about you? Did your wife get upset with you coming into work?'

Wise winced. That was the problem with personal chats. They gave others the opportunity to ask about his own messed-up life.

'Jean's away at her mother's at the moment. Her parents are getting old, and she wanted to spend some time with them. So, it was no problem working.'

Hannah turned to look at him. 'Well, I can imagine a weekend to yourself is nice every now and then, especially when you have kids.'

'It's uncomfortably quiet,' Wise said. 'Which house is Donny Reynolds'?'

Hannah told him the house number. It was towards the end of the street, a Victorian terrace house that, unlike most of its neighbours, hadn't been turned into separate flats. Wise manoeuvred the Mondeo into a parking spot and looked up at the building. Nine steps lead to a bright red front door and net curtains hung in all the windows, providing privacy from passersby. The window frames looked freshly painted as the bright white contrasted to the more subdued and pollution-stained windows of the rest of the street.

Hannah leaned forward to peer through Wise's window. 'Four floors all to himself? I think it's safe to say Donny Boy has some cash to splash.'

'Well, I don't think you give Beamers as presents if you're short of a few bob,' Wise said. 'Do we know what he does?'

'Something in finance. Brains tried explaining it to me, but it didn't make much sense to me. Something about buying foreign currencies from one bank and selling them to another bank — but not like a currency exchange. This guy deals with huge sums.'

'And is he expecting us?'

'Not exactly,' Hannah replied. 'I thought it better if we turned up unannounced and catch him by surprise.'

Wise nodded. 'Good thinking — as long as he's in.'

Both detectives got out of the Mondeo and climbed the steps to Reynolds' front door. There was a gold knocker in the centre of the red door and Wise happily gave it a good whack, the sound echoing through the house. He waited a few seconds and then gave the door another pounding.

'Alright, alright,' a man shouted from inside. 'Someone better be bloody dying.'

Wise glanced at Hannah, who grinned as they listened to a man stomp down the stairs.

'Someone's not an early morning person,' she said a second before the door was flung open.

A man stood before them, glaring away, wearing a red silk dressing gown and not much else. Unshaven, his hair all messed up and revealing more of his scalp than he probably liked, it was clear that he'd been asleep only moments before. 'This better be good,' he said with more than a touch of aggression, seemingly unbothered at finding a man of Wise's size on his doorstep, despite being a good six inches shorter. His accent was pure London barrow boy, but Wise wasn't sure whether it was put on or genuine.

Still, Wise knew how to deal with people like him. 'Donny Reynolds?' he asked, holding up his warrant card. And, just like that, the fight went out of the man.

'You're police,' the man said, all wide-eyed. He glanced back over his shoulder into the house, then turned back to Wise and Markham.

'We are,' Hannah replied. 'Are you Donny Reynolds?'

'Er ... yeah ... I am,' the man said, shuffling his feet. He made no move to let them in and didn't ask why they were there, as if he knew full well why two police officers were calling. At that precise moment, if Wise looked up the word *suspicious* in the dictionary, there'd be a picture of Reynolds with that look on his face.

Wise stepped forward. 'Can we talk to you inside, sir? We have some questions we'd like to ask you.'

'Right, er ... Okay,' Reynolds said. 'Do you mind waiting for a minute? I just need to tidy up. I wasn't expecting company and it's a mess from last night. Had a bit of a sesh, if you know what I mean. Two minutes and I'll come and get you?'

Wise stepped forward again, his bulk filling the doorway, forcing Reynolds to retreat into his hallway. Whatever Reynolds wanted to do in that time, he wasn't going to give him the opportunity, especially if he was going to try and do a bunk. 'Don't worry about that, sir. We don't mind a mess. It is early after all.'

'Well, let me tell my ... guest, at least, that you're here. Let her put some clothes on. Yeah?' Donny turned to face the stairs as Wise entered the house. 'Tasha! Wake up! The police are here!'

'What?' a woman called back.

Donny stood at the bottom of the stairs. 'The police. They're here.'

'Fuck.' They all listened to what sounded like Tasha falling out of bed, then scrambling around upstairs.

'While she's getting ... er ... dressed,' Reynolds said, 'we can chat in the kitchen? It's this way.' He practically ran from the hallway to the back of the house. Wise watched him frantically pick up plates from the island and dump them in the sink as quickly as he could. He was even faster turning on the taps, washing away what was on them. Wise doubted it wasn't last night's curry.

Wise followed, looked around. There were empty wine bottles and beer bottles, next to an overflowing ashtray. The air, unsurprisingly, smelt of stale smoke and sour booze. It was a high-end kitchen, though. All Italian marble, a six-burner gas range, a stainless-steel industrial-looking oven, and an island with stools for six people lined up on one side. The kitchen occupied one half of the ground floor, and no expense had been spared in doing the place up. Floor to ceiling windows overlooked a small, paved-over garden, with a rather sad table and chairs left out from when the days weren't quite so miserable.

'What's this about?' Reynolds said, spraying and wiping the island counter surface. He picked up a small, empty plastic bag — the type people kept either buttons or drugs in — and shoved it in his dressing gown pocket.

Somehow, Wise didn't think the man had been sewing new buttons on his coat late last night, either. He let it go for now though. 'We understand you used to date Justine Mayweather.'

Reynolds froze mid-wipe. 'Justine? This is about Justine?'

'That's right, sir,' Hannah said.

Reynolds straightened, confused, but just a little bit happier. His mouth twitched into a grin. Probably because he realised Wise and

Hannah weren't there to bust him for possession. 'I haven't seen Justine in six ... no, eight months.'

'But you were in a relationship with her?' Wise asked.

'Well, yeah. Kind of. You know, we hung out and stuff. It wasn't anything serious. Not for me anyway.' Reynolds cranked his neck back and gave his neck a roll, trying to act all Jack The Lad now he knew he wasn't getting nicked. Considering he was probably in his forties, it came across more than a little sad. 'Look, what is this about? Is Justine in trouble? Because, as I said, I haven't seen her in ages. Whatever she's done hasn't got anything to do with me.'

'I'm afraid Justine's dead,' Wise said.

And, just like that Reynolds' smile disappeared. His eyes bulged as he looked from Wise to Hannah and back again, his already pale skin going another three shades whiter. '*Dead* dead?'

Wise nodded. 'I'm sorry, sir.'

Reynolds put down his cloth and staggered around the island so he could sit on one of the stools. He let out a puff of air as he stared into space, lost in his own thoughts. 'Dead,' he said for the third time as if trying to give the word meaning and failing. He shook his head. 'No. I don't believe it. You've made a mistake.'

'I'm afraid we haven't, sir.' Wise watched Reynolds carefully. In his time as a police officer, he'd seen every type of reaction to such news and believed himself a good judge of when people were faking shock — after all, if Reynolds had killed Justine, then he would've already known she was dead — but his shock appeared as genuine as it got.

'How did she die?' Reynolds asked, finally looking up to meet Wise's gaze.

'I'm afraid we can't tell you that, sir,' Wise replied. 'We are, however, treating it as suspicious.'

'Suspicious? What? You mean she was killed?' Reynolds reeled once more at that information. 'Fucking hell.'

'Let me get you a glass of water,' Hannah said. She walked over to the sink, opened a cupboard, found a glass, filled it and passed it to Reynolds. He took it with shaking hands and managed to gulp down some.

He looked at the two detectives again. 'Fuck.'

'At the moment, we're talking to people like yourself, who knew Justine, and trying to build a picture of what she was like,' Wise said. 'What she did, who were her friends and so on.'

Reynolds rubbed his face, then blinked furiously. 'What she was like?'

'Yes, sir.'

'Right. Well, Justine's great … was great. I mean, she was a good girl. Fun to be with, you know? A good laugh. We always had a good laugh together.'

'How long were you together?'

'I don't know. Six months or so. Maybe a bit less.'

'Not that long then?' Wise said.

Reynolds shrugged. 'It was long enough.'

'Where did you meet?' Hannah asked.

'On one of those dating apps. Sparks, I think it was,' Reynolds said. 'I liked the way she looked. She liked me. We texted back and forth a bit and then met up. We got on and that was that.'

'Where did you go for your first date?' Wise asked.

'She picked the venue,' Reynolds replied. 'Some tiki bar in Battersea. It's all bamboo walls and flowery wallpaper. You drink out of coconuts. Her friend was the manager. Mark, his name was. I think she thought it was a safe place to meet.' He waved a hand. 'Anyway, we got on, saw each other again and that was that. As I said, she was a good laugh. We always had fun.'

'Apart from her being fun, what else can you tell us about Justine?'

'She was sporty. She loved going to the gym, doing pilates, yoga, all that shit.' Reynolds held up both hands. 'That was one of the ways we were different. I mean, I can tell you the best places to eat in the city and who has what wines on their lists. But I don't sweat or run around tracks.' He picked up the glass of water and drank some more. 'To be honest, I was quite glad when she went off to a class or hit the gym. It gave me a bit of a break. Justine could be … intense, if you know what I mean.'

'No, I don't actually,' Wise replied. 'In what way was she intense?'

'Well, she was just full-on, you know. All "I love you" from the start. She wanted to spend every minute of every day with me when she wasn't working, and she wasn't very subtle about wanting to get married.'

'And you weren't keen?'

'We'd only just met. To be honest, if I met me, I wouldn't think I was husband material. I'm not exactly reliable, if you know what I mean.' As if to punctuate the point, there was movement from upstairs, followed by footsteps on the stairs.

Two seconds later, a young dark-haired woman appeared in the doorway, clutching a fake fur coat to her chest and looking as rough as Reynolds. She wasn't quite sure who to look at. 'I'm ... er ... I gotta be somewhere.' She tilted her head towards the door. 'I'll ... er ... see myself out.'

'Can I just take your name and details before you go?' Hannah said, stepping towards her, notepad in hand.

'But I don't know nothin',' the woman said. 'I only met him last night.'

Hannah smiled. 'Still, just for our records. You can tell me on the way out.' She motioned towards the front door.

Reynolds' guilty look was back. 'As I said, I'm not exactly the marrying type.'

'Is that why you split up from Justine in the end?'

'Yeah. No. Maybe a little bit.' Reynolds shook his head. 'There were a few things that caused it, really. First, there was the marrying thing. Then there was the money — as in she loved spending my cash. She was very keen on getting spoiled, you know? She was always walking me past jewellery shops so she could just "happen" to see a new necklace or a ring that would just be "amazing to have". I mean, I do alright for myself but I'm not fucking Richard Branson. And she made me feel shit when I couldn't or wouldn't buy whatever it was.'

'But you did buy her a BMW,' Wise said.

'Yeah, and more fool me. I'd just got a bonus at work — a big one — and I got carried away, playing Billy Big Boots. She used to have this shitty Mini that used to keep breaking down, so after she dropped a hint that she needed a new motor for the one thousandth time, I thought why not? What a mug. I mean, she was good in bed, but she wasn't *that* good.'

'How did she take the break-up?' Wise asked as Hannah returned to the kitchen.

'There was a lot of screaming and shouting. A lot of name-calling. Then, when I asked for the car back, she went turbo on me. She got a bit violent, truth be told. In the end, I just walked away before she did some serious harm.'

'How violent?'

'A bit of kicking. A bit of punching. Nothing too serious, but still. I wasn't having that,' Reynolds replied. 'It wasn't my fault, everyone breaks up with her in the end.'

'Is that what she said?' Hannah asked.

Reynolds nodded. 'Yeah. But what did she expect? You behave like that, and blokes are gonna run, aren't they? And then there was the snoring.'

'The snoring?' Wise repeated.

'Yeah,' Reynolds chuckled. 'The snoring. She was loud. I mean, Foghorn Leghorn loud. It was hard to sleep sometimes. I used to take sleeping pills just to get through the night. Justine was pretty sensitive about it, though, so she must've had plenty of complaints. There were a few nights when I could've quite happily throttled her to get her to shut up.'

Neither Wise nor Hannah said anything. Reynolds must've realised what he'd said, because he suddenly looked panicked and held up both hands. 'Not that I did. It's just an expression.'

'An unfortunate one,' Wise said. 'Did Justine mention anyone else? Anyone who she might've had a problem with? Another bad break up?'

'The only bloke she always moaned about was her boss. Mac —

or some stupid name like that. He was always trying it on with her. Said he was really handsy. Justine joked that it would be good for her career if she slept with him, but he creeped her out.'

27

Wise and Hannah drove to Stephen Askins's home next. His place was in the back end of Ladbroke Grove, just passed the tube station, in St Lawrence Terrace. In many ways, it was a carbon copy of where Reynolds lived; all Victorian terraces, brown brick walls and white window frames and black doors. St Lawrence Terrace had more trees, though. It probably looked lovely during the summer, offering pockets of shade over the pavement but right then, in January, the branches were bare, shivering in the wind as they groped the grey sky.

'Boyfriend number two,' Wise said, finally finding a spot for the Mondeo just around the corner from Askins's house, in St Michaels Gardens.

Hannah checked her notebook. 'Stephen Askins, thirty-nine, a music producer. Apparently, he makes music for TV commercials and stuff like that.'

They both got out of the car and Wise grabbed his overcoat from the backseat, quickly putting it on over his suit jacket. The sky had brightened a fraction, but the day hadn't got any warmer. A cruel breeze raced down the street, pinching skin and stealing breath, forcing Wise to squint as they made their way back to St Lawrence Terrace.

Crossing the road, Wise noticed one house stood out among all the others, with its exterior painted a sky blue, with its steps a jet black leading up to a dark blue door. 'Bold colour choice,' he said.

'That's Askins's place,' Hannah said, pointing to the house.

'Not exactly subtle, is it?'

'Whatever floats your boat, I suppose.'

Wise let Hannah do the door knocking this time. She was gentler but just as persuasive in bringing another man to the door. If Reynolds had been a hungover mess, the man who answered the door was the complete opposite. Clutching a green coloured drink in one hand, the man was in full gym kit, covered in sweat and had a white towel draped around his shoulders. He did a double take when he saw the two detectives on his doorstep. 'Yes? Can I help you?'

They both held up their warrant cards. 'I'm Detective Inspector Wise and this is DS Markham. Are you Stephen Askins?'

'I am,' the man replied, the questioning look on his face intensifying. His hair, more silver than grey, was cut short, and contrasted with the almost sun-tanned colour of his skin.

'We'd like to ask you a few questions, sir,' Wise said. He pointed inside. 'Could we ...'

'Of course, Inspector,' Askins said. 'Please, come in. Do you fancy a coffee?'

'That would be lovely,' Wise replied.

'This way.' Askins stepped back from the door. He took the towel off his shoulders and wiped his face, then pointed down the hallway to his left. 'The kitchen's at the back. I've just made a pot.'

As Wise headed towards the kitchen, he noted that the house was clean, tidy and well-decorated. In fact, it was the sort of place his wife would love to have. Unfortunately, she married a police officer instead of a music producer. The kitchen itself was all teak cabinets offset against green-painted panelling with brass handles. Unlike Reynolds' place, there wasn't an island dominating the room. Instead, there was a teak dining table in the centre of the room with a bench on one side and chairs around the rest of it.

'Take a seat,' Askins said. He headed over to the cabinets above a stainless-steel sink, took out three mugs and filled them from a pot of coffee just to his right. He turned around. 'Milk? Cream?'

'Black for me,' Wise said.

'Milk for me,' Hannah added.

'Would you like me to froth it?' Askins asked. Somehow, he made it sound almost flirtatious and yet totally innocent at the same time. 'I have a gizmo somewhere.'

'No need, sir,' Hannah replied.

Askins placed Wise's cup on the table, then opened a concealed fridge to retrieve the milk. After adding a splash to both remaining cups, he placed them on the table and sat down on the bench. He wiped his face once more with the towel, then dropped it on the bench next to him. 'Now, how can I help you?'

Wise and Hannah sat opposite him. 'It's about Justine Mayweather,' Wise said, watching Askins's reaction.

'Justine?' He looked like he had to think about who she actually was to start with. Then, it clicked. 'Dear God. Is she okay?'

'I'm afraid she's dead, sir,' Hannah replied.

'Dead?' In many ways, Askins's reaction was similar to Reynolds; surprise, shock, disbelief and, finally, acceptance playing out across his face in milliseconds. 'How?'

'I'm afraid we can't tell you that,' Wise said.

'Christ,' Askins said. 'That bad?'

Wise nodded. 'That bad.'

'Do you mind telling us when you last saw Justine?' Hannah asked.

Askins took a sip of coffee. 'November, maybe?'

'How long were you together?'

'About six or seven months.'

'Was it a serious relationship?' Wise said, picking up his own coffee. It smelt wonderful. When he took a sip, he was pleased that it tasted even better. The man knew his coffee.

'It was serious as in we weren't seeing anyone else while we were together,' Askins said. 'But it wasn't serious in the way that ends up in marriage. Not on my part, anyway.'

'But it was for Justine?'

'I think she was in love with the idea of being in love, more than anything. When we first met, she was very upfront about the fact that she wanted to settle down, though. I had to tell her that I was very much a confirmed bachelor and that I wasn't looking for that kind of relationship.'

'How did she take that information?'

'She said it was okay, but I think she thought that she could get me to change my mind eventually.' Askins played with his mug, turning it in his hands. 'But I'm not that sort of guy. I'm too selfish. I enjoy women's company, but I like doing whatever I want when I want. I mean, I turned the upstairs' rooms into my own personal gym, and you can't do that if you have kids, can you?'

Wise thought about his own meagre set-up in the garage at home. Somehow, he didn't think Askins had a thirty-year-old punch bag and a single bench in his gym. 'It does get a bit more difficult with kids around,' he said, knowing that he'd give anything — sacrifice anything — to have his own family home again. 'Did it cause problems when Justine realised she couldn't change you?'

'Maybe. But things were coming to an end anyway at that point, so it wasn't a big deal,' Askins said. 'I think she'd met someone else by the time we broke up, so it worked out well for everyone.'

'Did she tell you she was seeing someone?'

'Not in so many words but she went from wanting to be with me all the time to suddenly being "busy" more often than not.'

'Did Justine mention any names or anything like that?'

'No, I'm sorry. It was more a feeling I had than anything. When I told her it was over, she almost looked relieved. The only awkward moment really was when she came over to pick up all her stuff from here.'

'What do you mean?'

Askins laughed. 'It's stupid really, but there was just so much of it. It was all just bits and pieces she'd left here over the months, but it felt like she'd been trying to move in by stealth, you know? She had to use a suitcase to fit everything in. She got a bit arsey with me when I made a comment about it.'

'Did you stay in touch afterwards?' Hannah asked.

'Not really. I sent her a card at Christmas but that's about it,' Askins replied. 'But that was more out of politeness than anything. We'd both moved on and I'm not big on hanging onto the past and all that.'

Wise finished the last of his coffee. 'Where did you meet Justine?'

'The same place I meet everyone. On Sparks. Saves a lot of messing around. None of this "I've got a boyfriend" nonsense after you've been chatting them up for an hour and buying them drinks. If they're on there, you know they're up for it. It's a good hunting ground.'

'Who swiped who first?'

'Funnily enough, it was Justine this time. She invited me to some tiki bar in Battersea for drinks. We got on and it went from there.'

'We've heard Justine could be quite materialistic,' Hannah said.

'She certainly liked the good things in life,' Askins said. 'But I didn't mind that. I do too.'

Hannah nodded. 'And did you split the costs of things between you, or did you pay for most things?'

'I paid for everything. Call me old-fashioned, but I was taught that's what gentlemen do.'

'Did she mention any problems with ex-boyfriends or any men in general?' Wise asked.

'Not really,' Askins replied. 'She said her boss was a twat but that was about it.'

Wise glanced over at Hannah, who nodded. He stood up. 'I think we have everything we need for now. Thank you for talking with us. You've been a great help.'

'Of course,' Askins replied. 'If you need anything else ...'

'We'll be in touch if we do,' Wise said.

As Hannah got to her feet, Askins did likewise and walked them to the door. 'I hope you find whoever's behind this,' he said as he let them out.

'Oh, we will,' Wise said. 'Thank you once again.' The two detectives walked down the black steps back down to the street. Neither spoke until they had crossed the road and were back on St Michaels Gardens.

'What do you think?' Wise asked as he unlocked the Mondeo.

'I think that Askins was a major upgrade on Reynolds but not by much. Justine obviously had a thing for emotionally immature men who only had enough space in their hearts to love themselves.'

'Askins certainly had a nice home. Very clean,' Wise said, opening the door. He climbed into the Mondeo as Hannah got in on the other side.

'It wasn't serial killer clean though,' Hannah said. 'As for Reynolds, that guy was a bum. His idea of getting rid of evidence was rinsing the coke off his dinner plate.'

'You noticed that?'

'How could I not? He probably thought we were there to nick him for sniffing a gramme of coke the night before.'

'Interesting that Justine met both men through Sparks,' Wise said. He turned the engine on, slipped the car into gear and drove out of his parking spot. 'Monique, the other day, said she was on the apps but maybe it was just the one she was using. Maybe that's where she met her Mystery Man.'

'We could give Emily Walker a call,' Hannah suggested. Walker was the CEO of Sparks. Wise and Hannah had met her back in September while investigating the murder of Mark Hassleman, the founder of Sparks. 'She could give us the names of everyone Justine had hooked up with via the app.'

'Good idea.' Wise said. Then a thought of his own crossed his mind. 'What if the killer is using the app to hunt for girls?'

Hannah turned her head, staring at Wise. 'Shit. He couldn't be. Could he?'

'It's a possibility.' Wise glanced over at her. 'As Askins said — it's a good hunting ground.'

'What about Justine's boss? That's two of them now who've mentioned him — plus Monique at Green.'

'Yeah. Let's add him to the list,' Wise said. 'I wouldn't put anything past that man.'

28

Sam had to admit he was nervous as he waited for Tom to pick him up for lunch. Jean's words rattled around inside his head, no matter how hard he tried to forget them. He was sitting in his armchair with the TV on, hoping to find something to distract himself, but there was nothing to watch, even with sixteen million channels to choose from.

'Haven't you told your dad that Tom's a murdering gangster? That he threatened you, me and the kids?' Jean screams.

Sam stood up. He could feel his heart racing. He felt sick. This was a mistake. How could he face Tom with all that nonsense clogging up his brain? He'd better cancel. Call it off. Make an excuse.

Sam marched over to the house phone, his mind made up, but when he picked it up, he realised he didn't know Tom's number. It was saved on his own mobile, of course, but where had he put that? It was turned off and put in a drawer somewhere. It was easier that way to hide from Si's calls. Easier to ignore his messages if he didn't have to read them. Besides, no one else called him these days.

There was only Simon and Tom. His mates down the pub didn't have to call. There were in the Oaks every night, rain or shine. All

Sam had to do was walk through the door of the boozer to have a natter if he felt like it.

He put the house phone back in the cradle and started opening drawers. Of course, it wasn't in the desk where the bloody house phone sat. No, that would be too easy. Sam went into the kitchen, hoping his mobile would be tucked away with all the takeaway menus that he kept but never ordered from. After all, it was a waste of money ordering food to be delivered when it was just him. But, after shuffling through the Indian, Chinese, pizza, kebab and fried chicken leaflets, he had to admit the phone wasn't there either.

Typical. The bloody thing must be his bedroom.

Sam had one foot on the stairs when the doorbell went. He turned around and saw a hulking shape through the frosted window.

Tom.

Shit. There was no calling it off now. Not when his kid was on his front doorstep.

Sam took a deep breath, found a smile from somewhere and stuck it on his face, and opened the door. 'Tom.'

'Dad,' Tom said, grinning himself. 'How are you, you daft sod?'

The two men stared at each other for a heartbeat, then they were hugging. And Sam was once again amazed that his little boy, whom he'd once carried about on his shoulders, was now this hulk of a man. Six feet tall and six feet wide. A tank. Tom smelt of cigarettes and aftershave, an odd combination that somehow worked for him and Sam realised he'd missed his son so very much.

When they let go, Sam had tears in his eyes. 'Good to see you, son.'

Tom gave him a playful punch on the shoulder. 'What you crying for? It's not been that long.'

Sam wiped his eyes with his sleeve. 'It's been too long. Sorry I've been hiding away.'

'So, you admit you've been hiding?'

A rush of guilt and fear hit Sam in equal measure so hard that he had to look away for a moment, trying to compose himself. 'Well, you know, not hiding. I just needed some peace and quiet. You know how it is.'

'Only too well,' Tom chuckled. 'Now, are you ready? We need to get over to Peckham before they give our table away.'

'Let me get my coat.' By the time Sam had his overcoat on and locked the house up, he'd calmed down enough to meet Tom's eyes again. 'You're looking well.'

Tom put his arm around his father's shoulders, and they walked down the street. 'Yeah, well. I bloody well hope so. I've been going down to the gym, trying to eat right and all that. I'm not getting any younger, after all.'

'Still on the cigs though.'

'A man's got to have some vices, Dad.' He stopped by a silver Audi TT, dug out some keys and beeped the doors open.

'This yours?' Sam said, staring at the motor.

'No, Dad. I just happened to find the keys lying on the ground and thought it'd be fun to nick it.' Tom laughed when he saw the look on Sam's face. 'Fucking hell, Dad. I'm just teasing you. Of course it's mine.'

'What happened to the Beamer?'

'Only wankers drive BMWs,' Tom said. 'Now, get in. We've got places to go.'

Sam opened the door, looked down at the leather seat and didn't fancy his chances of getting in. 'It's a bit low down, isn't it?'

'Here, let me help you,' Tom said, taking his arm. 'I keep forgetting my old man's an old man now.' Even with his son's help, it wasn't easy getting in the motor. Sam didn't know where to put his feet or what to hold onto and, by the time he was actually sitting down, it felt like his arse was an inch off the tarmac. Still, he had to admit, the car was beautiful. It was like sitting in a spaceship.

The whole car shook as Tom climbed into the driver's seat, seemingly taking up all the room in the car, his shoulder touching his father's. 'Buckle up, Dad.'

Sam did as he was told.

Tom turned the engine on, and it roared into life.

'I hope you're not going to drive too—' Tom was off before Sam could finish the sentence, wheel spinning his way out of his parking spot and off down the road. The speed of the thing thrust Sam back into his chair as Tom drove like he was doing a lap of Silverstone instead of navigating Streatham High Road. But that was nothing compared to when he got on the A23 and had some space around him. Tom accelerated, changing gears by pressing buttons on the steering wheel, and laughing his head off all the while.

Sam risked a glance out the window and saw everyone was watching the car go past. A few had that sanctimonious look of the outraged but most gawped with a good mix of envy and awe. Sam didn't blame them one bit for that.

'What do you think, Dad?' Tom asked.

'I think you should slow down before you give me a heart attack,' Sam replied.

'You boring old sod,' Tom replied, but he dropped the speed down all the same and Sam managed to sit a bit more upright in his seat.

'It's a lovely car, Tom,' Sam said. 'But you'll lose your licence if you carry on driving like that. There are cameras everywhere these days.'

'Fuck 'em. Soon they won't let you have any fun.' Tom glanced over at his dad. 'It is good to see you. I've missed you.'

'Same, son. Same.'

'I hope you don't mind, but I've invited someone else along for lunch today.'

'Oh yeah? Who's that?'

'Her name's Melanie.'

'Melanie?' Sam repeated.

'Yeah, Melanie.'

'Who's she, then?'

'She's my girlfriend,' Tom said.

'Your girlfriend?'

'Bloody hell, Dad. Are you going to repeat everything I say? Because if you are, this is going to be a very long, painful conversation and I'd rather skip to the good bit where I tell you that I really like her and I hope you do too, because this could get serious — if you know what I mean.'

'Serious as in marriage?'

'I'm thinking about it, Dad. I really am.'

Sam puffed out his cheeks. 'Wow. I never thought I'd hear you say that. She must be something special if she's got you thinking about hanging up your spurs.'

'I think she is, but you can see for yourself in a bit — just promise me you won't start flirting with her yourself,' Tom replied.

'Me?'

'Don't act all innocent with me, Dad. We all know what you're like around beautiful women.'

'Fair do, son,' Sam said. 'But it's not my fault women find me irresistible.'

'Well, I hope Mel doesn't decide to swap me for you.'

Rain started to fall on the windscreen, and as if by magic, the wipers sprang to life to wipe the offending moisture away. 'How did it do that?'

'Do what?'

'The wipers. You didn't turn them on,' Sam said.

'Everything's automatic now, Dad. The windscreen's rain sensitive.'

'A bit like you were when you were a kid, eh?'

Father and son laughed at a joke no one else would understand or find funny and that made it all the better.

'Dad,' Tom said, suddenly sounding serious and a little bit vulnerable. 'Before we meet Mel, I just want to check that everything's alright. I mean, really alright. We've never gone so radio silent before. Not even when I was ... inside. If something's wrong, you can tell me. If I've done something that's pissed you off ...'

'It's nothing,' Sam said, feeling guilty again. 'I just had a row with Simon — well, I was more angry with his missus really and, well, I needed some time to myself to get over it.'

'What was the row about?'

'A load of nonsense. She was pissed off about his job and she said stuff to me that she shouldn't have said. She was upset with Simon and hurt me to get back at him.'

'What a bitch,' Tom said.

'For once I'm not going to argue with you about that, but we all do stupid things when we're angry, don't we?'

'Still ... What did she say to you?'

Sam was aware that the mood had changed in the car. He could feel Tom's own anger growing without having to look himself. 'It was nonsense. Definitely not worth repeating. It annoys me even thinking about it.'

'I know, but she shouldn't be picking on you just because Simon's being a dick.'

'Simon's alright. You know he is. His heart's in the right place.'

'For a fucking copper.'

'Tom, please,' Sam said. 'I won't have you run your brother down to me. Same as I wouldn't let him do the same with you. You're both my sons, whatever your feelings are for each other.'

Tom took a deep breath, chewed on his lips for a moment, then breathed out. 'You're right. Sorry. I just don't like anyone having a go at you.'

'I know.' Sam took a breath. 'How's ... work?'

'Oh, it's good. Booming, in fact. Never been better.'

'What is it you're doing again?' Sam tried to make the question sound casual, but God only knew if he'd succeeded.

Tom cackled. 'You know, Dad. A bit of this. A bit of that. Anything that'll make a few bob.'

'But it's all ... above board, like? You're not doing anything dodgy?'

Tom turned to look at his father, the smile gone from his lips. 'Why would you ask that?'

'I just worry about you. That's all.' Sam tried to laugh but it came out faker than his mate Brian's Gucci sunglasses. 'I'm a worrier. I can't help it, can I? Not with you and Simon as my boys.'

'As long as no one's been saying shit about me.' Tom's eyes were on the road again, but it didn't make the mood in the car any less uncomfortable. Why the hell hadn't Sam just kept his bloody mouth shut?

'Why would they do that, son?' Sam said. He took a breath, calming himself. He was being stupid even thinking it. 'Now, tell me more about this Mel. She good-looking?'

Tom chortled and, just like that, the atmosphere changed back to the way it had been at the start of the journey. 'Good-looking? She's a stunner. A bloody twelve out of ten.'

'And you don't mind going out with someone who's blind?'

Laughter filled the car.

29

DC Millie Buchanan waited in the lobby of Justine Mayweather's building in Warriner Gardens more than a little bit pissed off. She wasn't annoyed because she had to work a Saturday. That came with The Job. If you were the sort of person who got upset at working weekends, you should never become a copper.

No.

Millie was pissed off because she finally had a good opportunity to do some serious police work, but Palmer and Riddleton were a pair of dicks determined to ruin it. So much so, Palmer had already goaded one of the others into breaking his nose. The news of which had sent the DCI into fits of bloody glee like he'd won the Pools or something.

'I'll have him kicked off the force,' he'd gloated, not caring that said officer had only buried his partner of thirty years on Tuesday and, while clearly a dinosaur, was by all accounts a damn good police officer. It didn't help that Hicksy reminded Millie of her dad in more ways than one and she hated the thought of someone messing with him just because Riddleton had a vendetta against Wise.

Millie couldn't even work out how she'd ended up being one of

Riddleton's lackeys. It was just bad luck that he'd been in charge at Hammersmith after she passed her exams, and he picked her to be one of his 'rising stars'. Since then, she'd found herself at a new station every few months, trying to get along with colleagues who thought that she was there to spy on them and fuck up their careers — which, in all fairness, she was — albeit very much against her will.

Before they'd gone into Kennington, Riddleton had told her and Palmer about this rogue team of corrupt cops that needed sorting out, claiming they were all on the take and as dangerous as the villains they went after. But Millie had to admit, she couldn't see it so far. Wise might look like a brute in a suit, but he seemed to genuinely care about his team and solving the case he was on. The same could be said about his team too.

And Millie was finally working for a Murder Investigation Team. It was all she had ever dreamed of. It was why she'd become a police officer to begin with. She didn't want to just be someone helping Riddleton climb the ladder, especially as she reckoned he was the sort of person who'd very quickly forget anyone and everyone who'd helped him get to the top once he was there. No, Millie wanted to go after murderers and put them away. She didn't want to be a spy to help someone's political ambitions.

She didn't want to move on in another couple of months, either, leaving behind ruined careers and bitter resentment, and be dumped into whatever mess Riddleton was using next to clamber up the ranks.

The truth was she had to work out how to disassociate herself from dear old Doug without ruining her own career in the process, because she knew that Riddleton would try to do that to her when she said she wanted to leave him. That's if there was a team left to be a part of. If Riddleton had his way, he'd nuke the whole damn lot just to get at Wise.

Millie sighed and checked the time on her phone. Palmer was late. Like he always was.

The lift dinged, drawing her attention. A man walked out and smiled as he caught her looking. He was old but in a good way, a

Pierce Brosnan way. His silver-grey hair was artfully styled, and he had a moustache and goatee equally well-taken care of. Despite it being a Saturday, he wore grey trousers with a faint pinstripe that set off well-polished brogues and complimented the black overcoat he had on.

'Hello,' he said as he came closer. 'I don't think we've met before.'

Millie took a breath. Despite his age, the man was all magnetism and he had it turned on for her. 'I don't think we have.' She held out a hand. 'I'm Millie.'

'I'm Marcus. Pleased to meet you.' He shook her hand but held onto it just a fraction too long. 'Are you new here or just visiting?'

'I'm just visiting, I'm afraid,' Millie replied. She could feel herself blushing under Marcus' gaze. He was looking at her as if she was the only woman in the world. Older men weren't normally her thing, but she had to admit there was something about Marcus she liked. 'It's quite an impressive building.'

Marcus smiled. 'Sometimes I think they tried a bit too hard with the décor, but I like it. And it's damn convenient for town. Who are you visiting here? Not your boyfriend, I hope.'

'No, not my boyfriend. I don't have a boyfriend.' Millie had no idea why she told Marcus that. She hadn't intended to.

He raised an eyebrow. 'That's good to know. Perhaps if you're bored one night—'

The front door opened, and Palmer bundled through, looking like he'd been in a car crash with his taped-up nose and black eyes. 'Sorry I'm late.'

It was like throwing a bucket of cold water over Marcus. The man stepped back, all his charisma turned off in an instant. 'Detective Palmer. You look like you've been in the wars.'

'It's nothing.' Palmer barely looked at the man as he walked over to Millie. 'You ready?'

'Yeah. Of course.' Millie turned back to Marcus. 'It was nice to meet you.'

'And you,' Marcus said but he was already moving towards the door. 'Have a good day.' And then he was out in the street and walking briskly away.

'What was that all about?' Palmer said.

Millie was still looking outside at the now empty street. 'Nothing. He just said hello. That's all.'

They headed over to the lift and Millie thought what a missed opportunity that was. She would've said yes if Marcus had asked her out. It was a shame he was one of those blokes who just didn't like coppers.

30

When Wise and Hannah returned to Kennington, it had just gone 5 p.m. They'd spent the afternoon speaking to Justine's other boyfriends, both of whom she'd also met via Sparks, and not come up with anything new. They had the same opinion of her as the others — she'd liked money and wanted to get married. Other than that, they had no complaints about Justine except both had made jokes about her snoring. As far as they were concerned, she was well-liked, good fun and they had no idea why anyone would want to kill her.

When Wise walked into MIR-One, it was as packed as it was normally on a weekday. For a moment, Wise felt a touch of guilt that his whole team had spent the day working but, when he saw all their faces, he didn't see any resentment or disgruntlement. Quite the contrary, in fact.

Apart from Palmer, that is.

He sat at his desk with his bruised eyes and taped up nose, looking as pissed off with the world as he ever did. The rest of the team, though? They all looked energised again and some of the darkness of the last few weeks seemed to have faded in the process.

Leaving Hannah, Wise walked to the front of the whiteboards and turned to face the troops. 'Can I have your attention please?' he called out over their chatter. 'Let's have a quick rundown from everyone on their progress and then we can shoot off and enjoy what's left of the evening. Palmer, Millie — do you want to start first?'

Palmer just scowled some more but Millie stood up and smiled. 'We've finished talking to everyone at Warriner Gardens. A few people knew her to say hello in passing but that's about it. They said she was friendly, out-going — the usual stuff. Didn't cause any problems. A couple recognised Stephen Askins from pictures, but no one had seen her with anyone new. One person ...' Millie checked her notebook. '... A lady called Amanda Potterton had an interesting bit of info though. She moved into Warriner Gardens at around the same time as Justine, so they had a bit more of a casual friendship than anyone else. Amanda said that Justine wasn't home much and, if she was, she was often coming home to change clothes to go out again, staying at her boyfriend's more than her own place.'

'That matches what we learned today,' Wise said. 'All her ex-boyfriends said she was very intense, wanting to spend every minute with them.'

'Well, this Amanda reckoned that all changed four or five weeks ago. Amanda saw Justine every day and she was worried that Justine had broken up with her boyfriend again. When they chatted, though, Justine told her not to worry and that she'd never been happier.'

'Did she say who she was seeing?'

Millie shook her head. 'Justine apparently said it was a secret for now, but Millie would be surprised.'

'Surprised?' Wise said.

Millie nodded. 'But she didn't say any more than that.'

'Maybe she was seeing someone her own age for once,' Hannah suggested. 'Instead of immature man boys.'

'Or someone poor,' Wise suggested. 'Thanks for that, Millie. Brains, how have you got on?'

'I've not got much to help us, I'm afraid. I've not come across any other cases where a body was dumped in the river. I've started looking at other murders but, as you know, sixty percent of homicides are female. I'm trying to eliminate some based on age, etcetera, but there's a lot to go through, especially as we don't know how far back to look or if he's just been hunting in London or elsewhere.'

'It looks like Justine was using the Sparks app to meet people,' Wise said. 'Hannah and I are going to get in touch with the CEO and see if there's a link there. Maybe that's where the killer is finding his victims too.'

'I have been going through her phone info as well,' Brains added. 'Call wise, she doesn't use it much, apart from conversations with people she works with, clients, etcetera. Even text messages are limited. They're mainly from delivery services and shops pushing promos.'

'That's a bit odd, isn't it? Do you think she had another phone?'

'It's not that uncommon. If Justine was using WhatsApp, for example, we wouldn't know who she was texting, and she could chat via that and not be charged any minutes or even data usage as long as she was connected to wi-fi.'

'Shit,' Wise said. 'What about her movements? Can we get anything from where the phone's been connecting to cell towers?'

'I've already been on that,' Brains said. 'And it merely confirms what Millie found out. The last few weeks Justine was only travelling from home to her office in Soho and then back again. There are early morning trips out and back four or five times a week to Battersea, but I did a bit of searching and found a gym in the vicinity. I called them and they verified that Justine was a member.'

'Palmer, Millie,' Wise said. 'Can you go down to this gym and find out if anyone knew Justine or saw her with someone? And see if they have any CCTV of her. It would be good to see Justine when she was alive and well. So far, we just have footage of her body in a bag.'

'Sure, Guv,' Millie replied.

Wise turned back to Brains. 'What about her movements over Christmas week and New Year's?'

'Now that is interesting in as far as she doesn't go anywhere — apart from the gym again and a few trips out during the day, probably to the shops. If Justine went out on New Year's Eve, she didn't take her phone with her.'

'No one goes out without their phone,' Callum said.

'Justine's other boyfriends said that she wanted to spend all her free time with them,' Hannah added. 'If she was as loved up as she made out with this Mystery Man, then she'd want to be with him over the holidays.'

'He might have been away,' Wise replied. 'Maybe he spent Christmas abroad?'

'Then she would've gone with him,' Hannah said. 'There's no way she'd let her boyfriend go away without her over Christmas and New Year. Not unless they broke up.'

'In that case, he spent the holidays with her at Warriner Gardens,' Wise said. 'And, if he was with her on New Year's Eve, then he's definitely our Mystery Man too. Callum, Donut — you two had any joy with the CCTV?'

'Not really,' Donut said. 'We've been going over footage for Monday — New Year's Day. We've checked the cars coming in and out of the Warriner Gardens' car park but it's only residents and not many of them.'

'Same with the front door,' Callum added. 'The view's not perfect but there's not many people coming and going until after midday but, with what we've got so far, we can match everyone to either residents, friends of residents or delivery people. Amazon's a regular. Plus food delivery people. We haven't checked if they are all legit yet, though.'

'Don't concentrate on those for now,' Wise said. 'We're looking for someone who knows the place well if he's spent every evening there with Justine. He'll fit in with the residents, so much so maybe no one's noticed him coming and going before the murder.

'Look for a man on his own. He used Justine's car to get rid of the body and then returned it to its parking spot, so he's definitely in the building from 4:30 a.m. Monday morning. We can assume he goes back to her flat. Maybe he carries on cleaning it but, at some point, he has to leave.'

'We're on it, Guv,' Callum said.

'We got Justine's bank details, Guv,' Hicksy said. 'I've been going through her statements and the only thing that stands out is that she's not blowing her cash each month like the rest of us. Her mortgage is her biggest expense but other than that its lunches at Pret, Yo Sushi and stuff like that. She doesn't even buy that many clothes.'

'That's because her boyfriends are paying for it all,' Hannah said.

'Yeah. I also don't think she's on the game or anything like that,' Hicksy added. 'Even if she was making dodgy cash, we'd see evidence of that somewhere — maybe paying off credit card debt or something like that but, once you take the stuff a boyfriend would pay for, the rest of it all lines up.'

'That's good,' Wise said. It didn't really make a difference as to how he'd carry on investigating her murder, but he was happy she wasn't up to anything illegal. It was at least one avenue of enquiry they could now ignore. 'What about the last six weeks with the mystery boyfriend? Any changes there?'

'No, Guv,' Hicksy replied. 'There are a couple of big-ticket items but they were probably presents. I'll dig deeper into those in case there's something useful.'

'Cheers,' Wise replied. 'What this tells us is that, true to form, Mystery Man's got cash. He's paying for stuff for her. So, Justine's not changed her type that much,' Wise said. 'What else could make him different?'

'I was thinking, Guv,' Hannah said. 'About why she went quiet on her socials. I mean, if she thought she had found Mister Right at long last, why keep it quiet?'

'Monique said she didn't want to jinx it.'

'Yeah, but by the sounds of it, she thought every boyfriend was Mister Right — so why's this one different?'

'He wanted her to keep it quiet,' Wise said.

'That's what I was thinking.'

'That's not surprising if he meant to kill her,' Hicksy said. 'He'll hardly want to be plastered all over Facebook before he suffocated her.'

'Yeah — but what if there was another reason?' Hannah said. 'Like he was married and didn't want his wife to find out. Or maybe he was her boss?'

'What? Not "Call me Mac"?' Wise said.

'He's the right age for her. He's got money. And Reynolds said he was pestering her.'

'And if you're shagging your boss, you wouldn't want that getting around the office,' Hicksy said. 'No one wants to be the office slag.'

'I wouldn't quite have put it like that, myself, but I agree,' Wise said. 'Mac is definitely worth talking to again. Find out where he lives, Hannah, and we'll go see him tomorrow.'

Wise turned to face the whiteboards. Donut had stuck up still images of the killer leaving Justine's car with her body in a bag. He peered again at the coat he was wearing, seeing again the graphics on the collar. 'Can someone investigate this coat the killer's wearing? It doesn't look like the sort of thing you can pick up in Marks and Spencer. Maybe there's something there that can help us.' Wise looked around the team. 'Hicksy, can I leave that with you?'

'Are you sure, Guv?' Hicksy replied, not looking exactly happy about the prospect.

'He's got a point,' Brains added. 'Hicksy's hardly Mr GQ.'

'Says the man who subscribes to *Geeks Weekly*,' Hicksy shot back.

'Everyone knows my drip's better than anyone else's here,' Callum called out.

'I don't know. Donut seems to have discovered fashion all of a sudden,' Hannah said. 'Maybe he's the man for the job.'

Donut blushed, saying nothing but looking pleased with the compliment all the same.

'Alright everyone,' Wise called out, smiling at the banter. 'I agree Donut is now, officially, the smartest dressed out of the lot of you, but Hicksy's the man for this. Find me that coat.'

'I'll do my best, Guv,' Hicksy replied.

'I know you will,' Wise replied. 'Right, go home all of you. Let your families, friends and loved ones know that you still exist. I'll see you all tomorrow.'

As everyone got up to leave, Wise turned to the whiteboards and started writing down notes from the meeting. He liked seeing everything up there, needing the visual reminders to jog his thoughts and perhaps see patterns hidden amongst it all.

One thing was clear, though: Warriner Gardens was at the heart of it all. Justine had spent the holidays there, undoubtedly with her killer. Had they just holed up in her flat, staying out of sight? Or did they go anywhere together?

If only the cameras at Warriner Gardens were working. They'd have everything they'd need on video. As it was, though, they still had nothing to point them in the direction of Mystery Man.

Unless it was there and he just wasn't seeing it yet.

31

The man put down his phone, having cancelled his date with Alicia, another girl he'd met on Sparks. He didn't like doing that. It was bad manners, after all, but seeing the police had unnerved him, even though he knew he was just one of many that they were speaking to. He was a name to tick off. A formality. They didn't know he'd been in a relationship with Justine. They didn't have anything to connect him to Justine in *that* way.

At least, he hoped they didn't.

He poured himself a whiskey, then headed over to the stereo. It took a few moments to pick a record to put on. In the end, he decided to listen to *Moon Safari* by Air, an original 1998 pressing. As *La Femme D'Argent* started to play, he sat down on the sofa and took a sip of his drink.

He'd cleaned Justine's flat from top to bottom, so he'd left no trace of himself there. The Thames would've cleaned her body of any DNA of his that he might have missed but he'd been diligent in scrubbing her clean too. And he'd always worn a condom when they'd had sex. After all, no one wanted an unplanned pregnancy to link them to a murder.

That just left the possibility of a witness seeing them together or getting caught on camera somewhere.

The man had been careful there too but, in a city like London, everywhere had cameras recording everyone all the time. It was impossible to be invisible and, as much as he'd encouraged her to stay in, they *had* gone on dates together. Never anywhere twice, though, and most times they'd not even travelled together to wherever it was.

In fact, he'd picked the venues every time bar one. Going for obscure places, dark places or packed places that wouldn't notice if the Prime Minister was having a drink in the corner.

But Justine had picked the venue for their first date. That damned tiki place. It was everything he hated. Utterly crass. Trying so hard to be ironically cool and failing miserably.

But there was a reason why she'd chosen it. What was it she'd said?

He took another sip of whiskey, thinking back.

'I feel safe here.'

And why was that, Justine? Why did you feel safe?

She'd said why. He knew that she had.

Why? Why? Why?

Oh yes.

'My friend, Mark, is the manager. I always come here on a first date. I like him to vet my possible boyfriends.'

Mark with his tattoos and his vintage denim jeans. Mark who'd brought them drinks. *'On the house.'*

Would Mark remember him?

Mark might.

The man put down his drink, walked over to the record player just as *All I Need* started playing and turned it off.

It was time to go out.

Time to pay Mark a visit.

32

It was nine o'clock when Wise finally found the courage to drive home. The irony wasn't lost on him that he used to resent work keeping him from his family but now he was using work as an excuse to stay away. At least when he was at Kennington, he had enough things to distract him from thinking about his personal life. Now though? There was just a sick feeling in his gut that grew and grew the closer he got to the place.

He stopped off on the way and picked up chicken tikka masala, rice and some samosas for his dinner. Jean would've told him off for spending money on a takeaway when there was food in the fridge, but he really couldn't face cooking for himself. As it was, he doubted he'd even finish the food he'd just bought. His appetite was another thing that had disappeared when Jean left with the kids. There was a good chance that, if things carried on the way they were going, his diet was going to be one hundred percent coffee.

At least he had plenty of homework to do when he got home. Wise was still getting to grips with all the information he'd been given at his meeting with Heer and Jamie, the UCO in Tom's crew, earlier in the week.

Wise had known that infiltrating his brother's crime organisation was about as dangerous a mission as they got but seeing Jamie's fear first hand had ratcheted up things another level. While Wise wanted Tom put away again so he could get his own life back, he certainly didn't want to get killed in the process.

Wise had just turned onto the A3 when his phone rang. He knew it wasn't going to be his kids calling him at that time of night, so his first instinct was that something had happened to do with the case. However, he was surprised to see his father's name on the caller ID. They'd not spoken since Jean had blurted out everything about Tom.

Wise pressed the green button to accept the call. 'Hey, Dad.'

'Simon!' his father said. 'I haven't got you at a bad time, have I?'

'No, it's good. I'm just driving home. I've been working.'

'On a Saturday? Bet Jean was happy about that.' His father's voice was full of forced cheerfulness, but his words only highlighted how long it'd been since they'd last spoken.

'She doesn't know, Dad,' Wise said. 'She moved up to Leeds before Christmas with the kids. She's living with her parents for now.'

'She left you?'

'Yeah. Basically. She's said she'd come back once …' Wise choked on what to say next. He didn't want to mention Tom's name. But he didn't want his father filling in the gaps either. 'She'll be back when things settle down. Hopefully.'

'I'm sorry, son. How are you holding up?'

'I'm surviving. It's not the best of times, if I'm being honest.'

'I can imagine.'

'Yeah, well. It is what it is. What about you? You doing okay?'

His father chuckled. 'You know me, son. You know me. Endless parties. Fighting the women off. Doing my best to stay out of trouble – but failing.'

'Yeah, I can imagine.' Wise knew the truth was quite the opposite. His dad really liked his own company, happier with a good book or watching crap on TV instead of talking nonsense with strangers. Even with the football, he'd rather watch it at home than in a crowded pub. 'I'm glad you've been having fun, but I've got to say I've missed talking to you, Dad.'

'Well, if you're ever bored, you know where I am, son. You're always welcome.'

Wise glanced down at the takeaway next to him. 'What are you doing right now?'

'Just watching TV.'

'You eaten?'

'Not really. I had a big lunch, so I was thinking of making a sandwich in a bit.'

'Fancy sharing a curry? I just picked one up and it's too much for me on my own,' Wise said. 'I could be at yours in about ten minutes.'

'Why not? I'll warm some plates up.'

'Don't go getting the fancy china out on my account.'

'You're lucky you're not getting the paper plates,' his dad replied. 'I'll see you in a bit.'

And just like that Wise's mood had done a one eighty flip. His studying could wait. Repairing his relationship with his father was much more important. He had no idea why his dad had suddenly decided to call him after six weeks of silence, but he was glad he had.

There wasn't much traffic on the road and Wise knocked on his dad's door exactly eight minutes later. He could hear the news blaring from the front room and smiled. The neighbours must love that.

Wise listened to his father's footsteps approach the door and then it opened, light spilling out and there he was. His dear old dad.

'Simon!' His father embraced him, a once giant man now barely able to get his arms around his son. Wise hugged him back with one arm, feeling an emptiness inside him disappear as he held on to the man that meant so much to him. Even the smell of his old man's aftershave had him smiling.

In the end, it was his dad who let go first and Wise saw his eyes were glistening. It was probably the closest he'd ever seen his dad come to crying. Even when Wise's mother had died, his father's reaction had been to bottle up every feeling and bury them deep somewhere so no one could see his pain.

'You better come in,' his dad said, stepping back. 'Otherwise, that curry will be stone cold by the time we get to eat it.'

'Lead on,' Wise said. After putting his overcoat on a hook by the door, he followed his father through to the kitchen and put the bag of food on the small kitchen table while his dad took out some plates from the oven and put them on the table. Wise's smile grew. His father was probably the last person who still insisted upon eating off a warm plate, but his dad always did like things a certain way.

'What did you get?' his dad said.

'It's just a chicken tikka masala, rice and some samosas.'

His dad had been fishing some knives and forks out of the cutlery drawer, but he froze. 'Bloody hell. I wish you'd told me that before I agreed for you to come over. You can hardly call that a curry, can you?'

'Sorry. I've always been a wimp when it came to heat.'

'Sometimes I really worry about you.' His dad plonked the knives and forks down and headed over to another cupboard. 'Good job I've got some chilli flakes tucked away. Might be able to save things.'

Wise sat down and started to take the lids off the containers. 'Where did you have lunch today, then?'

His dad froze again as he was rummaging in the cupboard. It was only for a second, but it was long enough for Wise to notice the hesitation. Then his dad sighed and, when he turned around, he seemed to have aged another ten years. 'I had lunch with Tom.'

'Tom,' Wise repeated.

'Yeah. He took me out for a steak over in Peckham.' His dad was still standing by the cupboard, its open door covering his body like a shield. 'I'd not seen him since ... well ... you know.'

Wise nodded. 'Since Jean.'

'Yeah.'

'It's alright, Dad. He's your son.'

His father emerged from behind the cupboard door and walked over to the table. 'He's your brother.'

'I know.'

His dad sat down. Neither man made any move towards the food. 'I hate all this.'

'Me too. And I'm sorry Jean said all that stuff to you. She was angry. She wanted to hurt me and, unfortunately, you were the easiest way for her to do that.'

His dad looked at him. 'I don't mean to be rude, Si, but Jean can be a right bitch sometimes.'

'I know that too,' Wise replied with a sad chuckle. 'How is Tom?'

'Tom's Tom. He always seems as happy as Larry. He introduced me to his girlfriend — not that you could call her a girl.'

'Oh yeah?'

'Her name's Melanie — Mel — and she was right posh,' his dad said. 'I don't know how he pulled her. She's waaaay out of his league.'

'Melanie? Melanie Hayes?'

'Yeah. That's right,' his dad said, then cocked his head back. 'How do you know that?'

'Her name came up in something. That's all,' Wise said, regretting blurting her name out like that.

'How? In your ... investigation?' Somehow, his dad managed to make the word sound like it ranked up there with kiddie fiddling.

'Melanie Hayes is quite a well-known criminal solicitor, Dad. A lot of the Met knows who she is.'

'She said she specialised in defending people wrongly accused of stuff by your lot.'

'I'm not sure that's quite right,' Wise said. 'She defends anyone who's got enough money. I don't think she cares if they're innocent or not.'

'So, you think she's a bad 'un as well, do you?' His dad pushed his chair back from the table. Away from Wise. 'Have you got her under "investigation" too?' Again, he added all the venom and disgust he could manage to the word 'investigation'.

'Dad, I don't go around just picking on people. We go after anyone who breaks the law. That's it. It's nothing personal.'

'So how come your involved in whatever nonsense your lot think Tom's done?'

'It's not through choice, Dad. Believe me, it's not.' Wise shook his head, suddenly feeling very tired. He looked at the food, his appetite gone. Even the smell of it now was making him feel sick. He pushed the nearest tin foil container to the other side of the table. 'Do you really want to talk about this?'

His dad sat back and crossed his arms. 'Yes. No. Oh, I don't know.'

Wise leaned over and put a hand on his father's arm, giving it a little squeeze. 'I feel exactly the same way. I really do. Because you're right — Tom's my brother and I want him to be happy, you know. I really do. I wish I could go for a beer with him or go to the football with you both as well. Be a family. I hate all of this.'

His dad looked up, his eyes glistening again. 'What happened, then?'

'I can't tell you much. But when I joined the police, I never told them about Tom,' Wise said. 'I thought that if they knew I had a brother who was inside for manslaughter, they'd not take me on. So, when this team, who were investigating this new gang that was trying to take over things in London, saw a picture of the man in charge, they thought it was me.'

'Because they didn't know you had a twin,' his dad said.

Wise nodded. 'When they questioned me, I didn't tell them about Tom either. I was just lucky that, when the picture was taken, I was with three other police officers so it couldn't have been me. I only started looking into what Tom was up to try and clear his name. I wanted them to be wrong.'

'Fuck.'

'Yeah. Fuck indeed.'

His father rubbed his face. 'So, it's true then? All that stuff Jean came out with?'

'I can't tell you anything. And it's better you don't know.' Wise sighed. 'He is your son. I'm glad you saw him. I'm sure he loves you as much as I love you.'

'What a mess. What a bloody mess. I'm glad your mum's not alive to see this.'

'Yeah, me too.' Wise watched as tears rolled down his father's cheeks. His heart breaking that little bit more with each one.

Sunday 8th January

33

Joshua McLean lived in a semi-detached townhouse in Savernake Road in Hampstead. The place backed onto Hampstead Heath and, judging by the cars parked alongside both sides of the street, you needed to be earning a pretty penny to live there. Needless to say, Wise's beaten-up Mondeo stood out like a sore thumb.

'He doesn't put all his money up his nose, then,' Hannah said as Wise parked the car.

'Apparently not,' Wise agreed as they climbed out the car. A man opposite was cleaning his own car — a BMW X5 — and looked rather disapprovingly as Wise locked the Mondeo. He gave the man a little wave back. 'Morning.'

'I don't think we fit in here at all,' Hannah said.

'I'm quite glad about that.' Wise opened a small black gate to enter McLean's property. A waist high green hedge protected separated the grey stone covered front garden from the street. The house itself was originally over three floors but someone at some point had converted the attic, so another window jutted out of the middle of the roof.

Wise knocked on the grey door. 'How are you feeling?' he asked as they waited for someone to answer. 'You fighting fit again?' He'd not had a good look at Hannah on the drive over but now, out in the daylight, he could see the dark shadows under her eyes.

Hannah kept her eyes on the front door. 'I'm fine.'

'Okay but if you want to go home after this,' Wise said, 'it's okay. I know it's a lot to ask of you to work a seven-day stretch straight after coming back from sick leave.'

The front door opened before Hannah could reply. A mousey-haired woman in a sweatshirt and jeans poked her head out. 'Yes? Can I help you?' The faint sounds of Soul II Soul drifted out from the house.

Hannah held up her warrant card. 'I'm Detective Sergeant Markham and this is Detective Inspector Wise. We'd like to speak to Joshua McLean.'

The woman's eyes twitched as Wise held up his warrant card as well. 'Mac? Has he done something wrong?'

'We'd just like to talk to him,' Wise said. 'Is he home?'

'Yes,' the woman replied. 'He's still asleep, though.' She stepped back, opening the door wide enough to allow the two officers to enter. 'You better come in. Excuse the mess. I was just playing with the kids.'

'No problem,' Wise replied. 'It is a Sunday, after all. How old are your children?'

'Daisy's four and Bluebell's two,' the woman replied. 'I'm Susanna, by the way. Mac's wife.'

Wise smiled. 'Nice to meet you.'

They passed a living room where two young girls looked up briefly from their iPads. The music came from a record player in the corner.

'I haven't heard Soul II Soul in ages,' Wise said.

'Oh, I love them,' Susanna said. 'But I've got to keep the volume down, so I don't wake Mac up. He was out late last night ... with clients.'

'On a Saturday night?' Hannah asked. They entered a combined dining room/kitchen area. Windows overlooked well-tended garden, where a bright yellow swing set had been installed at the far end. It looked forlorn against the bare tree branches behind it and the grey winter sky.

'It was a last-minute thing. It's hard to say no when they call. They do pay for all of this, after all. "The business has to come first,"' Susanna said, doing a bad impression of her husband and not sounding like she believed a word of it. 'Would you like a cup of tea or coffee before I get Mac?'

'We're fine,' Wise said, even though he could really have done with one right then. He'd had trouble sleeping the night before, his conversation with his father playing over in his mind non-stop. Even so, he was keener to talk to McLean.

'I'll go and get him then.' Susanna smiled, despite her obvious nervousness. She did a little hesitant two-step dance before heading up the stairs, as if she needed to summon up the courage.

Hannah glanced over at Wise and raised her eyebrows. They both listened as Susanna called her husband's name.

'What? Why are you waking me up?' he grumbled back.

'The police are here,' his wife replied.

'She sounds petrified,' Hannah whispered.

'The police?' McLean said. 'What are they doing here?'

'They said they want to talk to you,' Susanna said.

'Jesus Christ, woman. You could've told them I'm not here.' Footsteps thumped onto the floor. 'Tell them I'll be down in a minute.'

'Of course,' Susanna said, and Wise listened to her feet practically run down the stairs. 'He won't be long,' she said when she reappeared in the kitchen. 'He's not a morning person.'

'Lots of people aren't,' Hannah said. 'He's lucky you can look after the kids while he has a lie in.'

Susanna blushed. 'Well, I don't work.'

'I wouldn't say that,' Wise said. 'Two kids under four? That can be as tough as it gets.'

'That's kind of you to say—' Footsteps pounding down the stairs cut Susanna off.

McLean appeared, looking tired and angry, dressed in a black Adidas tracksuit, his white hair dishevelled. He did a double take when he saw Wise and Hannah. 'Oh, it's you two.'

'That's right,' Wise said, smiling. 'We just have a few questions we need to ask you.'

'And it couldn't wait till Monday?' McLean said. He still hadn't moved into the kitchen instead. He lingered, instead, by the stairs, half-hidden behind his wife.

'I'm afraid not, sir,' Wise said. 'Can we chat here or is there somewhere else you'd prefer?'

'No, we can talk here.' McLean put a hand on his wife's shoulder, making her flinch. 'Why don't you take the kids out somewhere? Give us some privacy?'

'But it's Bluebell's nap time,' Susanna said. 'I need to put her down in a minute.'

'For God's sake, she can sleep in her stroller,' McLean snapped back. 'The damn thing cost enough.'

'Okay.' His wife seemed to shrink as she slipped past him and headed into the living room. 'Come on, girls. We're going out.'

McLean pointed to the dining table. 'We can talk here but I have no idea what's so damned important that it can't wait.' There was none of the bonhomie of the last time they'd met. No request to 'call me Mac.'

They all sat down. McLean on one side, the detectives on the other. As they did so, Susanna appeared in the doorway, holding Daisy's hand and with Bluebell on her hip. 'I'm just going to take them upstairs. Bluebell needs changing.'

McLean waved her away without looking.

'It's about Justine Mayweather,' Wise said, as McLean's wife headed up the stairs with the children.

McLean rubbed a bleary eye. 'Well, I didn't think you were here to talk about the weather.'

'How would you describe your relationship with Justine?' Wise asked.

'Relationship? There was no relationship. She worked for me. That's all,' McLean replied. 'Look, I told you all this.'

'And it never went beyond that?'

'Beyond? What do you mean? What are you suggesting?' McLean raised his voice but, somehow, his outrage felt exaggerated.

'We've heard you enjoy spending time with your more attractive members of staff,' Wise said. 'And, specifically, that you ...' Wise turned to Hannah. 'What were the exact words?'

Hannah made a show of flicking through her notebook until she found the right page. '"He was always trying it on with her. Said he was really handsy. Justine joked that it would be good for her career if she slept with him, but he creeped her out."'

McLean's mouth dropped. 'You have to be joking.'

'I'm afraid we don't joke about such things,' Wise said. 'Now, were you trying to sleep with Justine Mayweather or were you actually sleeping with her?'

'No, I wasn't, and I object to you even asking me,' McLean roared. 'Who told you that? If it was one of my people, I'll have their job. It's bullshit.'

'We can't tell you who told us,' Hannah said, 'but it was more than one person.'

McLean shook his head. 'Ever since that bloody "Me Too" bullshit became popular, you can't even tell anyone they look nice without getting threatened with a lawsuit from some kid who wants to earn some easy money.'

'Is that what happened? You tried it on with Justine and she threatened to sue you?' Wise asked.

McLean went white. 'No. Certainly not. And don't think I don't know what you're doing. You're trying to make up some motive that would make it look like I killed her and it's just not true.'

'Where were you on New Year's Eve and New Year's Day?' Hannah asked.

'I was here,' McLean said. 'At home. With my family.'

'No, you weren't,' Susanna McLean said from the doorway, with

Bluebell on her hip and holding Daisy's hand. 'You were out all night, and you didn't get back until the afternoon the next day.'

34

'You were out all night, and you didn't get back until the afternoon the next day.' The words hung over all their heads as Susanna stared at her husband.

No one had noticed Susanna coming back down the stairs with her kids all dressed up and ready to go out, but now she had their full attention. She was white-faced and a myriad of emotions flickered across her face. Anger. Fear. Disgust. Sadness. Disbelief.

'What do you mean?' Hannah asked.

'Susanna, this has nothing to do with you,' McLean said, standing up, his face red, his voice full of anger. 'Take the damn kids out like I told you.'

'I'm sorry, *sir*,' Wise said, happy to add plenty of venom to the honorific. 'I suggest you sit down as I would very much like to hear what your wife has to say.'

McLean wasn't someone used to being told what to do but Wise was used to dealing with bullies and not many people had the balls to stand up to his requests. Sure enough, McLean gave him a good glare, still trying to act the big man, but his resolve broke quick enough and the man sank back down.

Wise waited a heartbeat more before taking his eyes off McLean and turning his attention back to Susanna. 'Now, Mrs McLean, can you repeat what you just told us? Just so I'm completely clear.'

'I'll just take the children into the other room,' Susannah said. 'Give me a moment.'

'No problem,' Wise replied.

Susannah ushered the kids through to the living room. She put the TV on and the intro music to *Peppa Pig* started playing. McLean's wife returned after that, taking her place in the doorway to the kitchen. She didn't appear to want to be any closer to her husband than necessary.

When Susanna McLean spoke, it was a cold, calm precision that did nothing to hide her anger. 'My husband told me he had to go out to a client's New Year's Eve party on Saturday night. It was all very last minute so there was no way I could arrange a babysitter to look after the children.' She glared at her husband. 'It was all *very* convenient. And, of course, he had to stay in town because it would be *impossible* to get a cab home from the West End.'

'And that's exactly what happened,' McLean said. 'You're making it sound like it was some devious plot of mine.' He turned to Wise and Hannah. 'I just didn't mention it to you because I know how it looks — how it could be so easily misconstrued — and I thought it would be easier to keep it to myself.'

'By lying about where you were when Justine's murder took place?' Wise said. 'By claiming you were at home instead of admitting you were in London at the very same time she was killed?'

'As I said, I knew how it could be misconstrued.' McLean looked from Wise to Hannah and back again. 'Surely you can see that?'

'I think it makes you look a very viable suspect,' Wise said. 'Innocent people don't tend to lie to us.'

'Not to mention it's an offence to waste a police officer's time, Mr McLean,' Hannah said. 'It's also an offence to obstruct us in the course of our duties.'

'You're not the one who's times being wasted,' McLean said. 'I am. This is all nonsense. You should be out looking for Justine's killer. Not bothering me.'

Wise smiled. 'I think we should continue this conversation down at the station, Mr McLean. Get everything on tape. Make sure there are no misunderstandings.' He stood up. Hannah followed suit.

The only person who didn't move was McLean. 'You have to be joking. I'm not going anywhere. I want you to leave my house. Now.'

'If you don't want to come with us voluntarily, we can arrest you,' Wise said.

Hannah produced her handcuffs.

McLean looked over at his wife. 'Tell them this is all nonsense. I would never do anything to hurt anyone!'

His wife shrugged. 'I'm not sure that's true. What about the time you threw books at me for not getting the kids to bed on time? Or punched me because Daisy's crying woke you up?'

'Christ, Susannah, it wasn't like that,' McLean spluttered. 'You're making it sound like I'm a monster or something.'

'You are,' she replied.

'Why you—' McLean lunged for her, his arm already pulling back, his fist clenched. Wise grabbed him before he managed to do anything more, twisting his arm so it was behind his back and one ounce of pressure away from being popped out of his socket. He slammed McLean's face into the kitchen table for good measure — not hard enough to do any real damage but hard enough to let him know there wasn't going to be any more nonsense.

'I think we might need those handcuffs now, Hannah,' Wise said.

Hannah didn't need asking twice.

'You fucking bastards. I'll have your jobs for this,' McLean snarled into the table as the cuffs went on, but it was all just noise.

'Joshua McLean, I am arresting you under section five of the Criminal Law Act 1967, for wasting police time in the course of an investigation, and under section five of the Public Order Act of 1986 for threatening behaviour with intent to do harm. You are being taken into custody for further questioning as I believe you are both a flight risk and a threat to the safety of others,' Wise said, lifting McLean up by his arms.

The man was red-faced and wild-eyed. 'This is fucking ridiculous.'

'You do not have to say anything, but it may harm your defence if you do not mention when questioned something you later relay in court. Anything you do say may be given in evidence.'

'You're all mad,' McLean exclaimed. 'Mad. I haven't done anything.'

Despite McLean sticking his heels in, Wise and Hannah marched him to the door as his wife watched, shaking her head. 'If they let you out, you're not coming back here,' she said. 'I'll have the locks changed by this afternoon.'

'But it's my house! My kids!' McLean shouted as Hannah opened the front door. Wise 'You can't do that, you fuck—'

He lunged towards his wife again, but Wise had a good hold of him. He all but lifted McLean off his feet as he hauled him out of the house. 'I suggest you keep quiet for now.'

Unsurprisingly, McLean didn't take that option. 'You're insane! She's insane! You can't arrest me. I haven't done anything!' he shouted as Wise and Hannah led him down the steps to his house, out through the black gate and over to the Mondeo.

The man opposite, who'd looked so disapprovingly when Wise had arrived, was still washing his Beamer, and his mouth fell open as Wise put McLean in the back seat of the Mondeo. Wise pointed to the back of the man's car. 'You missed a spot.'

The man's bewilderment made him chuckle as he climbed into the driver's seat. As he put on his seat belt, he looked over his shoulder at McLean. 'Have you ever been to Brixton nick before?'

35

Kennington police station was more of an administrative building these days. It was closed to the public and its interview rooms and holding cells were long decommissioned. As a result, anyone arrested by Kennington's murder teams had to book their suspects into Brixton nick, have them processed there and hold all their interviews in that station.

It was a bit of a pain in the arse logistics-wise, but it also meant that officers had to be well-prepared before talking to anyone, making sure they had everything they required to carry out an interview. There was no 'just popping upstairs' to get something if they didn't have it with them. The police could only keep a suspect for twenty-four hours without formally charging them with an offence so a trip to Kennington and back burned precious time.

Once he became a DI, Wise used to hate not carrying out interviews himself and let others do it on his behalf. But now he understood the benefits of watching from an observation room. It allowed the interrogators to concentrate on the conversation while allowing him to take in everything else.

Often it wasn't just what the suspect said or didn't say, as they'd often go 'no comment'. It was how they behaved under questioning that told Wise so much and helped guide the interrogation.

Was the suspect a pack of nerves from start to finish or did they just react to a certain question in a certain way? Were they all brash confidence or bored by what was going on? Would they meet the detectives' eyes or avoid looking at anyone at all? Did they appear prepared for the questioning, providing rehearsed answers or were they genuinely engaged, giving the detectives helpful information?

It helped that Hannah had turned out to be great at interviewing people and she was wonderful at thinking on her feet. He'd partnered her up with Jono to great effect, the veteran's more grandfatherly/man-of-the-people approach complementing her more all-business style. But Jono was dead now and, instead, Wise had brought Hicksy in to work with her.

Considering the rather antagonistic nature of their relationship when Hannah first started, Wise wasn't sure if it was the best decision to make but, as short of resources as he was, he didn't really have much of a choice. There was no way he was putting Brains in front of a suspect. The man might be a genius with computers, but he didn't do human-to-human contact that well. Callum was too inexperienced and Donut ... well, the new year might have brought a rather dramatic transformation in the man, but he still had a long way to go. That just left Millie and Palmer as possibilities, but Wise didn't trust them as far as he could throw them for now. They were Riddleton's people after all, and there was no way to know they wouldn't screw things up just to make Wise look bad.

Wise watched the interview room on two screens. One was focused on Hannah and Hicksy and the other on Joshua McLean and his solicitor. McLean was still in his Adidas tracksuit. The few hours he'd spent in a custody suite hadn't helped his hangover and now the man looked like he'd do anything to be a million miles away from where he was. His solicitor, a gentleman called Robert Godwin, all dressed in a three-piece suit, sat next to him. Apparently, the man came from McLean's agency's legal firm rather than one specialising in criminal law, but the unfamiliar surroundings didn't deter Godwin from auditioning for the part of the smuggest man in London.

'I'd like to read a statement from my client,' Godwin said once the tapes were rolling in the interview room. He sounded like all of it was beneath a man of his talents and he picked up the prepared statement with a flourish. '"I, Joshua McLean, strenuously object to my treatment by Detective Inspector Wise and Detective Sergeant Markham this morning at my home. I was arrested without cause and in such a way as to cause embarrassment to me in front of my family and neighbours. I will be lodging a formal complaint with the Metropolitan Police Service as well as pursuing all legal avenues in regard to compensation to redress their Gestapo-like tactics.

'"In regards to why I failed to inform the two detectives about my correct whereabouts on the night of 31st December, 2022, I was simply trying to protect my wife from the knowledge of my ... infidelity. Against my better judgement, I have been involved in an extramarital affair for the last twelve months with a colleague, Miss Naomi Kable, and I spent New Year's Eve and New Year's Day at her home in Greenwich. Miss Kable will be happy to confirm this.

'"My only relationship with Justine Mayweather was that of employer and colleague. And no time did it become intimate, nor did I want it to be. Anything else you may have heard can simply be put down to malicious gossip."'

Godwin put down the paper, gave his neck a brief stretch and then smiled. 'With all that in mind, I request you allow my client to return to his family so he can begin to repair the damage done by your behaviour this morning.'

Hannah looked over at Hicksy, who chuckled.

That infuriated Godwin. 'I assure you this is no laughing matter—'

Hannah held up a finger. 'We will, of course, check everything with this Naomi Kable but that doesn't really change why we're here. Your client's statement is, in fact, a confession that he deliberately wasted our time this morning by lying to us.'

'What?' Godwin said, looking like he'd just had all the smugness slapped from his face.

Hicksy chuckled again. He looked at McLean. 'I hope this fella's not charging you a fortune. So far, he's established that you're a liar, a cheater and, if I'm not mistaken, you're someone who'll quite happily get his leg over someone he works with.'

Now it was McLean's turn to splutter. 'What? How dare you? I won't be insulted by the likes of you.'

'I'm sorry. No offence meant.' Hicksy held up both hands, not looking the least bit regretful. 'What bit of that did I get wrong?'

'I ... I ... I ...' McLean looked to Godwin for help, eyes wide and desperate.

'My client has no further comment to make,' Godwin said.

Hannah nodded. 'In that case, we'll terminate the interview for now and have Mr McLean returned to his custody suite while we contact Miss Kable.'

'Is that really necessary, Sergeant?' Godwin asked. 'My client didn't murder anyone!'

Hannah smiled. 'I'm sure you can appreciate we can't just take your word for that. We do actually need to corroborate Mr McLean's new version of what he did on New Year's Eve. Now, the custody officer will be along shortly to take him back to his custody suite.'

Hicksy formally ended the interview and turned off the tapes. The two detectives then left and joined Wise in the observation suite.

'What do you think, Guv?' Hannah asked as she walked in.

'Let's check out his alibi and go from there,' Wise said. 'But, even if his girlfriend says he was with her all night, we need more than just her word on his whereabouts. Let's check his phone for a start and see if it was anywhere near Justine's at the time of her death.'

'Naomi was the hot receptionist's name at Green, wasn't it?' Hannah said.

'Fucking hell,' Hicksy said. 'Good job you said that and not me. It's not very PC to call someone hot these days.'

Hannah smiled. 'Maybe not in your case. I can get away with it, though.'

'That's just not fair,' Hicksy replied. 'Then again, I can't even remember the last time I saw a hot receptionist.'

'What do you think of McLean?' Wise asked.

Hicksy shrugged. 'He didn't say much, did he? But first impressions? I think he fancies himself and he likes getting his leg over young girls. Probably makes him a shit husband but I'm not sure he's our man. He was shitting himself in there.'

Wise nodded. 'Yeah. He doesn't strike me as someone who could calmly clean up a flat after killing Justine. I don't think he's ever touched a mop in his life for one thing and he's all emotion for another. Our guy has ice in his veins.'

'Unless he's a really good fucking liar,' Hicksy said. 'This could all be an act to convince us he's just a twat and not a murderer.'

'There is that very distinct possibility,' Wise agreed. 'He wouldn't be the first one to try that act.'

'So where does that leave us?' Hannah asked.

'We push on,' Wise replied.

36

Hannah was hunched over a Diet Coke in Brixton nick's staff canteen, feeling like crap. The fluorescent lights weren't doing her headache any favours, either. In an ideal world, Hannah probably needed to sleep for at least a month before she'd be anything back to normal. As it was, she was only averaging about three, maybe four hours a night at the moment, which meant every day she was feeling worse, not better.

Shit. She should really take some time off. Get herself sorted. But how? The team was running on fumes as it was. The governor needed her, even if she was only working at a fraction of her capabilities.

Her hand went to her pocket, found the pack of paracetamol with added codeine, and popped two out of the blister packet with practised ease. They were in her mouth a second later and Hannah washed them down with a slug of Diet Coke. How many had she taken so far that day? Hannah had no idea, which meant it was too many, but the tablets were the only things keeping her going. They made her headache bearable at least. Without them, she reckoned she'd be bashing her head against a wall.

Christ, she shouldn't be at work. Let alone on a Sunday. Wise would understand if she said she had to go home and get some sleep. How many times had he asked if she was okay anyway? Too many. Like the tablets, that was another big red flag that she was not in a good way.

Hannah pinched the bridge of her nose and puffed out her cheeks. All she needed—

'Bloody hell, you're back!'

Hannah looked up and saw DC Samira Sathiah standing by her table. They had worked together when Hannah was stationed at Brixton and Hannah counted her as much a friend as a colleague. Even so, Hannah had to force a smile. A chat about old times wasn't what she needed right then. 'Hey.'

'I don't see you for months and then—' Samira stopped, and twisted her head as she took in Hannah. 'Shit, girl. You okay? You look as rough as they get.'

'Thanks. You always did know how to make me feel special,' Hannah replied.

Samira slid into the seat next to Hannah. 'I'm serious. You look like death warmed up,' she said in a whisper. 'Are you okay?'

'I got banged up a bit in a ... car accident a month or so ago,' Hannah replied. 'It's just taking me a bit of time to get over it.'

'It must've been a bad one.'

'It was.' Hannah didn't mention her car had been rammed by a van full of crazed gangsters and they'd dragged her out of the car with the intention of shooting her dead. She shook the memories away. 'Anyway, how've you been?'

Samira hesitated in replying as she didn't quite want to leave the conversation about how crap Hannah looked but then her enthusiasm got the better of her. 'I think I might've picked up a murder last night. The call out said it was a traffic accident, but I found a witness who said some bloke shoved the victim in front of a bus.'

'Oh, yeah?' The news perked Hannah up a bit. She was happy for her friend. When they'd worked together, most of their time was spent filling out burglary reports and dealing with drunken assaults.

It didn't feel like real police work and that was one of the reasons why Hannah had pushed to join Wise's team despite their bad reputation.

'I mean, I know I shouldn't be so happy about it. A man died after all. But a murder? Beats the normal crap I have to deal with every day.' Samira was beaming with excitement. 'Talk about a great start to the year.'

'Any idea why someone would've wanted your victim dead?'

'Not yet. The man was no one special. He ran a tiki bar on Lavender Hill and, as far as I can tell, everyone liked him. Maybe he was sleeping with someone else's girlfriend or whatever.'

A thought stirred in the back of Hannah's pain-addled brain. 'Did you say a tiki bar?'

'Yeah, it's called Sugar Tree. The inside's done up like a Hawaiian shack with bamboo everywhere and coconut drinks. It's a bit tacky if you ask me, and maybe a little bit racist.'

'Hold on.' Hannah dug her notebook out of her pocket and flicked through to her notes from the interview with Donny Reynolds the day before.

'What is it?' Samira asked.

Hannah ignored her as she scanned her notes. Looking for what she knew was there. Or was it? Had she been mistaken?

No. There it was. Justine's first date with Donny. *Some tiki bar in Battersea. It's all bamboo walls and flowery wallpaper. You drink out of coconuts. Her friend was the manager.*

'Fuck,' Hannah said.

'What is it?' Samira repeated but Hannah was reading on, moving to the Stephen Askins interview. She found what she was looking for quicker this time. *She invited me to some tiki bar in Battersea for drinks.*

Hannah looked up, her headache forgotten. 'I think I might have your motive.'

Samira sat back. 'You do?'

'Yeah. What's the name of your victim?'

'Mark Temple.'

'Let me make a call.' Her hand went to her other pocket and

grabbed her mobile. She rang Askins, who answered on the fourth ring.

'Hello?'

'Oh, hi, is that Stephen Askins?' Hannah asked.

'It is,' he replied. 'Who's this?'

'It's Detective Sergeant Markham. We met yesterday.'

'I do remember,' Askins said, not sounding too happy about another chat with the police.

'Sorry to bother you on a Sunday but I have a really quick question for you.'

'Yes?'

'You said you went to a tiki bar in Battersea with Justine for your first date,' Hannah said.

'That's right.'

'Do you remember the name of the place?'

'Yeah, it was called the Sugar Tree.'

Hannah could feel her pulse pick up. 'And do you know why Justine picked there to meet?'

'Her mate was the manager. Nice bloke. Had tattoos up both arms. Gave us a few drinks on the house.'

'Do you remember his name?'

'Er ... it was a while ago. Um ... Mike? Matt? Mark? Definitely one of those.'

That was good enough for Hannah. 'Thank you ever so much. You've been a massive help. I'll let you get back to the rest of your weekend.'

'Cheers,' Askins said and hung up.

'So?' Samira asked but Hannah was already dialling Wise.

'Hannah, what's up?' he said on answering.

'Can you meet me in the canteen? A friend of mine is investigating another murder that I think is connected to ours,' Hannah said, enjoying the look on Samira's face as she listened. And for the first time in an age, Hannah was grinning for real. Maybe she didn't need a month's worth of sleep to feel like her old self again. She just needed a damn good lead to chase.

37

Once Hannah had updated Wise about the death of the tiki bar manager, Wise had ushered both Hannah and her friend into his Mondeo so they could head straight over to Lavender Hill.

It was only a fifteen-minute drive away but Wise was impatient to find out more and the journey felt like an age.

'You don't think this is just a coincidence?' Samira said from the backseat.

Wise looked at her via the rearview mirror. 'There's no such thing as coincidences when it comes to murder. This is definitely connected to our enquiry.'

'If Justine always arranged to meet any potential new boyfriend in Sugar Tree because she felt safe there,' Hannah added, 'then it stands to reason that she took her killer there too.'

'And the manager would've seen him,' Wise said. 'Maybe he even knew Mystery Man's name as well if Justine gave Mark a briefing on who she was going there with. Maybe bringing the free drinks over was his way of getting close enough to form an opinion of her suitor.'

'And Mystery Man knows Mark's a potential witness,' Hannah said. 'Hence ...' She mimed a push in the back.

'Shit,' Samira said.

'Shit indeed,' both Wise and Hannah said together.

Wise smiled, enjoying feeling in synch with Hannah again. He glanced over. Some of the darkness had gone from her eyes and he knew she was feeling the buzz too. Mystery Man had been working in a very controlled environment when he'd killed Justine. There'd been no one else in the flat and he'd had the time and privacy to clean up after himself. He'd been further helped by Justine's building being camera-free. He'd been practically invisible.

But if he was the one who pushed Mark Temple in front of a bus on a busy London street ... well, there was a damn good chance one of the city's many CCTV cameras had caught him doing it.

God, he hoped so.

There was no parking outside the tiki bar itself so Wise had to drive around the block until he found a spot opposite the Four Thieves, a pub offering two floors of every type of entertainment possible, including private karaoke rooms, arcades, live music, and a DJ-hosted dance floor. The place was already in full flow despite it being 6 p.m. on a Sunday if the thump thump of music coming out of the place was anything to go by.

He noticed Hannah wincing as they walked by, and the haunted look returned to her face. He thought about asking her if she was okay again but dismissed it. She'd only repeat that she was fine, like every other time he'd asked.

They turned left onto Lavender Hill. It was typical of many high streets in London; both sides of the street lined with restaurants and fast-food outlets offering everything from jellied eels to Vietnamese, and about five or six estate agents pushing million-pound properties.

'The Sugar Tree's just there,' Samira said, pointing to a building four hundred yards ahead of them. There was a small wall behind which six feet high bushes provided privacy to whatever was going on inside. The bus stop was right outside the bar. 'The bar shut at 1 a.m. but Mark stayed on to clear up and lock up. He left at just gone 2 and set off, heading east. The bus that hit him had just picked up passengers but there wasn't any traffic on the road, so it was doing thirty by the time it struck Mark.'

'Where did he go under the bus?' Wise asked.

'Just up ahead by the magistrates court,' Samira said, pointing to a Sixties concrete block of a building. 'On the corner of Kathleen Road. The witness was about five metres behind the victim. He said he saw a man walk out of the doorway from the shop on the corner and head diagonally towards Mark, reaching him a heartbeat before the bus, and shoving him into the road. He didn't see where the man went after that. He was too shocked at the sight of Mark being run over.'

'Did your witness give you a description of this man?'

'Only that he was tall, wearing a black long coat with a hood up. It wasn't raining but it was freezing cold, so he didn't think anything of it beforehand.'

'That definitely does sound like our Mystery Man,' Wise said. He looked over at the doorway where the man had waited, imagining him there still. Hunched, hood up. Trying to be invisible. Watching for Mark to leave the bar. Had the plan always been to push him under a bus or was that just an opportunity he seized? A spur of the moment decision so unlike the murder of Justine. A desperate act.

The shop itself was boarded up, with signs proclaiming the premises were available to buy or rent. There were no cameras though. The owners probably thought them not necessary to protect an empty shop. Judging by the graffiti covering the boarded-up windows, they didn't care about a bit of mindless vandalism. Ignoring it was probably the cheaper option than trying to prevent it.

Still, this was London. If one place didn't have cameras, there were plenty of other places that would have them.

Like a magistrate's court.

'The court must have lots of cameras,' Wise said, walking towards the junction where Mark had died.

'I spotted two that should cover the incident,' Samira said, following just behind. 'Unfortunately, we can't get access to their systems until 8 a.m. tomorrow, but I've arranged for someone to be here when they open up.'

'Well done,' Wise said. He nodded towards an estate agent's on the opposite side of the street, painted bright white in contrast to all the other buildings in their dark blues, blacks and greens. 'They've got a camera, too, that could help us.'

Samira made a note. 'I'll check that as well.'

Wise stood on the corner of the road and looked around. Christmas lights dangled across the street from one side to the next, looking more lost and forgotten than festive. The street itself was still relatively busy, though, with people bustling along to collect their Sunday dinners, or nipping out for a crafty drink or two to make the most of what was left of the weekend. He didn't see too many happy faces though. January wasn't that type of month. It was too cold, too dark and most people were too broke after Christmas.

Wise spotted a family bustling along, the dad struggling along with supermarket carrier bags full of the weekly shop and the mother holding the hands of two young children. The kids must've been about four or five and, suddenly, he was back in time to when his kids were around that age, him and Jean so in love with each other, not quite believing they had a family, thinking every day was just going to be full of fun and laughter, before life's disappointments had a chance to kick the crap out of their happiness.

Before Tom reared his vicious head again.

'Guv?' Hannah said.

Wise blinked. 'Sorry. Did you say something?'

Hannah gave him a raised eyebrow in response. 'I was just asking about the bus cameras, Guv. They all have them now, covering every angle, inside and out.'

'Shit,' Samira said, closing her eyes for a moment. 'I didn't think about getting those.' She dug her phone out of her jacket. 'I'll make a call.'

'It's okay,' Wise said, not wanting the DC to feel bad. 'You're doing really good. You could've easily have written this off as an accident, but you didn't. You've been asking all the right questions and there's a lot to think about with murder enquiries.'

'Thank you, sir,' Samira replied.

Wise winked. 'I don't really like being called "sir". Makes me think of my dad. You can call me Simon or Guv if you want.'

Samira glanced over at Hannah, then back to Wise. 'I feel a bit awkward with both of those. I mean, you're a DCI so I can't call you Simon and, well, you're not my governor.'

'Not yet anyway,' Wise said. 'Let's go check out the Sugar Tree.'

As the three detectives walked back to the tiki bar, Samira made a call about the bus footage. After a quick conversation, she looked much happier. 'They said they were wondering when I was going to ask for it, so they've already packaged it up. It'll be in my email in the next ten minutes.'

'Excellent. We can look at that next,' Wise said, pushing the door to the Sugar Tree open.

There were a few people drinking inside but the atmosphere was muted to say the least. There was only one person working as far as Wise could tell, an older woman with olive skin and long, dark hair pulled back into a ponytail. She looked up as they entered, and Wise recognised the expression on her face only too well.

Grief.

He held up his warrant card. 'I'm Detective Inspector Simon Wise,' he said. 'And DS Markham and DC Sathiah. We're looking into the death of Mark Temple.'

The woman screwed up her face for a moment as if summoning every last iota of strength to stay on her feet. Then she breathed up and Wise could see tears forming in the corners of her eyes. She brushed one eye with the back of her hand. 'Sorry. I still can't believe it. I should've stayed closed for the night, but I need the money. Not that my mood's helping people have a good time.' She brushed the corner of her eye again. 'Not when I keep bloody crying.'

'Can I just have your name to start with?' Wise asked, keeping his voice soft, caring.

The woman let out a sad chuckle. 'Of course. Of course. Sorry. I'm not thinking.' She held out a hand. 'I'm Jem Chiesa. The owner.'

'You're not Hawaiian then?'

'God no. My father's Italian and my mother's from Bermondsey.

The tiki thing is just to give the place a bit of character, you know? Otherwise, you're just another boozer.'

'And Mark Temple was the manager?'

'Yeah. Mark's great … was great at dealing with the punters and stuff. You know, a natural. This was his career, not just a job he was doing while he looked for something else,' Jem replied, her voice cracking here and there.

'How long did he work here?'

'About five years, I think. As I said, he was good and worth keeping so I made it worth his while staying.'

'Did he ever have any trouble with anyone? A customer maybe?'

'No, not at all. Mark got on with everyone — apart from his boyfriends, that is. He had terrible taste in men. He liked bad boys, if you know what I mean.' Jem cocked her head then. 'Why do you want to know? He died in a road accident.'

Wise smiled. 'We have to ask all sorts of questions, I'm afraid. Most of it's a formality. But, as it turns out, we were planning on talking to Mark this week, about a friend of his who also died.'

'Oh dear,' Jem said. 'That is awful.'

'Her name was Justine Mayweather.'

'I don't think I know her.'

Wise looked over his shoulder to Hannah. 'Do you have a picture of Justine?'

Hannah found one on her phone and showed the bar owner. 'Do you recognise her?'

Jem stared at the picture for a second and then they all saw the change in her face. 'Oh yes, I know her. Her and Mark were as thick as thieves. She was just as bad as he was when it came to the men. She used to bring her new fellas here for Mark to okay — not that it did either of them any good. Mark was bloody useless in spotting a wrong 'un. Me, on the other, I can spot them a mile away. Of course, it took me two divorces to get that good.'

'Do you remember the last time you saw Justine with Mark?' Hannah asked.

Jem shook her head. 'Maybe before Christmas sometime but I

don't really know. I never pay much attention to that sort of stuff. There are people who've been coming here since we opened, and I couldn't tell you what they looked like.'

Wise looked around the bar. 'What about cameras? Do you have any CCTV?'

'Yeah. I've got one covering the bar, one covering the tables and then one outside. You have to have them in case it kicks off. I have security on the doors on a Friday and Saturday night and it protects them as much as me.'

'How long back do you keep the footage?' Wise asked.

'Unless there's been a bit of aggro, I delete them after a week. It's a waste of a hard drive otherwise.

That wasn't what Wise wanted to hear. 'The period we're looking at is about six weeks ago — so mid-November to the start of December.'

Jem shrugged. 'I can look when I get home but I can't promise anything.'

Hannah handed her a card. 'That would be great. You never know what might help.'

Jem nodded at the picture of Justine. 'I take it someone did her in?'

'I'm afraid so,' Wise replied.

'And you think Mark's death might have something to do with it?' Jem asked.

'We don't think so,' Wise said. 'I'm sure this is a horrible coincidence.'

'Dear God. I really am going to have to shut up tonight,' Jem said. 'I need to go home and have a good cry. At least the two of them are in heaven together now.'

Wise smiled as if he agreed but he wasn't sure he believed in heaven anymore. In fact, he wasn't sure if he believed in anything anymore. The world was fucked. 'Take care, Jem. Let us know if you find anything.'

'I will,' the bar owner said.

As the detectives left, Wise's phone rang. It was Hicksy.

'Alright, Guv,' he said. 'Just wanted to let you know I've spoken to McLean's mistress, Naomi Kable, and she confirmed that they were together. Said he never left her side the whole time. But she did say that she got blind drunk and passed out before midnight and didn't wake up until midday on the First.'

'McLean could easily have left her and gone over to Justine's then,' Wise replied.

'Easily,' Hicksy replied. 'As alibis go, it's not the slam dunk McLean's solicitor thought it was.'

'And we've got another murder that looks like it's connected to our case. One of Justine's friends was pushed under a bus last night and our friend, Mac, was out and about in town.'

'That's a nice coincidence,' Hicksy said.

'Yeah, that's what I thought too.'

'So maybe he's not as innocent as we all thought?'

'Who is?' Wise puffed out his cheeks. 'Tell his smarmy solicitor we're going to be interviewing him later tonight and we'll be keeping him in for the full twenty-four hours. Me, Hannah and Samira are going to look at some video footage, then we'll be back, and we can question McLean again. We can blindside him with the information about last night's killing, and see how he reacts then.'

'Sounds good to me,' Hicksy replied. 'But who's Samira?'

'A friend of Hannah's. She's helping us out at the moment. The other murder is her case.' Wise waited for some sort of wisecrack or complaint from Hicksy but none came.

'See you later,' he said instead. 'I'll carry on checking up on McLean's movements.'

'Cheers.' Wise hung up the phone and turned to the others. 'Shall we go back and watch Bus TV?'

38

Back at Brixton, Wise sat in a small meeting room with Hannah and Samira, watching Mark Temple's murder on a large monitor affixed to a wall. London Transport had provided clips from the front, sides and rear of the vehicle that struck Mark.

'I knew they had cameras recording the interiors,' he said, 'but I never knew they had the exterior covered like this as well.'

'You're not really a bus guy, are you?' Hannah replied.

'You've got a point there.'

'They need them for insurance claims. You can get a big payout if you get hit by a bus.'

'Must be easier ways of earning some cash.'

'Not for some.'

Wise glanced over at Samira who was operating the laptop with the clips on it. 'Let's see the front-of-bus view again.'

The big screen came to life once more. The camera was set up in the centre of the bus window, and offered a view just above the driver's head so the detectives got his view of the road in front of him.

Lavender Hill was fairly quiet with a few cars going by in either direction but the bus had a fairly clear run of it. The sad Christmas decorations looped over the road offered a little light but otherwise the street was awash with light from the various takeaways still open and the streetlamps every ten metres or so.

There weren't that many people on the street either and Mark was easy to spot as he left the Sugar Tree and turned left, past the bus stop, to head up Lavender Hill. Six people got on the bus, including one very drunk man who took an age to tap his Oyster card for payment, allowing Mark to get quite far ahead of the bus.

Then the doors shut, and the bus set off, quickly picking up speed. Not speeding, but catching up quickly on Mark.

It was almost shoulder to shoulder with the bar manager as it came up to Kathleen Road, with the Magistrates Court lurking on its corner. Mark suddenly lurched to his right, into the road and the bus's path.

Even though it was the third time he'd seen it, Wise still flinched at the point of impact and again a heartbeat later when Mark went under the bus. The bus driver braked as quickly as he could, but it was all too late. Sixteen tonnes of bus had already run over him.

'The poor driver,' Hannah said. 'He'll be haunted by this for the rest of his life.'

'Go back to where Mark is pushed into the bus,' Wise said.

Samira did so. 'There's a dark shadow just to his left.'

It was clearly a man, but the footage just showed no more than a black shape. There was nothing identifiable from it. 'Go back slowly,' Wise asked.

Samira clicked it back in slow motion. When the driver's view was wide enough to take in the doorway of the boarded-up shop, Wise told her to freeze the film. 'You can't see anyone in the doorway.'

'He must be hiding in the blind spot,' Hannah said.

'Move it forward again,' Wise asked.

Samira advanced the film frame by frame. Somehow the shadow, when it began to move, managed to stay on the edge of the film frame. 'No way he's doing that on purpose,' Hannah said. 'That's just luck.'

'Maybe,' Wise replied. He didn't like the idea of a killer with luck on his side as well as skill. They got to the point of impact again, watched Mark Temple die again. 'Keep moving forward.'

The film advanced in jitters again. 'There's no sign of the shadow man,' Hannah said.

'Switch to the kerbside camera,' Wise requested.

Samira did so. The camera view was distorted, curving as it did to pick up as much of the left-side as possible. The right-hand edge of the screen stopped about three metres in front of the bus while the left-hand edge went as far as the rear of the bus.

They watched the impact again. This time, the shadow man was visible as he emerged from the doorway in his long black coat, the hood up, closing in on Mark Temple. The bus reached them at the same time as the killer reached Mark. The detectives watched the shadow man's hand dart out and Mark tumble into the road.

Samira stopped the film a frame before impact.

'There's your murderer,' Wise said. 'But is it our guy?'

'He's got every reason to kill him, especially if Justine confided everything with Mark,' Hannah said. 'Mark could've known his name, address, occupation — the lot — as well as being able to identify the killer.'

'I agree.' Wise turned to Samira. 'Let's see the rest of the footage.'

Samira hit play. The killer turned one hundred and eighty degrees to his left so that his face was always away from the bus's camera and then headed back towards the Sugar Tree, head down and hidden in his hood.

'He's not lucky,' Wise said. 'He's smart. He knows where cameras are or might be and he does everything he can to keep himself hidden. Even if using the bus to kill Mark was opportunistic, he's still as calm as can be while carrying it out, making sure cameras don't catch his face.'

'Do you think it's McLean?' Hannah asked.

'I don't know,' Wise said. 'They look like the similar height and build but is it him? All we know for sure is that he was in town last night.'

'Shall I head over to McLean's house and see if I can find the coat? If we can get our hands on that, we can link him to both murders.'

'Good idea. Take Samira with you.' Wise looked at his watch. It was 7:15 p.m. 'We'll talk to McLean again at 10. He should be good and tired by then.'

Hannah laughed 'And irritable.'

Wise smiled. 'Perfect.'

Hannah stood up and looked over at her friend. 'Come on then. Let's go coat hunting.'

'Hold on a minute,' Wise said as Samira got to her feet. 'Who's your gaffer? I need to give them a call and let them know we're taking over your case.'

'My DCI's Sharon Glass,' Samira said, looking crestfallen.

'I know her,' Wise replied. 'I'll give her a call. By the way, do you think she'll mind lending you to us as well? We could do with your help.'

That perked Samira back up. 'You want me on your team?'

'Just a secondment for now but yes — if you're interested.'

'I am.'

'Excellent,' Wise said. 'We'll chat later.'

As Hannah and Samira left, the thought crossed Wise's mind that Riddleton would want to be informed before he called DCI Glass, to at least to maintain the illusion that Riddleton was in charge, but it was late on a Sunday and Wise just couldn't be arsed.

He could deal with any fallout in the morning.

Wise leaned over and turned Samira's laptop so he could play the film clips again. He watched mark die and he watched the killer walk away, head down like he didn't have a care in the world.

Was it McLean? Did he have this heartless bastard in a cell downstairs? God, he hoped so.

39

It was 10 p.m. and Hicksy was dog tired. Not that Hicksy was complaining about that. He'd rather be working than sitting at home, pounding the whisky while trying to not think about how shit life was.

They had fancy pants McLean waiting for them in an interview room with his smarmy, smart-arse solicitor, but first he was being updated on everything the governor and his two PC sidekicks had found out since he'd last seen them. And by PC, he meant Politically Correct, because the new girl, Samira or whatever-her-name was, added at least two more ticks on the team's diversity quota, what with her being a woman and of ethnic origin as well. No doubt the governor thought she'd be a good replacement for Sarah Choi, the traitorous little bitch.

Of course, if Jono had been around, Hicksy could've made some gag about how most people preferred an Indian to a Chinese anyway, but he wasn't and there wasn't anyone else around who'd appreciate the joke. And, knowing Hicksy's luck right then, he'd just find himself on another charge of racism to go with the assault on Palmer. Not that Hicksy considered punching that prick in the nose an assault, but that was the problem with the modern police force. In the old days, it was encouraged to sort out problems within teams with a little fisticuffs. Now, all it achieved was a trip to bloody HR.

The new girl seemed alright, though. Even if she was so bright-eyed and bushy-tailed that it made Hicksy want to feed her tranquillisers. No one should be that on-the-fucking ball.

He shook his head and concentrated on what Diversity was saying. He had to be the one that was on the ball in the interview room. He'd have to have a coffee before he went in, though. Maybe with a little dram in it. He had a hip flask in his pocket, after all.

'We didn't find any coat that looked like our killer's, Guv,' Hannah was saying. 'And his wife said he's never owned a coat like that. She let us search his house and his car.'

'That's a shame,' Wise replied. 'We got anything on his phone yet?'

Hicksy shook his head. 'I've got requests in with his phone company but no one's going to look at those until tomorrow, let alone action them. It's the same with Digital Forensics. I've passed his actual phone to them so they can have a nose inside, but they just gave me a sob story about being swamped. Apparently, they'll get back to me before the next blue moon.'

Wise sighed. 'It's not their fault. The whole police service is running on fumes. Have you and Hannah worked out your interview strategy?'

Hicksy chuckled. 'We argued over who got to be bad cop and who was good cop but in the end we both agreed I do nice better than anyone.'

Wise just raised an eyebrow and so Hicksy and Hannah went over their plan for the interview with the governor.

'It's pretty wafer-thin,' Wise said when they were finished.

Hicksy shrugged. 'It's not like we have any new evidence to slap McLean around the face with. The truth is we've got jack shit to link him to either murder.'

'Only that he knew Justine and was in town for both of the murders,' Hannah said. 'And he's a dick.'

Wise nodded. 'Unfortunately, he's our only suspect right now. I think it's worth having another poke at him to see if we can get a reaction. If it's going nowhere, call it quits and we'll let him loose.'

'We'll do our best,' Hannah said.

'That's all any of us can do,' Wise replied.

Five minutes later, Hicksy and Hannah entered the interview suite. The solicitor, Godwin, jumped to his feet straight away, spouting out his protests. Hicksy didn't bother listening, though, as he sat down and placed his cup of coffee (whisky-free) in front of him. After all, there wasn't anything the man could say that he hadn't heard at least a hundred times before.

Hicksy gave his neck a little roll, trying to loosen the kinks, but it was a waste of time. Somehow, he didn't think an army of Thai masseuses could sort out the tension in his body. Then again, he wouldn't mind putting that theory to the test.

Maybe he should put in for some leave. Get signed off for stress for a bit. He could have a holiday and justify why he'd punched Palmer in the nozzle at the same time. Any tribunal would accept minor mental health issues as justification for the bap in the nose and Hicksy could get off to Bangkok for some much-needed R&R.

Bringing his thoughts back to the job at hand, he saw that Godwin was still babbling away on his feet. With a sigh, Hicksy furrowed his brow and fixed his eyes on the fancy pants solicitor. 'Why don't you sit down and stop pontificating. Because we can't ask our questions while you're showboating. And, if we can ask our questions, we all might actually have a chance to go home tonight.'

Godwin glared back for a moment but, as threatening looks went, it was about as intimidating as Frank Spencer having a wobbly. So, Godwin plonked his fat arse down and Hannah did the honours of introducing everyone for the benefit of the tapes.

McLean sat against the wall, looking every bit like a peacock that had its feathers roughly plucked by an angry gorilla. Then again, that was only to be expected. The man had been trying to sleep off a hangover when Wise and Hannah had nicked him and spending the rest of the day in one of the Met's finest custody suites was never going to get him fighting fit again.

'We spoke to Naomi,' Hannah said to McLean. 'She confirmed that you were with her on New Year's.'

Both McLean and Godwin perked up at that bit of news, so Hicksy was happy to put the dampener on things. 'Unfortunately for you, Mr McLean, she says you got her so pissed that she passed out before Big Ben got to do his ding donging for the new year and she didn't open her eyes again until lunchtime the following day. Therefore, given her general sense of unconsciousness, you could've quite happily left her place, popped over to Justine's, killed her and made it back to Naomi's without anyone being any the wiser.'

Sure enough, McLean didn't take that bit of news too well. 'But I didn't. I stayed there the whole time.' He turned to Godwin. 'Tell them!'

'Unless Mr Godwin was in the room with you while you watched Naomi sleep, I'm afraid your solicitor can't tell us anything,' Hicksy said.

'What did you do while your date was unconscious?' Hannah asked.

'Unconscious? She was sleeping!' McLean protested. 'You'll be accusing me of drugging Naomi next.'

Hannah arched an eyebrow that portrayed just the right amount of scepticism. 'Did you?'

'This is outrageous!' Godwin said.

'I don't think it is, Mr Godwin,' Hannah said. 'I think your client is a clever man. It's exactly what a clever man would do. I mean, Naomi's young. I'm surprised she could get that drunk so quickly. Normally, girls her age can handle their drink better than most and I doubt she was pounding shots with Mr McLean. It's hardly what you do on a rare romantic night in with your married lover.'

'She'd been out during the day,' McLean spluttered. 'Some brunch thing. She was already drunk when I got there.'

'Were you annoyed about that?' Hicksy asked. 'Were you pissed off that she'd got pissed up?'

'No,' McLean said. 'It was frustrating, but I wasn't angry.'

'I mean, lying to your wife to get a night out with your much younger bit on the side and she passes out before you can get your leg over?' Hicksy shrugged. 'Who wouldn't get upset about that?'

'I ... I ... ' McLean didn't know what to say.

'What did you do while Naomi was unconscious?' Hannah asked.

'She was sleeping!' McLean said again.

'I'm no expert,' Hicksy growled, 'but I'd say "sleeping" was the very definition of unconsciousness. I'm not sure what you don't like about that word.'

'Because it implies I made her that way,' McLean said.

'Did you?'

'No!'

'I must protest at this aggressive questioning,' Godwin interjected. 'My client ...'

'... Is a suspect in two murders,' Hicksy said. 'So, forgive me if I don't say "please" and "thank you" enough.'

'Two murders?' If Godwin had looked out of his depth before, he looked like he was drowning now. And McLean? If the man went any whiter, he'd have a tag on his toe.

'Where were you last night, Mr McLean?' Hannah asked.

'Last ... last night?' McLean repeated.

'And don't say you were home because your wife told us earlier you were out,' Hicksy said.

'I wasn't out *killing people!*' Either McLean was bloody Laurence Olivier or he really was shitting bricks right then.

'So where were you?' Hannah asked, sounding just a little bit bored.

'I ... I was out with ... with ... with clients,' McLean said.

'Names?' Hannah clicked the end of her pen, so the point popped out, ready to write.

'No ... no comment.'

It was Hicksy's turn to perk up then. Why was McLean going 'no comment' all of a sudden? 'Why don't you want to say who you were with?'

McLean wouldn't meet any of their eyes. 'No comment.'

'Where did you go with these clients?' Hannah asked. 'Surely you can tell us that?'

'No comment.'

'If you don't want to tell us who you were with or where you went,' Hicksy said, 'you know we're going to think the worst, don't you? If you've got nothing to hide, then you should tell us.'

'Only guilty people go "no comment",' Hannah added.

'I think I need to talk to my client alone, please,' Godwin said.

Hicksy exchanged looks with Hannah, then nodded.

'Interview terminated at 22:17 hours.' Hannah turned the tapes off. 'Let us know when you're ready to talk.'

The two detectives stood up and left the interview room. Two minutes later, they were with Wise and Samira.

'What do you think, Guv?' Hicksy asked.

'He's scared,' Wise said. 'Whatever he was doing last night, he doesn't want us to know what it was.'

'Did you see how white he went when we mentioned the second murder?' Hicksy said. 'You can't fake that. He crapped himself.'

'But was that because he'd been found out, or because he just couldn't believe the shit he'd found himself in?' Hicksy said.

There was a knock on the door and a uniform officer poked her head around the door. 'Mr McLean's ready to continue.'

'We'll be right there,' Hannah replied.

'Good luck,' Wise said as they left the observation room.

Hicksy walked into the interview room with Hannah to find McLean and Godwin already in their seats. Hicksy noted there was another piece of paper on the table in front of them. The two detectives took their own places, Hannah turned on the tapes and ran through the formalities once more.

'You had your chat, then,' Hicksy said. 'Ready to tell all?'

Godwin glanced at his client, before facing the detectives and picking up the paper. 'I would like to read the following statement on behalf of my client. "I, Joshua McLean have nothing to do with either Justine Mayweather's murder or the victim of any other murder. I have no further comment to make."'

Bloody wonderful.

'So, you're not going to tell us who you were with last night?' Hannah asked.

'No comment,' McLean replied.

'Where did you go?'

'No comment.'

'Were you with clients?'

'No comment.'

Hicksy watched McLean as he continued to knock back all of Hannah's questions with yet another 'no comment.' The man looked ... Not guilty. But ... sad. Maybe even a bit ashamed.

It was a look Hicksy knew only too well. He saw it most mornings in the mirror.

Hicksy leaned forward, his forearms pressing on the table, making it groan. 'Look, Mr McLean, I'm not normally known as the nice one around here. I mean, I started off in the police when it was expected of you to crack a few heads together to get a result, if you know what I mean. Anyway, if you're going all "no comment" because you did something stupid last night — something illegal perhaps — I really don't give a shit. Within reason, of course. All we care about is whether you killed Justine Mayweather and another gentleman last night. That's it.' He turned his hands over and showed his empty palms. 'So, if you were cavorting around a crack den with a dozen prostitutes and a nappy on your head, I really couldn't give a shit. Just tell us where the crack den was so we can eliminate you from our enquiries.' He watched McLean and saw the man look up for a second, before dropping his head once again. 'But, if you go make us run all over London for the next few days, digging into your every move, using everything at the Met's disposal, only to find out that you kept your gob shut because you are too ashamed to admit you were playing *Dungeons and Dragons* in Mayfair with Miss Whiplash, well then ...'

Hicksy rolled his neck and everyone in the room heard the crack. 'We will lock you up for wasting our fucking time, throw away the key and I will make sure they put your fancy pants arse into the most horrible part of Pentonville you can imagine. Do you understand me?'

'Detective Sergeant Hicks, I must—' Godwin said before Hicksy held up a finger, silencing him.

'We're hunting a very dangerous man,' Hicksy said. 'So, no, we haven't got time to pussyfoot about your client's guilty fucking secrets.'

'Alright,' McLean said in a whisper. 'Alright.' He looked up, tears in his eyes. 'But you can't tell anyone. Not my wife or anyone. I'll be ruined.'

'We're the souls of discretion,' Hicksy said, and hoped he didn't look too smug himself.

'I'd like my solicitor to leave,' McLean said.

'Joshua, I really don't recommend that,' Godwin said. 'I—'

'Leave!' McLean said through gritted teeth.

'You're making a mistake,' Godwin said as he got up, made a show of shuffling his papers and left the interview room.

'Okay,' Hannah said. 'So, it's just the three of us now. What's your big secret?'

Monday 9th January

40

Wise clutched his coffee as the team updated each other on the events of the weekend. It was his second proper cup of the day, not counting the espresso he had necked on the way from Luigi's to Kennington, and the caffeine was doing its best to make him feel human. He'd got home late from Brixton the previous evening, his empty house feeling even more depressing at that time of night as it sat in cold darkness waiting for him.

Even the silence inside had felt accusatory, damning him for failing to keep his family within its walls, for destroying the safety of their own home. He'd spent an hour in the kids' rooms, staring at the empty spaces they should've filled, feeling even more guilty for not talking to them over the weekend. Sure, he'd been busy, but Wise knew he'd used work to stop himself thinking about the mess his life was in. Now though, he had no distractions. Nowhere to hide. Nothing to smother the pain he felt.

In the end, he couldn't face going into his own room and had headed downstairs to lie on the sofa. Finally, after scrolling through pictures of happier days on his phone, he'd fallen asleep, only to be woken what felt like minutes later by his alarm going off.

Now, he stood in his usual place in front of the team, trying to pretend his life wasn't falling apart, while Kat updated the whiteboards with all the new information that had been gathered. Of course, the fact that Kat was standing where Sarah Choi should've been felt like a stab in the gut as well. Another reminder of someone he'd failed.

What was worse was that he kept seeing Jono out of the corner of his eye, sitting among the troops but, when he looked directly at Jono's desk, there was just an empty chair glaring back, adding to his guilt.

One day, he thought, there would be so much of the damn stuff piled up on his shoulders that he'd break in half. Right then, that moment didn't seem that far off.

Wise's mood wasn't helped either by Riddleton's presence at the DMM. He'd plonked himself down in a far corner of the room, not hiding the look of disapproval on his side, as he listened to everything that was being said. Naturally, Millie and Palmer stood with him. As displays of loyalty went, it wasn't the most subtle, but it was effective. Wise wouldn't have been surprised to find they were wearing t-shirts that said 'Team Riddleton' under their work shirts.

At least it was good to have Samira with them. Her DCI had okayed Wise taking over the Mark Temple murder and given permission for Samira to help without any hesitation. She'd given the junior detective a glowing reference in the process.

'She's wasted with me,' DCI Glass had said. 'Samira's got a sharp mind and a good heart. She needs to toughen up a bit, but The Job will make that happen naturally enough.'

That was true. Sometimes, Wise imagined meeting his eighteen-year-old self. He doubted either would recognise the other now. He was worn out and battle-weary, whereas the optimism and drive he had when he joined seemed impossible to conjure up now.

He took a sip of his coffee and focused his attention back on Millie and Palmer, who were going over how they'd spent their Sunday.

'We went to Justine's gym yesterday,' Millie said. 'Members must use a card to get in and out so every time they visit, it's logged in the system. That made it easy to find out when Justine was in the place. Once we knew that, the manager let us access CCTV footage of those dates.'

'We went back to mid-November,' Palmer added. His eyes were still a vivid purple, but the swelling had gone down somewhat. 'She went to the gym a lot, but she was always on her own. She didn't even talk to anyone while she was working out.'

'So, no Mystery Man helping her lift weights?' Wise asked.

'No. No one,' Palmer replied, his face blank, his voice flat.

'That's a shame,' Wise said, 'but at least that's another avenue to scratch off. Brains? How did you get on?'

'Not great. There're more than a few unsolved old cases that are similar to ours in London and from across the country,' Brains said, 'but none of them are identical enough for me to say it's our man's work. If we had a suspect, it'd be a different matter, of course. I could use the data of where he was living and at what dates to see if there are any murders that match with those locations and times, etcetera. From there we could build a list of other likely victims but without a starting point, I'm a bit helpless.'

'But the fact of the matter is that you have no proof whatsoever that your killer has struck before,' Riddleton interjected, making no effort to hide his irritation. 'You've gone fishing and caught nothing.'

'As I mention on Friday, sir,' Wise replied, 'it is highly unlikely that someone this good at covering their traces has not killed before. There was nothing rushed about Justine's murder and the way he cleared up afterwards was of a professional standard. This definitely isn't his first time.'

Riddleton waved the comment away. 'Supposition.'

'Well, we might not have any earlier murders we can directly connect to our Mystery Man, but we do have a more recent one that we can.'

Riddleton stiffened. 'What do you mean?'

Wise took a breath. 'You've not met DC Samira Sathiah yet, have you? She's based over at Brixton nick on DCI Glass's team.'

The sudden change in subject threw Riddleton. He looked over in surprise as if noticing Samira for the first time. 'No, I haven't.'

Wise turned to address the whole team. 'Samira was called out to a fatal road accident at 2 a.m. yesterday morning. A man, Mark Temple, the manager of a bar called Sugar Tree, was hit and killed by a bus at Lavender Hill. While at the scene, Samira spoke to a witness that saw a man, in a long dark coat and with the hood up, push Mark into the path of the bus. CCTV footage from the bus in question corroborated the account. Hannah, can you play the footage?'

Hannah ran an edited clip of Mark's murder on the incident room's main screen to the side of the whiteboards. There was no doubt he was murdered.

'What's this got to do with anything?' Riddleton asked. 'It's hardly the same MO.'

Wise pressed his lips together for a second to stop himself from smiling. 'Mark Temple was Justine's best friend. She always took any potential boyfriend to the Sugar Tree to get Mark's approval. Apparently, they talked about everything.' Wise could see that bit of information ripple through the team but not everyone caught its significance.

'But what has that to do with him being pushed in front of a bus?' Riddleton said.

'Justine would've taken this Mystery Man to the Sugar Tree to get checked out,' Hicksy said as if talking to a three-year-old. 'Therefore, Mark would've been able to identify him. Depending on how much information Justine shared with her BFF, this Mark probably knew his name and cock size as well. Therefore, Mystery Man was removing a threat to his secret identity.'

'And, as you can see from the footage, Mark's killer is wearing the same coat as the one Mystery Man wore to dispose of Justine's body.' Wise walked over to the screen and pointed to the murderer. 'You can see the same white markings on the collar.'

Riddleton glared at the screen, his face reddening.

Wise continued. 'There's no hesitation in pushing Mark under the bus either, nor does he allow his face to be seen by any possible cameras. This man kills as easily as I drink coffee. And you don't get that good without practice.'

'Right,' Riddleton said. 'But you still have no leads as to who this "serial killer" is?'

'We do have a possible suspect in custody. Joshua McLean was Justine's boss, and he had a reputation for trying it on with his staff. Justine had complained about his attentions to several people. When DS Markham and I went to interview him, he claimed he was at home with his family on New Year's Eve. However, his wife refuted those claims. He'd supposedly gone out with clients at the last minute and not come home till late the next day — the exact time period Justine was murdered in. When McLean tried to attack his wife for telling us this, we arrested him.'

'And?' Riddleton asked.

Wise went over the interviews with McLean and his refusal to say where he was the previous night.

'Sounds guilty as hell to me,' Riddleton said.

'Except, after dismissing his solicitor, McLean confessed that he had spent the night cruising various gay bars in Soho before going home with a man he picked up in Her Soho.'

'I thought you said he was sleeping with women he worked with?' Riddleton said.

'Turns out Mr McLean likes it every which way,' Hicksy said. 'He's a very modern man of insatiable appetites.'

'Not that he wants everyone to know that, least of all his wife,' Wise added. 'Nor his solicitor.'

'How do we know he's telling the truth?' Riddleton asked. 'It's all a bit convenient.'

'Apparently, he has a secret phone with video and pictures in his desk at work. Hicksy's going to pick it up after this meeting. The images should all be date and time stamped, so they'll confirm what he claims. We'll get them checked out for authenticity but, considering we've had him in custody since 10 a.m. yesterday, I think we can be pretty sure he's not had time to fake them.'

'You'll have to let him go then,' Riddleton said. 'He's innocent.'

'I'm afraid so,' Wise added.

'And you're back to square one with a growing body count.'

'These things take time, sir.'

'Best get on with it then,' Riddleton said as he stood up. 'I'll expect updates later.' With that, he marched out of MIR-One.

Ignoring the man's ill manners, Wise looked over his team. 'Samira's chasing down CCTV for the Temple murder. Donut, Callum, you're doing the same for Justine. Brains, keep digging. Millie, Palmer, can you help with that? Maybe you'll spot something in the old cases. There might be a clue buried in all that data that will help us today. Hannah and I are going to see the head of Sparks, the dating app Justine liked to use, in case she met Mystery Man through that.'

He took another sip of coffee. 'And Hicksy, can you sort out getting an extension on McLean's custody before you go? I expect we're going to have to release him, but I'd rather keep him here all the same until we get everything checked out.'

'Yeah, of course,' Hicksy grunted back. For the first time in an age, though, Wise was glad to see that he didn't look hungover. Hopefully, it was a sign that Hicksy was coming to terms with his grief.

'And don't forget to look into the coat when you get time,' Wise added.

'Wouldn't dream of it, Guv.'

'Excellent.' Wise winked at the veteran detective. 'Alright, everybody. We've got lots to do, so let's get to it.'

As everyone began to disperse, Wise heard his desk phone ringing in his office. He jogged over and entered the small room. Putting down his coffee, Wise picked up the phone. 'D.I. Wise.'

'I told you I wanted to be kept updated on your investigation,' Riddleton snarled down the line. 'And that means before a bloody DMM. Do you understand?'

'Yes, sir,' Wise replied, biting his tongue to stop himself from saying what he really thought.

'Do it again and shit will rain down from heaven on you and your career.' Riddleton slammed his phone down, ending the call.

What a dick, Wise thought as he put his own phone down. As if he didn't have enough problems to deal with. And to think he used to complain about Roberts.

He took the lid off his coffee, saw there was a mouthful left and gulped it down. He threw the empty cup into his bin and turned to head back out into MIR-One, only to be stopped by the chirp of his mobile.

It was DCI Heer from SCO10. Immediately, he felt his pulse quicken. He answered it. 'Morning. I wasn't expecting to hear from you for a bit.'

'You free tomorrow to meet?' Heer said.

41

The Sparks office was in Rathbone Square. It was a giant U-shaped building made of steel and glass. Wise and Hannah had first visited the building while investigating the murder of Sparks's founder, Mark Hassleman.

Wise's first impression was that the place was more like a university campus than a place of business and not much had changed since then. As they walked through the revolving doors, he was confronted by people who looked like they should be in an art gallery or a nightclub, with their distressed clothing and outrageous fashion sense. He smiled at what his father would say at the sight of all the tattoos, piercings and combat trousers on display. Sam Wise was very much a belt and braces type of man who always wore a proper shirt and trousers with a razor-sharp crease, even though he'd retired ten years before. Sparks would have him tutting in disapproval within two seconds of walking through the door.

They headed over to the long, white reception desk, staffed by three would-be models with cheekbones that could cut glass. One, a woman with red hair tied up into two bunches on the sides of her head, smiled as the detectives approached. 'Good morning. Welcome to Sparks.'

'We're here to see Emily Walker,' Hannah said, showing the receptionist her warrant card.

If she was surprised to see two police officers turn up, she didn't show it. She just smiled again. 'One moment.' She tapped a message on her tablet, then looked up again. 'If you'd like to take a seat, Ms Walker will be with you shortly.' She indicated towards a seating area made up of a mixture of bright red lip-shaped sofas and giant orange bean bags.

'Thank you,' Wise said and headed over towards the seats. When he got there, he didn't sit down.

Hannah nodded to one of the sofas. 'Not keen on putting your backside on one of those?'

'I suppose it's meant to be some satirical statement about arse-kissing or something,' Wise said with a smile. 'But it just looks uncomfortable to me.'

'You'd probably break it anyway.'

'Very true.'

The clacking of heels on the concrete floor drew their attention. Emily Walker strode towards them, looking as Amazonian as ever. Her jet-black hair was shaved at the sides and the top was slicked back and pulled into a ponytail. Like every other time Wise had met her, she wore an all-black outfit. Today it consisted of a flared, full-length skirt, with an all but transparent shirt under a leather jacket cropped at the waist.

'Inspector Wise, Sergeant Markham. I wasn't expecting to see you both so soon,' she said in her transatlantic accent. 'Or rather, I was hoping I wouldn't see you again.' She smiled. 'Nothing personal.'

'I don't blame you. It's hardly ever good news when we turn up somewhere,' Wise said.

'Well, who's died today?' Walker asked.

'Can we talk somewhere a bit more private?' Hannah asked.

'Of course, I was just being a tad facetious,' Walker replied. 'I have a meeting room reserved for us upstairs. This way.'

Wise and Hannah followed Walker up the central escalator to the first floor. They passed various meeting rooms, named after celebrities such as Madonna, Jagger, Lennon and Monroe. All were packed full of people having earnest conversations, pondering how to get more people dating via the Sparks app, no doubt.

Walker stopped by a door. 'We're in Springsteen.' She pushed it open and stepped through. Inside, the long, green meeting table was set up with sparkling water, coffee, cups and biscuits. 'Help yourselves,' Walker said as she sat down. She picked up a small bottle of Perrier and twisted the lid. It came off with a small fizz and she poured it into a glass.

'That's very kind of you,' Wise said, taking a seat across from the CEO. 'Everyone looks very busy out there.' He picked up a coffee pot and poured himself a cup, then looked over to Hannah, who shook her head.

'You wouldn't believe it. We're growing at a rate of twenty-three percent every quarter. Apparently, the more shit the world gets, the more people look for love.' She held up both hands. 'And we provide the Sparks.'

Miraculously, Wise managed not to groan. 'We're investigating the murder of someone who used your app to meet potential boyfriends. We believe her latest man killed her. But unfortunately, he left us very little in clues, so we were hoping you could give us her user history. Whoever she met last is our prime suspect.'

'Oh my God, that's terrible,' Walker said. 'What's the name of the victim?'

'A young woman called Justine Mayweather,' Wise replied.

'Let me just make a phone call.'

'Certainly.'

Walker produced a phone from a pocket and scrolled through her contacts until she found the number she was looking for. She hit dial and put the phone next to her ear. Whoever she was calling answered almost immediately. 'Yes, it's me,' Walker said. 'We're in Springsteen. Yes, bring them as well.'

Walker ended the call and put down the phone. 'They won't be a minute.'

'And they are?' Wise asked.

'The right people to have in the room for this conversation.' Walker smiled back. There was no warmth in it and, once again, Wise was reminded of a panther thinking about lunch.

They sat in awkward silence for a couple of minutes. Then the door to the meeting room opened and two men and one woman marched in. Unlike everyone else in Sparks's office, the newcomers were suited and booted. Wise knew who they were instantly.

Lawyers.

Walker stood up. 'I thought it best that our in-house solicitors joined us. This is Terrence, Samantha and Khalid.'

Wise and Hannah got to their feet and shook hands with the trio, introducing themselves.

Khalid was obviously the one in charge as he sat next to Walker. He placed a phone on the table. 'I hope you don't mind if I record this conversation? As I'm sure you know, I find it stops any misunderstandings later.'

So, it was going to be that sort of meeting. Wise sighed. 'Of course I don't.'

Khalid hit record, then smiled. If Walker was a panther, Khalid looked like a shark, his small, dark eyes fixed on Wise. 'Now, how may we help you?'

Wise repeated what he'd told Walker.

'Ah,' Khalid said, when Wise was finished. 'First of all, may I say how saddened all of us are at the news of this poor woman's death. It's a real tragedy.'

'It is,' Wise repeated, waiting for the 'but' he knew was coming.

'I would like to know, however, what connection you have to suggest ... Justine met her killer via our app?' Khalid asked.

Wise pursed his lips for a moment. 'I can't go into those details right now.'

'But you do have proof? Hard, irrefutable evidence?' Again, Khalid smiled but there was no warmth to it, no humour. It was more of a 'fuck you' smile and Wise felt the urge to lean over the table and punch the man.

'Again, I can't go into the details of an ongoing investigation.'

'Well then, I'm afraid we have a problem. As much as all of us want to help the police in any way we can, we can't just divulge confidential information about our customers without the necessary details to justify doing so,' Khalid said. 'Our hands are tied, as it were.'

'We want to stop someone from using your app to kill people,' Wise said, his voice rising. 'Surely that warrants you giving us the help we need.'

'Inspector. I appreciate you can't tell us what evidence you may or may not have, but I warn you that if you make that statement anywhere else and it gets reported in so much as a Tweet, then Sparks will have no choice but to sue you personally and the Metropolitan Police for any damages such a statement would inevitably cause. I would imagine we would seek restitution in the region of several million pounds if we were feeling generous — and I can't remember the last time that happened.'

'Are you being serious?' Wise said. 'You won't help us?' He looked from Khalid to Walker, who was just staring through the glass walls to the meeting room, watching the world walk past.

'It's not that we don't want to help you, but we can't,' Khalid said. 'Of course, if you bring me a court order, then it will be my pleasure to give you the information you want.'

'A court order could take weeks to get,' Wise said. 'That's time I don't have.'

'I'm afraid we're all just at the mercy of the law, Inspector,' Khalid replied.

Wise looked at Hannah, who just shook her head. She knew as well as Wise that there was no point trying to fight a battle they wouldn't win.

'Okay. Fine. But I just want you all to know that if we catch this bastard and find out that he was definitely using your app to hunt his victims, then I'll make sure that every media outlet refers to him as the Sparks Killer,' Wise said. He jabbed a finger towards Khalid's phone. 'And you can play that back to yourself as many times as you want, just in case there's any sort of misunderstanding.'

The two detectives both stood up. 'Thank you for your help,' Hannah said.

Walker finally returned her gaze to them. 'Good luck, detectives. I hope you catch you man.'

'We'll see ourselves out,' Wise said.

'Good seeing you again,' Walker called out after them as they left the meeting room.

Wise was fuming as he walked back to the escalator and made his way down to the ground floor, not even pausing to see if Hannah was keeping up with him. So much for cooperation! So much for public spirit.

Wise marched across the foyer, not caring who might be in his way, his mood alone parting the crowds before him. He barged into the revolving door, his anger growing when it resisted his momentum, and he was forced to wait for it to make its slow revolution.

When he finally stepped out into the courtyard, he was about to howl with rage when he felt a hand on his shoulder.

It was Hannah. 'Don't, Guv. They'll be cameras and they could be watching. Don't give the shits the satisfaction of knowing they wound us up.'

'Jesus Christ, though,' Wise said through gritted teeth. 'I just wanted to smack the crap out of that stuck-up little wanker.'

'Yeah, me too. But let's get away from here, eh?'

Wise took a deep breath, letting the cold January air fill his lungs and cool his rage. 'You're right. I don't know why I let it bother me. But why the hell did Walker agree to meet us if they were only going to stonewall us like that?'

'I don't know,' Hannah replied. 'Maybe because they wanted to be on record saying that they wanted to help us, even when they had no intention of doing so.'

They walked quickly through a tunnel of green arches into Stephen Street. So close to midday, office workers were already leaving their buildings to seek something to eat or just a respite from their desks. Most likely, it was going to be the only bit of daylight they saw all day long because it'd be dark by 4 p.m. And no doubt like Wise, they'd travelled to work in the dark as well.

By the time they reached the Mondeo, Wise was feeling better or, at least, calmer.

Then his phone rang. It was Hicksy.

'Yeah, what's happening?' Wise said.

'Riddleton refused to apply for an extension for McLean,' Hicksy said. 'We've had to let him go.'

42

Hannah had never seen Wise so angry and that was saying something. He drove back to Kennington gripping the steering wheel so tight his knuckles were nearly popping through his skin. Needless to say, there wasn't much conversation going on either.

In the end, Hannah had just stared out of the window, watching London whizz by. At least, she was starting to feel more of her old self. She'd noticed her concentration was getting better and she was starting to think she could ride her bike again without worrying that she'd kill herself by running a red light or something stupid like that.

Her headache had improved too. It was now just a dull ache rather than the constant pounding that she'd been enduring. But maybe that was more to do with the paracetamol and codeine tablets she was popping. She'd been taking a couple every few hours to manage the pain. Hannah knew it was too much, but it made everything easier to deal with. She even felt calmer, no longer jumping at shadows twenty-four hours a day.

Of course, that didn't mean she didn't flinch every time she saw a white van drive by. It didn't stop the flashbacks of the car crash, of Sarah being dragged from their vehicle and the gun pointed at her own head, the sense of helplessness she'd felt as the gang had dragged her from the car as well. God, even now she could feel the bile rising in her gut. Why was she thinking about it again?

She glanced back at Wise, but he only had eyes for the road, his eyebrows knitted together in fury.

He really hadn't taken the news of McLean's release well, despite the fact that none of them really believed he was the man they were looking for. Especially after Hicksy had picked up McLean's second phone from his office.

Hannah and Wise hadn't seen the pictures themselves yet but, according to Hicksy, who was never one to mince his words, the images showed McLean 'balls deep up some bloke's backside' at the time of Mark Temple's murder.

Hicksy had shown Riddleton the images, though, and as a result, the DCI had refused to put forward any request for a custody extension or approve any additional digital forensic work on the images to check their authenticity as it 'would be a waste of his budget'. Instead, he told Hicksy that he'd better pray that McLean didn't sue the Met for wrongful arrest before ordering the man to be released.

It was already starting to feel dark by the time they pulled into the car park at Kennington, despite the fact it wasn't even 2 p.m. As Hannah got out of the car, she shivered at the cold, damp air quickly leaching all the warmth from her body. She did up her motorbike jacket, but it was already too late, so Hannah stuck her head down and marched into the station, eager for its antiquated heating systems to do their job.

The fluorescent lights made Hannah blink as she walked into the old reception area of the station, and she hoped it wouldn't set off her headache again. For a moment, she was tempted to take more painkillers, but it'd only been an hour or so since she'd last swallowed some. Instead, she took deep breaths in the empty foyer and concentrated on the fact she was back in the warm again. That was something to be grateful for, at least.

All the same, Hannah was glad there was no one behind the old reception desk watching her. After all, no one was stationed there as Kennington was no longer open to the public. Apart from three Murder Investigation Teams and some senior officers, most of the people working out of Kennington were paper pushers.

Not that Hannah minded that much.

She quite liked the fact that the place was like their own private kingdom. It meant that she didn't have to wade through drunks, druggies and other general scallywags each time she went in and out of the station. Hannah had had enough of that while she'd been stationed at Brixton. The sad thing was that she definitely found the dead easier to deal with than the living.

The main door opened behind her and Hannah turned to see Wise enter with his face still like thunder. He saw her looking and stopped, straightened and he visibly shook his head and rolled his neck.

'Sorry,' he said, almost looking back to his normal self. 'Those ... people at Sparks really riled me up and then to hear ...' He shook his head again. 'I don't even think letting McLean go was the wrong decision. I know he's not our killer. He's just a narcissistic arsehole. It just drove it home that we have nothing — nothing — to point us towards our killer.'

'We'll find something, Guv,' Hannah replied. 'You know we will.'

'Do I? I'm not sure I know anything these days.'

Hannah puffed out her cheeks. 'Do you fancy getting a coffee over at that place you like? The one across the road? Luca's or whatever it's called?'

'Luigi's,' Wise said. 'Please tell me you've been in there at least once since you joined us.'

Hannah smiled. 'I haven't. Coffee's just coffee to me. I don't care if it's instant or freshly ground by Sicilian monks.'

'Stop right there or I'm going to have to ask you to transfer off my team.'

'Do you want to show me what all the fuss is about then?'

Wise looked up the stairs to MIR-One, then back out into the cold, damp afternoon. When he turned back to Hannah, he was smiling. 'Yeah, why not?'

Hannah made sure her coat was done up tight, then she followed Wise back out of the station, through the carpark and out onto Kennington Road. The traffic was all but at a standstill, so the two detectives hurried between the cars to cross over to the other side of the street and hurried down to the cafe three doors down.

A large man in a white apron was behind the counter, his dark, curly hair a mere whisper of what it once had been. He looked tired but his face broke out into a large smile when he saw Wise. 'Inspector! I wasn't expecting to see you again today.'

Wise walked over, grinning himself. 'Luigi, I'd like to introduce a colleague of mine — DS Hannah Markham. She's been on my team for about six months, and, for some insane reason, she's never had one of your coffees.'

Luigi looked past Wise to Hannah. He raised his eyebrows. 'Is this true?'

'I'm sorry,' Hannah replied. 'I have no excuse.'

'Well, you're here now. No?' Luigi said.

'I am and I'm expecting great things.'

Luigi bowed theatrically. 'It will be the greatest cup of coffee you have ever had in your life.'

Wise pointed to a table by the window. 'We'll be over there.'

Luigi smiled. 'Three minutes.'

The two detectives sat down and, for a moment, neither said anything. Hannah watched the world outside their window grow ever darker. All the cars had their lights on and anyone walking by had their heads down as they hurried along.

Luigi was soon back with two small espresso cups in his hands. He placed them in front of Wise and Hannah. 'There you go. It's made with Pacamara beans from Columbia, which was then roasted in Florence. I use a medium grind, and the coffee is brewed with water at ninety-four degree Celsius for two minutes, twenty-three seconds exactly. I think you'll find this is a very attractive cup that will delight all your senses.'

Hannah smiled. 'Wow. I normally just dump some granules in a cup and pour in boiling water.'

'Please, do not say such things in here,' Luigi said in mock disgust. 'You have not been drinking coffee. Today, you start.'

'I can't wait.'

'Enjoy!' Luigi headed back to his counter as Hannah picked up her cup. If the aroma coming off it was anything to go by, the barista's efforts hadn't been wasted. It certainly didn't smell like the instant Nescafe she normally drunk.

As Hannah raised the cup to her lips, she saw that Wise was watching her. 'It's just coffee,' she said.

'I know,' he replied. 'I know.'

Keeping her own eyes on Wise, Hannah took a sip. She didn't know what she was expecting but even so the flavour took her by surprise: delicate, almost ... flowery with a hint of ... lemon? 'This doesn't taste like coffee,' she said.

'But you like it?' Wise asked.

Hannah grinned. 'I love it. I can kinda understand why you drink so much of the stuff now.'

'Luigi's coffees are next level.' Wise took a sip of his own cup.

'You feeling better now?'

'Yeah, I am. Sorry again about earlier. I don't even really think my mood had much to do with the case at all.' He put down the cup and twisted it on the saucer so the handle was at a perfect right angle. 'It's just everything's been a bit shit lately.'

'Yeah, it has,' Hannah replied.

'How's things with you? I was worried about you for a bit last week.'

Hannah took another sip of coffee to buy herself some time before answering. She thought about lying for a moment, but she'd done enough of that lately. 'As you say, it's been a bit shit. It's taking longer than I thought to get over ... what happened. I've had headaches and ... nightmares.'

'I'm sorry. Have you talked to anyone about it?'

'No.'

'After Andy was killed last year, someone recommended that I see a psychiatrist,' Wise said. 'I didn't want to go. I thought everyone would think I was weak or something if I saw a shrink. I mean, we're cops, right? We're supposed to be able to deal with stuff, you know. Just shrug it off and make a bad joke or two. But, I couldn't let it go. I was having nightmares all day and all night long. I didn't even have to be asleep to see him die yet again.'

'I didn't ... I didn't realise,' Hannah replied.

'Why should you? I think I got pretty good at pretending everything was okay, but it wasn't. Anyway, I went to see Doctor Shaw. It was uncomfortable at first to talk about myself — my feelings — but I'm not exaggerating when I say she saved my life,' Wise said. 'So, you know, if you need help ... We have resources in the Met. Or you can talk to me about it at the very least.'

'You've got enough on your plate without me adding my problems to them,' Hannah said. 'But yeah, I might take up the offer of help from the Met. I think I could get into trouble otherwise.'

'I don't want that. You're too important to the team.'

Hannah felt her cheeks redden. 'I don't feel that way.'

Wise chuckled. 'You'll see it yourself one day. Trust me.'

Hannah took another sip of coffee. If anything, the flavour was improving each time. 'So, what are we going to do about finding Mystery Man?'

'We do what we always do,' Wise replied. 'We keep going until we catch the bastard.'

43

Wise sat back in his chair and played with his coffee cup for a moment, twisting it this way and that in its saucer. He felt calmer now. In control. Thank God Hannah had suggested going to Luigi's. If he'd gone up to MIR-One or run into Riddleton, his career could well have been over.

He was glad, too, that Hannah had opened up about what was bothering her. Hopefully, she'd get some help now. There was no way he could lose her. Not after everything that had happened, the others he'd lost.

'I keep thinking the answers are in Warriner Gardens,' Hannah said.

Wise looked up. 'Why's that?'

'If Justine was as intense with Mystery Man as she was with her other boyfriends, she'd have been with him all the time, right?'

'Yeah, especially if she was as loved up as she said she was,' Wise said.

'So, I reckon she would have been with him every night at Warriner Gardens.'

'And yet no one's seen him.'

. . .

'BECAUSE MYSTERY MAN IS INVISIBLE,' Hannah replied. 'No one's seen him come and go from her building at all. Not the residents that live there, nor us on whatever CCTV footage we've been able to find.'

'It would've helped if the building's internal cameras were up and working.'

'But they weren't. And he must've known that,' Hannah said. 'But someone must've seen them together.'

Wise shrugged, then picked up his coffee. 'This is London. I've lived in my house for nine years and I'm not sure I'd be able to identify my neighbours if they were in a line up, let alone notice who they were dating.'

Hannah smiled. 'You've got a point there.'

Wise finished his coffee. It was as good as ever and he could feel the caffeine working its magic in his brain. 'Staying at her flat is new though. Normally, she's at the boyfriend's place.'

'But that could be down to him being married or something like that. Maybe his place wasn't an option? That would tie in with her social media blackout as well.'

'Yeah, maybe,' Wise replied but he wasn't convinced. 'The "married man" angle doesn't seem right to me, the more I think about it. She's been hunting for Mr Right all this time, looking for someone to settle down with — to move in with, even if it's by stealth. So why pick a married man as a boyfriend? And if she's vetting potentials with her mate, Mark, why would she take such an obvious no-go to meet him?'

'That makes sense,' Hannah said. 'Okay, in that case, we can say Mystery Man is single and he's got money to pay for her first-class lifestyle. We know he's tall, fairly strong as well — he carried her body without any sign of difficulty, after all.'

'Yeah,' Wise agreed. 'And all her other boyfriends were Caucasian so we can assume he'd be the same as well.'

'Single, white male. Sounds just like every other type of serial killer.'

'Yeah, but it's not enough to track him down. Without knowing where they met and how, we've got nothing.' Wise shook his head. 'If only those idiots at Sparks had actually helped us — they could've told us exactly who she was seeing.'

'*If* that's where she met him,' Hannah said. 'Maybe she broke her pattern with this one too. Maybe she'd had enough of meeting useless fuck boys that way?'

'How do people meet these days?' Wise said. 'It's been a long time since my dating days.'

Hannah shrugged. 'The same places as before: work, bars, or through friends.'

'Justine doesn't seem to have any friends though. She just has boyfriends.'

'And she's not going to bars unless it's on a date.'

'So that just leaves work,' Wise said.

'But not McLean,' Hannah added.

'No, we wasted enough time on him. It was stupid of me to even go down that route.' Wise stood up. 'But, if we're looking for a tall, wealthy, well-built, single white man in her ad agency, I reckon we'll find that there's not a big list we'll have to look at.'

Hannah got to her feet. 'Yeah, you're right there. From what I remember, the men I saw would struggle to punch their way out of a paper bag.'

'Let me go pay for the coffees and then we'll head back,' Wise said. They both walked over to the counter.

Luigi greeted them with another smile. 'And what did you think of your first coffee from Luigi's?' he asked Hannah.

'It was incredible,' she replied. 'Life-changing.'

'That makes me so happy,' Luigi replied. 'I hope I'll see more of you, Sergeant, now you've seen the light.'

'I think you will.'

'Excellent!'

Wise held up his debit card to pay for the coffees, but Luigi waved him away. 'These are on me. My treat, as they say.'

'Are you sure?' Wise asked. In the ten years he'd been buying coffees from Luigi, he'd never been given a free cup before.

Luigi looked around as if to make sure no one was in earshot. 'If my wife was here, she'd tell me I was a fool, but she's not and, for this afternoon, I am the king of my own business. And I say your drinks are on me.'

Wise had to laugh. Luigi's wife, Maria, frightened even him. 'You're a brave man, my friend. And thank you. But, if it causes a problem, just let me know. I can still pay tomorrow.'

Luigi shooed him away. 'Go. I am my own man. It's alright.'

'I'll see you tomorrow,' Wise said, fully expecting to receive the bill when Maria was back. Still smiling, he and Hannah left the cafe and hurried back to Kennington as quickly as they could, trying to outrace the rain that had now decided to fall.

Even so, they were more than a little soaked by the time they made it into the station, and Wise had to shake the water off him like a dog. They dripped their way upstairs to the third floor and entered MIR-One.

Brains, Palmer and Millie were working away in one corner of the room going over old cases, while Donut and Calum were still going over CCTV footage on their monitors. They'd done a good job so far, but Wise couldn't help but wonder if Sarah Choi would've come up with something important by now. She'd always been so brilliant in piecing together events via footage taken from London's one million cameras.

Hicksy was there too, a heavy scowl on his face. He got up when he saw Wise and Hannah walk in and headed over to meet them. 'Sorry, Guv. I did my best.'

'It's alright, mate,' Wise replied, squeezing his shoulder. 'For what it's worth, I think Riddleton made the right call — but don't tell him that.'

'You should've seen his face when I showed him the films,' Hicksy grunted. 'I thought he was going to have a heart attack.'

'That bad?'

'Yeah. I thought I was pretty broad-minded but that bloke got up to stuff that shocked even me.'

'You sure you weren't just a little bit turned on?' Hannah said with a chuckle.

'Not in the slightest,' Hicksy grunted. 'But each to their own and all that.'

'Hannah and I were just chatting, and we think we should have a proper look at the people Justine worked with at Green, McLean's agency. Just in case that's where she met Mystery Man.'

'And you'd like me to do that?'

'If you could. Hannah can help. I might be tied up with … something else in the morning,' Wise said. 'I might join you afterwards, though.'

'Yeah, sure. Why not? Anyway, I do have a bit of news for you,' Hicksy said. 'Might be good news but I don't know yet.'

'Oh yeah? What's that?' Wise asked.

'Come and have a butcher's at my computer.' Hicksy walked back to his desk with Wise and Hannah following. Hicksy sat down. 'You know you asked me to look into that coat the killer's wearing?'

'You found something?'

There was the beginning of a smile forming on Hicksy's lips. 'Well, as you know I'm not exactly Mr Fashion, am I? But I didn't have anything to do after I had to let McLean go and I needed something to take my mind off those videos of his.'

'And?' Wise said.

'So, I googled expensive coats. And, let me tell you, I can't believe the money people spend on something that's going to get rained on half the time.' Now, Hicksy didn't hold his grin back. 'Anyway, I came across this.' He turned his monitor so Wise and Hannah could see the screen. It was open on a website for a clothing brand. There was a black jacket on a blue background. It had white writing around the inside of the collar.

'That looks like Mystery Man's coat,' Hannah said.

Wise leaned in closer to get a better look. 'I think you're right.'

Hicksy held up a screen shot of Mystery Man taken from one of the bus's cameras. 'I know it's the same coat.' He pointed to a small patch on the sleeve. 'This is the brand emblem as well. What we're looking at is a Saint Clair hooded down jacket.'

'Well done, Hicksy,' Wise said, looking from the screen to the still image and back again. 'You're right.'

'There's more,' Hicksy said.

Wise straightened. 'What do you mean?'

'If you notice, this jacket sells for just under three and a half thousand quid. That is a lot of money.'

'It is.' Wise remembered complaining to anyone who'd listen after he spent two hundred quid on his overcoat, thinking that outrageous.

'I rang the company and spoke to a very helpful young woman,' Hicksy went on. 'And she told me that they only sold five of these coats last year.'

'Five?' Wise couldn't believe it.

'Five,' Hicksy repeated. 'I mean, it's not that surprising at that price, is it? Anyway, she was so helpful, she said she'd find out where they were sold.'

'And, if we know that, we can find out who they sold them to,' Wise concluded.

Hicksy winked. 'Bingo.'

'Thank God he didn't get it from Marks and Sparks.' Wise laughed. He couldn't believe it. This could be the breakthrough they were looking for.

44

Millie's eyes burned. It'd been a long day spent reading about cold cases of murdered women. Of looking at pictures of people who'd had their lives stolen from them and had yet to find any sort of justice.

Millie didn't believe in ghosts, but it was easy to imagine the spirits of those young women still roaming London in confusion, howling for someone to bring them peace.

It was heart-breaking in every way.

But something else had happened to Millie as she read one horror story after another. She felt for the first time that she was doing what she was meant to do. She belonged on a murder squad, hunting the perpetrators of these awful crimes.

Not helping the career of a dickhead like Riddleton.

The man had made a right tit of himself this morning, trying to score points when there was no need. Everyone was working their backside off to get a result and his jibes only made him look out of touch with everyone else. Even Palmer had kept quiet afterwards — and if *he* wouldn't defend Riddleton, then that summed up how bad the man had been.

At least, they were making progress on the cold cases by

narrowing down the overwhelming list of dead women into something that was a little bit more manageable.

She'd sat with Brains and Palmer and worked out ways of eliminating some of the cases. They began with age, cutting out anyone under eighteen and over thirty-five. They then decided to remove anyone who was married. Palmer had wanted to focus on cases where the victim had been smothered but neither Millie nor Brains had agreed with that. Somehow, it didn't feel right to assume he'd used the exact same approach each time. Nor did they concentrate on bodies fished out of the Thames, the sea or any other rivers or canals. Brains had made the point that Mystery Man was most likely getting better with practice, refining his approach each time he killed, learning more about how to remove evidence that could give him away and stuff like that.

'I bet the first one was as messy as hell,' Brains said. 'A spur of a moment thing or, if he'd been thinking about it for a while, he had to work his courage up to do it. Somehow, though, he got away with it and then decided he liked killing. So, he did it again and again, each one getting easier and easier.'

'How far back do we go?' Millie asked.

Brains shrugged. 'Depends on how old Mystery Man is. If he's the same age or thereabouts as Justine, then I'd say no more than seven or eight years. But, if he's older, then we might have to go back ten or fifteen years maybe.'

'That's too much,' Palmer said. 'We should keep the search to the last five years or we'll be doing this forever. We can always go further back later.'

They'd all agreed, and Brains had done his data-crunching. He might be a bit of an oddball, but Millie was impressed at how well he manoeuvred his way around HOLMES 2, the police's database. Millie had done all the courses herself, but it still seemed like eating soup with a fork every time she tried to look for something. But Brains? He was bloody Mozart with the damn thing.

By the time they were finished, they had sixteen cases to go through. Sixteen unsolved murders of women around the same age as Millie.

No wonder she felt frazzled now. She glanced at the time on her phone. 5:45. Maybe she could do another hour before calling it a night. Maybe …

Her phone rang. There was no name on the display, just the number. A number she didn't recognise.

'Hello, DC Buchanan,' she said on answering.

'Oh hi,' a woman's voice said. 'This is Amanda Potterton. We chatted the other day at Warriner Gardens? About Justine?'

'I remember,' Millie replied. 'How can I help you, Amanda?'

'It's silly, really, but you said to call you if I remembered anything that might help you.'

'And you have?'

'Well, I have but I have no idea if it's of any use. It's just that I remembered there was someone else in the building that Justine was friendly with. Maybe not in a boyfriend/girlfriend way but they definitely hung out together. I saw them having coffee one morning at Marco's.'

'Marco's?'

'The coffee shop around the corner on Forfar Road.'

Millie made a note. 'And who was the friend?'

'His name's Marcus. Marcus Short.'

Millie remembered the man who'd spoken to her in the lobby of Justine's building. She could see Justine being attracted to him. 'Older man, looks a bit like Pierce Brosnan?'

'That's him,' Amanda said. 'You've met him?'

'I have.'

'Well, you should talk to him again. He probably knew Justine better than anyone in the building.'

'I will do,' Millie said. 'Thanks for calling.'

She put down her phone and turned her chair to face Palmer. 'Hey.'

'Yeah?' he replied, not looking up from his screen.

'Did you interview a Marcus Short at Warriner Gardens?'

'Yeah, I think so. Didn't get anything of use from him but that might've been because the Neanderthal with the broken nose thought the bloke was gay. Why?'

'Someone just rang me and said he and Justine were mates — but maybe not in a dating kind of way. She said he might know something.'

'Well, he wouldn't be dating her if he was gay, would he?'

'No,' Millie replied, even though she couldn't see how anyone could think the man she met was gay. Far from it. 'Still, have you got his number? I'll give him a call?'

'Yeah, hold on a minute.' Palmer finally tore his eyes away from the screen, delved into his suit jacket pocket and pulled out his notebook. He flipped through the pages until he found what he was looking for. He scrawled a number on a post-it note, and passed it over. All without meeting her eyes once. What a knob. 'Here you go.'

'Cheers.' Millie took it and picked up her phone again. She dialled the number, but it went straight to voice mail. She left her name and number and asked Marcus to call her back, just a little surprised that she felt disappointed at not being able to speak to him straight away.

She ploughed on for another hour like she promised herself, but her head was throbbing and Millie knew she wasn't concentrating properly. She stood up and stretched. 'I'm going to call it a night,' she said to Brains and Palmer. 'I'm knackered. I'll come in early and catch up then.'

'No problem,' Brains called out. 'Thanks for all the hard work today. It was a massive help.'

'My pleasure,' Millie replied, meaning it.

Palmer still hadn't looked her way.

'Night, Palmer,' she said, not giving in to his attitude. She had no idea what had pissed him off. Maybe he thought she was being too friendly to the 'enemy'.

Whatever.

Not waiting for a reply, she headed out of MIR-One and trotted down the stairs, eager to get some cold air to clear her head. It was just starting to spit with rain when Millie made it outside, but she didn't care. Tucking her hands into her coat pockets, she left and headed towards the tube station. It was only a two-minute walk away and it served the Northern line so she could be home in Balham within fifteen, twenty minutes max — something else she liked about working with Wise's team.

Millie was just about to enter the station when her phone rang. She looked at the caller ID and recognised Marcus Short's number. She hit the green accept button. 'Hello, DC Buchanan.'

'Oh hello,' Marcus said. 'I'm not disturbing you, am I? I just got your message to call.'

'Not at all,' Millie replied, stepping back out onto the pavement. 'Thanks for getting back to me so quickly.'

'How can I help you?' Marcus asked.

'We've been looking for people who knew Justine Mayweather, the woman who was murdered from your building.'

'Yes, that's right. I spoke to two of your colleagues.'

'It's just that we had a call from someone who said you were friends with Justine.'

'Really?' Marcus sounded surprised.

'She said she saw you having coffee together.'

'I'm sorry but I'm really confused. Someone said that I did what?'

'You were having coffee together at Marco's. Ama— the witness said she saw you there.'

There was a pause. 'Oh, *her*? That's who was murdered? I didn't even know her name. I was in Marco's, just finishing up my coffee and a Danish and this woman came in. We recognised each other from the building and said hello. She bought her drink and asked to share the table as the place was packed. I don't think we spoke more than five sentences to each other before I left.' Marcus let out a sigh. 'That was the poor girl who was murdered. Wow. I can't believe it.'

'Yes. That was Justine Mayweather,' Millie said. 'Do you mind if I come over and take a statement from you? Just for our records, to show I've followed up the line of enquiry?'

'Of course. It'd be lovely to see you,' Marcus replied. 'And, as I said, anything to help. Is tomorrow afternoon okay? It's just that I'm on my way out now for a dinner meeting.'

'Sure. No problem,' Millie said. 'What time tomorrow is best?'

'Shall we say 4?'

'I'll see you then.'

'I'll look forward to it,' Marcus said, sounding like he meant it.

Millie ended the call and slipped her phone back into her pocket. There was something about Marcus she liked. After all, how many men did she know who were happy to have a police officer call on them?

None.

Millie was smiling when she entered the tube station, eager to get home.

Tuesday 10th January

45

The one good thing about his family being up in Leeds was that Wise didn't have to explain why he wasn't wearing a suit. He'd chosen to dress in jeans, with a black hoodie under a leather bomber jacket instead. He had a baseball cap on as well, doing his best to hide his face, but he was also aware that, because of his size, he could hardly walk around inconspicuously.

Thankfully, when he reached the Travelodge by Waterloo Station, it was still dark and miserable out and the only people in sight were doing their best to stay dry in shop doorways or hurrying along to wherever they were going with their heads down.

The interior of the Travelodge was all but identical to the one he'd visited in Finsbury Park, right down to a monosyllabic receptionist, who really couldn't give a monkey's who walked through the door. The Waterloo building only had three floors though, so Wise could at least take the stairs up to the fictitious Andrew Simon's room, clutching fresh coffees from the hotel cafe.

Once he reached the room, Wise had to awkwardly knock with a single knuckle so he didn't spill a drop from one of the drinks. A shadow fell over the spy hole, then there was a moment's hesitation before Jamie opened the door.

Wise held up the drinks. 'I brought you coffee.'

'Cheers,' Jamie said, stepping aside to let Wise enter.

As Wise passed the UCO, he noted the man looked a wreck. God only knew when he'd last slept. Wise headed over to the desk in the corner of the room and put the drinks down as he heard Jamie push the room door shut and lock it.

When Wise turned around, Jamie had a small revolver pointed straight at his face. 'Who introduced us?' Jamie snarled.

'What?' Wise couldn't believe it. He could tell the man wasn't playing around. He'd shoot Wise if he had to.

'Who introduced us?' Jamie repeated, pushing the gun forward so it all but touched Wise's nose.

'DCI Rena Heer,' Wise replied. 'From SCO10.'

'And where did we meet?'

'Thursday morning in Finsbury Park.'

The gun wavered as Jamie stared into Wise's eyes, fear and uncertainty battling away within the UCO. Long, agonising seconds passed as the gun stayed pointing at Wise's head and all Wise could think was that Jamie was going to shoot him.

And there was nothing he could do to prevent it.

He took a breath, wishing he'd spoken to his kids that morning. Had a chance to tell them that he loved them. Christ, if only he could've hugged them one last time.

He closed his eyes, ready for the bullet. Ready to die.

And waited.

'Fuck,' Jamie said. 'I'm sorry. I'm a mess.'

Wise opened his eyes. Jamie staggered back and put the gun down on the sideboard.

'I haven't slept,' the UCO said. 'Your brother's got me paranoid. He ...'

Wise wasn't listening. He shook his head, still not believing he was still alive. His legs felt weak. He wanted to be sick. He stepped back, then all but fell onto the bed, quaking at how close he'd come to getting killed. To it all being over. 'What the hell was that about?'

Jamie sat down at the table by the window and rubbed his face.

'I'm sorry.' He glanced up at Wise. 'You really do look just like him. And you know what? Turning up here, pretending to be you is exactly what he'd do. Tom would think it was fun, letting me believe everything was good before letting me know just how in the shit I really was.'

Wise could believe that. Tom had always had a cruel sense of humour.

'Here.' Wise passed the UCO one of the coffees. Jamie took it, removed the lid, and had a sip. Wise did the same. The two men didn't speak, and Wise could feel his heart rate slowing back down. Colour was returning to Jamie's face as well. 'Feeling better?'

Jamie let out a sound that could've been a sob. 'Better? I don't even know what that is anymore. I'm alive and I didn't kill you, so that's something.'

'Yeah, that's something.' Wise had another sip of coffee. It wasn't in the same league as Luigi's, but it was warm and strong and, right then, it was exactly what he needed.

'I am sorry,' Jamie said again.

'Don't be. I can't even imagine the strain you're under.'

'I've worked undercover most of my life,' Jamie said. 'I've helped put some really bad people away — but this case?' He puffed out his cheeks. 'It's going to be the death of me one way or another. If your brother doesn't whack me, then the stress will get me.'

'But you're safe? Your cover's still good?'

'If it wasn't, I wouldn't be here. It's as simple as that. Hell, if Tom even suspected I was Old Bill, he'd have me fucking tortured, then strung up. The man doesn't mess about. He doesn't take chances.'

Jamie didn't have to tell Wise that.

'If I see you walking down the same street as me,' Tom says, 'I'm going to get very upset, and when I get upset, things get messy. All sorts of people can get hurt. Especially innocent bystanders ... How are the kids, by the way?'

Not for the first time, a million doubts flooded his mind about this crazy plan of his to pretend to be Tom and infiltrate his gang. If he messed it up, if he got caught, then he could only hope Tom would kill him quickly and not go after his family as well. The trouble was, the more he learned about Tom, the more that seemed like a fool's hope.

Jamie must've seen something on Wise's face. 'Having second thoughts?'

'I was just wondering if I was mad for trying to do this. I have family that I don't want hurt.'

'Yeah, me too,' the UCO said. 'Look. It's not too late to back out. No one would blame you. Going undercover isn't an easy thing to do. You've got to forget who you were originally and be the person you're pretending to be. In this room, I'm Jamie Aspinal, an upstanding police officer with commendations coming out of my arse. But out there? I'm Jamie Gregs, an ex-con who'd nick the fillings out of his granny's teeth if he could make a bit of scratch.

'When you're a copper, the world's black and white. We follow the rules and uphold the laws. But when you're pretending to be a piece of shit drug dealer or whatever you are, the world is nothing but grey. There are no rules to follow except one — you do what you have to do to stay alive. If that means you have to stay up all night snorting gack, then you get sniffing. If you have to beat someone up who owes you money, you break their fucking leg and not think twice about it.'

'What if Tom wants you to kill someone?' Wise asked.

Jamie shook his head. 'Tom knows I don't do that shit, so he doesn't ask me. Besides, he's got plenty of lads who won't think twice about cutting some poor sod's throat and, of course, he's more than happy to do it himself.'

'How many people has he killed?'

'I don't fucking know,' Jamie said. 'I've personally seen him off four people, and I've been there when he's ordered the deaths of at least three others.'

'Christ, and we still can't arrest him?'

'You know it's not as easy as that. One eyewitness isn't enough. He'd only produce a hundred others that said he was in another part of the country when the murders happened. Then you'd find me with my throat cut somewhere.'

Wise puffed out his cheeks. 'We better get on with my lessons then. The sooner Tom is put away the better.'

Jamie nodded. 'Yeah — but let's work out a code so I know it's you when we meet next. Because, I swear to God, I'll shoot you if I ever have the slightest doubt it's you.'

Wise looked at the gun. 'No rules except one, eh?'

'Damn right. And don't think I don't know how to make a body disappear if I have to.'

Wise smiled. 'I wouldn't want to put you in that position.'

'So, what's going to be our code?'

'What does Tom call you? By your name or by a nickname?'

'He calls me "Jamie" most of the time, "Knobhead" occasionally, and "You fucker" every now and then when he's pissed off.'

'What if I call you Jimbo when we meet?' Wise said. 'It keeps it simple, and it won't draw any attention if someone overhears us.'

Jamie nodded. 'Yeah, that works.'

'Good. Now where's DCI Heer? Shouldn't she be here by now?'

Jamie looked at his watch. 'Yeah. She should.'

Wise took out his phone, scrolled through his contacts until he found Heer's number and hit the green button. He listened to the dial tone until the phone ended the attempted call, unable to connect.

Both men looked at each other, neither hiding their concern.

'That's not good,' Jamie said.

'It doesn't have to be anything bad.' Wise tried to call again and had the same lack of response.

'Fuck this. I'm off,' Jamie said. 'Who knows what's going on, but I'm not staying here.'

'How can I get in touch with you?' Wise asked. 'If something's happened to Heer?'

Jamie shook his head. 'You don't.'

'But—'

'But nothing.' Jamie headed to the door, then stopped. He looked over his shoulder at Wise. 'I'm not going to get myself killed for The Job.'

And then he was off out the door, leaving Wise alone in the hotel room, wondering what the hell had happened. He tried reaching Heer again, and failed to reach her for the third time. With a sense of foreboding in his gut, Wise followed Jamie out of the door.

46

Wise changed into his suit when he reached Kennington and, by the time he entered MIR-One for the Daily Management Meeting, no one would've known his morning hadn't started the same as it always did.

His thoughts kept drifting, though, as he listened to the team's updates, wondering what had happened to Heer and why she hadn't been in touch. He couldn't come up with one good reason to justify her silence, only a hundred bad ones. He decided he'd call her DS, Brendan Murray, after the meeting to see if he knew anything.

'We've got fifteen possible murders that could, perhaps, be linked to Justine's,' Brains said.

'Fifteen?' Wise repeated, forcing himself to concentrate.

'They're just possibles, though,' Brains said. 'Not definites. The means of death is different in all of them — we've got knife wounds, strangulation, blunt force trauma etcetera. But what they do have in common is an increasing lack of evidence at the scene of crime or on the bodies. So, in these cases, it's the lack of evidence that links them.'

'It's something at least. Go through the case files and see who was interviewed and maybe you'll spot a name of someone we've spoken to pop up in one of those cases,' Wise said.

'Will do,' Brains replied.

Wise looked over to Donut's team. 'How are you getting on?'

'Not great,' Donut said. 'We haven't come across anything new that could help. We've made a compilation of all the clips we have of Justine coming and going from her building during the weeks leading up to her murder, though. Including whenever she's driven somewhere. We're matching them to her phone data movements as well, but that's about it.'

'Okay. Keep at it. Once you have all the routes mapped out, start looking for other cameras that we might not have access to but might have picked up Justine. Private ring cameras and such. It'll be a bit of leg work, but it might pay off.'

Donut scribbled his instructions down on his notepad. 'Yes, Guv.'

'And can you send me the compilation of Justine you made? I wouldn't mind looking through it myself.'

'Absolutely.' Donut tapped away on his keyboard. 'I've emailed it to you.'

'Thanks,' Wise replied. 'Samira?'

'I've been chasing CCTV on Lavender Hill, but I haven't got anything useful,' Samira replied. 'Mystery Man was picked up by a few cameras after he killed Mark Temple, but he always keeps his head down and then we lose him after he turns down Lavender Gardens. There's no CCTV down there. I was going to look for private cameras today.'

'Good thinking,' Wise said. 'Hicksy, do you want to update everyone about the jacket?'

Hicksy stood up and ran through everything he'd learned about the Saint Clair jacket. The information got the team visibly excited. They all knew this development, more than anything, could be the breakthrough they were looking for.

'Obviously, any of the five people who bought this coat will become a person of interest in our enquiry,' Wise said. 'And if one of them is someone we've already talked to, then they will become our prime suspect.'

'Hicksy, you genius,' Brains said.

'I just try my best,' he replied with a nod of his head.

Everyone laughed, except Palmer, who glowered at the veteran detective.

'Alright, everyone. Hannah and Hicksy are also going to go back to McLean's agency today and look at the staff there, in case Mystery Man worked with Justine,' Wise said. 'And just a reminder, we're looking for someone who is tall, strong enough to carry Justine's body with ease, single, most likely Caucasian and wealthy — so much so that he can afford to use a three and a half grand coat to kill people in. So, keep your eyes open and good hunting.'

As everyone got up to start work on their actions, Wise headed back to his office. Sitting behind his desk, he took out his phone and tried to call Heer again but, as before, she didn't pick up.

Wise found her DS' number next. This time, the call was answered in seconds.

'Yeah?' Murray said.

'It's Wise.'

'Look, this isn't a good time to chat,' Murray replied. 'Why—'

'I was supposed to meet your DCI this morning,' Wise said before Murray could continue. 'She didn't show up.'

'Yeah.'

'What's going on?'

'She's gone missing is what's going on. No one's seen or heard from the boss since last night. I'm at her place now and there's been a struggle.'

'Shit.' Wise stood up and walked over to his window to peer down onto Kennington Road. 'You think she's been taken?'

'Someone tried to grab her at least,' Murray replied. 'Maybe she got away and is lying low somewhere but, if that was the case, she would've called for help by now. So, yeah, we think she'd been snatched.' He didn't say what the other alternative was. He didn't have to.

'You think it was Tom?'

'It could be anyone — the boss has been a copper for a long time

— but, if I was to draw up a list of people that would want to hurt her, his name would be the first one I write down.'

'What are you going to do?' Wise asked.

'If it was down to me, I'd round up every officer in the bloody Met and go kick in every door associated with that cunt of a brother of yours,' Murray said. 'But it's not.'

'If there's anything I can do ...' Wise said.

'Yeah, we'll be in touch,' Murray replied. 'Now I've got to go.'

The line went dead.

Wise put his phone down on the table, his mind replaying the conversation. It was a bold move if Tom had snatched the head of the team investigating him. Really bold. There was no way the Met would allow that to go unanswered. Tom would become public enemy number one — if he wasn't that already. They would spare no expense to hunt him down.

So why do it?

There had to be a reason.

Tom wouldn't have done it for the hell of it. Had Heer discovered something that made snatching her — killing her — a necessity?

Wise stared out his window, his eyes no longer taking in the outside world. Instead, he imagined the fear Heer must be feeling wherever they had her imprisoned — if she wasn't already dead. And Wise had no doubt that would be her final fate. No one kidnapped a DCI and just let them go.

Especially not Tom.

47

Considering the excitement everyone had felt after the DMM, Millie had to admit that the rest of the day had failed to live up to expectation. Saint Clair hadn't come up with who had bought their outrageously expensive coats yet and her team hadn't found any connection between the cold cases and the current investigation.

It was as annoying as hell. Still, she plodded on, hoping to find something that would help the team, wanting to do her bit in catching the killer.

Then, just as she was thinking about leaving to go and see the bloke at Warriner Gardens, Palmer's desk phone rang. It was an internal call and Millie's heart sank. There was only one person who could be on the other end of that line. Riddleton.

Palmer picked up the phone. 'DS Palmer. How can I help you?' God, even the way he answered the phone annoyed her. 'We'll be right down.'

Great.

Of course, Palmer jumped up out of his seat like a good little boy the moment Riddleton called. 'Come on, the boss wants us.'

With a sigh, Millie stood up and followed Palmer down to the second floor. He stayed three steps ahead of her, no doubt eager to be the one who knocked on the boss's door.

'Come in,' Riddleton called out when Palmer rapped away. He had the door open and marched in a second later, leaving Millie jogging the last bit to catch up.

'Oh good,' Riddleton said. 'Take a seat.'

'How are you, boss?' Palmer said as he sat down.

'All good here,' Riddleton replied. 'How are you, more importantly?'

'The swelling's going down but my nose hurts like hell,' Palmer said.

'I hope you are going ahead with the complaint against DS Hicks.'

'Of course, sir. The man's a drunk and doesn't belong on the force.'

Millie looked down at her feet, not wanting to be asked her opinion. From what she'd seen of Hicksy, he seemed a pretty decent bloke who'd just lost his partner of twenty-odd years. Not many people would blame him if he'd been having a few too many drinks while he was getting over that, and he had found the information about the coat.

Besides, Millie had thought about decking Palmer plenty of times. He was an irritating twat.

'How's the rest of the investigation progressing?' Riddleton asked.

Palmer ran through everything that had happened over the last twenty-four hours. 'The cold case angle seems like a blind alley to me,' he added. 'Me and Millie have wasted two days sat on our arses, blowing cobwebs off files just so Wise can turn this into another serial killer case. It's just ego if you ask me.'

Riddleton templed his fingers. 'That's what I thought. It shows poor resource management on his behalf, something we can ill afford these days on our limited resources. What about the rest of the team?'

'The one they call Brains is alright,' Palmer replied. 'A right computer nerd. Probably useless with people but he can work a keyboard. The others? Hicksy's a drunk and the other DS, Markham, fancies herself a bit. Likes being Wise's shadow. She wouldn't be worth keeping once you get rid of the fucking gorilla. As for the other two? One's a kid who doesn't know what he doesn't know, and the other one is a bit of a Johnny Try-Hard but he's alright.'

Riddleton leaned forward. 'Any signs that they're bent?'

Palmer shrugged. 'Not that I've seen so far but it's only been a week and I'm not exactly their confidant.'

'What do you think, Millie?'

Riddleton's question took her by surprise. She looked up, hoping she didn't appear too startled. 'Think?'

'Do you think Wise has any more bad apples on his team?' Riddleton asked.

'They all ... seem pretty decent to me,' Millie said.

'Well, keep your eyes open. Don't trust any of them,' Riddleton said. 'We'll have DS Hicks out soon enough and then we can bring in another one of us to help get things back on track.'

'Yes, sir,' Palmer said.

Millie just nodded and felt shit for doing even that. Maybe she should have a word with Wise and tell him what Riddleton was up to? It felt like the right thing to do but if Riddleton found out, she could kiss any hope of a career goodbye.

'Okay, you best get on,' Riddleton said, picking up some paperwork.

Dismissed, Palmer and Millie got up and headed back to MIR-One. Palmer didn't say anything, which suited Millie because she just felt sick from the whole bloody meeting. She didn't want to be anyone's spy. That's not what she signed up for.

Back at her desk, she picked up her coat. 'I'm going over to Warriner Gardens and talk to that bloke that had the coffee with the victim.'

'Do you want me to come with you?' Palmer said but he was already going through the paperwork on his desk and had no intention of moving from the warm office.

'I'm a big girl,' Millie said, her voice dripping with sarcasm. 'I think I can manage without you.'

'If you're sure,' Palmer replied, fitting AirPods in his ear.

'Wanker,' Millie muttered as she stormed out of MIR-One. Fuck him and Riddleton too.

Millie felt better when she was out of the station, even if it was pitch black already and freezing cold. It felt good being on her own for once, a feeling that only grew with every step she took down Kennington Road, away from Riddleton and Palmer.

The bus stop she needed was by the Imperial Museum and her luck was in too. Her bus was approaching just as she crossed the road. Pulling out her Oyster card, she hopped on the moment the doors opened and tapped the ticket machine before grabbing a seat on the bottom deck. Making things even better, there were only three other passengers on the bus, so she had plenty of space around her. She hated it when the bloody things were so packed she couldn't breathe.

The bus took her almost straight to Warriner Gardens, so she spent the twenty-odd minutes it took scrolling through her socials and laughing at the crap her friends were posting on Instagram. Her mate, Christina, was only a junior account executive in a PR agency but she acted like she was some big shot influencer, narrating her whole bloody life for the world to see. She was only twenty-four and yet she was already pumping her face full of shit to stay young-looking and keep her lips full.

Millie looked up and saw her reflection in the bus's window, imagining what she'd look like if she did that, and decided she was happy the way she was. Not that she could afford cosmetic surgery on a copper's salary. Then again, she wasn't sure how Christina could afford it either on what she was earning. The woman was living on credit.

That got her thinking about the victim, Justine Mayweather. Always hunting for a rich boyfriend to pay for everything. So bloody keen to settle down. Justine was probably worrying about getting old at twenty-seven, of getting passed up. Maybe she was afraid she'd have to settle for someone who was less than ideal. All stupid nonsense and it did her no good.

She still ended up dead in the river.

Poor woman.

Millie got off the bus by Battersea Park Library, crossed the road and walked up Alexandra Avenue before turning left into Warriner Gardens. Justine's apartment building was only fifteen metres ahead, so she jogged the last bit, eager to be out of the cold.

Walking into the building, Millie had the same surge of envy that she always felt there. It was the kind of place people lived in on TV shows. It was a glamorous life she'd never experience. Not unless she met a rich bloke like Justine had wanted to do.

Millie unbuttoned her coat as she headed over to the lift. She pressed the call button, and the doors opened immediately. She smiled. Her luck was definitely in. Stepping inside, she pressed the button for the fifth floor.

As the lift went up, Millie had to admit she was looking forward to chatting with Marcus Short.

How Hicksy and Palmer thought the man was gay was beyond her.

48

Wise was in his office, worrying about things he had no control over. However, there had been no updates on DCI Heer's whereabouts since his conversation with Murray earlier that day and he couldn't help but fear the worst.

Tom had to have taken her. She was leading the investigation into his criminal empire, after all. And, if he had, Heer was either already dead or soon would be. In fact, the only reason Tom would keep her alive would be because he wanted information from her. And to get that information, his brother would use any and all means possible. That meant that, if Heer was still alive, she was being tortured.

Goddamn it.

He stood up for about the thousandth time and walked over to his window. It was dark, wet and miserable out there. As he glanced down though, he saw Millie on her own, striding down the road to the bus stop. Even from that distance, he could tell she didn't look happy and wondered what had got her worked up. They'd obviously not had any luck going through the cold cases or someone would have fetched Wise from his office to share the good news.

He'd not heard from Hannah or Hicksy either. He wasn't surprised, though, as his gut told him that checking staff at Green was going to be yet another dead end. Maybe he should call them back and stop wasting their time. But to do what when they got here? He hated to admit it, but his team were running out of avenues of inquiry. This damn Mystery Man had left them fuck all to go on — apart from the coat.

He picked up his phone and rang Hicksy.

'Guv,' the DS said.

'Hicksy,' Wise replied. 'How are you getting on over there?'

'We've got nothing. There's no one here that even comes close to our killer's profile. To be honest, most of the people look like pretentious, unemployed art students. There's no hidden millionaires lurking among them.'

Wise puffed out his cheeks. 'I thought as much. What about the coat people? Have they got back to you yet?'

'Not yet but I'll give them a bell now and chase.'

'Cheers. Let me know how you get on.'

'Will do.'

Wise ended the call and returned to his chair. He pulled his laptop closer and opened up Donut's compilation video of Justine coming and going from Warriner Gardens. He'd watched it a few times and nothing had jumped out at him, but what was the harm in looking again? It was something to do at least.

He hit play and sat back and watched.

On screen, Justine walked out of the front of the building, dressed in workout gear and carrying a rucksack over one shoulder. The time stamp said it was 7:05 a.m. She returned at 8:25, clutching a coffee and a brown paper bag from Starbucks — containing her breakfast most probably. The next time she came out, it was at 9:15, wearing smart trousers and her hair tied up. A computer bag dangled from one shoulder. Off to work.

The next clip was in the evening, at 7:43. Justine walked into the building, with her computer bag — returning from the office. The entrance to the building was busier, with other residents going in and out.

He carried on watching as Justine did more or less the same thing each day, occasionally going out in the evenings but, on the whole, she stayed in at home. But that didn't make sense. She had a boyfriend. She was seeing him, spending time with him. So where was he?

Surely, if he was visiting her every day, or most days, and staying over, he'd be on the footage somewhere. But he wasn't. There were only residents going in regularly.

Only residents.

Residents.

Of course. How could he have been so bloody stupid? For someone called Wise, he could be an idiot sometimes.

The boyfriend wasn't visiting each day. He lived in the building with her. That's why Justine spent so much time at home in the leadup to the holidays.

Wise went back to the CCTV compilation, fast-forwarded past the gym trips and the mornings in general, concentrating on the times Justine went out in the evenings and when she came home. He wasn't watching her this time, though. He concentrated on anyone entering or leaving the building at the same time, looking for a tall, strong, white, single male. He discounted anyone with families or in an obvious relationship. Struck off anyone who wasn't Caucasian.

Suddenly, someone stood out. Someone who could be their man.

Wise went through the compilation again. Checking what he'd seen. Testing his theory. Growing more certain by the second.

He froze the frame on one image of the man as he was coming out of the building. Justine was just ahead of him, only her leg still in shot.

Wise got up from his desk and headed into MIR-One. It was fairly quiet. Brains and Palmer were working in one corner and Kat was at her desk, but thankfully the other people there were the ones Wise wanted.

'Lads,' he said as he walked over to Donut and Callum. 'I need your help.'

'What do you need, Guv?' Donut asked.

'Have you got pictures of all the residents at Warriner Gardens?' Wise asked.

'Yeah, like you asked,' Donut replied.

'Can I have a look at them?'

'Sure.' Donut tapped away at his keyboard, then turned the monitor so Wise could see the screen. As he did so, Callum got up from his chair so he could see as well.

'Just scroll through the pictures until I tell you to stop,' Wise said.

Donut did as he was asked, slowly clicking from one picture to the next, Wise scanning each one, waiting for one face to appear.

Mystery Man's face.

They'd gone through about thirty people before Wise told him to stop. 'Who's he?'

Donut checked his notes. 'Marcus Short. He lives in 5C.'

'What else do we have on him?' Wise asked.

'Not much. Hicksy and Palmer saw him. It says here that he has a partner, a George Meadows, but he was out of the country and not returning until ... today.'

'So we didn't do any checks on him? Not even asked where he was when Justine was murdered or anything like that?'

Donut shrugged. 'If we did, there are no notes.'

Wise turned and called over to Palmer. 'Can you come here for a sec?'

Palmer got up with a huff and a puff and took his time ambling over. 'What is it?'

Wise pointed to the picture of Marcus Short. 'I hear you and Hicksy interviewed this man.'

'Yeah. So?' Palmer grunted back.

'There's no records of what he was doing when Justine was murdered or any checks into his background on our part,' Wise said, ignoring his rudeness.

'Well, no, but he was obviously not who we're looking for.'

'How do you know that?' Wise asked.

'We're looking for someone who was shagging Justine. This bloke had a live-in boyfriend.'

'Did you meet the boyfriend?'

Suddenly, Palmer's attitude shifted as he realised he might've screwed up. 'No. He was ... he was out of town.'

'Brains,' Wise said. 'Can you check if there's a George Meadows registered as a resident in Warriner Gardens?'

'On it,' Brains replied. He tapped away at his computer, then leaned in to check the screen. 'Nope. No George Meadows. Nearest man of that name lives about eighteen miles away.'

Palmer went white. 'We saw a picture of Short and his boyfriend. They had their arms around each other.'

Wise ignored him. 'Brains, I want you to find out everything you can about Marcus Short, resident of 5C, Warriner Gardens.'

'Is he our man?' Brains asked.

Wise fixed his eyes on Palmer's battered face. 'I think he could be.'

Palmer's mouth fell open. 'Fuck. Millie's gone to see him. She's seeing him right now.'

'What?' Wise said.

'Someone rang her and said Short knew Justine, that they were mates. She's gone to interview him.'

'Call her now and tell her to get out of there,' Wise said.

49

Marcus Short opened the door and greeted Millie with a white-toothed smile, looking every bit like James Bond on his day off. He had an untucked long-sleeved black shirt on, open to halfway down his chest, showing off tanned skin, plus black, loose-fitting trousers and no socks or shoes. Somewhere, music was playing. Millie didn't recognise the ambient sounds, but she liked it.

'Hi,' Marcus said. 'Good to see you. Come in.'

Millie smiled as she entered the man's flat. 'I don't often get greeted like that in my line of work.'

Marcus shut the front door. 'Well, I wouldn't be so pleased to see you if you'd come to arrest me, I suppose. Can I take your coat?'

'Thank you.' Millie shrugged her overcoat off and passed it to Marcus. He took it, pressed his hand against a panel in the wall and a cupboard opened. He selected a hanger and placed the coat on it, before slipping it in amongst his other coats. He gestured to a door off the hallway. 'Come through to the living room. I've just put the kettle on.'

Walking into the living room, Millie's building envy shot up another level. It looked like it'd been put together for an interior design magazine. The brown leather sofas were a bit too masculine for her tastes but that was her only complaint. Maybe she could see why dinosaurs like Hicksy and Palmer thought he was gay, after all. No doubt they didn't believe a straight man could like home furnishings. 'I like what you've done with the place,' Millie said as she sat down on one of the sofas.

'It's just stuff I've picked up over the years,' Marcus said, walking to the other end of the room where the kitchen was located. 'Would you like tea or coffee?'

'Tea please.'

'Milk or sugar?'

'Just a splash of milk.'

Marcus opened white cupboards and pulled out two equally white mugs. Opening a jar, he found two tea bags, dropped them in the cups and then poured boiling water from a white, beautifully designed kettle. It wasn't the sort of thing you'd find in IKEA.

Marcus ambled back a minute later, clutching the two mugs. He passed one to Millie. 'I hope I didn't put too much milk in it for you.'

She looked down at the caramel-coloured drink and smiled. 'No, it's perfect.'

Marcus sat next to her on the sofa. 'Now, what can I help you with?'

Millie had to shift in her seat so she could look at him properly. 'It's just a follow up really. I know you spoke to two of my colleagues, DS Hicks and DS Palmer …'

'I spoke to two detectives, but I couldn't tell you their names,' Marcus replied. 'I'm terrible at remembering these things. I know one of them had a broken nose and the other was rather grumpy looking.'

'Yes, that's them.' Millie stifled a smile. 'Anyway, as I mentioned when I called, someone said they'd seen you having coffee with Justine …'

Marcus made an awkward grimace. 'Yes, but it wasn't really like I was having coffee with her. We shared a table for about two minutes.

That's all. I didn't even know her name. She was just someone I smiled at whenever I saw her in the building.'

'But did you talk about anything with Justine?'

'I might have made a comment about the coffee or the weather. Or moaned about nothing working in the building. That sort of thing, you know, but I can't really remember. I like keeping myself to myself most of the time. Small talk kills me.'

'I'm the same,' Millie replied. 'People ask "how are you?" but they're never listening to the answer. They're just words people are expected to say.'

Marcus held out his mug to clink Millie's in agreement. 'Exactly. Why bother?'

Millie sipped her tea. The man was charming. 'Did you run into Justine apart from the coffee shop?'

'Of course, we lived in the same building. I think she was on the floor above me. We'd nod at each other in the lift and stuff like that. She didn't tell me anything that would help your case, though, I'm afraid.'

'What did you think of her?'

'Think of her? Hmm. She seemed nice. Good-looking — but not like you.'

Millie felt herself blush. 'What do you mean by that?'

'Oh God, I haven't put my foot in it, have I?' He cringed. 'Sorry if that was inappropriate. I just meant she was good-looking in a fairly obvious way. You're far more elegant. People would photograph Justine whereas they'd want to paint or sculpt you.' Marcus held up his hands. 'Sorry, it's the artist in me. Again, no offence.'

Millie smiled. 'None taken. It's very flattering of you. What type of artist are you?'

'I paint,' Marcus replied. He nodded towards the hallway. 'That's one of mine over there. It's the only one, though. It's a bit naff to have your own work hanging on the walls.'

'I don't know,' Millie said. 'If I could paint like that, I'd have them every—'

Her phone rang, interrupting her. Putting her cup of tea down, she took her mobile out of her trouser pocket and checked the screen. It was Palmer. Well, sod him. She declined the call.

Almost immediately, he rang again. She declined the call again.

'If you need to take that ...' Marcus said.

'It's just a colleague who's been driving me mad. Whatever it is, it can wait.'

Her phone rang again. This time the caller ID said WISE. 'Oh, this is my boss,' Millie said, looking up. 'I'm sorry. I have to take this.'

Marcus smiled. 'Go ahead.'

'I'll just go into the hallway,' she said, standing up and answering the phone. 'Guv.'

'Millie,' Wise said. 'Just give me yes and no answers if you can.'

Millie stopped, surprised by the seriousness in Wise's voice, then forced herself to walk into the corridor. 'Yes, I can do that.'

'Are you with Marcus Short right now?' Wise asked. He was in a car by the sounds of it. Moving fast. She could hear the siren wailing.

'Yes.'

'Okay, I want you to tell him I need you back at the station as another case has come in and get out of there as quickly as you can. We're heading over now. We'll meet you around the corner in Alexandra Avenue.'

A chill ran through Millie. 'Yes. Okay. I'll see you back at the station.'

'Call me back the moment you're clear of the building,' Wise said. 'We're on our way.'

'Bye, Guv,' Millie replied and ended the call. She turned, calling out as she did so. 'I'm sorry but my boss wants me back— Oh!' Millie jumped back in shock. Marcus was standing a foot away from her. 'You startled me there.'

'Is everything okay?' he asked, all the humour gone from his eyes.

'Just a new case that's come in. The boss says it's all hands on deck.' God, even Millie didn't think she sounded convincing. 'I've got to go.' She turned, looking for the coat cupboard. 'I just need my coat.' She fumbled along the wall, found the door, pressed it and it popped open. 'Sorry. Sorry.'

Millie reached and started moving coats along the rail, looking for hers. She moved a black coat with a hood, saw the white letters on the inside of the collar. SAINT CLAIR. She stiffened, all doubt gone about why Wise wanted her out of Marcus's flat.

A hand grabbed her hair, yanking her back off her feet.

50

Hannah waited outside Green's offices on Dean Street while Hicksy made a call. She had her bike with her, but she was regretting that decision now. Her headache was back with a vengeance and the street and car lights were only making it worse. Blinking furiously, she turned her back to the road and popped two more paracetamol and codeine tablets out of the blister pack in her pocket.

Hannah turned so her back was to Hicksy, then dry swallowed them, wincing at the taste. She'd taken too many that day and was taking too many in general. So much so, that she'd started buying boxes from different chemists around both where she lived and the nick. After all, she didn't want anyone else knowing she had a problem. It was bad enough she knew.

But it was only temporary, she told herself. She'd stop once she got better.

Her phone rang. It was Wise.

'Where are you?' he said before she could say anything herself. His voice sounded rushed.

'We're just finishing up at Green's,' she replied. 'Is something happening?'

'I think our killer is a resident at Warriner Gardens,' Wise said. 'A man named Marcus Short. I'm just driving over there now with Palmer, Callum and Donut.'

'Do you want us to head over too?'

'Yeah. Millie was talking to him in his flat when we found out. I told her to get out and meet us around the corner. She was supposed to call us the moment she was clear, but we've not heard anything. Now she's not picking up.'

'That's not good.'

'Yeah,' Wise replied. 'We're on our way but we're still about ten minutes out.'

'And we're on the wrong side of the river. Shit,' Hannah said. 'But I've got my bike. Maybe I can beat you there.' She was already thinking of the route. If she cut down The Mall and then past Buckingham Palace ... Really opened up the throttle ...

'Don't do anything stupid,' Wise said, as if reading her thoughts.

'I won't, Guv. See you there.'

Hannah slipped her phone back in her pocket and turned to see Hicksy coming towards her.

'You'll never guess who bought one of those coats,' he said. 'The fucker lives below Justine.'

'Marcus Short,' Hannah replied. She put her helmet on while Hicksy stared at her open mouthed. 'Wise just called. They know it's him. They're on their way there now.'

'You heading over there?'

'Yeah, Millie was with Short earlier and now they can't get hold of her. They need everyone at Warriner Gardens as quickly as possible.'

'Fuck.'

'See you there?'

'Yeah.'

Hannah went to go to her bike, but Hicksy grabbed her arm. 'Be careful, eh?'

They locked eyes, then Hannah nodded. 'I will.'

'Go then.' He let go of her arm then and Hannah ran for her

Ducati, her head pounding with the beat of her heart. Shit. Why did this have to happen now when she was in such a state?

Climbing on her bike, memories of the ambush played through her mind, of Sarah being dragged from the car, of them coming for her. She thought about Jono being buried, of Sarah's body still in a morgue somewhere, waiting for permission to be released.

Hannah wasn't going to let Millie end up like them.

No way.

51

'Why the hell did you let her go there alone?' Wise said as he accelerated down the Albert Embankment towards Vauxhall. He had the blues and twos flashing away and his siren wailing but it was 5 p.m. on a Tuesday and the whole world and their mother were trying to get home. The road was jammed.

'She was just going to get a follow up statement,' Palmer said in the seat next to him. 'How the hell was I supposed to know he was the bloody killer?'

'For fuck's sake, you're her bloody partner,' Wise snarled back. 'You're so busy telling everyone else how to do their job, you forgot the basics yourself.' He swerved the Mondeo into the bus lane, and, for a few glorious moments, he had a clear stretch to charge down.

'I would've gone with her if I'd known,' Palmer muttered back but the man's words had no fight in them and Wise didn't push the point further. Palmer knew he'd screwed up. The shit could hit the fan about his conduct later after they got Millie back safely.

'Callum, call Millie,' Wise said. 'See if she's out yet.'

'Yeah, Guv,' Callum replied from the back seat. He had Donut next to him. Wise had brought the pair of them just in case things got hairy down there. He'd rather have too many people than not enough.

As Callum made the call, Wise spotted two buses up ahead, blocking his way. The main lanes were still bumper to bumper, giving him no option to go that way, but then he spotted a petrol station next to the road.

Wise accelerated, closing the gap on the buses in seconds, then, at the last minute, he swung the car left, powering into the station forecourt, hoping his siren would make any pedestrian get out of his way. He lost his left wingmirror clipping a black cab that was filling up with diesel, and then steered the car back into the bus lane, having overtaken the two double-deckers that had been in his way.

'She's not picking up,' Callum called from the back. 'It went to voice mail.'

'Shit,' Wise spat as he turned left onto Lambeth Place and went under the train tracks, forcing the Mondeo across four lanes and through a red light to get onto South Lambeth Road. They were still going too slowly though. 'Palmer, call for back up. Maybe there's a patrol car nearby. We need to get bodies there now.'

Palmer grabbed the radio mic. 'Calling all units. Urgent assistance required. Officer in possible danger,' he said and rattled off the address. 'Suspect is a Marcus Short. He is believed armed and dangerous. Approach with caution.'

'This is Yankee Two Zero Delta,' a young man's voice came back. 'I'm one minute from that location.'

'Be warned: the suspect is wanted for two murders. We believe he has DC Millie Buchanan with him.'

'Are there any firearms on the premises?' the police officer asked over the radio.

'We have no reason to believe that,' Palmer replied. 'But take all precautions.'

'Roger that. Pulling up outside the building now.'

52

Marcus Short didn't understand how everything had gone wrong, but he knew that it had. He'd known the moment the police officer had got the phone call. One minute she was batting her eyelashes at him like they all did and the next she couldn't get out of his flat quick enough.

And, if he'd had any doubts whatsoever, the way she'd reacted when she saw his coat was all the confirmation he needed.

He grabbed her by the back of her hair and hauled her off her feet. 'Stupid girl,' he said as he dragged back into the living room, her feet kicking out, leaving scuff marks on his nice, clean floor. 'Watch what you're doing.'

Marcus threw her against one of the sofas and she hit it with a thump, before collapsing on the floor in a heap. He curled his lip in disgust. What a mess. And to think he'd been attracted to *her*.

Millie looked up, eyes already wet with tears. 'Please, just let me go. I promise I won't say anything.'

It took everything he had not to kick her. Maybe if he was wearing shoes, he would've. Kicked her and stamped on her. She'd made him that angry. 'Your colleagues — are they on their way here?'

'No, no,' Millie said, sniffing up snot. 'They just told me ... told me to go back to ... to the station.'

'Liar! You're a liar,' he shouted. 'I hate liars. Claire was a liar. She did nothing but lie, lie, lie until I had no choice but to strangle her. Do you want me to do that to you?'

'Please, just let me go,' Millie said, shivering away. 'I—'

He threw his teacup at her. It was a good shot too, catching her on the forehead despite her attempt to duck. The mug shattered on impact and Marcus was glad to see he'd drawn blood as well as hopefully knocking some sense into her.

He jabbed a finger in her direction. 'Stay there and be quiet.'

Millie, for once, did as she was told.

Marcus marched into his bedroom, grabbing a holdall and throwing clothes into it. Why hadn't he planned for this? Been prepared? It was so unlike him. But the truth was he'd never ever thought the police would suspect him.

He shook his head. He'd been too confident.

Marcus had enjoyed having Millie around this afternoon. Enjoyed flirting with her. Why, he'd even considered asking her out, thinking what fun it would be to date a police officer who had no idea what he was really like.

Well, she was going to find out now, alright.

He put shoes on and, carrying the holdall, headed back into the living room, stopping on the way to pick up a nice, big, sharp kitchen knife. 'Get to your feet,' he told Millie, letting her see the blade.

Using the sofa to help her, Millie did as she was ordered. She glared at Marcus though, trying to act defiant, trying to show her hate for him, but he could see the real emotion in her eyes.

The fear. He loved seeing the fear.

'The hallway,' he said, motioning her towards it with the knife.

'Where are we going?' she asked.

'We're going on a little car ride,' Marcus said. 'Now, if we see anyone on the way, I want you to pretend that we're just a happy couple on their way out. Say anything, do anything contrary to that, and I'll shove this knife in one side and out the other. Understand?'

Millie sobbed and Marcus took that as a yes.

When they reached the front door, he realised he needed a free hand. 'Carry the bag.'

When Millie took it off him, he had to smile. She was already following his orders like a good little dog. 'Open the door,' he said, holding onto her arm just in case she thought about running, knife ready to strike if she did so.

'This ... this is a mistake,' she said but he ignored her and marched her out into the hallway and down to the lift. He pressed the call button but saw the lift was already in motion. Already heading up.

A shiver of fear ran through him. 'Is that them?' He snarled at Millie. 'Are your friends in the lift?'

'I ... I don't ... I don't know,' she whimpered back.

The lift was on the third floor. Fourth.

He couldn't risk it. 'This way,' he said, dragging her towards the stairs. They were halfway to them when he heard the ping of the lift arriving. Heard the doors open.

'You there!' a man called out. 'Stop! Police.'

53

By the time Wise pulled up alongside the patrol car outside Warriner Gardens, five minutes had passed since the officer had arrived on the scene. Five long minutes and they still couldn't reach Millie or get an update from the unnamed officer. Yankee Zero Delta wasn't answering his radio either.

'Callum, stay down here. The rest of you with me,' Wise said as he swung the car door open and then he was sprinting into the building without waiting for any sort of answer. He raced over to the lift. As he did so, he spotted the stairwell to his right, a red glowing exit sign above it. 'Donut, take the stairs. And be careful.'

Wise and Palmer entered the lift and Wise hit the button for the fifth floor. As it began to climb, he hoped that he'd not find another dead team member waiting for him. How could Millie have gone off like that without anyone with her? How could Palmer let her go?

But he knew why.

Everyone had too much to do with too little resources. It was easy to cut corners and not follow standard procedures — and it was always the police officer's life that got put at risk. It was like the uniform who'd answered their call for help. He was on his own too.

When Wise had joined the Met, that would never have happened. Police officers used to always travel in pairs.

Everyone needed someone covering their back. But not now. The Met couldn't afford it.

The lift climbed to the fourth floor, then the fifth.

It stopped. Both men heard the ding announcing its arrival. The doors opened.

'Shit,' Wise said, seeing the body on the floor. Blood pooled out across the floor. He rushed over, praying the poor sod was still alive and wished he'd asked the uniformed officer for his name when he'd answered Wise's call for help.

Palmer got on the radio. 'We need an ambulance urgently,' he said. 'Officer down and critical. Repeat, officer down and critical.'

Wise turned the uniformed officer over, searching for the wound and found it. Dark blood bubbled out of a wound in his neck. He checked the man's wrist, searching for a pulse, noting how pale he was and how much blood had already leaked out of him. For a moment, he could not feel anything except the man's cold skin. 'Come on. Don't die on me,' he whispered. But ... no ... wait. There it was. Faint, but a heartbeat all the same.

He looked up at Palmer. 'He's still alive. Try and keep him that way. I'm going into the apartment.'

'Go,' Palmer said.

With blood over his suit and staining his hands, Wise ran into Short's flat. Would he find Millie dead in there?

The layout of the flat was identical to Justine's on the floor above which helped Wise move quickly, checking each room, looking for Millie's body.

Thank God, it wasn't there and there was no sign of Short either. Wise ran back out to the main corridor. The uniform must've turned up just as Short was leaving with Millie. Did they take the lift — no, there was a bloody handprint by the stairs. Short must've gone that way.

Wise yanked the door open and ran into the emergency stairwell. He peered down the central well, looking for Short and Millie, looking for Donut too. He didn't see anyone, but he heard footsteps, heard voices — a man telling someone to hurry up.

'Donut!' Wise called down, his voice echoing in the stairwell. 'They're on the stairs. Coming down to you. Watch out, he's armed.'

'I'll get him, Guv!' Donut called back.

Wise took the stairs down himself, moving fast, jumping down two or three steps at a time, his right hand on the banister, using it to help keep his balance. Down and down he went, around and around.

'Stop, police!' Donut shouted from somewhere below. 'Ow, fuck!'

Wise picked up his pace, imagining the worst. He reached the third floor, the second. He jumped from step to step, his heavy weight crashing down each time like an out-of-control boulder eager to reach the ground.

Wise found Donut just after the first-floor landing. He clutched his side, where blood leaked through his fingertips.

'Sorry, Guv,' he said.

'Are you okay?' Wise asked.

'It's just a scratch,' Donut replied. 'Looks worse than it is. Go after him. He has Millie. He's gone to ... the parking lot.'

Wise ran on. Down the stairs, past the ground floor, his heart racing. He had to stop Short, rescue Millie. Two officers were already injured, one critically. He couldn't let any more join that list. Couldn't let anyone else join Andy, Jono and Sarah. Die because of him.

Wise reached the parking level. A grey steel door greeted him with a white 'P' painted on it. He pulled it open and sprinted through, his footsteps echoing around him, his ghosts keeping pace.

But there was no sign of Short and Millie. No sign at all.

Shit. Had the man gone out through the ground floor exit after all? Should he go back ...

No. They were down there. Wise could feel it. He walked slower now, looking for his quarry, wary of an attack. The man had a knife and Wise only had his fists.

There was enough florescent light to see by, but not enough to banish the shadows that filled the corners and lurked behind the pillars. Cars occupied most of the spaces, providing even more places to hide.

Which car was Short's? Maybe that's what he was after down there.

Wise checked the numbers under the cars nearest the stairwell. They belonged to the first floor on the left, the second on the right. The fifth floor's spaces should be the third block of cars along then, on the left.

He started to move quicker, watching the apartment numbers, checking the shadows, looking for—

An engine roared to life up ahead, lights blazing bright. It accelerated out of its spot, wheels spinning as it turned, leaping forwards, coming straight for Wise. He froze on the spot, dazzled by the headlights, then the car turned, heading for the exit ramp, leaving Wise blinking and blinded. As his vision came back all blurred, he ran after the car, chasing its red rear lights, pulling his radio out of his pocket as he did so.

'Calling all units. Suspect is fleeing in a grey Tesla Model 3, heading up ramp to exit the building. He has Millie with him. Repeat, he has Millie with him,' Wise said as he ran. He rattled off the registration numbers. 'Someone bloody stop him.'

Because it wasn't going to be Wise as he watched the Tesla accelerate up the ramp and out of the street, leaving him far behind.

54

Hannah turned into Warriner Gardens, grateful to still be alive. The journey from Soho had been a nightmare. The myriad of lights that illuminated London at night had played havoc on her headache and caused her vision to blur on more than one occasion, making it impossible to tell what was what. And the more she'd struggled to see, the worse her concentration had got.

In the end, she'd had to reduce her speed just to have any hope of joining the others, promising herself on the way that, if she did make it, she'd see a doctor about what was wrong. There was no way she could pretend she was fit to work anymore, no matter how many pills she popped to get through the day.

As she approached Justine's apartment building, she saw Wise's Mondeo parked up next to a marked patrol car, its doors open and blue lights still flashing. Callum was next to it, radio in hand, looking worried.

Hannah stopped the Ducati beside him. 'What's going on?'

'The governor's inside chasing the bastard, but he's already stabbed a uniform and Donut's been cut up bad too. He—'

'Calling all units,' Wise's voice boomed out through the radio. 'Suspect is fleeing in a grey Tesla Model 3, heading up ramp to exit the building. He has Millie with him. Repeat, he has Millie with him.' Wise called out the registration numbers. 'Someone bloody stop him.'

Just then, Hannah and Callum both heard a screech of tires and turned as a car leaped out of the apartment building's car park and swerved a hard right into the street. It was Short's car.

Hannah didn't think. She just gunned the Ducati and charged after it. There was no way she was going to let that bastard get away, especially with Millie.

The road was narrow with cars parked on either side, restricting Short's options, and Hannah closed the gap quickly, her bike's engine far more powerful than anything the Tesla could offer. And thankfully, the streetlamps were few and far between, helping her focus.

Anger surged through her as she accelerated again, drawing so close that she could almost touch the corner of Short's car. How the fuck was she going to stop it though? She had her expandable baton in her jacket pocket. Maybe if she could get that, she could use it to smash his window ...

She looked up. Saw a junction fast approaching. Saw the stop signs. Saw cars driving in both directions across their path ...

Hannah engaged her brakes as the world switched into slow motion. Her speed dropped down rapidly as she used her whole body to keep the bike upright and not let it go into a skid, while the Tesla shot forward, still charging towards the junction. Hannah saw the cars travelling along Alexandra Avenue, oblivious to the maniac about to cut across their path. She wanted to shout a warning, but she was still braking, still slowing, only too aware that she might not stop in time either.

The Tesla was halfway across the junction when an SUV struck it on the passenger's side, crumpling metal, sending both into spins. They both hit more cars, coming from every direction. Glass exploded everywhere as the noise of each impact echoed back and forth across the street.

In Hannah's mind, she also saw her own car crash, being hit by that bloody van and the monsters within it. She could feel the impact in her bones, feel the fear rising in her gut, hear the voice telling her to run away.

But she couldn't. She climbed off her Ducati, her eyes fixed on the suspect's car, still moving in slow motion, praying that Millie was alright and, if anyone was hurt in that tangle of metal, it was Short.

By the time everything stopped moving, Hannah counted six cars all crunched together in an unholy mess, with Short's Tesla at its epicentre. Crash bags filled the windscreens of all the cars, making it impossible to tell who was hurt and who wasn't, but Hannah had seen enough accidents to know that it would take a miracle for everyone involved to walk away unhurt.

Then the driver's door of the Tesla opened as far as it could. It smacked against the side of a Fiesta wedged into the front corner of the car and Hannah only hoped that Short would be too trapped to get out but life didn't give a shit about her hopes. Of course it opened just enough.

Hannah started to run towards the Tesla as a man climbed out, bleeding from a cut on his forehead, and clutching a kitchen knife in his other hand. It had to be Short. He staggered as he dragged his body out of the wreckage, his eyes already searching for a way to escape.

'Stop! Police!' Hannah shouted as she charged towards him, using her momentum to cancel her fear. He turned to face her as Hannah jumped onto the bonnet of the Fiesta. She saw the knife come up as she launched herself at him, screaming with as much fury as fear.

She hit him hard, knocking him back into the Tesla, bending him over what was left of the bonnet. He might've cried out, but Hannah couldn't tell. She was too busy punching the bastard in the mouth. He went down, all but dragging her down too, but Hannah found her feet, steadied herself. Short had dropped the knife so Hannah kicked it out of reach as she spun him around. She yanked his arms behind him, then dropped her knee and all her weight into his back. He definitely cried out that time and it was bloody lovely to hear. Hannah was smiling as she handcuffed the bastard's hands together.

With Short secured, she looked up and into the Tesla, saw Millie sitting upright, eyes open but clearly dazed. 'Are you hurt?' Hannah shouted. 'Are you hurt?'

Millie shook her head and that was all Hannah needed to know right then. Thank God.

Reassured, she leaned over Short and spoke clearly and slowly into his ear. 'Marcus Short, I am arresting you for the murders of Justine Mayweather and Mark Temple. You do not have to say anything, but it may harm your defence if you do not mention when questioned something you later relay in court. Anything you do say may be given in evidence.'

55

Once again, Wise stood outside a flat in Warriner Gardens, dressed in a white forensic suit, waiting to be invited in to have a look around. Hicksy and Hannah were with him and in no hurry to go home despite the lateness of the hour.

Martin Short had been taken off to hospital to have his injuries seen to before he could be taken to Brixton to be formally charged and interviewed. Millie and the drivers of the other cars were being checked over but Wise was pleased to hear that, apart from being banged about by the crash, the young DC was relatively unhurt.

The same couldn't be said for the uniformed officer who'd answered Wise's call for help. PC Thomas Simpson was in critical condition and word was it was unlikely he'd make it through the night.

Donut, on the other hand, had only needed a half dozen stitches for his knife injury. The lad had been lucky, and Wise would be eternally grateful for that.

He glanced over at Hannah. 'I know I keep asking you and you always say no, but are you sure you don't want to go home? Get some rest? You've certainly done enough to warrant heading off.'

Hannah smiled. 'Don't get me wrong, Guv. I definitely need some time off after this and, maybe, I came back to work a bit too soon after everything that happened a few weeks back, but there is no way I'm leaving you now.' She nodded towards the open door of Short's apartment. 'Not until someone comes out of there and tells us we've got enough to lock that bastard away for the rest of his natural.'

'Even without Justine and Mark's murders, Short's definitely going to prison — for the ... attempted murder of PC Simpson and kidnapping Millie,' Wise replied. 'But we'll have more than that, I promise you. Brains is already going through the cold cases to see if any can be linked to him.'

Hicksy shook his head. 'I'm sorry I fucked up when I interviewed him, Guv. My head wasn't on straight, and I made assumptions that were bang out of order.'

'You had a lot going on, mate,' Wise replied. 'Maybe it was too soon for you to come back to work as well.'

'Still, there was a time I would've spotted that wanker's bullshit for what it was,' Hicksy said.

'You weren't on your own when you interviewed him,' Wise said. 'Let's save the pity party for later. We've got a result tonight. Let's concentrate on making sure all his victims get justice and we can worry later about what we could've done better.'

'Alright. Sounds fair.' Hicksy didn't look convinced though and Wise hoped he wasn't going to beat himself up too badly over what happened. He wasn't sure any of the team had been particularly on the ball with this case, himself included.

A SOCO emerged from Short's apartment. They pulled down their hood and removed their mask. 'Inspector,' Helen Kelly said, with a smile.

'Good to see you again,' Wise replied. 'Please tell me his flat's not as spotless as Justine's?'

'No, it's not, but it's close. The man's a clean freak, that's for sure.'

'Please tell me you've got some good news.'

Helen gave her eyebrows a little wiggle. 'I can do better than that. I can show you.'

'Really?' Wise said, feeling a sudden surge of excitement.

'Hoods up, masks on, keep to the treads,' Helen said. 'And follow me.'

Doing as they were told, the three detectives followed Helen back into the flat. She led them through to the bedroom. Helen stopped in the doorway though. 'As you'll remember from Justine's flat, there are two built-in wardrobes on the far wall. What I'm going to show you is in the second of those wardrobes.'

'Curiouser and curiouser,' Wise said.

Helen nodded towards the bedroom. 'This way.'

The bedroom was very different from Justine's in every way. It was very masculine, with the walls painted a dark grey, with matching grey bedsheets and a steel bedside table. There was a small picture frame on the table. Wise glanced down and saw a picture of a grey-haired woman smiling at the camera. 'His mother?'

'Perhaps,' Helen replied. 'Whoever it is, he obviously likes her a lot. There's a better picture in here.' She walked over to the far wardrobe and opened it. 'I give you Marcus Short's shrine, Inspector.' Helen stepped aside so the detectives could see what was within.

A portrait in an ornate gold frame hung from the wall. It was of the same grey-haired woman. There was a small table underneath it with gold jewellery neatly arranged along its surface. There was a watch, two bracelets, a necklace with a locket attached and some rings.

'It's definitely a shrine,' Wise said.

'If I was to make a guess, I'd say the woman is his mother as you suggested. With that in mind, and going by the very old-fashioned nature of the bling here, I'd say the jewellery is hers as well.'

'Creepy, but how does that help us?'

Putting the locket back, Helen reached underneath the tabletop, pressed something and a hidden drawer popped open. 'My team found this.'

Helen pulled the drawer out. Inside were more items of jewellery. However, the pieces were very different from the ones openly displayed above. Wise was no expert, but some looked very expensive indeed whereas others looked like they cost no more than a fiver. Still, he couldn't help but smile when he saw them. 'Trophies.'

'Looks like it,' Kelly said.

'Okay. I don't need to tell you how to do your job, Helen, but we need to be really careful with these. If there's any DNA from their owners still on them, we could match them to any bodies we've found over the years.'

'Christ,' Hannah said, peering over his shoulder. 'How many women has he killed?'

Wise glanced back at her. 'Too many.'

Wednesday 11th January

56

Wise only managed to get a few hours' sleep before he had to return to Kennington. Despite that, he felt energised. Not only did they have Marcus Short under arrest, he'd received news first thing that PC Thomas Simpson's condition had stabilised and the doctors were now feeling hopeful that he was out of danger. As far as he was concerned, things couldn't get better than that.

Marcus Short had also been checked over by doctors and they'd given the okay to take Short to Brixton nick around 5 that morning. They had already formally charged the man with the kidnapping of Millie and the attempted murder of PC Simpson, so no one had to worry about the custody clock ticking down while they went through everything they'd found at Short's flat and his electronic devices. In particular, Forensics could take their time processing any DNA they found from Short's souvenirs. Hopefully, they could then link him beyond doubt to Justine's murder and any others he had committed. Considering the SOCOS had found fourteen different sets of jewellery, Wise expected the man's final murder tally to be high.

However, he was painfully aware he'd not updated Riddleton on anything that had happened and, considering it had been one of his people that Short had kidnapped, Wise had no idea how that meeting would go. Knowing Riddleton, Wise was sure he'd find something to complain about.

And, of course, there was no news from SCO10 about Heer.

He was still ten minutes away from the station when his phone rang. Caller ID said the call was coming from Kennington.

'Wise,' he said on answering.

'Hi, Guv, it's Kat — from the station,' the voice said, as if Wise wouldn't recognise her Yorkshire bur.

'Hi, Kat. Is everything okay?'

'Er ... I think so but Detective Chief Superintendent Walling has asked that you go straight up to his office when you get in,' Kat said.

'Sure. Can you let him know I'm nearly at the station?'

'Will do and ... er ... you'll see when you get here but just so you know — the press are outside,' Kat said. 'They're asking about last night's arrest.'

'Now I know why Walling wants to see me,' Wise replied. 'Hey, I hate to ask but could you do me a massive favour?'

'Er... depends what it is,' Kat replied, but he could hear her smiling.

'Can you go to Luigi's and get me an espresso? I'll give you the money when I get in, but I have a feeling I'm going to need the caffeine if I'm going to get through this morning.'

Kat laughed. It was a lovely sound. Warm and genuine. 'It'll be my pleasure, Guv.'

'And get yourself one too, if you want.'

'I'm not into coffee but you might treat me to a cake if I see anything nice.'

'It'll be a pleasure,' Wise said and ended the call.

In many ways he wasn't surprised that the press found out. The mass pile up at the Warriner Gardens and Alexandra Avenue junction would've been enough to get their attention, not to mention everyone being taken off to hospital and then there was an officer in critical condition.

He only hoped no one had been talking to them. It was exactly the salacious type of story they'd love — a serial killer hunting single women — and an officer would make a few quid selling inside information. Then he remembered the promise he'd made to the solicitors at Sparks after they'd refused to help him. They were lucky that Justine had met Short in her apartment building and not through their app. Otherwise, Wise would've been tempted to leak a bit of inside knowledge himself.

Sure enough, when he got to the station, he had to wait for uniformed officers, drafted in from Brixton no doubt, to clear a path for him to enter the car park. From what he could see, everyone was there from the BBC to LBC.

Camera flashes chased him to the car park and the uniforms had their work cut out for them as they stopped the reporters from swarming in as well.

'Inspector!' they called out. 'Inspector!'

'Did you catch the killer, Inspector?'

'How many women did he kill?'

'Inspector!'

Wise just kept his head down and marched into the station. Kat was waiting for him in the reception area, espresso in hand. 'Kat, you're a life saver.'

'I do my best, Guv, and thanks for the cornetti,' Kat replied. 'It was lovely.'

Wise had the lid off the espresso before he'd got one foot on the stairs up and he'd drunk it before he'd reached the first landing. 'God, I needed that. Are the troops in yet?'

'The ones that aren't all bashed up and bleeding are,' Kat replied.

'Great. Get everyone helping Brains in matching Short with any of the old cases. And make sure Forensics fast track the DNA checks on the trophies we found last night.'

'Will do,' Kat said. 'And good luck with the big cheese upstairs.'

Wise smiled. 'Appreciated.'

Leaving Kat, Wise made his way to Walling's office on the top floor. The door was closed so Wise knocked.

'Come in,' Walling boomed from the other side.

If Wise's office at the back of MIR-One was a shoebox, Walling's was a palace. Not only was his desk twice the size, but it was old in a 'valuable antique' kind of way rather than the 'it needs to be thrown on a skip' type of old like Wise's.

There was also room for a sofa and two armchairs set up around a coffee table and Wise noted there was a tray with a coffee pot and two cups on it.

Walling, in full uniform, rose from behind the desk. 'Simon. It's good to see you. I hear you've had quite the start to the new year.' He waved towards the sofa. 'Take a seat.'

'Thank you, sir,' Wise replied, just a little confused. There had been occasions when Walling hadn't let him even sit on one of the normal guest chairs, let alone on the sofa. 'And yes, it's been quite the start.'

Wise sat on the sofa while Walling perched on one of the armchairs. 'Coffee?'

'Oh right, yes.' Wise reached over to pick up the pot, but Walling brushed him away.

'I'll be mother,' Walling said as he poured coffee into the two cups. 'Milk? Sugar?'

Wise shook his head. 'Black's fine.'

'Before you tell me about last night,' Walling said. 'I need to update you about DCI Heer.' Walling was one of the few senior officers who knew about SCO10's investigation into Wise's brother, Tom. 'It's not good news, I'm afraid.'

'No?'

'No. As you know, she was taken early yesterday morning from her home, and we've not heard a word since. We've had troops on the streets searching for her. We've spoken to every informant we have. We've even raided some of your brother's businesses and clubs, but everyone has come up empty-handed. We've not even found anything illegal in any of his premises to charge anyone with possession of a Class C substance. It's like he cleared everywhere out before he snatched her.' Walling paused to take a sip of his coffee. 'I don't have to tell you we're more than concerned for DCI Heer's safety.'

'I suppose there's no doubt Tom took her?' Wise asked.

'We're looking at other possibilities, but no one seriously thinks anyone else is responsible.'

'But why now? Taking Heer escalates things to a whole new level.'

'No one knows but, as I'm sure you can imagine, people are nervous about your involvement, Simon.'

'I—'

Walling held up a hand. 'I know you haven't leaked information to your brother, but the timing doesn't look good. After all, we showed you all that we knew a few weeks ago and the next thing we know, your brother has taken the person running that very investigation.'

'Please believe me, I haven't—'

'I do believe you,' Walling said, cutting him off again. 'If I didn't, you'd be in handcuffs right now. But have you told anyone — said anything to anyone that could've got back to your brother?'

A memory of eating curry with his father, the two of them talking about Tom, flashed through Wise's mind. Christ, had he caused all of this? Was he responsible? He shook the thought away. He'd been vague enough. 'No, I haven't.'

'That's good,' Walling replied. 'For the moment, though, I'm afraid we can't have you involved like we hoped.'

Walling's words felt like a punch in the gut, but he didn't blame Walling for making that decision, especially if something he — or Jean — had said to his father had made its way back to Tom. 'I understand.'

'Good. Now tell me about this case you've been working on.'

Wise told the Chief Super everything, leaving nothing out, including the initial mistake when Hicksy and Palmer interviewed Short.

'We found fourteen items of jewellery that we believe belonged to women Short has killed,' Wise said in conclusion. 'We're running DNA tests on them all right now so hopefully we can match the items to their original owners.'

'Fourteen, eh? That lot out there will go wild when they hear that,' Walling said.

'I know, sir. But, if I'm being honest, we got lucky. Really lucky.'

'You know what Napoleon said. "I'd rather have lucky generals than good ones." You got a result, Simon. A good one. Let's concentrate on that, eh?' Walling said. 'In the meantime, I'll work with the press team to get a holding statement put together to keep the great unwashed press hordes at bay for a while.'

'And Hicksy, sir? He's a good copper. I don't want his career ruined because he was provoked into punching Palmer.'

Walling nodded. 'I think we can sort things out. Perhaps it might be best if he were to take some sort of stress leave for now, though.'

'Thank you, sir. I'll speak to him,' Wise said. 'Do you mind if I ask if there is any news regarding DCI Roberts?'

'Not yet. These things move slowly, Simon.'

'She saved lives doing what she did, sir.'

'No one's disputing that, Simon. But we all have rules to follow. But I'm sure everything will work out well for her too.'

'I hope so too,' Wise replied. 'I'll be much happier when she's back.'

Walling arched an eyebrow. 'Things not going well with Doug Riddleton?'

'We just have very different personalities, sir,' Wise replied with as much diplomacy as he could manage.

'Do I need to have a word with him for you?'

'No need, sir. I can handle things.'

'Good to hear,' Walling said, standing up. 'Well, I'm sure you've got plenty to be getting on with.'

Wise got to his feet. 'Yes, sir. And thank you. I appreciate the support.'

'I know we haven't always seen eye to eye, but you are doing a great job,' Walling said.

Wise nodded. Somehow, getting praise felt more difficult to accept than the various rollockings he'd received in that office. He smiled. 'Thank you, sir.'

57

When Wise walked into MIR-One, the room felt emptier than ever. Kat was there, along with Callum, Hannah and Brains but that was it. He'd told Millie to take at least a day off to recover from her ordeal and Donut wouldn't be in after getting carved up the night before, but he was surprised that Palmer and Hicksy weren't at their desks yet.

However, Wise was halfway to his office when he heard laughter from the corridor and turned to see the two detectives enter MIR-One, clutching mugs of tea and obviously in very good moods.

'Morning, you two,' Wise said.

'Guv,' Hicksy replied, whereas Palmer, despite his apparent good mood, just grunted.

Wise ignored the rudeness. 'Can I have a quick word with you in my office, Hicksy?'

'Sure,' Hicksy said. 'I wanted to have a chat with you myself.'

The two men walked together over to Wise's office. Due to its small size, Wise had to go in first and squeeze around to his side of the desk before Hicksy could enter and sit down opposite him.

'Do you want to go first?' Wise said. 'What did you want to talk to me about?'

'Well, it's like this.' Hicksy rubbed the back of his head, not meeting Wise's eyes. 'I think these last few weeks have shown that I'm not dealing with stuff like I should. I know that sounds crap, but ...'

'It's nothing to be ashamed of,' Wise replied. 'I know only too well how hard it is to lose a partner. I'm still not over Andy's death and it's been six months at least. You're doing the right thing in acknowledging you're struggling. The old ways of coping — pretending nothing's wrong, drinking yourself stupid — don't work.'

Hicksy looked up then. 'I tried the drinking thing a bit too much. It just made me feel even more shit.'

'So, what do you want to do?'

'I got the doc to sign me off for a bit. I know that leaves you short-handed, but I need to get away from here — from this place and The Job and get my head sorted.'

'Funnily enough, that's what I was going to talk to you about. I spoke to Walling earlier and he suggested you take a break. He's also going to sort out the bullshit with Palmer. Make sure he doesn't press charges.'

'That's good of the Chief Super, but I don't think Palmer's going to do that anyway. Me and him had a chat this morning. He knows he's been a dick. And that fuck up with Short? That was on both of us. He knows he's got to make up for that too.'

'Bloody hell, what time did you get in this morning to get all this done?' Wise laughed.

Hicksy shrugged. 'Turns out it's easier to get out of bed in the morning if you've not drunk a bottle of whisky the night before.'

'You didn't find out what his first name is while you were getting all matey with him?'

'Nah, but I reckon he looks like an Archibald or some shit like that.'

'Sounds like a nickname made in heaven.' The two men laughed together, and Wise had to admit it felt good. It'd been too long. He wiped a tear away. 'Any idea what you'll do with your time off?'

'I was thinking a trip to Thailand might be nice. Either that or go visit my sister in Brighton.'

'Either way, a bit of sea air will do you good,' Wise chuckled. 'Take it easy wherever you go and I'll see you when you're ready to come back.'

'I'll look forward to it. Cheers, Guv.' Hicksy stood up, gave him a wink and left the office.

58

It was 10 p.m. and Jamie hadn't left his flat since he'd got back from the meeting with Wise the previous day. None of Tom's crew knew where he lived, so it was as safe as anywhere to hole up while he worked out what was going on.

Or rather, he *had* felt safe up until five minutes ago when his phone had beeped with a message from Tom.

And not just a message. A summons.

Jamie stared at his phone, reading the text over and over again, trying to work out if he should run or not.

We need you at the warehouse now. Move your arse.

It was innocent enough. Too innocent?

There was no need for Tom to say what warehouse. It had to be the one in Ealing. The one Tom was using for his headquarters at the moment. Jamie had been there plenty of times, so asking him over wasn't an unusual request. But still, the place was just out of the way enough so Tom could commit bloody murder there without anyone hearing anything.

And, right then, Jamie didn't want to be anywhere that could happen. If he had to leave his flat at all, he wanted to go somewhere with crowds of eyewitnesses to stop one of Tom's boys putting a gun against his head.

But was his cover blown? Did they suspect him?

Christ, Heer going missing had him jumpy as hell.

Tom had to have taken her. It was the only thing that made sense. Why would anyone else care about her? Heer's unit was only investigating Tom and his gang. No one else.

She was a threat to Tom and only Tom.

But had he grabbed her and killed her or grabbed her and made her talk? If it was the latter, God only knew what she'd told him by now. It'd been over thirty-six hours since she'd gone missing. Enough time for Tom to force her whole life story out of her — and Jamie's.

Yeah, Jamie should definitely fucking run.

He had a go bag packed and ready in his wardrobe, so he headed there first as he thought about his next moves. There was no way he was going to head back to his real home. Not yet anyway. If Tom was after him, Jamie wasn't going to lead that psycho back to his wife and son.

No, he'd find a B&B somewhere and lie low until he could find out just what the fuck was happening.

After collecting his go bag, Jamie put on his coat, then picked up his gun from the table in the hallway. It was a Taurus 905 .38 special revolver, with six rounds in the chamber and totally illegal. Jamie liked it because it packed serious stopping power, but it was small enough to carry easily without any tell-tale bulges. Jamie tucked into the waistband of his jeans and pulled his t-shirt over it. He also picked up a small switchblade, which he slipped into his jeans front pocket.

Feeling better, Jamie opened the door — and found Gorgeous Gary standing in his way.

So much for no one knowing where he lived.

Shit.

One of Tom's most trusted henchmen, Gorgeous Gary wasn't called Gorgeous because he was good-looking. Far from it. The man had a face only his mother could love, made even uglier over the years from a career in illegal bareknuckle boxing. His nose was just a flattened blob above a crooked mouth and his ears looked like people had bitten chunks out of them just for shits and giggles. Which they might well have done.

Gorgeous was a cruel bastard and Jamie had seen first-hand what damage he could do.

'Jesus,' Jamie said, trying to cover up his shock. 'You frightened the life out of me. What the fuck are you doing here?'

'You off somewhere?' Gorgeous asked, but it sounded more an accusation than a question.

'Just got a message the boss wants to see me,' Jamie replied, trying to stay calm. The bloke filled the hallway. There was no way he could push past him and make a run for it.

'Funny that, because he asked me to come and pick you up,' Gorgeous replied. 'Big Tony's downstairs with the motor.'

'We better get going then,' Jamie said and headed towards the stairs. He thought about shooting Gorgeous there and then, but a gunshot would alert Big Tony and that would be it. Tony would pump him full of bullets the moment Jamie stuck his head out the front door. Better to wait till they got to the car and shoot Gorgeous and Tony then. Use the surprise to kill them both.

'What's in the bag?' Gorgeous said as they walked down the stairs.

'Just some shit I have to dump in my car. Stuff I need later.'

'Might as well bring it with you. You leave it in your motor now, some scrote bag will probably nick it. You know what this neighbourhood's like.' Gorgeous let out a laugh that chilled Jamie to the bone. If anyone looked in that bag while he was with Tom, the boss would know he was doing a runner. 'Only tossers live here.'

Jamie ignored the insult. 'Nah, I'll chuck it in the car all the same. There's nothing worth nicking and it sure as hell ain't worth lugging across London to see the boss.' Jamie knew whatever Gorgeous said or did next would tell him how much trouble he was actually in. If Gorgeous stopped him from going to his car, then Jamie was a dead man walking. If he let him, life was fucking roses.

'Fair enough,' Gorgeous grunted and Jamie had to stop himself from smiling. He was golden. Panicking about nothing.

They reached the downstairs and Jamie ambled out of the building like he didn't have a care in the world. Big Tony was leaning against the corner of his car, a black Range Rover, puffing away on a fag. 'Alright, Jamie,' he called out.

'I am now I've got you playing chauffeur,' Jamie called back. He held up his go bag. 'Just going to dump this in my motor and then we can be off.'

Tony rolled his eyes. 'Fucking hell. No rush, eh? It's not like I get paid by the hour.'

'Be quick,' Gorgeous said. 'The boss don't like waiting.'

'I know that,' Jamie said with a wink and jogged over to his car, a blue VW Golf. It didn't look flashy, but it had some serious kick to it when it was needed. He popped the boot open and chucked the bag in. As he did so, he watched Gorgeous and Big Tony. Both men were watching him and his paranoia kicked in again. He thought about his gun and how he might well be better off just walking back to the two thugs and popping them both in the head. But, if he did that, he'd really be in the shit. Tom would put a contract out on him and The Job wouldn't protect him. They'd see it as murder.

But he didn't want to get killed either.

'Oi, hurry up,' Tony called over. 'Tom's promised to take us all out for dinner later and I'm already starving.'

'You're always hungry,' Jamie said. He was sure now. He was safe. Best to go with it. See Tom. He could always run later if he had to. Jamie walked over to the Range Rover like he was Top Cat. 'Shouldn't you be wearing a peak cap and a suit if you're driving me?'

'Fuck off,' Tony replied, grinning, 'and get in.'

Jamie went to climb in the back but Gorgeous put a hand out and stopped him. 'You sit in the front. I'm having the back seat to myself for once.'

Somehow, Jamie managed to smile himself even though the thought of sitting with his back to Gorgeous got him scared again.

He'd seen *The Godfather*. He didn't want to get shot like Paulie. 'Kinda ruins the whole chauffeur experience, don't it?'

'Not for me it don't,' Gorgeous replied.

'You got a point there.'

The drive over to the warehouse took about twenty minutes. The three men chatted about this and that but none of it was anything important. Just the normal piss-taking amongst friends. And every minute that passed without Gorgeous shooting him in the back of the head, the better Jamie felt. In fact, by the time they reached Ealing, Jamie was feeling as safe as he'd ever done as an UCO, confident that his cover was secure but aware that one slip up could still get his throat cut. No wonder he needed to pop a load of sleeping pills every night to get some shut eye.

The warehouse was in the middle of an industrial park but most of the businesses were dark now with only outside security lights illuminating the surrounding areas. Tom's unit was located towards the back of the estate, far from any passing traffic. That allowed for any late-night comings and goings to go unnoticed.

Tony parked the Range Rover by the main door and the three men climbed out, their breath misting in the cold night air. 'I've had enough of this miserable weather,' Gorgeous said. 'It's proper brass monkeys.'

'What do you care?' Tony said as he opened the door. 'I thought you'd lost your balls years ago.'

'That's what your missus said to stop you worrying about what I do to her while you're out,' Gorgeous replied.

Jamie was laughing as he walked inside but he stopped the moment he saw what was waiting for him.

The floor was covered in clear plastic sheeting for one thing and, in the middle of the empty warehouse, DCI Rena Heer was tied to a chair, black tape covering her mouth. By the looks of things, she'd had the shit kicked out of her real good. Her clothes were covered in blood.

Gorgeous reached over and took Jamie's gun from under his t-shirt while he was still standing there, gobsmacked. Then Tony punched him in the face and knocked him to the ground. As he spat blood onto the plastic, a boot flipped him over and Gorgeous took the knife from his pocket.

'Over to you, boss,' Gorgeous said, stepping out of sight.

Tom leaned over. 'Hello, Jamie. Nice of you to pop round.'

'What's ... what's going on?' Jamie said, still acting, still hoping.

'You see this woman?' Tom said. 'She's filth. Detective Chief Inspector Rena Heer to be precise.'

'Yeah?'

'She's heading up a special unit investigating little old me, and she's been doing a good job of it from what I hear. So, I decided to have a little chat with her and find out how she was managing to discover shit she shouldn't know.'

Jamie sat up. He still wasn't sure if Heer had told Tom about him or if Tom just suspected he was a copper too. His mind raced trying to work out the angles, what he could say to walk out of there alive. 'But what's that got to do with me? Why's Big Tony trying to knock my teeth out?'

Tom smiled. It was the scariest thing Jamie had ever seen. 'Well, funny you should ask. You see, I reckon the plod have got someone on the inside helping them out. Now, this bitch denies it — even after Gorgeous plucked her fingernails out with the pliers and I gave her a good slap around.'

'Maybe it's the truth then,' Jamie said.

'Yeah, or she's just a tough old bird,' Tom said. 'Anyway, I got to thinking about my crew and, if anyone was a snitch, who would it be.'

'Well, it ain't me. I swear on my mother's life.'

'I'm glad to hear that. It's just that the others — like Big Tony and Gorgeous — I've seen them do stuff that no copper would ever do. In fact, the only person who's not killed anyone in front of me is you.'

'That don't make me a snitch,' Jamie said. 'I'm just not a killer. That's not my thing.'

Tom winced. 'And that's the fucking rub, Jamie me old son. I mean you say that but you still brought a pistol along with you tonight and what's the point of that if you're not going to use it?'

'It's just for show. To scare people if I have to.'

'Yeah, well. Those days are gone.' Tom stepped back so Jamie could see Heer in the chair, her eyes wide with fear, panting through her nose because she knew every breath could be her last. 'I've decided that if I'm going to trust someone with my life and liberty, I want to know one hundred per-fucking-cent that they're not a cop. So, right now, you've got an opportunity to prove that to me — or you're going to end up wrapped up in plastic just like the DCI here.'

'What do you want me to do?' Jamie asked.

'I want you to shoot the copper in the head.'

'What?' Jamie couldn't believe it.

'Kill her and we go on as normal. Say no and Gorgeous will pop you instead.' Tom shrugged. 'It's as simple as that.'

'Okay,' Jamie said, climbing to his feet. Blood dribbled from his split lips. 'Give me my gun.'

Tom looked over his shoulder to Gorgeous. 'Give him back his shooter.'

'I thought you'd never agree to do it,' Gorgeous chuckled as he handed Jamie back his Taurus. 'You've got balls after all.'

Jamie took the gun. After all, Tom had left him no choice. He flipped the safety off and looked up. 'You really are a mad bastard,' he said to Tom.

'So I've heard.'

Jamie raised the gun and aimed it at Heer's head. She gave the slightest of nods as if giving him permission to kill her.

Well, fuck that too.

Jamie swung his arm around, aimed the gun at Tom and pulled the trigger. The hammer went click as it struck an empty chamber. Jamie couldn't believe it. He pulled the trigger again, got another click. 'Fuck.'

Big Tony hit him again and knocked him down for the second time. Gorgeous joined in and both men kicked the shit out of Jamie while Tom laughed his guts out.

'I knew it,' Tom said when his flunkies stopped their assault. 'Fucking knew it.' He turned to Gorgeous. 'You owe me twenty quid.'

Gorgeous pulled a note out of his pocket and passed it over. 'Bastard.'

Tom then bent down and picked up the Taurus and opened it so Jamie could see the empty chamber. 'Gorgeous took all the bullets out before he gave it back to you. Good job he did, eh? Otherwise I reckon you would've tried killing us all to save this bitch's life.' He passed the gun back to Gorgeous. 'Load it up.'

Jamie watched the ugly bastard carefully slot all six bullets back into the chamber. Tears ran down his face as he thought about his wife and little boy back home. They'd probably be asleep right then, unaware that their dad was about to die. Not knowing they'd never see him again.

The gun loaded, Gorgeous passed it back to Tom. 'Thank you very much,' he said, then walked over to Heer. He placed the gun against the DCI's head, checked that Jamie was watching, then pulled the trigger.

The chair with DCI Heer toppled to the ground a heartbeat after her brains hit the floor.

Tom smiled and walked over to Jamie. He crouched down and pointed the gun at Jamie's left eye. 'I fucking hate snitches.'

Jamie stared back, mustering all his hate. 'Fuck—'

THANK YOU

Thank you for reading *Into the River Dead,* the fourth Detective Inspector Simon Wise thriller. It means the world to me that you have given your time to read my tales. It's your support that makes it possible for me to do this for a living, after all.

So, please spare a moment if you can to either write a review or simply rate *Into the River Dead* on Amazon. Your honest opinion will help future readers decide if they want to take a chance on a new-to-them author. Leaving a review is one of the greatest things you can do for an author and it really helps our books stand out amongst all the rest.

DI Wise will be back in LONDON'S DYING.

Thank you once again!

Michael (Keep reading to get a free book)

GET A FREE BOOK TODAY

Sign up for my mailing list at www.michaeldylanwrites.com and get a free copy of Dead Man Running, and discover exactly how DS Andy Davidson ended up on that rooftop in Peckham with a gun in his hand.

Plus by signing up, you'll be the first to hear about the next books in the series, special deals and maybe a bit about my dog too.

THE DI SIMON WISE SERIES

Out Now:

Dead Man Running

Rich Men, Dead Men

The Killing Game

Talking of The Dead

Into The River Dead

Printed in Great Britain
by Amazon